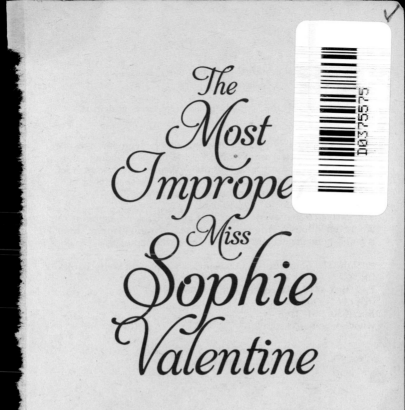

The Most Improper Miss Sophie Valentine

JAYNE FRESINA

sourcebooks
casablanca

Published by Sourcebooks Casablanca, an imprint of Sourcebooks,
Inc.
P.O. Box 4410, Naperville, Illinois 60567-4410
(630) 961-3900
Fax: (630) 961-2168
www.sourcebooks.com

Printed and bound in Canada.
WC 10 9 8 7 6 5 4 3 2 1

To Lynne

Chapter 1

ENDANGERING THE PRISTINE QUALITY OF HER NEW white muslin gown, Sophia Valentine leaned over the stone balustrade, assessed the shadowy distance to the lawn below, and wondered exactly what steps were necessary to "gird one's loins." She hovered on the brink of an abyss and felt this was surely the very moment for such an action, if she only knew how it might be done, for tonight she faced several dark dilemmas. Enlarged by an overly active imagination and one too many cups of punch, they seemed monstrous in dimension.

Much to her chagrin, precarious situations were prevalent in Sophie's life, and good common sense less frequently encountered, appearing long after it was needed, in company with that most frustrating of all commodities: "hindsight." She was generally in too much haste to stop and find the quality of prudence whenever it was most in need. Her reaction to situations of perceived emergency often created calamity of a genuine nature, rather than any escape from them. She knew all this but couldn't seem to stop herself. At nineteen, Sophie recognized she had yet to grow into anyone very admirable. She was a young woman with little beauty, many failings, and considerable desire for rebellion with no real direction, and was the first to admit her own shortcomings. But she had occasional signs of hope—when she chanced to catch her reflection in flattering light or heard herself saying something witty. Neither happened often.

Behind her, muffled by French doors, the music of a dignified quadrille currently led the other guests around a ballroom. Soon the rumor of an unseemly encounter would dance its own insidious steps through the crowd, causing Sophie to be pointed out, yet again, as a Young Lady in Need of Firmer Direction. This, however, was the least of her problems. Foremost among all her quandaries was this one: Where, for pity's sake, were all the real heroes? Where was her fiercely sculpted, steely-eyed knight on a fine black warhorse, charging up to carry her off over his shoulder? Did they exist only in novels? If they were real, they didn't appear to be looking for her. Perhaps, she mused unhappily, they came only for radiant maidens with cupid's-bow lips, limpid blue eyes, and alabaster brows. In which case, mediocre girls like she were destined to be cornered by Achingly Polite Milksops, Old Gropers with snuff-stained nose hairs, and the ever-annoying, self-proclaimed Rakehell, who fancied himself irresistible to all women, and whose greatest concern was whether the running at Newmarket was likely to be firm or soft that week.

And then there was James Hartley, a young man of considerable advantages, who had—much to her bewilderment—just proposed marriage. Most folk who knew them both would say it shouldn't have been such a shock to her, since they'd known each other for years, and he'd paid her many attentions she didn't deserve. But he had never courted her officially. His grandmama did not approve. Sometimes Sophie thought that was exactly why he'd chased her to London, and she, flattered to have his notice, encouraged it.

Now that he'd actually proposed, the game was over. She'd enjoyed it for the laughs and excitement but never expected to win. It was fun to play in James's world occasionally. Not so much fun, she suspected, to live there forever, forced to conform to the rules. She saw how it wore on *him*, and he'd been raised in it, whereas she was just a gawky country girl beneath her fancy new gown.

But this was the time of reckoning. They could no longer go on being merely friends. The cards would be put away, the chips counted. No more playing. Suddenly, it was serious.

She clutched her glass of punch as the brisk air cooled her face, and she struggled with her fears. Surely she was ready to fall in love—better now than at twenty-five or thirty, when she was too old to enjoy it. And there was much to be said in favor of her suitor. She and James had a great deal in common. Both were frequently in a hurry, and both preferred a lively country-dance to a subdued minuet. James, she suspected, had never paid attention to a sermon in his life. As for she, rather than read books written for the guidance of young ladies, she read sentimental novels and silly romances—although she skimmed the pages and never finished any. With a similar desire for mischief and instant gratification, they were, in many respects, two like souls. So she ought to be in love *now*, with Mr. James Hartley. After all, she could be at the peak of her "beauty," in which case, she should take this chance, grab James before he realized his mistake.

He was exceedingly handsome and would, one day, come into a large fortune. There was nothing more a young woman like she should dare ask for. However, there was something else she wanted, and it wasn't the sort of thing young ladies could talk about. Sophie wasn't even sure she knew the right words.

That evening, James had made love to her for the first time, apologizing profusely throughout the two and a half minutes it lasted. When a couple of stray guests had entered the billiard room and found them using the green baize surface for something other than billiards, Sophie was still waiting for the heavens to part and showers of stars to rain down on her. She was completely unaware that it was already over. So much for the romance and passion for which she yearned.

Soon, whispers of that scandalous encounter would travel the length of Lady Honoria Grimstock's glittering ballroom, to make yet another black mark against her. A guest of her fine Grimstock relatives, Sophie had been in London precisely one week, and was already accused of showing her ankles in public and using a curse word over a game of whist. But this latest transgression would surely outdo all that. She wouldn't mind so much if it had been actually worth all the fuss.

Now, here she stood, wondering if she was right to accept his proposal. A small voice inside her was screaming in protest. She began to feel boxed in by other people's expectations, stripped of her own.

Playing for time, she'd sent James off to find her velvet shawl, but he would return all too soon; hence the necessary girding of loins. A decision must be made.

If they hadn't been caught on that billiard table, would he still have proposed, or had he been cornered into it, much as she felt the same pressure to accept?

Her mind sputtered and sparked with questions, flaring to life and petering out, like fireworks in rain. Would it be fair to him? She really couldn't think what he saw in her.

And what if, somewhere out there…?

The punch made her light-headed. Swaying, she looked down again over the balustrade. Darkness had yet to descend but was only a breath away as dusk finally surrendered its sultry grip and slid behind a distant line of precisely manicured hedge. She should have worried about catching cold, but the crisp, uncluttered night air was a welcome relief from the stifling warmth and thick, waxy perfume of the ballroom.

She blinked drowsily as her gaze searched the lawn below. She thought she saw someone standing there, staring up at her. As the next brittle breath shattered in the cool air around her mouth, the shadows shifted again, and the shape was gone. Although she dismissed the vision as a result of too much punch, her heartbeat took on a new rhythm, and it seemed to say, *Jump, jump, jump, and I'll catch you*, over and over again.

She glanced back through the glass-paneled doors and saw James strolling around the perimeter of the dance, looking for her. A young maid, holding a tray of empty glasses, stood aside for him to pass, but he stopped. And then Sophie saw him slyly check over his shoulder before raising a hand to the girl's blushing cheek. He stroked it with one finger and gave her chin a tweak. It was a brief gesture and went unnoticed in the crowded ballroom, but Sophie, standing on the outside looking in, saw it all. He whispered in the girl's ear, and her lashes fluttered, her blush deepening. She was a plump, well-developed girl, slightly younger than Sophie. Her hair was very dark, almost raven. So were the adoring eyes she raised to James Hartley's face.

Sophie stepped back and stumbled against the balustrade.

As she clutched the mossy stone, she turned and gazed out over the wind-ruffled ivy. That vast lawn undulated softly, daubed by alternate splashes of moonlight and shadow, a magical carpet waiting to carry her far away.

Jump, jump, jump, and I'll catch you.

It would be a considerable leap, but suddenly flight into the unknown was preferable to facing the predictable future.

She heard voices below, people moving about in the quilted shadows.

"Where 'ave you been, boy?"

"Trimmin' the ivy, sir."

"You shouldn't still be out here now. What can you see to trim in the dark? Oh…" There was a pause. "I see what kept you, young scoundrel!"

She heard a low "*ouch*" followed by a mumbled curse. "You didn't 'ave to do that, sir. Now me ears are ringin'."

"And so they should be."

"I weren't doin' no harm. Only lookin'."

"Listen, boy, these fancy folk don't want their evenin' spoiled by seeing the likes of us about. Remember what I told you? We're not to be seen, only the results of our hard work."

And the young man answered, "Then we don't exist to people like them? People like her—up there?"

Alarmed, she stepped away from the balustrade. Since she'd been unable to see them, she'd assumed they wouldn't see her either.

"That's right, boy," came the distracted reply. "No. Leave that now and get out o' sight. You can fetch it in the mornin'."

The rustling stopped, the voices drifted away, and a great heaving sadness settled in Sophie's throat, because she wanted to shout down to the boy, but she couldn't. It wouldn't be proper, and she was in enough trouble as it was. Taking her anger out on her long white evening gloves, she wrenched them off as if they contained stinging nettles. What was the point of trying to look coolly elegant, when, on the inside, she was an ill-tempered, dissatisfied hussy?

Soon James would realize where she was and come

to fetch her; time was running out. Could she marry him and be happy? Could she make *him* happy?

He was only a few feet from the French doors now, his gaze scanning the dancers, but she couldn't go back into that stifling ballroom. She needed just a few more moments alone, in peace. Swept up in the desperate drama of the moment, she drained her cup of punch, tucked her skirt over one arm, and climbed up onto the mossy ledge, where she swayed slightly.

The door handles behind her began to turn with a loud squeak. She hated subjecting her new gown to the possibility of a stain or a tear, but there was nothing else to be done—there was no other way out. And so she leapt from the balustrade into the fast-creeping darkness, expecting, in the fearlessness of youth, to escape the fall with nothing more than a few grass stains.

Chapter 2

Ten and a half years later

LAZARUS KANE HAD WAITED UNDER THE LAMPPOST for some time, with no sight of anyone coming in or going out of the gentleman's club. He finally turned his head at the distant sound of a dog bark, and noticed a hefty figure as it rounded the corner, swinging an ivory-topped cane and checking a pocket watch. Eyes narrowed, Lazarus stepped back out of the circle of lantern light and carefully observed the approaching shape.

The other man hummed softly as he made his way down the street and apparently never noticed Lazarus standing so still and silent in the twilight. His destination appeared to be a tall, narrow white building in the midst of a row that curved gently to embrace the border of a very pleasant little park. The portly figure advanced with a brisk step, cane tapping the pavement, while the trace of a stiff smile lingered on his face.

Lazarus could almost smell the man's desperation,

the eagerness to get through that door with its polished brass knocker in the shape of a lion's head. Inside, a gentleman could enjoy several hours of uninterrupted contentment in the warm embrace of a leather chair, read the racing papers uninterrupted, play a few hands of cards, and partake of whatever wagers could be had that evening.

He watched as the man raised a gloved hand to the door knocker.

Eventually, the door opened, and a grim face peeked through the narrow crack. "Yes, sir?" the footman intoned with all the glee of an undertaker.

"It's me, Peters, Henry Valentine."

Aha! Lazarus smiled slightly in the shadows. The very man he'd waited there to meet.

"So I see, sir. I bid you good eve." The footman began closing the door, and Henry shoved his booted foot in the gap.

"Peters! What is the meaning of this?"

"Sir, you are no longer permitted here."

"How very amusing, Peters. Who put you up to this? James Hartley?" He glanced over at the bow window.

The steadfast footman repeated that he could not let him in, and Lazarus watched Henry's jowls shake. "Let me in, at once! I insist. You take a jest too far."

"Sir, you have been…removed…from the membership list."

Henry demanded to know why, and the old footman blinked slowly. "I fear, sir—one unpaid debt too many." Then he gave the door another push, and Henry withdrew his foot with an anguished curse. "Good eve, sir," said the footman so respectfully no one would guess how much he relished his task, unless, like the watchful Lazarus, they happened to catch the wild gleam in his eyes.

With a cool thud, the door closed, leaving Henry on the steps of the club, clutching his cane and the last remnants of his dignity. He felt hastily for something in his waistcoat pocket, but his fingers were too clumsy, and he seemed to forget what he was doing with them. Turning, he stumbled down the steps to the pavement, his face crimson.

Only then did he notice Lazarus under the lamppost, near enough to hear every word of his exchange with the footman. He looked as if he would walk by with no acknowledgment, but Lazarus stepped in his path.

"Is your name Valentine? Did I hear correctly?"

Henry stopped and looked at him, gloved fingers wrapped tight around his cane.

"I'm on my way to the village of Sydney Dovedale and have business there with someone by that name," Lazarus explained.

"I know nothing of Valentines or any place called Sydney Dovedale."

"But I thought I heard…"

Henry marched off across the street, and Lazarus watched him go, more amused than annoyed by the slight. He'd planned to approach this matter properly and respectfully, but now Mr. Henry Valentine could blame only himself for the shock he was soon to get.

⁂

The following day bloomed with a fine spring morning. Under a clear, harebell-blue sky, the earth warmed, and the grass shook off its dewy tears, for something new was in the air. Change was coming.

Lazarus Kane felt it in his very bones.

He walked along the verge with a long stride, a swinging arm, and a whistle on his lips. The arm not swinging held a large box on one shoulder, and this carried all his possessions, apart from those he wore, the hat on his head, and the boots upon his feet. These boots were the only clue as to the distance he'd traveled, for the heels were badly worn down, the toes scuffed and splashed with dried mud.

He stopped at the peak of a slight hill and ran a hand along the rugged bark of a primeval oak—rumored to be the oldest in England—and gazed out over the cluster of thatched cottages nestled around a Norman church in the distance. The village was surrounded by timbered hills, and what were once open fields and meadows were now seamed with hedgerows and low stone walls. Thin trails of smoke left the rooftops, adding a little twist of coal ash to the pottage of fragrance.

Nearly there. Excitement, tempered by a little anxiety, traveled swiftly through his veins. Better not stop, for then his feet hurt. As long as he kept moving, he didn't feel the pain.

Suddenly a tribe of young women in white frocks tumbled down the sloping lane, chattering and laughing, bonnets nodding like a row of droopy daisies. When he tried stepping out of their way, they giggled. The sound rose and fell in a frenzied cacophony as they surrounded him on all sides like a gaggle of excited geese. Then they were ahead of him, running away. He watched as they took turns climbing a stile. When they joined hands to run across the breeze-dimpled meadow, he realized where they were headed. In the distance, a tall maypole waited, bedecked in ribbons.

He smiled and followed the path of his merry daisies, the box of belongings still perched on his shoulder. Several villagers now observed his approach. Sydney Dovedale was not the sort of place to which people came unless they passed through on the way to somewhere grander, and the sight of a stranger would, no doubt, be cause for concern. So he kept his face merry, his stride confident. Let them see he came in peace.

Just as long as no one gave him any trouble.

He set down his box and leaned against a five-barred gate, squinting in the bright sun as the pink-cheeked, boisterous young girls circled the maypole.

Now, which was the woman he came here to find?

Moving along the hedge, he stood in the soft shade of a chestnut tree, where the grass was still wet and the dank earthiness tickled his nostrils. He'd just removed his hat to comb his hair back with the fingers of one hand, when something dropped on his head. One corner of it narrowly missed his left eye, and it bounced to the grass at his feet. A stifled curse trickled down through the branches, but when he looked up into the tree, all was very still. If it was possible to hear breath being held, he was certain he heard it. The fingers of a small hand slowly retreated like stealthy caterpillars through the leaves.

"Good morning," he called, holding his hat to his chest.

Nothing but a low sigh. Might have been a breeze trailing through the leafy branches.

When he stooped to retrieve the slender book that had fallen, the tree made a tiny, agitated mewl of distress. And no wonder. The pictures printed in this book were shockingly clear, detailed and instructive, not generally the sort of reading matter one expected to find a lady perusing on a sunny spring morning in the branches of a chestnut tree. Or anywhere, for that matter. He couldn't read a word printed there, but the pictures spoke a universal language.

"I didn't mean to disturb you," he shouted up into the tree even as he wondered why he apologized, since it was her indecent book that almost took out his eye. He knew it was a woman. Her presence rippled against his skin like the soft, sun-warmed waves of a calm but curious sea.

The tree, however, stared down at him, haughty and proud. And silent.

He ought to shake the wench out of her hiding place like a ripe chestnut.

Snapping the book shut, he tucked it inside his waistcoat and turned back to watch the dancers around the maypole. His lips puckered in a careless whistle while he deliberately ignored the tree. His gaze now traveled over the other women.

No. She was not among them. These girls were all too young.

A wasp buzzed his ear. He batted it away and then, in his peripheral vision, saw a booted foot, followed by a long, shapely leg in a torn stocking, slide slowly down the tree trunk. When her skirt and petticoat snagged on a branch, she halted and cursed under her breath in short, irritable gasps. A second leg emerged.

As did the intriguing sight of delicate lace drawers.

He'd expected her to hide up there until he was gone, but apparently she wanted that book back, and badly enough to show her face—and her drawers.

He should have looked away at once, but being a young man of lively humor and certainly no saint, turned his head to watch. She wore no bonnet, and her hair, the color of honey and sun-gilded wheat sheaves, spilled down her back, falling from a ladylike and ineffectual knot at the nape of her neck. He felt the instant stirring of interest.

She was lucky—very lucky. Lazarus Kane was currently masquerading as a gentleman and on his best behavior.

Her boots finally reached the safety of damp grass, and the ripped skirt dropped, covering her legs. Only then did she glance over her shoulder to be sure he hadn't seen, and her eyes widened when she found him staring brazenly back at her, enjoying the view.

Without a word, she held out her hand. She was an agreeably rounded creature, with delicate but well-defined features and a stunning pair of bright hazel eyes that shone full of stars, even in daytime and under the tumbled shade of the chestnut tree. He couldn't guess her age, although by the shape of her, she was clearly no child, despite her obvious proficiency in climbing and hiding in trees. Something about the way she held herself, the proud chin and determined set of her mouth, made him stare—that and her stunning resemblance to a solemn-faced angel he'd once seen painted on a domed ceiling inside a grand house where he worked. Yes, she was an angel. Clearly, in this case, a fallen one. Perhaps the tree broke her fall, he mused. Mesmerized, he slid one hand into his waistcoat and withdrew the slim volume.

There was no word of thanks. She advanced a step, her gaze on the book in his hand. With a second thought, regaining some of his playful wits, he brought the book back to his chest and held it there, daring her with a narrow-eyed challenge. She hesitated, fingers fidgeting with the pleats of her skirt, lips slightly parted. He imagined his own mouth on hers. He could taste those sweet, soft petals, could feel them shyly parting for him. The pink tip of her tongue darted out, sweeping left to right, dampening the lower lip. He was so absorbed in his imaginary kiss, he barely noticed the slender scar across her cheek.

Then he saw it. And he knew he'd found her at last.

Relief swept him until he was almost giddy. It was she. She wouldn't know him, of course, but for ten years she'd been his guardian angel, bringing comfort in some of his darkest hours. Without her image engraved on his mind—that hope of one day finding her again—he would never have survived.

He finally held the book out to her again, but when she reached for it, he forgot his newly adopted "gentlemanly" manners. So much for them. With his free hand, he captured hers and held it tight, drawing her closer through the long, shady grass.

"A kiss, madam," he muttered. "Is that not a fair exchange?"

He expected her to struggle away, but she glanced

anxiously over the hedge toward the merry revelers. She gave no shout of alarm, no sound but the smallest of startled yelps. It occurred to Lazarus she was more eager not to be seen there than she was to alert any of the villagers to her aid. The book, of course, he mused.

What good fortune it fell upon his head this morning and none other. Lucky for her too, since he knew how to keep a secret. He had plenty of those himself.

He tugged again, and she stumbled over a gnarled tree root, falling against him. Wide-eyed, she looked up at his face, and he felt those quick, anxious breaths ripple through her warm, generously shaped body. With every exhale, her breasts pillowed against his chest, and as she tried to settle her balance on the uneven ground, her hip inadvertently stroked his thigh. There was still no protest from her lips; instead, a curious light quickened in the sultry hazel depths of her unblinking gaze.

Was the lady ready for a little practice to go along with the theory she studied in her wicked book?

In that case, he would readily oblige. Lazarus ruthlessly cast aside all previous intentions of chivalry, recently acquired along with his new set of clothes, and reverted once more to the basic actions of a young man who'd learned most of his life lessons in the dark alleys and back streets of London.

His mouth sought hers, claiming it with neither mercy nor apology. Somewhere a bird sang, and his skipping pulse soared along with those high notes. She tasted as sweet as she looked, and although this kiss was bartered, it was neither coldly offered nor resentfully given. It was tentative but surprisingly gracious. She bestowed it like a blessing. Or a forgiveness.

How could she know, yet, she had anything to forgive him for?

He was calmed by it, briefly humbled even. And then he wanted more.

The delightful, teasing friction of her body against his had whetted Lazarus Kane's appetite. He let his tongue slip between her lips, distracting her while he released her small hand and slid his arm around her waist to pull her more securely against him. He parted his feet for balance, ran his splayed hand along her spine, and let his tongue delve deeper. She shivered. Her lashes lowered, trembling against her cheek. Dappled sunlight fell through the trees gently to dust the side of her face with verdigris and copper. When he felt her tongue touch his, growing bolder, he wanted to laugh, the joy taking him by surprise. His kiss turned demanding, his mouth slanted to hers, and his hand anchored at the nape of her neck.

And still he wanted more.

But she, it seemed, had given enough. He felt her pulling back. As much as he wanted to keep her, he knew better. For now, they were obliged to be civilized.

She stepped back, took her book from his hand, and ran off, disappearing into the covert of trees.

Lazarus laid one hand to his heart and felt the little bump beside it.

His angel was even more than he could have hoped for, and certainly more than he deserved. Each new day was already a precious gift not to be taken for granted.

His endangered heart pounded with a renewed burst of enthusiasm. Lazarus returned to where he'd left his box of belongings, heaved it up onto his shoulder, and continued on his way.

❧

His destination lay just on the border of the village, on rising ground from which he could see over the thatched rooftops and chimneys of Sydney Dovedale. In the opposite direction stood a somewhat forbidding stone fortress, moss clad and unprepossessing. His first impression, formed as he stared up at the dark, shadowy structure in the distance, was of a ruin, uninhabited and abandoned, so he turned his eyes instead to the house immediately before him. There, wedged into the flint-and-pebble wall by the gate, a carved sign proclaimed the name of the farmhouse— Souls Dryft.

He set down his box and pushed on the tall iron bars of the gate. As he lifted the latch, there was a groan of despair, and the gate dropped from the rusted top hinge. The bottom opposite corner fell to the ground with a thud, nestling in a deep ridge carved in the dirt, where it obviously felt at home, for it stubbornly refused to move farther. He struggled a while then made up his mind to find another route.

He climbed speedily up the rattling, protesting bars and leapt down into the yard. His mind, which was just as nimble as his body, had already taken note of the house's potential. His smile remained unchallenged, even as he found the shutters at the windows rotted and wormholed, the roof falling apart, and the walls bowed at such an angle it was a miracle they still stood upright.

Before he could fit his key in the lock, the door opened, and a wizened grey figure appeared, like a genie from a lamp. "Ye the fellow what leased the old place from the admiral, then, eh?"

"I am indeed."

"Heard the rattling and thought it was that tomcat leaping over the gate again after the new chicks."

Lazarus held out his hand and introduced himself.

The old man's prickly brows rose like startled bird's wings, and he lurched forward on bowed legs. "Lazarus? Like him what came back from the dead, sir?"

"The very one. But please call me Kane—not sir. And you must be Tuck."

"Aye." He sniffed proudly. "Been here, man and boy, nigh on sixty winters. Served a dozen masters, and sixteen mistresses betwixt 'em." He squinted. "Ye alone, then? No wife?" This last was uttered hopefully.

"No wife, Tuck. At least"—he grinned—"not as yet."

"Better off without one. Wife means woe. Better off without 'em." Seeing the large box sitting by the broken gate, his face gathered in folds of distress. "That's yern, is it?"

Lazarus laughed. "Worry not, Tuck. I carry my own luggage, but I'll mend that gate first. I should be grateful for some luncheon and a mug of ale, if one could be found."

Sniffing again, Tuck lumbered back into the farm-house and beckoned for Lazarus to follow. "Should 'ave come round the back. There's a bit o' broken wall in the orchard big enough to get through. Youngsters use it to scrump apples in autumn."

Ah, he thought, another item on the list of things to be mended. "Is that how you get in and out?"

"Oh no. I use the gate," the old man explained. "There's a trick to it."

Lazarus nodded. Yes, there was a trick to most things. Rolling his shoulders to ease the soreness, he stepped down into the house and looked around eagerly. Mellow sunlight filled the musty interior, but the year was not yet far enough advanced for any real warmth to muster against stone much before noon. And although shafts of gold fell through the leaded windows, waking the house from its slumber, they lacked the steady heat necessary to touch that flagged floor. Tuck had begun cleaning the place for a new tenant, but despite the breeze through the open windows and the burning coals in the fireplace, the air was still thick with dust. Furniture was sparse and looked to be as old as the house itself.

Lazarus stood at the window and ran a finger along the deep stone ledge, gathering a cobweb.

"The admiral en't been home in nigh on thirty years," Tuck explained, shuffling off to the pantry. "He leaves everything up to the solicitors in Yarmouth. They take care o' the leases, and I take care o' the house and farm."

That explains it, then, thought Lazarus. He'd been somewhat disheartened by the sight of saggy-fleeced, depressed-looking sheep in the rough pasture, of fields overgrown with flowery thistles and tall, angry weeds. There was no activity such as he'd seen on other farms along the way, and a plow abandoned in the yard was too full of cobwebs to have seen much use in a few years. The hay cart he passed had oats and reedy grass growing between the planks where fallen seeds were left to do as they pleased. Rot and mustiness hung so heavily in the air he could bite it.

Tuck reappeared, bearing a tray of bread, cheese, pickled onion, and ale, which he set before Lazarus with a disapproving sniff. "I don't know why the admiral don't sell the place and have done with it. Might be best for the village to have a constant fellow here—not just one stranger after t'other." He wiped his nose with the back of one claw and gloomily surveyed the tray as if it might be the last supper for a man about to be hanged. "Folk here don't care for strangers, and no one stays in this 'ouse long enough to make a difference."

Lazarus pounced on the hastily assembled luncheon, both arms on the table as he shoveled food into his mouth. "That old ruin up on the hill—is that part of this property too?"

Tuck's expression struggled between a scowl and a grin. "That *ol' ruin* is the residence o' Mr. 'Enry Valentine, but he won't take kindly to 'earing it called such. And whether or not 'tis part o' this property, well…" He finally conceded defeat in a dour chuckle. "That's a matter in dispute. Mr. 'Enry Valentine's father, God rest his soul, gave this house to the admiral to clear a debt. But Mr. 'Enry says it were only a temporary arrangement for the lifetime of his father and Souls Dryft should come back to him now old Mr. Valentine is dead and gone. The admiral reckons otherwise."

"Are there no records of the transaction?"

"Oh, aye," Tuck flung over his bent shoulder. "The solicitors 'ave fancy papers of all sort, on both sides. All of 'em as genuine as 'Enry Valentine's lush head o' hair."

Lazarus paused, ale tankard halfway to his lips. Then he laughed abruptly, shook his head, and continued his meal. Wiping his mouth on his sleeve, he gazed at the grimy window, eyes narrowed. With two work-roughened fingers, he rubbed a clear patch to look out and survey the cobbled yard.

There was a lot to be done to get this place in order, and he wasn't entirely sure where to begin.

Perhaps with the acquisition of a little property of his own. Time to stake his claim. He'd waited long enough.

Chapter 3

LAVINIA VALENTINE STRETCHED OUT ON THE OLD Grecian couch and kicked off her slippers to free her stubby pink toes. "Stop it, Sophia," she hissed at her sister-in-law. "I feel your bitter resentment burning holes in me even as I lie here with my eyes closed, trying to nap. No wonder my head hurts and my stomach churns, with you so miserable and bitter and glaring at me. And to think, I'm a well-brought-up lady from a fine family, yet I'm reduced to this...exiled to this dark, damp, dull place with no society of fashion. When I think of what I might have had!"

She wriggled like a plump grub and adjusted her bosom—an appendage frequently in need of some handling, apparently. Sophie thought a well-brought-up woman from a fine family should probably not punctuate every small insult by plumping her bosom like two saggy pillows. But there was no point remarking upon it, for she would be reminded only of how *she* was once caught *in flagrante* with a young gentleman whose breeches were around his knees. So she was hardly in a position to question anyone else's etiquette.

In the cooler months of the year, the residents of the fortress spent most of the day and evening in the cookhouse for the sake of economy. The fire must be lit, in any case, to warm water and cook food, so the family gathered here too, saving all the coal otherwise required to heat the drafty tower keep with its dank walls and icy-cold stone floor. Lavinia had ordered this button-tufted couch moved into the cookhouse, because she found the other chairs and benches insufficient cushion for her delicate posterior. "At the very least," she'd complained to her husband, "I might be permitted the comfort of a cushioned seat, even if I must be reduced to a life in the servants' quarters."

This morning, Lavinia wore yet another ostentatious new gown, although she intended to do nothing in it but lie on her couch: a well-fed sow napping in the warmth of the fire, eyes closed, and multitude of chins trembling like a naughty child's slapped buttocks.

By midday—or sooner should it become stained—that gown would be changed for another similarly ugly garment, made with an excess of expensive material and trimmings. Sophie, having quietly observed this extravagance on several occasions, suggested the need to budget a little better, as well as consider the burden of laundry.

"I wear what I please, thank you very much! I shall be glad when I'm treated with the respect I'm due in this house! Never have I been so put upon. If Henry had any care for my comfort, he would be rid of you once and for all! Scratching at me with your scornful comments. It's jealousy, of course. I wouldn't be surprised if you tried to poison me, and that's why I feel so ill today. Henry ought to send you away." Her mean little eyes caught sight of Aunt Finn giggling under her quilt. "And that wretched, old crone can go to the workhouse with you!"

Sophie bowed her head to hide her expression and continued her sewing. She should have known better than to raise the subject of economy, for any advice she tried to give Lavinia dropped into small, ineffectual ears muffled by ringlets and attached to a very small brain incapable of understanding any will but its own.

"To be thus attacked and criticized in my own home. Me, a married woman of consequence and property, from good family and well brought up! To be lectured daily by a tight-lipped spinster who's here only on my husband's charity. I've never heard of such a thing. I am outraged that *you* think to tell *me* how to behave!"

The wisest course of action would be to ignore her. After all, Sophie should be accustomed to it by now. It was apparently her lot in life to always be in the way, unequal to anything and unwelcome to everybody. But even as her conscience politely reminded her she was almost thirty and ought to be darning stockings by the fire with her aunt, only occasionally discussing the ins and outs of her health with no one who cared, she simply must relieve her anger somehow.

She was supposed to be a reformed character these days. Alas, the same naughty, rebellious imp that once urged her to leap from a balcony, not knowing how far she had to fall or what lay directly below, thrived inside her still. It would not sit in a corner and be quiet.

She stood quickly, set aside her sewing, and walked out into the yard and round the corner. There she waited a moment, fists at her side, gaze darting back and forth.

"Put upon," she muttered. "*Put upon?*"

She turned in a tight circle, bristling with anger.

Aha! There were two large sacks of chicken feathers and goose down against the wall, waiting for the pillowcases she and her aunt were sewing. Grabbing a stick from the woodpile, she ran up to the sacks and began beating them, imagining they were her sister-in-law.

"You should be put upon and often," she hissed. "And if your husband dislikes the duty, I'll gladly do it!"

A cloud of feathers flew up as the first sack burst open, and she found the sensation so satisfying she turned her wrath on the second sack, until the air was full of feathers. She swung that stick so wildly she heard the stitches ripping at her shoulder, but it felt too good to stop. When she tossed the stick aside, she picked up the sack and emptied the last of the feathers, shaking it hard overhead. "One of these days," she gasped, "I'll clap the side of your big head with the bacon kettle!" Dropping the sack to the ground, she stamped on it, grunting.

"I beg your pardon, madam, I tried the bell by the gatehouse, but there was no reply."

She spun around and found him right behind her, his hat under one arm, a pair of darkly curious eyes studying her in part bewilderment, part amusement.

Goose down drifted all around her, and her hairpins were falling loose, but she was frozen to the spot.

It was he: the man who'd stood under her tree earlier and undressed her with those same sinister eyes—the eyes of a barbarian. The man who'd made her kiss him. Shocked by it, she'd tried to put it out of her mind, as if it never happened. Now here he was again to remind her.

She puffed out a breath of surprise, along with several small feathers. When his fierce gaze moved to the torn shoulder of her gown, she felt the heat on her exposed skin, as if it were burned by the sun. She quickly placed her left hand over the tear, and her fingers fumbled to cover the ripped stitches. He'd made her kiss him before; what would he make her do next?

As if he'd read her mind, his smile widened.

She scowled, blew another chicken feather from the tip of her nose, and backed up a step. Face to face, yet again, with this black-haired, gypsy-eyed stranger, Sophie Valentine—the reformed version—sensed trouble. The untamable creature was still very much alive within her, however, and it scented something else. Something new and exciting.

Lavinia must have spied the stranger crossing the yard, for she finally ventured from her couch to see what he wanted. "I am Mrs. Valentine, sir," she chirped as she waddled around the corner. "Can I be of assistance?"

He was still looking at Sophie, holding her trapped in his steady, thorough regard. "Then you are *Miss* Sophia Valentine?"

She held up her sleeve and backed away with as much dignity as her bedraggled appearance could allow.

He followed her, smiling slowly, and she knew he too thought of earlier, when they'd met under the shade of the chestnut tree. He'd seen her book, her legs, and the Lord knew what else. If she was of a more ladylike constitution, she supposed she might have fainted. Instead, because she was a widely acknowledged, wicked hoyden, she felt remarkably well. Her heart was beating only a little faster than usual, because twice now he'd caught her doing something she shouldn't.

Had he just winked at her?

❧

She wore a stained apron over a blue gown, which had the appearance of something well loved, oft worn, and long past new. Her face was heart shaped, her eyes bright as a buttercup-sprinkled meadow, the two brows above them curved upward. When he looked into those eyes, he was pulled forward, every nerve and tendon in his body drawn to attention. Then she looked down at the cobblestones, dampening the hot spark that glowed under her lashes, and, for the first time in his memory, Lazarus Kane was unable to read a woman's mind. Challenged, he searched her small, prim face for the clues that were usually so abundant, but she closed herself off like a hedgehog retreating under its prickles.

Earlier, when he kissed her under the tree, she had not been so defensive. But then, of course, they were alone, witnessed by no one. And she evidently enjoyed her secrets.

The other woman lifted on tiptoe, creeping back into his view. "Did my husband expect you, sir? He said nothing of any visitor."

He looked down at her, vaguely irritated she was blocking his path. This one wore no apron. Her frock was arrayed lavishly with ruffles and bows. As if unable to choose between the many trimmings, she'd settled for all at once. Her dark hair was curled into ringlets so tight they shot out sideways from her head, their only movement a slight vibration when she twitched nervously.

"No, madam, I doubt your husband would mention me. I'm the new tenant of Souls Dryft. But it's Miss Sophia Valentine I've come to see."

"What on earth do you want with *her*?"

He looked over her head at the feather-strewn woman who, like a child knowing she's about to be punished, tried slipping away around the corner. "I come in answer to her advertisement."

"*Advertisement?*"

"For a husband," he said calmly. "I've come to marry Miss Valentine."

ം

Sophie had written that advertisement in a very foul temper after another quarrel with her sister-in-law, who took every opportunity to remind her she was in the way and a burden on her brother's finances. Throughout the writing, blotting, sealing, and posting, her fury remained in high heat, but as soon as the letter left her hands, she regretted it, as she did many other rash decisions before this. When her temper had cooled, she wished the entire thing undone, but it was too late.

If only she could prevent herself from these reckless actions, but the ideas popped into her head always when she was at her most desolate. Even the advance of years failed to dampen the urge for mischief, much to her chagrin. Thus it was with a mixture of feelings, none cordial, she looked at the man who had come that morning.

Was he actually so desperate for a wife he sought one in a newspaper? He did not look as if he should have trouble finding women. He saw too much, pried inside her with those dark eyes, and had thought nothing of bribing her for a kiss earlier. At her age, she was quite done with the sort of misadventure he offered. At least, she should be.

She'd backed up all the way into the cookhouse, but he continued walking forward, eyes agleam with amusement. Strands of her hair slowly tumbled to her shoulders. Her ladylike hairpins had not been enough to withstand the force of her violent tantrum, and she felt those ill-behaved tendrils curling wistfully against the throbbing pulse in her neck, whispering and slithering over her hot cheek.

He was swarthy, with a tumbled mess of coal-black hair falling almost to his shoulders, which appeared to span beyond the width of the door. Only their sheer breadth probably prevented him from stepping over Lavinia and following his quarry into the cookhouse. Sophie's gaze traveled downward, and she noted four things in quick succession: the scarred knuckles of his hands, his snug breeches, his filthy, scuffed boots, and then his snug breeches once again, just for good measure. Her brow quirked. Very Good Measure.

But then she already knew that, having been thrust up against his body earlier that morning. Again, it was something she'd tried to put out of her mind, in case she might be obliged to admit it happened. That she'd allowed it to happen.

Finally she forced her attention back to his face. A warm, satirical spark broke through the wariness in his steady gaze, and suddenly his eyes were devilishly enigmatic, drawing her in and whirling her about until she was dizzy.

Her pulse scattered like spillikins.

Perhaps she could...

But she really shouldn't.

Lavinia was squawking and flapping, something about his coming back later when Henry was home. As the stranger watched Sophie slip farther away into the shadows, he gave her a quick bow and departed in haste. She went immediately to the nearest chair and sat before her knees gave out under the strain. If she'd had a fan, she would have used it, but the little puffs of breath shot out from the curve of her lower lip would have to suffice as a cooling agent instead.

Once, years ago, her heart palpitated for the sight of a broad-shouldered warrior riding to her rescue. Now here he came, and the old adage, "Be careful what you wish for," ran giddily through her mind.

Chapter 4

"I SHALL FAINT, MARIA, I'M SURE OF IT! OF ALL THE things your sister has ever done, this is the very worst. We shall never recover from the shame of it."

"What has she done now?" The rector's wife, Sophie's younger sibling, had arrived for her usual morning tea and gossip.

"Your sister has procured a husband from an advertisement! Oh, my heart races. I'm giddy. I cannot breathe!" Lavinia fell back onto the groaning couch, where the imprint of her broad posterior was already worn into the upholstery after three years of constant contact. "Dark as the Devil, he is. Eyes that looked right through me, and a smile...a smile, Maria, that was surely the wickedest I've ever seen." Clearly she would have crossed herself had she the energy and required strength in her limbs at that moment. "We are all undone."

"An advertisement?"

"She wrote one and sent it to the newspaper."

"Oh, Sophia," Maria exclaimed, "I thought Henry confiscated your writing box, ever since you wrote all those protests to our local member of Parliament."

Sophie hid a smile behind her book. "Someone had to point out that man's inertia and incompetence."

Her sister barely heard. "Now, once again, you put pen to paper and cause trouble. This is surely the matter to end all. What will Henry say?"

Sophie said nothing and studiously turned a page.

Unable to sit still, Maria declared she would run down to the oak at the crossroads and wait for the mail coach, which passed through the village soon on its way between Yarmouth and Norwich. Henry was due to return on it from Morecroft that day. "I'd better meet him there...otherwise he might hear of this from someone else first."

She hurried off on her mission, while Lavinia resumed her loud lament, which was by turns mournful and irate but never comprehensible.

⤫

As it turned out, Henry was already aware of his sister's latest scandalous prank. While in Morecroft, he'd heard about the advertisement, and when he entered the cookhouse with Maria at his heels, he threw a copy of the newspaper across the table, ignored his wife, and demanded Sophia read it out for all to hear.

She picked it up and read quietly, "Wanted, one husband, not too particular. Age and size not an issue. Must have patience for recalcitrant females. Small dowry, several books, sundry furnishings, and elderly aunt included. Idlers, time wasters, and gentlemen with other attachments should not apply. All enquiries, Miss Sophia Valentine, Sydney Dovedale."

Lavinia promptly melted into the next stage of

hysteria, moaning and swaying, her ringlets vibrating. Next came apparent exhaustion, at which she fell down—always onto something conveniently comfortable—and required the application of smelling salts. It usually had the desired effect of returning all attention to her, but today no one was very interested in her antics. She realized this and recovered enough to make tea, or at least to supervise Maria in the making of it, while Sophie quietly explained why she chose to place her advertisement in the *Norwich and Morecroft Farmer's Gazette*, among the livestock for sale. "It is surely the most appropriate venue. I thought you'd be pleased, Henry. With Aunt Finn and me gone, that is two less burdens on your hands. And I'm under Lavinia's feet. Daily she reminds me…"

Henry's teaspoon tapped angrily against his china teacup, waking Aunt Finn from her nap.

"We shall all be murdered in our beds!" the lady cried, clutching her patchwork shawl to her chin and looking around with wide, frightened eyes. "Bonaparte has come—he has come!"

Sophie gently reassured her Napoleon Bonaparte had not invaded the village, no French soldiers had come, and they were all quite safe.

"But, Sophie dear, I heard gunshots."

"The war is over, Aunt Finn. Remember Waterloo? I'll pour you some tea." She tucked a blanket around the lady's knees and fetched another teacup from the dresser.

Henry folded his arms. "I don't like the sound of this fellow. Not one bit."

"He must be an oddity," Lavinia exclaimed. "By

answering such an advertisement, he proves himself a lunatic. You ought to pay him a visit, my husband." Her eyes gleamed with spite. "Find out what he's up to. I daresay he needs to be told the lay of the land, and who better to tell him than you? I suppose he thinks by marrying into this family, he might get a foot up on the social ladder."

Always amused by Lavinia's overinflated view of Valentine importance, Sophie let out one low chuckle, which, as she tried to prevent it, turned into an unladylike snort.

Henry turned stiffly in his chair and observed her with a cold eye. Nothing could cause such a wintry chill as her brother's dour, disappointed expression. "I think, Sophia, you've had your fun. You would do well to remain silent and show repentance for such a foolish prank."

But in the innocent, everyday act of pouring her aunt's tea, Sophie pondered the stranger's face, the darkness of his hair and eyes, the square jaw held without fear.

She couldn't marry him, of course, a complete stranger. The idea was patently ridiculous, yet he came all this way—wore down the heels of his boots—to find her. And that was her fault.

Her family assumed the advertisement to be another prank, and, in the beginning, she might have confessed it was so. But now that someone had actually come in answer to it, she was forced to take stock of her circumstances.

There was only so much loneliness a soul could take. Surely even a scarred woman with scandal in her past was entitled to a companion and partner. She didn't expect anything more than that. Or she shouldn't.

There seemed to be an excess of "shoulds" and "shouldn'ts" in her life lately. The wayward, opinionated creature that still dwelt inside her, just below the ladylike surface she'd carefully cultivated over the last decade, had begun to bristle at the sound.

Every day, for almost eleven years, she'd gone through the motions, doggedly following the same routine, and for the last three of those years, she did it all to the accompaniment of Lavinia's whines. Today, however, someone had thrust a pin in the clockwork mechanism, and all the cogwheels were stuck...jammed. Finally, something new had happened. A man had come out of nowhere and kissed her. Kissed her like no other man ever had.

"Sophia! The tea!"

She'd almost overpoured.

Maria, exhaling cake crumbs as rapidly as they were previously inhaled, exclaimed indignantly, "As if my sister would truly entertain such an idea! Marry a complete stranger?"

"Our sister's temper has once again got the better of her," said Henry, "and, as always, it falls in my lap to undo the damage."

Sophie's lips tightened. She gingerly carried the very full cup to where her aunt sat, then she picked up her sewing to mend the skirt she'd torn that morning. But her eyes couldn't concentrate on the stitches; she was too distracted by the restless pacing of her heart. She could hardly blame Aunt Finn for thinking Napoleon Bonaparte had invaded the village, for everything was turned upside down, and her own nerves spun about like tumbling maple seeds.

Now her family, with no input from her, were discussing the stranger and his motives.

"I've never seen such coarse hands on a gentleman of means," said Maria, crumbs falling from her busy lips as she stuffed cake into her mouth with more greedy alacrity than one might expect from a rector's wife, especially one who so frequently lamented the tightness of her stays.

"It depends by what *means* he became a gentleman," Henry replied as his fingers ran over his straining waistcoat buttons.

"Quite!" his wife agreed. "What sort of gentleman travels so far—on foot—to marry a woman he's never met and knows nothing about?"

If they only knew he'd already kissed her, she thought mischievously. Oh, if they only knew how his hand had touched her, stroked her spine and the nape of her neck. She was all goose bumps at the mere memory of that, not to mention the brazen shape of his arousal as her hip pressed up against it. He'd taken possession of her mouth as if she owed it to him, as if he'd waited a long time to claim it, and she hadn't offered up the slightest argument to dissuade him of that amorous notion.

Of course, strangers were rare in Sydney Dovedale, and they were most often merely passing through. She certainly hadn't expected him to creep up on her again a few hours later with marriage in mind.

"The stranger has leased the property at Souls Dryft from the admiral, they say, for a considerable sum," Maria exclaimed. "He must be quite rich."

Henry sighed deeply and disdainfully. "If it's true he has money, it's only new wealth. The fellow may be rich, but he clearly has no social standing, no rank, or he would not seek a wife in the *Farmer's Gazette*." He glared across the room at Sophie and added with icy calm, "I know exactly why she posted that advertisement. She wrote it for the same reason she wrote those letters to the newspaper about why women—*women*, of all things—should be permitted the vote. To cause mayhem and make me look ridiculous. Well, she might have caused a ruckus with her preposterous opinions and misguided wit before this, but she shall not goad me into an apoplexy, no matter how she tries."

When Sophie pricked her finger and cursed aloud, her aunt exclaimed, "Are you cold, my dear? You look pale. I hope you're not coming down with a chill. I promised my dear brother, God rest his soul, I would look after you all!"

Sophie smiled. "Another cup of tea, Aunt Finn?"

"No, no, my dear, or I shall need the chamber pot again. You know it goes right through me."

Lavinia sighed loudly. "Well, I'm sure I don't want to hear about your bodily functions. Henry, tell her!"

But they all knew whatever one said to Aunt Finn generally went in one ear and came directly out the other, or, if it chanced to linger, was misinterpreted en route in some way that might be deliberate. Parsimonious with his time and speech, Henry wasted none on ladies from whom he could gain nothing. He leaned back in his chair and fumbled for the watch chain in his waistcoat pocket. "I must be going, my dear. Life continues as usual, despite everything."

Nobody ever asked Henry what he had to do with his day, but he was more often out than he was home, with no real occupation and no inclination for any. From their father, he inherited the ancient fortress and land upon which they lived, but he took little interest in the management of it, leaving all that to his steward.

Sophie watched as he stooped to kiss his wife's fleshy pink cheek, and Lavinia informed him of her need for a new parasol. Henry promised to purchase the item for her on his next visit to the town, even though he must know this would appease her for no more than half an hour, until the newness of her parasol wore off and she spied something else she must have.

Needs. Sophie sighed and studied her clumsy stitches. Some women knew what they wanted—or thought they knew—and demanded it at the top of their lungs. Some women kept their needs to themselves, afraid of them. Of course, as a consequence, the second sort of woman never got what she wanted, while the loudest voice, accustomed to getting its own way, never felt the value of what it had. It was never satisfied, never content. With the acquisition of a silk parasol agreed upon by her husband, Lavinia now returned her thoughts to the true cause of her upset that morning. Abruptly her tone changed from wheedling and cooing to the sharp bark of a discontented lapdog. "You should call on this stranger, find out who he is and where he comes from, Henry!"

He studied his pocket watch, lips pursed. "I shall consider what must be done. In the meantime, I expect discretion from all of you. Sophia"—he fixed her in his hard glare—"you will not go near the man until I have spoken with him and ascertained his true purpose."

She looked up from her sewing with as much innocence as might be mustered, and bowed her head in mute agreement.

"We don't want this spread about the village," he added, his stern gaze turning to their younger sister. "Do you pay heed, Maria?"

Maria was tying her bonnet ribbons under her chin and not listening to Henry at all. She checked her reflection in the silver teakettle. "Oh, Sophia," she exclaimed, "the flowers in the church are quite tired and miserable. You'd better bring some new before Sunday. I see yours are blooming so well already, and yet my garden is in a very sad state. You've been quite lax at seeing to the church flowers lately. I cannot think why, as you have little else to do. Lord! When I think of how busy my day is compared to yours. If you had my life...with two children to raise...you would be rushed off your feet with no time for that little school of yours."

No one in the family considered Sophie's teaching of the village children to be a worthwhile enterprise. Henry disapproved the very idea of a school that would distract the local children from their work in his fields, and had tried in the beginning to make her abandon the enterprise. But she dug in her heels, and eventually, having far less energy than his sister to pursue a cause, he gave up and merely resorted to the occasional scornful comment about the damage an education could do where it was unwarranted. Maria, on the other hand, distantly indulged the subject of her elder sister's school with the mellow forbearance of a busy mother tolerating a small child's collection of dead insects. She patted Sophie's clenched hand and kissed her sullenly proffered cheek before hurrying after their brother, who continued with dire warnings about holding her tongue.

While Lavinia returned to her listless, lounging pose on the couch, Sophie cleared away the tea things and wondered what Henry meant to do about the stranger. It would, no doubt, take him a few days to decide. The only impulsive choices Henry ever made were those regarding racehorses and hands of cards.

Chapter 5

SOPHIE ESCAPED INTO THE WALLED GARDEN, EAGER TO gather her thoughts in peace. She carried cake crumbs in her apron to disperse for the industrious spring birds, and then sat on a small bench in the shade of the wall. She was so still and quiet the birds landed within a few inches of her feet, pecking for the crumbs she'd thrown and finding the bonus of an occasional worm. One bird was a big, bossy fellow with a speckled chest. He bobbed about and supervised the others—all noise and strutting with very little productivity. Another bird flew in and perched on the garden wall, watching slyly, assessing his competitors with a keen eye. He had shiny black feathers, slightly ruffled by the playful breeze. He twitched his head and winked at her, just as the stranger did that morning.

It was almost as if he saw inside her, to where all her ideas and daydreams clicked back and forth. Almost as if he knew her, and she, somehow, knew him.

Her thoughts turned suddenly to James Hartley, the man to whom she was once, very briefly, engaged. She'd not seen him in many years. In the beginning, when she first came home after the accident, he wrote to her almost daily. But over time, his letters became shorter, his handwriting more slanted and hurried, as though hastily slathered across the paper in a last-minute dash. Finally, they stopped altogether. She couldn't resent him for it. After all, she was the one who broke off the engagement.

James lived in London now, returning occasionally to visit his grandmother in Morecroft. Although he had a very handsome yearly allowance, she held the purse strings to a vast portion of his fortune until he reached the age of thirty-five—an extremely stringent, but probably wise precaution written into the terms of his inheritance. Whenever Sophie asked about her old beau, Henry would say only that James was "still insufferable and still richer than Croesus." Henry blamed James for giving her one too many cups of punch at the Grimstock ball ten years ago, when she was unaccustomed to the heady effects.

The scandalous events of that tragic evening were still occasionally spoken of, although time exaggerated many "facts" about it. This included the number of witnesses to their brief coupling on a billiard table, which grew from a mere two to an incredible dozen. The latter number included Lady Rosemary Grimstock-Pritchett, who swore she could no longer look at green baize without needing a sit-down and a tonic. Yet, in truth, she was not even present at that particular ball.

All that happened in another lifetime. Today came a new man, a very different sort of man. She felt an odd flutter in her breast. The stranger was nothing like

James Hartley. His hair was distinctly unkempt, just as unruly as those eyes. He dressed well, the fabric of his clothes obviously of luxurious quality, but there was something about him…something…misplaced, like an off-key note.

He was altogether too…altogether too…

The blackbird on the wall suddenly took flight, skimmed low over her head, and landed on the willow arbor.

Wild. That was it. Wild. Only masquerading as tame.

Showing off for her, the blackbird dived down into the shrubbery and plucked a worm out from under the speckled bird's complaining beak.

The stranger was trouble. No doubt about it. His hands were large, square, and restive. Like his eyes, they held an unquiet spirit. And promise.

She glanced over at the cookhouse to be sure no one was watching, and withdrew her copy of *Fordyce's Sermons for Ladies* from where it was folded up in her woolen shawl. Inside the pages of that worthy tome, she kept another—one propriety required disguising in such a sly fashion. This second book was a small, slim volume she'd once found hidden in her aunt's sewing box. With each perusal of its illustrated pages, Sophie felt anew that little thrill of venturing into a forbidden world. Now she examined it again with the eagerness of a truly irretrievable hussy, too lost to be saved from her own wickedness by the estimable Mr. Fordyce and his sermons.

Her nervous fingers rediscovered a much-thumbed page. *Chapter three, figures i and ii - The Male Anatomy in Repose and Erect.* She studied the sketches, her lively imagination transposing a pair of breeches over the detailed drawing, comparing it to what she saw that morning. The stranger was neither figure i nor figure ii, but had the latter occurred, it would definitely strain the confines of his breeches. Her imagination drew a new sketch: figure iii - The Male Rampant. She snapped the book shut, quite disappointed in herself for having such a prurient interest in the poor man. He didn't deserve her mental undressing. And what must he think of her already, having seen the sort of book in which her interest lay? Not to mention her zealous, uncalled-for abuse of a sack of innocent chicken feathers.

Sophie shook her head, disgusted with herself. Under no circumstances could she ever think of the stranger again or yearn for what she thought he might give her. Marriage was completely out of the question. She knew nothing about him, except he was darkly handsome and altogether too forward. At her age, she must think practically.

Now, if it was an elderly gentleman in a bath chair who had answered her advertisement—someone in need of tender nursing in his dotage—well, then she would consider it. But marriage to a daring, vigorous young man like him? Impossible. Ridiculous, even.

She could almost hear her brother exclaiming in hushed, brittle tones, "What will our noble relatives, the Grimstocks, think of this?" That would be his first concern. The Grimstocks' easily offended sensibilities must always be considered.

Thirty-six years ago, when Lady Annabelle Grimstock eloped with Jeremiah Valentine, a respectable, hardworking gentleman farmer with only modest savings and no title, the Grimstock family never forgave her. Jeremiah was a solemn fellow, what might be called "plodding" in nature, whereas Sophie remembered their mother as being full of ups and downs, veering from tragedy to airy delight, often all in the space of one afternoon. Her daughters took after her in spirit, while Henry resembled their father, growing up to be a stern fellow with graying temples and a prematurely receding hairline. When Annabelle and Jeremiah died within a year of each other, the children had only one adult remaining in their immediate family, Jeremiah's spinster sister, Finn. But it was Henry who ruled the household, taking miserly delight in ordering his sisters about, especially Sophie. In his opinion, she'd always got away with far more than she should.

Henry was eager for his sisters to make advantageous marriages and, therefore, no longer be a burden on his finances. He had written a groveling letter to his mother's Grimstock relatives, offering an olive branch. They agreed, most condescendingly, to send the girls to a ladies' academy and then, should they turn out to be presentable, invite them to London for a Season.

This turned out to be a very unfortunate idea. The Billiard Room Incident and The Accident sent Sophie back to Norfolk within a month. Maria, two years younger than her sister, didn't wish to stay in London without her, so they returned together to Sydney Dovedale. It would seem as if Henry were stuck with the burden of his sisters once again. Only a few years later, however, exuberant chatterbox Maria surprised everyone by falling in love with quiet, unassuming Mr. Bentley, the rector, and bullied him mercilessly until he married her.

Sophie smiled as she thought of her little sister. Maria, like their mother, had a very romantic view of life: everyone deserved to be happy. In their childhood, when the volatile tempers of Sophie and Henry clashed, it was Maria who ran to tell tales and get help. Though she was usually caught in the middle of their squabbles, she was also, on occasion, the unwanted peacemaker. Her nosy curiosity was exceeded only by an inability to keep secrets.

With this in mind, Sophie severely doubted her sister would manage to hold her tongue about the stranger's purpose in Sydney Dovedale. It probably would not be very long at all before the mortifying truth was out.

Chapter 6

As Sophie was daydreaming through Mrs. Cawley's parlor window the following afternoon, she suddenly saw the stranger appear between two cottages and cross the market square. She moved quickly away from the window and tripped, almost dropping her teacup. Anxious to see what was causing her sister such distress, Maria nudged the drapes with her shoulder and peered out.

"There he is," she exclaimed. "The stranger!"

Maria was immediately shoved aside by the impertinent shoulder of Miss Jane Osborne, a determined, horse-faced creature, who considered any unmarried gentleman in the village to be her own personal property until she declared him unsuitable for herself.

"He's too dark for an Englishman," the young woman neighed through her ponderous buckteeth. "I wouldn't be at all surprised to hear he's a foreigner. Amy Dawkins said he's a Spaniard."

"He has no accent," Mrs. Cawley assured her. "I heard him speak already."

"As did I," agreed Mrs. Flick, taking smug pride in the fact. "I detected no accent at all, and if there was one, I assure you I would know it. Amy Dawkins wouldn't know a Spaniard from a Scot."

They clustered around the window and watched the stranger pass, each falling silent as they greedily assessed his appearance. Even Sophie cautiously looked out again, unable to resist temptation.

He was pronounced by the room in general to be "exceedingly tall," although Sophie was sure it only seemed that way because of his confident manner of walking. His shoulders, it was also decided by the other ladies, were uncommonly broad. With this state-ment, she could brook no argument. They all agreed his profile had a certain interesting and unusual quality; it was not, by any means, unpleasant to look upon. While Mrs. Flick declared his nose lacked nobility, she could also allow it was not too large and showed no signs of overindulgence in the Demon alcohol. His black hair was rather long, but then, as Miss Osborne pointed out, it might be the fashion these days for gentlemen to wear their hair longer and somewhat tousled. Sydney Dovedale being so far from London, it was often the case that fashion had already come and gone before it arrived in the village. This was a great frustration to younger ladies like Miss Osborne, who pondered sketches of fashionable gowns in old copies of *La Belle Assemblee* with the awe and amazement other folk might reserve for detailed accounts of new discoveries in science and medicine.

"He could be a Russian Cossack," Jane whispered. "He has that look about him."

"What look would that be?" demanded Mrs. Flick. "What Russian Cossack have you ever seen?"

Miss Osborne had nothing to say to that, having never been outside the county of Norfolk, let alone the country.

"Walking about in his shirtsleeves," Mrs. Flick muttered. "What can he be thinking?"

"He could catch cold," said Mrs. Cawley, although that was, of course, not the reason for the other lady's concern.

"He looks as if he's about to burst out of his clothes," Jane Osborne exclaimed.

Again they all fell silent, watching as he walked away in his shirt and waistcoat, his narrow hips and tight buttocks not remarked upon but certainly observed. By Sophie, in any case.

"He's hosting a party at Souls Dryft," Mrs. Cawley muttered as she lifted her spectacles to watch the fading figure. "He called here yesterday to invite me in person."

Maria swiftly snapped her lips shut and looked across at her sister. Even as Sophie frowned and shook her head, she saw Maria struggling with their secret, so full of stifled energy. The sudden announcement of a party being planned without their brother knowing would surely bring her to the bursting point. Henry Valentine considered himself the most important person in the village, and no party of any kind ever happened without his permission.

In a huff, Maria left the window. She resumed her seat at the table and fidgeted with the buttons on her gloves, her countenance peevish.

Sophie quietly suggested they might all return to their discussion. As a founding member of Sydney Dovedale's Book Society, Sophie was also the most enthusiastic reader. These days she no longer skimmed pages but read books from cover to cover, having far more time on her hands to do so and no lively beaus to drag her away from them. The other women, she suspected, joined the book society for tea and gossip as much as they did for any intelligent, insightful conversation about novels. Maria would read the beginning and the end; Miss Osborne read the cover and ascertained from that what the story was about; Mrs. Flick fluttered through the pages for any passages that would allow her to condemn the book; Mrs. Cawley, while making a valiant attempt to read every chapter, usually found too much else to take her attention away from it and could never quite "get to grips with the story."

Sophie glanced around the small parlor and thought what a pity it was that Mrs. Cawley's niece, Ellie Vyne, was not there. At times like these, Sophie missed the distraction provided by her dear young friend very much. Ellie always had plenty of opinions to express, usually contrary to those of her fellow society members, even though Sophie suspected Ellie never read the books either. If Ellie were here today, she would have mocked them all for being so intrigued by the stranger. She would probably have cornered him already and found out everything there was to know about him, including his shoe size, thereby ending all the silly speculation. Although she was five years younger than Sophie, she was far bolder, quite dangerously fearless at times.

But Ellie would not be back to visit her aunt until the summer, and Sophie must plow bravely forward without her. It's not every day a girl is proposed to by a perfect stranger, and she could use her best friend's counsel.

As she opened her mouth to begin the discussion, she was interrupted before the first sound formed on her tongue.

"He has a scar upon his chest," Jane Osborne sputtered. At once all the ladies turned to look at her. "The Misses Dawkins saw him with his shirt off, mending his gate." She, too, returned to the table, and the other ladies followed, gathering eagerly like pigeons around bread crumbs. "It is a little bump," she added, "right by his heart."

Immediately, they were all agog, and Sophie watched her younger sister begin to perspire, fingers working frantically at the tiny, much-abused buttons on her gloves.

"It seems to me," said Mrs. Flick curtly, "the Misses Dawkins spent rather more time than is proper, inspecting the fellow without his shirt. They should have turned their eyes away at once."

They all agreed aloud the Misses Dawkins were quite at fault.

"And how is dear Finn?" Mrs. Flick suddenly inquired of Sophie.

Relieved by the change of subject, she replied, "My aunt is quite well, thank you."

But Maria exclaimed, "All this business about this new person coming to the village has upset her. Strange men coming to mar—" Sophie nudged her, and she stopped with a small yelp.

"I shall take Finn some calves' foot jelly," Mrs. Cawley exclaimed, beating her knees with her fists as if she ought to have thought of it long before now. "There's nothing like it for strengthening the blood."

Sophie ground her lips into a smile, but Miss Osborne, who couldn't care less about Finn Valentine's state of health, exclaimed merrily, "His name is Lazarus! Of all things…Lazarus!"

Her nerves scattered, Sophie studied the carpet. She could almost feel the building tremors of her sister's righteous indignation shaking her Hepplewhite chair.

"What will my dear Mr. Bentley think of a name like that?" Maria grumbled. "It might be a biblical name, but it's not a solid, plain name like Peter, Paul, or John. Lazarus—he who was raised from the dead." She shuddered. "I can't imagine what my dear Mr. Bentley will have to say, but surely he will not approve. Of course, I'm never one to judge, but such a name…and dark as a gypsy he is. The moment I knew Souls Dryft was let to a single man, I said to my dear Mr. Bentley, *It will only be trouble*. The admiral cares nothing about this village. If he did, he wouldn't let his house to people called Lazarus."

Sophie licked her lips, desperately searching for another subject, but Maria picked up speed, her flighty gaze dancing back and forth in a rowdy jig around Mrs. Cawley's cozy, tranquil parlor, her breath coming in little spurts like steam from a nearly boiling kettle.

"A stranger—a single man—all alone…moving into that house…Well, it's none of my business, and I take no interest in his comings and goings. Henry says he wouldn't be surprised if he was"—she lowered her voice—"*from the colonies*. Those are not the hands of a gentleman...not even a glove in sight...I wouldn't be surprised...not a bit...An advertisement for a...well, really! Who ever heard of such a thing?"

Sophie cleared her throat. "If we might return to the book—?"

"I suppose he made a fortune in investments." Maria mowed over Sophie's words as if they were nothing more than the drone of a fly.

Wilting in her chair, Sophie tried desperately to restrain her sister with little nudges of the knee and elbow, yet nothing worked. One may as well strive to uncurl a pig's tail as stop her now. Maria was about to burst out of her stays.

"It could be money smuggled out of France," she exclaimed. "He must be a mercenary soldier. Hence the wound."

"Very few men of wealth came by it honestly," said Mrs. Cawley. "Show me a man with great fortune—as my dear Captain Cawley would always say—and I'll show you a thieving tinker. Ah, my dear captain. God rest his soul."

The clock on the mantel wheezed out another soft, steady thunk, and the departed captain's old parakeet, recognizing his master's name, gave a proud squawk from his tall cage by the window.

Maria raised her chin another inch, ignored her sister's polite request for more tea, and then out it came.

"He has come to find a wife." It fell into the quiet, comfortable air of the room like clumsy, hobnail boots dropped from a careless hand. "He has come to marry Sophia, because she advertised for a husband in the *Farmer's Gazette*." With every eye now turned in their direction, Maria assumed an innocent face and sipped her tea, unblinking. She might as well have disowned the very statement her lips just delivered, leaving Sophie to take the brunt of their amazement and disbelief.

Miss Osborne opened her mouth, but perhaps it was simply the size and placement of her teeth that prevented it from closing again when no words emerged. Mrs. Flick looked smug, as if she could possibly have had an inkling of it, while Mrs. Cawley blinked in astonishment, bearing more than slight resemblance to her husband's bird, whose crest was now raised as he jumped from one foot to the other in agitation.

The secret undone, Maria had nothing left to lose. It could not very well be put back under her tongue. She consoled herself out loud with the reassurance that "nothing ever remains secret very long in Sydney Dovedale. I suppose you would all have found out soon, in any case."

Mrs. Flick nodded, her lips pressed tight, and Mrs. Cawley's expression drooped with pity for the poor, desperate, scarred woman in their midst. Jane Osborne covered her mouth with one small hand, and Sophie suspected she was struggling to restrain a spiteful giggle, one she would let out as soon as she had the chance to relate this story to another.

Sophie wished fervently for a trapdoor under her chair and someone braver than her to pull the lever. There was no one, of course. Making a hasty and nonsensical excuse of being needed at home to make jam tarts, she leapt to her feet and left Mrs. Cawley's parlor.

✧

Lazarus whistled softly as he strode down the narrow, muddy lane, arms swinging. His thoughts were so far away he didn't see anything in his path until the toes of his boots hit the edge of a deep, wide puddle. He stopped abruptly and looked up to assess whether he could make it over with one jump.

And then he saw Sophie Valentine on the other side of the puddle, apparently pondering the same problem. She carried a bonnet in one hand, a book in the other. Her coat was unbuttoned, her face flushed, and her hair in disarray, as if she'd been running again and was in considerable temper. Her eyes widened when she saw him at the exact moment he saw her. She stepped back, her heels squelching in mud. He followed the path of her gaze as it tracked from left to right and measured the verge on either side. There was only a narrow strip of grass before the stone wall on one side and a high, steep bank of weeds and thistles on the other. Finding dry footholds would require the balance of a circus acrobat.

Well, he couldn't let her get her petticoats wet, could he? Lazarus rolled up his shirtsleeves and sloshed forward into the water, his stride long and determined. Alarm and surprise took turns possessing her pretty face. It seemed she was too stunned to move away, and when he finally reached the spot where she stood, he swept her up easily into his arms, swung around, and carried her slowly across the puddle. They did not speak. Her arm reached across his chest, her hand resting on his shoulder, clinging to the ribbons of her dangling bonnet. He felt her breath, unsteady and shallow, as it trembled through her light form. His own heart thumped away, beating in his ears and boldly disregarding the metal lodged nearby.

Carefully, he set her down. He wondered if he should say something, but he didn't want to spoil the peaceful moment.

At first he thought she meant to walk away and say nothing, but apparently her temper—something he'd already witnessed being released on a sack of feathers—got the better of her.

"What made you think I needed your help?" she demanded primly, chin up and eyes aflame. "I suppose you assumed I was just waiting to be rescued."

He scratched his head. "You *were* standing there looking desperate."

"Desperate? *Desperate?*" Something about that word raised her temper another notch. Whatever had put her in a bad mood already, his sudden appearance in the lane had done nothing to appease it. "I'll thank you to know, sir, I am quite capable of finding my own way around a small obstacle. I am twenty-nine years of age and managed to survive quite well on my own all these years. Do you suppose I was waiting all this time for you?"

He said nothing but rubbed his jaw slowly with one hand, taking her in from muddy feet to the wayward straggle of honey-colored hair.

"I might not have wanted to cross the puddle," she

added. "I might not be going this way. You didn't even ask."

He cocked his head to one side.

"Why do you look at me in that manner?" the haughty madam demanded.

"Miss Valentine, may we—?"

"Don't speak to me!" She held up her hand, palm in his face. "I cannot converse with you."

"Why not?"

"Because it's most improper. You're a single man and a stranger."

"But you're speaking to me now," he pointed out.

"Indeed I am not," she exclaimed boldly with the aplomb of a woman accustomed to telling fibs.

His gaze swept down to her feet again. "You've got mud on your gown."

"I know that, for pity's sake. Don't you think I have enough people to point out my faults already?"

"Well, I—"

"If there's one thing I do not lack, it's other folk trying to direct my life."

"I only pointed out the mud—"

"I may be a woman, but that does not make me an imbecile. Neither am I crippled. I am perfectly capable of negotiating a puddle. Things may be different wherever you come from, sir, but here in Sydney Dovedale, gentlemen don't sweep ladies off their feet."

He smirked. "I'm sorry for the ladies, then. Good thing I'm here, ain't it?"

"That is not what I meant, and well you know it." Her cheeks darkened another shade. "They do not put their hands all over ladies without permission."

"I'll ask first next time, then." And one of these days, he mused, his blood roused, he'd make her beg for his touch. "*Ma'am*."

"Well, you are refused—"

"I didn't ask yet."

"—in advance," she sputtered, wrapping her bonnet ribbons around her fingers. "Besides, your hands are dirty," she added with a grand flourish, as if she'd been searching for more insults. "Dreadful, impertinent man."

His hands were dirty? Was that the best she could do?

He gave her a moment, and when that produced no further comment, he took matters into his own filthy hands.

Bending his knees slightly, he scooped her up again, this time vertically, with his arms around her hips, and carried her back across the puddle. He set her down again, doffed an imaginary hat, and left her there as he walked onward down the lane. He had no doubt the ungrateful wench watched him go, so he kept his gaze forward and resumed his merry whistle.

Chapter 7

As the day wore on, the sky brightened, not a cloud in sight. Then, slowly, it began to soften, like a watercolor painting that became too wet and crinkled the paper. By late afternoon, Lazarus's view of the horizon from the roof of the farmhouse rippled with merging, fuzzy layers of blush-pink, cobalt blue, and burnished copper. The busy birds still chirped, but less frantically now, their notes dampened and warped like the sun.

Lazarus was taking a short break and sitting astride the peak of his roof, when he spied Henry Valentine arriving at his gate to yank impatiently on the bell rope. He'd expected this visit yesterday, but evidently, Valentine had decided to make him wait. Fine. If that was the way he wanted to play. Lazarus would let Tuck deal with him first. He'd finish his work and then go down. Mr. Henry Valentine could take his turn waiting.

In answer to repeated clangs of the bell, Tuck finally emerged from the house, his ambling, crooked gait in no hurry.

Henry bellowed through the iron bars of the gate, "I haven't all blessed day. Where is he?"

"Hold yer horses," Tuck exclaimed, moving no faster, plainly careless of Valentine's noble pretensions.

Lazarus smiled as he felt the hot blast of Henry's frustration even from that distance. Tuck unlocked the gate, and Henry barged ahead into the house, leaving the old man to hobble after.

Almost half an hour later, Lazarus strolled leisurely through the farmhouse door, a jolly whistle on his lips. He saw Henry seated by the window, gripping his cane in both hands and rattling on about his time being very important. At the sound of the door opening and Lazarus's careless whistle, Henry stiffly turned in his seat. Shock and horror quickly consumed his features, and Lazarus wondered if it would have been proper to put his shirt on before he came in. It hadn't occurred to him. He tried to keep that shirt as clean as possible, so he never wore it when working around the house and farm.

Henry's gaze fell to the small bump on Lazarus's bare chest before it swept back upward. Recognition must have slapped him hard and quick when he realized this was the man he'd recently encountered lurking under a lantern outside Morecroft Gentleman's Club. The man who knew he was in debt.

He rose quickly. "Kane, I presume!"

Still wiping his hands on an old rag, Lazarus nodded his head. "And who might you be?"

Henry tapped his stick indignantly upon the flag-stones. "I, young man, am Henry Valentine."

"Ah," Lazarus said slowly. Of course he knew who it

was standing in his house, but he made the man admit it this time. "Please forgive my state of undress..." He extended a hand toward Henry, the great bulk of muscle in his arm and shoulder making the gesture rather more menacing than welcoming.

"I've waited here long enough," Henry snapped. "I have many other matters of business today, so I shall tally no longer and get directly to the point."

Lazarus retrieved his unaccepted hand. "I'm grateful for your haste, Valentine. I, too, am busy."

Henry's face grew redder with every breath. "I understand you came here with plans to marry my sister. Had you consulted me first, I could have saved you the trouble. Sophia will not marry. I must ask you to forget you ever read that advertisement."

"Oh?"

"My sister is prone to whimsical ideas, all in the purpose of her own amusing sport. The advertisement was merely a result of that same regretful impulse for mischief, which has, in the past, caused us similar trouble. Sophia is a difficult, contrary creature, her temper as changeable as the wind. That advertisement, written in one mood, she now already wishes retracted."

A sharp pain stabbed his chest. Lazarus caught his breath, placing his hand over the little bump there. "Why does she not tell me this herself?"

"It is not fitting for a well-bred lady to speak with a bachelor like yourself, in any matter." He paused. "I regret you came all this way for naught. You've traveled a great distance?"

Lazarus gave no answer but walked to the window

and turned his back to Henry, trying to get his thoughts in order, his temper under control.

"You were a soldier, Kane?"

"I've been many things." He looked back at the red-faced man, who seemed to inflate further with every angry breath. "The lady changed her mind, is that it? Perhaps I don't suit her fancy."

"My sister has no wish to marry. She's resigned to spinsterhood."

"'Tis an odd thing for a young woman like that to be so resigned," Lazarus replied steadily. "I'll talk to the lady myself."

"You certainly will not approach my sister," Henry exclaimed, breathless and perspiring. "I warn you to let the matter rest."

Lazarus stared at the flagstones under his feet and rubbed the back of his neck with one hand. Every sore muscle in his shoulder heaved then settled. He should have known there'd be trouble. Nothing worth having in life was easy. "I see how it is," he said finally. "How much do you need to pay off your debts? What will it cost me?"

"You misunderstand, sir, and willfully, I suspect," Henry blustered, almost exploding out of his waistcoat.

"Oh no, *sir*, I understand you perfectly." Lazarus looked up again, smiling slowly. "You're disinclined to give your sister away for free. Can't blame you for that. I'll buy her from you."

"My sister is not for sale!"

"She neglected to mention any price in her advertisement, but I suppose I should've known…Well"— Lazarus stroked his chin, assuming a thoughtful pose—"I do like the look of her. Fine bones, bright eyes, good hair, and, I assume, she's hearty breeding stock, although untried."

"How dare you!"

"Yes, she'll suit me very well. I'm not averse to the challenge. If what you tell me of her wayward character is true, the sooner I take her in hand the better." He laughed, a hollow sound that echoed around the farmhouse.

"If you persist in this matter, you will regret it!" Henry sputtered.

"But I want a woman, and she'll do nicely. You've convinced me."

"I warn you, Kane! You will not lay one finger on my sister, or I'll call you out."

Abruptly, Lazarus stopped laughing, the tendons in his neck and jaw held tight. He'd fought one too many battles in his life and came here to get away from all that, but if this fool continued to push his temper...

He stretched out his back, slowly and carefully, giving his anger another moment to cool. "As you wish it," he said quietly. There was no elaboration. He'd let Henry Valentine interpret that however he preferred.

The man cursed under his breath and almost dropped his cane.

"Behind you is the door, Valentine. You fit through it well enough one way without an invitation. I daresay you'll fit through it quicker going out again with my boot up your backside."

Henry gathered another lungful of arrogance, took one last scornful sweep of the house interior, and then strode out the door, his hat almost knocked off his head by the low lintel.

Lazarus kicked the door shut behind him.

Evidently, the lady had changed her mind and sent her ridiculous brother to warn him off. He looked down at his rough hands. No amount of fine clothing, it seemed, could cover all his worn edges, although he'd imagined they shared a spark of understanding when they met. That kiss under the tree yesterday had surely lit her flame as much as it did his. Her tongue had not withdrawn from his, and when he felt her move against him, it was not to push away. She was ready to explore. Perhaps, he thought grimly, it was merely wishful thinking on his part. The way she launched into him this afternoon for carrying her across a puddle would suggest she regretted giving him that kiss. Perhaps she didn't yet know what she wanted. Her brother plainly meant to stop her from marrying him, and if she already wavered…

He glanced at the window, caught his frowning reflection there, and felt the heat of deep, fathomless anger bounced back at him. His time was running out. Hadn't he overcome enough obstacles to get here? His Maker clearly thought not.

"Nothing stays secret long in this village, ye should know." Tuck chuckled softly. "'Tis an odd place for a feller to come, if he means to hide. Ye can't do that here."

Lazarus rounded on him. "Hide? Who said anything about hiding?"

Tuck nodded and smirked. "That's ye real name, is it, then?" he croaked wryly. "Lazarus?"

He had no reply to that.

Tuck got on with his work, and Lazarus returned to his outside.

∽⊱

Her basket overflowed with wallflowers and anemones from the garden. Sophie moved quickly through the gate, the hem of her gown dampened by the dewy kiss of meadow grass. She took the long footpath to the church that evening, enjoying the sweet promise in the air and the low, comforting call of the wood pigeons. Her earlier bad temper had melted away. In fact, her thoughts were unusually merry, her spirit several pounds lighter that evening, so she even hummed a tune as she walked along the shady pine grove amid the bluebells. The countryside was at peace as it settled in to embrace the evening, like a mother with her arms around a play-weary child.

She entered the church from the vestry door and stepped down into the cooler shade. Her nose twitched at the clammy odor of old stone. Time had its own scent here. All was peaceful, and she had no expectation of meeting anyone inside the church. But when she rounded a fat stone pillar, she discovered she was not alone.

The stranger sat in one of the front pews and was staring up at the tall, arched stained glass window above the pulpit. Luckily, she was walking along the strip of worn carpet that led from the vestry, so he hadn't seemed to have heard her steps yet. Her breath hitched in her chest, and she backed up a few steps, pressing her shoulders to the pillar. Once she'd gathered her wits, she peered out again and saw him there still, recognizable by his thick black hair and broad shoulders. Usually, when people were at prayer, they bent their heads and knelt. But not him. He was gazing at the bejeweled colors of the tall, sun-drenched window, apparently absorbed in them.

While she watched, he scratched his left ear, revealing those rough hands again. Maria and Lavinia agreed he couldn't be a gentleman with hands like those, but at least the hands of Lazarus Kane wouldn't fumble with naïveté.

Instantly, she admonished herself. *Stop it, you wanton hussy. What would the Grimstocks think?* Had she not already made up her mind to keep that man at a distance?

She peeped around the pillar and watched him examine a prayer book found on the pew beside him. He turned it over in his hands, flipping through the pages. Then he stopped and raised it. Although his pose was that of a man quietly reading, he held the book upside down. Sophie watched as he turned another page, pretending to read. Finally, he tossed it down in a frustrated gesture.

Gripping her trembling basket of flowers ever tighter, she straightened her shoulders and aligned her spine with the cool stone of the pillar. She would walk up the aisle. She really should apologize for being rude to him in the lane today, when he'd tried only to help her. Although really, it was all his fault for coming in answer to her silly advertisement, forcing her to face the consequences of her mischief.

Suddenly, he stood, and she ducked back behind the

pillar. His footsteps echoed down the aisle. Her breath blew hard and fast, her heartbeat uncontrollable as she tried to think of a suitable greeting. They still hadn't been formally introduced. Was there any etiquette to observe when dealing with a man procured through an advertisement? A man who introduced himself with a kiss?

"Miss Valentine."

He'd seen her, or part of her, protruding from the shadows of the great pillar. Too late to run away now.

She swallowed hard and walked fully into the stream of sunset that gilded the aisle. "Mr. Kane." She could barely get the name out. Would he try to kiss her again?

Probably. He didn't seem the sort to unduly trouble himself with rules.

"You bring flowers?" he muttered inanely as his dark eyes swept her basket.

She nodded. *Speak, fool. Say something.*

His rough hands hung at his sides, fingers flexing. "They are quite lovely."

Who cares about the dratted flowers?

A moment passed…and then another. There were so many things she needed to say, and yet she couldn't think where to start. An apology. Yes, that was it. Apologize for her terrible, unladylike temper.

Her gaze fluttered over his waistcoat buttons. Just as she thought she'd found the right words, he reached out with one hand, swept a lock of hair back from her cheek, and tucked it under her bonnet and behind her ear.

"Your brother tells me you changed your mind,

Miss Valentine. Is this true?" His words echoed softly around the stone walls of the church.

"I...yes...I'm afraid I could never...It was a mistake." Her face was hot, her tongue thick and sluggish, resenting the words she made it form. He didn't appear to hold any bitterness for the things she'd said earlier by the puddle. Most men would have commented sternly on her display of bad temper, but it seemed he had thicker skin.

"A mistake?"

"I could never marry a stranger." There. That was better. Sounded bolder.

He considered her thoughtfully, his head on one side. "We can become better acquainted."

The touch of his fingertips still resonated on her skin, although his hand was at his side again, as if it had never moved. Her heartbeat thumped so hard she was sure even the pigeons plumping their feathers in the belfry would hear it.

"Take a leap, Miss Valentine," he said, "and I'll be there to catch you."

She couldn't breathe. Copper sunset kissed his face, dazzled her eyes. Yes, he would catch her. She had no doubt he was strong enough. He had carried her across that puddle today as if she weighed no more than a lamb.

"I'm too old to jump," she muttered.

"But not too old to climb trees?" A slow smile bent his lips. Leaning closer, he whispered, "Very nice drawers, by the way."

She licked her lips. Her cheeks were very warm. "French lace," she muttered. It was the only extravagance she ever allowed herself: frilly underthings ordered from Norwich. To know that she had them under her clothes where no one else could see was another clandestine indulgence cherished—like the naughty book.

"Not very patriotic, is it? French lace?"

She sighed, rueful. "I suppose not."

"Well, I won't tell. Your secrets, Miss Valentine, are safe with me. All of them."

She suddenly heard another voice approaching from her right. It was the rector, Maria's husband, coming through the vestry and softly muttering little reminders to himself. Confused, Sophie didn't know which way to turn. They were standing far too close. Lazarus Kane was discussing her drawers and looking at her mouth as if he would kiss it again, regardless of who saw.

Mr. Bentley would tell Maria he'd seen them together—or have it wheedled out of him. Maria would never be able to keep it from Henry or the rest of the village.

This man was a complete stranger and could be a murderer, for all they knew. Look how he had already put his hands on her...and his lips.

But in that moment, even with all her doubts, she wanted him to do it again. And he seemed of the same mind.

He raised his hand once more and let his fingertips trail along her jaw, lifting it as he bent his head.

"Marry me, Miss Valentine. Don't tell me I came all this way for naught."

She felt his breath on her lips. Any moment now good, gentle, quiet Mr. Bentley would catch them being wicked together. And what of her promise to Henry—her vow to behave and cause him no further trouble? Look what happened the last time she leapt into the unknown. She raised one hand to the scar on her cheek.

"No," she gasped. "It is quite impossible."

"Your mind is made up?"

"Yes."

His lips still hovered above hers. "Then I'll just have to make you change it, won't I?"

"You're wasting your time." She shook her head, hand dropping from her scar.

"I'm not going away, Miss Valentine. I came here for one thing only, and I won't rest until I have it. I'm very"—he drew a finger across her lower lip—"very determined."

"Are you, indeed?"

He nodded slowly. "And perhaps it works to chase other men away, Miss Valentine"—he stroked upward along her jaw with the backs of his fingers—"but all the temper tantrums and insults in the world won't work this time. Not now you've tempted me with those lovely lace drawers."

"Please…Excuse me."

She was ashamed of the way he made her feel, afraid of what he might do, and wary of the latent strength in his hands. She made a dash for the church door, leaving him standing alone in the glow of sunset.

She hurried back through the graveyard, angry with herself and the world in general. Even with her fondness for French lace.

Chapter 8

HE STARED AT THE GREAT ARCHED DOOR THROUGH which his future bride had just disappeared. He wanted to go after her, but he knew he couldn't. She needed time, yet. Unfortunately, he didn't have all the time in the world to woo her properly. He pressed a hand to his heart again, thoughtfully running a finger over the small bump. He might have years, months, or only days. No one knew.

Hearing footsteps, Lazarus turned to see a man in a black coat rounding the stone pillars. "Aha! You must be Mr. Kane." The rector smiled warmly and extended a firm hand. "How glad I am to see you here. Please...do not let me chase you out. The church is especially beautiful at sunset, with the light through the stained glass."

Lazarus agreed. In fact, he'd studied the window for some time and felt a little guilty not to be at prayer. He'd been too distracted by the angel depicted at the top of the arch, who looked down on him with her wings uneven and her halo oddly askew. "I was reminded somewhat of Miss Sophia Valentine," he explained, gesturing toward the window as they walked up the aisle together.

"Really? I had not noted the resemblance, but I suppose...Yes, there is a likeness."

"When I first saw Miss Valentine, there seemed to be a halo of light around her..." He stopped, feeling foolish. "In any case..."

The rector sorted through books on the lectern but still smiled distantly, letting Lazarus know he was listening.

"I came here to marry her. Did you know?"

A Bible almost fell to the floor, but the rector caught it. "Marry? Sophia? Ah yes...the advertisement. My wife mentioned—"

"I fear she's changed her mind, however."

The rector sighed. "Women *are* changeable creatures."

"So I see. I hoped you might advise me, Rector. You know the lady well, I presume?"

"Indeed. I am married to Miss Valentine's sister. My name, by the way, is Bentley."

"Then perhaps you can advise me, Mr. Bentley. I'm sore in need of good counsel in the matter of Miss Valentine."

The rector hesitated. "Surely, sir, you know as much about the fairer sex as do I. Probably a great deal more."

"Yet you're married to a Valentine."

"And that, sadly, does not make one an expert. There is much I shall never understand about women, and being married to a Valentine introduced me to just as many mysteries as it uncovered." Mr. Bentley struggled to explain. "When I married my wife, it was really her idea. I merely went along with it." He paused, smiling wearily. "I find it easier to let the lady take the upper hand. I strive for a life of peace. That is my aim."

Suddenly, Lazarus burst out, "Do you believe a man might find an angel on earth, Mr. Bentley? That an angel might come to fetch a dying man up to heaven?"

"A dying man?"

"Well...we are all dying men, Mr. Bentley. From the day we're born. We must make the most of every day we have."

The rector nodded. "Indeed."

"That's why I'm here—to achieve something good with my life before it's too late."

"I see. Then I wish you every good fortune in your quest." The rector was solemn, but his eyes were kind. "I should like to see Sophia more happily settled, but my wife and I were resigned to the idea of her remaining unwed."

"I've not yet had the chance to discuss the matter at length with Miss Valentine," Lazarus admitted. They'd had only a moment just now in the aisle, and she seemed to have trouble with her tongue. Yet earlier, when he'd carried her across that puddle, she'd had plenty to say. There apparently were two sides to Miss Valentine: one very proper and circumspect, the other full of hot, passionate temper and considerable mischief. With the former, she tried to quell the latter. It wasn't working, he mused as he glanced again toward the arched doorway through which she'd vanished so speedily.

"Her brother and I have not begun on the best of terms," he murmured.

"Ah." Mr. Bentley's smile turned sympathetic. "Yes. Mr. Henry Valentine is a force to be reckoned with. Yet his sisters are equally stubborn in their own way. Don't let Miss Valentine's quiet manner deceive you. She knows her own mind."

Quiet manner? Oh no, he was not deceived. If the real Sophie Valentine thought she could hide from him behind her tightly laced corset, she was very much mistaken.

❧

Tonight, Sophie couldn't settle her mind to anything. Instead, she paced about, opened and closed cupboard doors, picked up books, only to toss them aside again, pushed food about her plate at supper, and fussed with her fingernails. One she discovered unforgivably chipped and so nibbled away at it with unladylike ferocity. Finally, she retrieved her sewing and flopped into a chair by the hearth to attack a torn skirt as if her very life depended on it. For once, she had no argument with Lavinia. She completely forgot her existence.

Aunt Finn inched forward in her chair and whispered, "Would you partake of a little gin, my dear? I find it calms my nerves very well."

Lavinia stirred slightly, smacked her lips, and repositioned her weight on the creaking, protesting couch. Her snores resumed almost immediately, her breath unsettling the stiff ringlets that fell across her drool-encrusted cheek.

Sophie managed a slight smile. "Thank you, Aunt Finn, but I think I should keep a clear head."

Finn chuckled, her eyes bright with mischief, not unlike those of her niece. "I've never found much benefit in a clear head. I prefer my edges softly foggy. It makes everything look so much nicer, and I appear younger when I look in the mirror."

Sometimes Sophie felt much older than her aunt. She envied the lady her ability to be so completely without care for what anyone thought of her. At what point, she mused sadly, did all her caution and anxiety set in? Whenever it was, Aunt Finn had apparently skipped that year. Not that anyone knew with any surety exactly how old she was. The lady not only lied about her age but frequently forgot what she last said it was.

Sophie sighed heavily and glanced over at Henry, who sat in the corner and was going over his accounts by the wavering light of a candle stump, trying, no doubt, to make the numbers grow by some magical means.

That evening at supper, he'd told her Lazarus Kane did not want to marry her. According to Henry, the stranger came there only because—hearing the name Valentine—he expected a good dowry. Now he knew there was only a very small one to be had, he'd rejected her.

She knew, of course, this was a falsehood. The man she met earlier in the church had made his intentions clear, and they did not match Henry's words. But she did not want her brother to know she'd defied him by speaking to Kane against his express wishes. Better she stay silent in the matter. Perhaps it might all die down and be forgotten in a day or two.

Ha!

She turned her eyes turned back to her sewing and
shook her head, knowing she was trying to fool herself
with vain hopes. Thanks to Maria's flapping tongue,
the entire village would now know why the stranger
had come. There could be no hiding it.

In that moment, she saw herself again at the balustrade, setting down a cup of punch and preparing to
leap into the darkness to embrace the unknown. If only
she'd stopped and reconsidered, she wouldn't have this
scar today, and many things might be different. She
could be safely married to James by now and have a
handful of children to fuss over. There would be no
time for mischief, then.

She closed her eyes tight and sought the past
through that soft, velvety darkness. She saw James's
sly glance over one shoulder, followed by the stolen
caress of a blushing cheek. She heard the music, just as
it played that night years ago while she stood outside
in the chill September air. Her heart had raced as she
watched the maid's lashes flutter and her tray of glasses
tremble. And again, she caught the edge of James
Hartley's knowing smile. He'd never touched *her* so
fondly as he caressed the cheek of Lady Grimstock's
young housemaid.

Perhaps, like other wives, she might have learned
to overlook his dalliances. On the other hand, perhaps
she could never have turned the necessary blind eye.

Sadly, if she was there again, hovering on the
precipice, there was every likelihood she would still
jump, even now.

∽◦∾

That evening while it was still light, she walked out to the gatehouse with a small, shallow bowl of water for the hedgehogs. If she left her shutters open when she went to bed, their little mating snuffle could be heard every night. She stood a while, staring down the lane to the dark, ungainly shadow of Souls Dryft. They had no candles or torches lit, yet. Tuck, she remembered with a smile, always waited as late as possible before he lit the candle in the lantern under the door arch—ever the good economist.

The sun, like a playwright with all the winding threads of his imagination exhausted, put down his quill and dipped his weary head to rest. Long shadows slowly crept across the ground, the bronzed fingers of sunset stretching to ease the cramp of a long day's writing.

And, stirred out of its dreams as if it felt her watching, the house down the lane appeared to open one eye, a flickering orb against the inky shadows. It was Tuck, of course, lighting the first candle of the evening and setting it on a window ledge where the shutters were left open.

As that house squatted there, waiting, its eyelids—all but for that one—closed and its mouth half-sunken into the earth, it might easily be mistaken for a dead thing, which is what it wanted any casual observer to believe. Only by lingering long enough might one witness that bowed belly move, softly exhaling, unsettling the weeds around it. Some might mistake that exhalation for a breeze that shattered the delicate puff of dandelion seeds by the wall, or else a mouse, moving through the tangled grass. But they would be wrong. It was the house letting out a gentle snore.

Sophie had spent the happiest years of her life in that house. She knew every inch of it, had whispered all her secrets and dreams into its walls.

Well, it seemed she would never go back there again. One day it would have a new mistress— someone bold enough to accept the rough hand of mysterious, reckless Lazarus Kane. It couldn't be her, of course. After all her daydreams of dark warriors riding to her rescue, in the end, she didn't have the gumption to leap into his arms. He'd called her bluff.

With a sigh, Sophia left the bowl of water and went to bed.

Chapter 9

"You've heard, of course, what she's done now?"

"My dear Mrs. Flick, of course I heard. Poor Sophia."

"Poor Sophia, indeed! She makes her own trouble, does that creature. Fancy placing an advertisement in the newspaper! We're fortunate only one man came. We might have been overrun. At my time of life, the less of *that* there is, the better."

"Henry must be at his wit's end."

"He should have reined her in before now. We reap what we sow."

Just then, Lazarus—hiding under the arch of the bridge—saw the very object of their animated discourse moving slowly down the lane toward them. Immediately, her critics turned, still gathered in a knot, and headed for the church gate.

Whether she saw them or not, her face betrayed nothing, and her gaze wandered along with the bubbling stream. She came to a halt and looked up into the branches of the blossoming hawthorn tree at the foot of the bridge. Something had caught her eye and held it. She used the bridge wall to boost her height and reached up into the tree, leaning precariously. Intent on the elusive object she sought with her fingers, she failed to see the man below, half-hidden in the shadow of the bridge, watching and listening.

For a brief moment, Lazarus took her for a spirit or an angel again, so ethereal was her appearance framed by the sharp light of that May morning. But the whispered curses coming from her lips were not the words of an angel.

She leaned farther, and a few tendrils of amber hair fell loose from the knot in which it was kept. Her slender arm stretched out, and her face colored with the effort of reaching. He feared she would fall, but if he called out a warning, he'd give his presence away.

Her lips broke apart with a sigh of frustration, and he saw the pink tip of her tongue before her teeth closed upon it. Her slender eyebrows lowered. Her eyes—the rich, unusual color, visible even from a distance—considered their prey with fierce determination. As she leaned and stretched, her body dipped, her back arched, and the low collar of her coat parted, the motion causing the weight of her breasts to nudge the material. It was a slight swell at first, but the farther she reached, the more it grew, her ladylike corset apparently unable to contain the complete fullness.

Lazarus drew back and suffered considerable agony of a sort most inappropriate for a Sunday. Still, he mused, God made her to be appreciated. He was, therefore, doing the Good Lord's will.

Aha! She had what she'd sought and, victorious, tucked it under the peak of her bonnet. Out of all the flowers, many closer to her reach, she'd chosen that one in particular for some reason and put herself to all that trouble for it. To him, the flower looked just like all the others, but she had set her heart on it and would have no other. Now she slid back, out of his view, leaving the sky above him empty again and dull.

❧

That sprig of hawthorn flowers peeking out from Sophia Valentine's bonnet was surely a sign of defiance and rebellion. The fresh white petals, newly blossomed, stood out like luminous clouds as she came down the aisle and took her place in the pews. She stared up at the stained glass window, so deep in thought she must be somewhere else entirely. Her body was merely holding a place on the pew beside her brother. Lazarus sat at the very back of the church in a seat from which he could unobtrusively observe Miss Valentine and her nodding posy...and the back of her brother's head with its crimson-tipped ears.

Several faces turned to look at him on that first Sunday, but theirs did not. Arms folded, he leaned back and studied the Norman arches of the little church as he breathed in the dampness of the ancient stone and listened to the dull echo of the rector's sermon.

Suddenly, he became aware of a face turned his way—a pale blur amid the bonnets. It was a young woman with a bland face, very prominent teeth, and large eyes that blinked rapidly now as she inclined her head in his direction. A little way farther on, two more ladies turned to nod in greeting until the elderly woman seated between them hastily drew their attention back to the sermon with quick pokes of her elbow.

He looked ahead to watch three little boys giggling in a pew across the aisle, making faces at one another, fighting and paying no heed to their mother's frantic whispers and threats. They all looked to be under the age of ten, and as sharp-eyed as fox cubs. One of them saw Lazarus watching and stuck out his tongue. He would have stuck out his tongue in return, but at that moment, Sophia Valentine, seated in front of the boys, turned her head and dropped a folded piece of paper into the ringleader's lap. Disregarding Henry's stern frown, she whispered something to the boy, and he quickly relayed it to his companions. All three looked at the folded paper and then settled down considerably.

After the service, the rector waited at the door to see his parishioners on their way. At his side stood his wife, a rather noisy, restless creature—another Valentine—whose lips were in constant motion in a conversation that trailed on without pause and with little encouragement from the reluctant listeners. Although she wore the pert look of someone disinterested, her husband was obliged to introduce her. She had dark hair, unlike her sister, and her eyes held no haughty air of mystery. They pinned him to the spot with a demanding curiosity, as if she could measure each limb just by looking. When she opened her mouth, that breathless speech tumbled out like apples from a dropped basket, rolling all around him in every direction. Meanwhile, Henry Valentine steered his other sister hurriedly away down the path, not allowing her to stop and greet anyone.

At last, Lazarus managed to interrupt Maria with, "I hope you will attend my party next Friday, madam? I mentioned it to your husband when we met."

She glared at the rector, who immediately crumpled in weary apology, aghast at having forgotten to tell her of the invite.

"Oh, really!" She bounced on her small feet. "Frederick, you're so forgetful. I'm always the last to know anything!"

"You will come, I hope? All of you?" Lazarus persisted.

"Well I…" She looked at her sad, repentant husband.

"I think we might attend, my dear," he offered gently.

"Yes, I suppose so." And her eyes narrowed as she sought the figure of her brother, who was now almost out of sight, vanishing under the lych-gate. "If I am able to come…"

"I hope to see you there." Lazarus bowed and walked on, leaving her to nag at her husband, probably for another five and twenty minutes about being so absent of mind.

As he passed through the gate, he glanced right and saw Sophia by the stream with the three little boys, helping them float that paper boat she'd made for them in church. In answer to their eager pleas, she showed them how to fold more boats, using pages torn from the back of her prayer book. Soon, each in possession of their own vessel, they proceeded to race them down the quick-flowing stream while she perched on a worn stone marker that pointed the road to Norwich in one direction and Yarmouth in the other. The boys ran back and forth, tripping over the grass and shouting to one another and to the smiling woman who watched, that nodding sprig of hawthorn flowers reflected in the glow of her cheek.

Her pose, seated on that marker, was very prim and ladylike: her gloved hands gathered in her lap, her shoulders pressed back. But there was something about that woman, something that warned she was not what she appeared to be. However somber her appearance, however determinedly she sought to pass herself off as a meek, virginal spinster, she utterly betrayed that act by giving in to an apparently greedy appetite for misbehavior. She couldn't help herself, it seemed, and had a wanton disregard for her own safety. The same spirit that caused her to write an advertisement for a husband had also set her mind upon the retrieval of a blossom far beyond her reach, when any other, much closer and easier to attain, might have done just as well. There was also the matter of two secretive hazel eyes, which claimed dutiful timidity even as their mistress privately flaunted the rules by climbing trees and studying naughty books. Finally to be considered: the undeniable existence of an extremely well-made figure that could not be disguised, even by stiff stays and an ugly coat. Miss Sophia Valentine was a wolf in lamb's fleece.

But she refused to acknowledge the existence of that wild creature inside her. It was up to him, therefore, to lure it out. He'd warned her he would.

He took only one step in her direction before he was unfortunately apprehended by a young woman who leapt in his path, dragging with her a startled-looking elderly gentleman with thick, fluffy white sideburns.

"Oh, Mr. Kane, I know this is most improper, and

I should wait for an introduction, but I shall plow ahead in any case and cock my nose at the ensuing *scandal*!" She tittered gleefully while he squinted down at her. "My name is Miss Osborne, sir, and this is my dear papa."

Her father, it turned out, was a prosperous dairy farmer, the owner of a property he'd passed and admired upon his arrival in the village. Within a few minutes, he was invited to Sunday luncheon, and Miss Osborne would take no excuse. She hastily linked her arm under his, and with her father on her other side, she drew them back down the lane away from Sophia.

Chapter 10

WHEN LAZARUS PUT HIS HEART AND MIND TO A project, there was no stopping until it was complete. He worked on the repairs to that farmhouse—so Tuck observed aloud—as if he had a demon nipping at his heels.

To which Lazarus replied, "Not a demon, just an angel."

One morning as the old man stumbled out into the yard, still not quite fully awake, he remarked that his master must have more energy than he could ever expend in a full lifetime. "Will ye never rest, lad?"

"When I'm dead, Tuck. Plenty of time to rest then."

Tuck shook his grizzled head. "Ye'll be dead soon enough, lad, carryin' on like this."

Lazarus laughed as he made his way down from the roof. He was already sweating so early in the day, having been up since cockcrow. He saw Tuck glance sideways at the wound on his bare chest, but the old man never asked about it. Instead he said, "'Tis supposed to be the master watching the servant at work, not the other way about."

"Once I'm awake, Tuck, I can't lie abed. Mind's too busy, body's too restless."

Tuck gave a low chortle, much like the cooing doves currently watching from the flint wall. "When ye get to be my age—*if* ye do, lad—ye'll welcome a few extra hours abed in the morn."

Lazarus shrugged. "When I have a wife to delay me."

"I told ye—wife makes woe, and ye're best off without one."

He turned away to wash his arms in the water trough. "Perhaps."

Sophie occasionally passed along the lane beyond his gate. He never let her know he saw her. Instead, he threw himself frantically into his work.

Still washing off his chest and arms in the water trough, Lazarus asked, quite casually, "Sophia Valentine has lived with her brother ever since the accident that left her scarred?"

"Aye, and none too happy with the arrangement now that harpy wife of his moved herself in."

"I'm surprised she never married."

"Oh, she were engaged, but after the accident, nothing came of it. Fellow was too fine and dandy, I reckon. Couldn't do with a scarred wife."

He straightened up and pushed back from the trough. A sharp pain stabbed his gut, like a sneaky punch delivered before he was prepared. He hadn't known about any other engagement, and now he wished he hadn't asked. Perhaps that was why she refused to consider him—her heart was with another man.

"She keeps herself busy," Tuck added, "with the schoolhouse in the village."

"The schoolhouse? She's an educated woman, then."

"Only by chance. When they lived here, Master 'Enry had a tutor for science, geography, and whatnot, but the young lad never cared much. It were Miss Sophie who read all the books and sat listening when she weren't supposed to. She were always studying books. Liked them better than dolls. Frustrated her mother, it did. Miss Sophie always wanted to make use of herself. She'd say to me, 'I won't sit about and be stupid, Tuck. I'll do something useful with my life.'"

Lazarus glanced again toward the gate as he slowly trailed the fingers of one hand over that scar by his heart. He'd been searching for a way to win her over. Like most things, he thought, there had to be a trick to it.

Tuck had just given him a clue.

❧

"Matthias Finchly, pay attention. I hear you whispering..." She'd just hurried between the rows of benches to reprimand her most trying pupil, when a terrible clattering noise startled the entire class and set her heart into a gallop. "What on earth...?"

A bird had come down the chimney and now flew madly about the small schoolhouse, swooping over heads and scattering little white droplets all over the place. The children leapt to their feet and ran about screaming. Few had the good sense to clamber out of the way, under benches and desks. Most danced about, trying to evade the bird's aim or else attempting to capture it.

Sophie ran to the window and flung it open. She

hoped the bird would find its way out. Instead, it fluttered up to the beams under the thatched roof, perched there, and chirped excitedly. She opened the door and grabbed the broom from its corner, meaning to shoo the creature out. The Finchly boys, meanwhile, attempted to reach the bird by standing on each other's shoulders, despite her angry shouts at them to sit down. Little Molly Robbins lay flat on the earthen floor, screaming she feared her eyes would be pecked out.

The bird flew from one beam to the next, apparently in no hurry to leave. It occasionally swooped down again, narrowly missing a head and causing another chorus of screams and shouts.

Into this chaos came Lazarus, who must have heard the ruckus and then quickened his pace down the horse path to stand in the open doorway and look in.

She was horrified. He was the last man she expected to see in that moment…the very last man she wanted to see her as a helpless female again.

He walked over and tried to extract the broom from her grasp. "I think we might dispense with this," he said.

"Oh…but…"

He smiled and leapt onto one of the desks.

"Do be careful, Mr. Kane."

He looked around at the children, one finger pressed to his lips. At once they all nodded and then fell silent and watched in awe. Sophie crossed her arms, slightly miffed.

The bird fluttered back and forth, singing happily. He whistled back at it.

She scowled. What *was* he doing? Of course, he had the recklessness of youth on his side. She had not asked his age. It would surely be improper to ask such a personal question. It would also probably give him encouragement to tease her. But he was young. As she saw him today, surrounded by the schoolchildren, and the way he'd formed an immediate alliance with them, his youth was more evident than ever before.

She was holding her shoulders stiffly, and they began to ache. She would not relax. She was too determined to disapprove the brazen young fool's antics. He was no better than the troublesome Finchly boys, and not far advanced in years, it seemed.

He stepped across to another desk to move closer to the bird. It swooped, and he ducked.

Again she warned him, this time with a slight edge to her tone. "*Do* be careful, young man. An ounce of caution is worth a pound of cure." He glanced down at her, and she quickly added, "I wouldn't want you breaking anything. In my schoolhouse."

The bird came back again, crisscrossing the room, almost as if it were taunting him. Lazarus whistled softly. He raised one hand. As the errant bird circled his head, Molly Robbins shuffled close to Sophie, hugging her legs and hiding her face in her teacher's skirt.

Lazarus moved suddenly. The schoolroom held its breath. All was still.

Stunned, Sophie watched as he climbed down from the desk, his large hands cupped gently around the bird. He grinned at her with supreme arrogance and then carried his prize to the window. The children followed him as if he were the Pied Piper.

There he lifted his arms and released the bird into a cornflower-blue sky, much to the cheering delight of his little followers.

Sophie's heart finally found a more even pace, although it was still not, by any means, calm or slow. He was watching her, waiting no doubt for her astonished praise and dutiful swooning. She'd turned him down once, yet he still bothered to smile and flaunt himself before her. The secret ache grew inside, but those heated yearnings must be suppressed. It would do neither of them any good. She was not the woman he needed, and he was, most certainly, all wrong for her—too young, brash, and forward. What she needed was someone quiet, placid, and respectable, not a man bent on turning the world upside down. Certainly not a man capable of reading her filthy, shameful thoughts. A woman had to have some secrets.

When nothing came out of her mouth, he prompted her. "It was a good thing I came to your rescue again, Miss Valentine. Wouldn't you agree?"

As she briskly set the room back to order, she finally allowed a small nod. "Thank you, Mr. Kane. I'm sure we're all very grateful. Are we not, children? Now back to the lesson, please."

While the children complained and slouched back to their benches, Lazarus slowly crossed the room to where she stood. He had a very powerful frame, an overwhelming presence when he was near.

"Miss Valentine?"

He was standing too close. Did he have no sense of propriety? Every pore on her body felt his heat; every lock of hair sprang to life, tempted to curl itself.

"I was not passing by chance today," he said. "There is a matter I wanted to discuss with you."

She clasped a slate to her chest and looked away. "I'm presently occupied, as you see."

"It won't take long. May we talk privately?"

"Privately? I'm afraid that wouldn't be proper." She lowered her voice. "Have I not told you that before?"

"Outside. Just two minutes"—his voice grew husky—"of your time."

Finally, and most reluctantly, she agreed. She left instruction for Matthias to continue reading the passage aloud, and led the way outside into the sun. Her hands were shaking, so she gripped them tightly around the slate in her arms, hoping he wouldn't notice.

"What do you want, Mr. Kane?"

"I'm in need of your talents, Miss Valentine."

"My talents?"

"I need a tutor. A private tutor."

"For what purpose?"

He looked around sheepishly, hands behind his back, and then leaned down toward her. "I cannot read or write, Miss Valentine. Well…I can a little. A very little. It pains me to admit it. I should like to master the skill for something beyond the marking of my own name."

Her fingers tapped against the slate. "I don't give private lessons." She turned hastily to go back inside. He blocked her way, his shoulder propped against the door frame.

"But you owe me, Miss Valentine."

She swallowed. "I owe you for what exactly?"

"Must I remind you? I came here thinking I'd

found a wife, but now I'm obliged to begin my hunt all over again because you refused me so callously. Am I not entitled to some kindness, some compensation, considering the disappointment?"

So he was trying to make her feel guilty. As if she didn't already.

"You owe me a bride, Miss Valentine. The least you could do is help me get one by softening my rough edges."

She looked up at him, wondering why he thought he needed her help. He had no shortage of wily charm and a certain persuasive quality. She might be in danger herself, if she were ten years younger and a great deal stupider. "Believe me, Mr. Kane, I'm very sorry I ever posted that advertisement. I don't know why I did it."

"Don't you? I do."

She clamped her lips tightly.

"Because you wanted me to come and find you," he said calmly.

His sheer arrogance goaded her temper enough to reply, "And what would I want you for, pray tell?"

He treated her to a slow, arch grin. "Shall I show you here and now?"

Alarmed, she stepped back.

"You may pretend to the whole world, Miss Valentine, but you can't lie to me. You need me."

She clung desperately to a few shreds of practical thought. "Mr. Kane, if you cannot read, how did you find my advertisement?"

"The landlady at the Red Lion in Morecroft read it out one morning at breakfast." He was looking at her hands around the slate. "It caused some amusement among her guests."

"Of which you were one."

"A guest, yes, but I was not amused. I was intrigued. Then I found you climbing out of that tree, and my curiosity increased."

She took a quick, tight breath. "A gentleman wouldn't take advantage of a lady and bribe her for a kiss."

"You made it necessary to kiss you. I was undone." The overgrown boy grinned down at her. "Vixen."

To her utter despair, Sophie felt a chuckle tickling her throat. Despite the ridiculousness of his statement, it was impossible to keep a straight face. She looked away, anxiously checking the lane at the end of the horse path that ran along the side of her schoolhouse, not wanting anyone to see them standing together. At least, with the door half-closed, the children couldn't see, and having been left untended for a few moments, they were already loud enough not to hear a word of the conversation taking place outside.

At last she recovered enough to muster a gentle reply. "I understand you've been disappointed, Mr. Kane. But that is not entirely my fault."

"Oh?" He folded his arms, settling against her door frame.

"I should never have written that advertisement, but you should never have come in answer to it, when you'd never met me. I wonder what you expected to find."

"Nothing like this," he replied dryly.

She sighed. "I believe I made my feelings clear.

I cannot speak with you further on this matter, Mr. Kane. Good day."

He still blocked the doorway. "The least you could do, Miss Valentine, is agree to tutor me, turn me into a proper gent who wouldn't embarrass a fine lady. A gentleman even a Valentine would deem worthy enough to smile at." He stopped again, those devilish eyes narrowed thoughtfully. "Not that a gentleman is what you truly need."

She tried scowling but suspected it came out more as a wince. "Mr. Kane, surely you have other women to torment."

He was staring at her lips in a very odd way and then he took a step toward her. Sophie thought she could duck under his arm and get safely inside, but he must have read her thoughts. He backed up again, just as she advanced. Now they were both in the doorway, separated by mere inches and with his arm blocking her escape once more.

"I suppose you think this amusing," she muttered, "to come here like this and tease me. As if I could ever agree to give private lessons to an unmarried man."

He moved even closer. Her heart thumped so hard her hairpins were coming loose.

෨෧

Lazarus was intrigued by this prim-faced little woman with the deliciously tempting lips, this chaste spinster in French lace drawers. She was moving directly up against his arm into his ready embrace—exactly where she professed she didn't want to be, and exactly where he yearned to have her.

He was incredibly aroused just to be this near. The scent of her hair made him quite light-headed. He could see every rapid breath she took, her breasts straining against that tight corset. His throat was dry, his loins heavy.

Her lips wobbled for a brief moment, and he heard a slight groan, as if she were trying to restrain something. His heart lifted. Was she going to laugh? Yes. He saw it in her eyes—a warm amusement with him, with herself, and with their circumstances. He even felt her body tremble, ready to give way to a fit of giggles.

But she controlled herself, straightened up, and resumed her stern and proper schoolmistress voice again.

"I have other things to do with my day than wait around for some shallow young rake to make a greater fool of me than I can make of myself. There are plenty of other women here, and you may perform for all of them, but I'm not so easily impressed. I know a brash, vainglorious fool when I see one, and I stopped being breathless and wide-eyed over your sort when I was a great deal younger even than you are now. *Perhaps* you'll grow out of it. Most little boys do. Good day, sir!" She turned swiftly, ducked under his arm, and slammed the door in his face.

Lazarus stared, thinking how easily he could break apart those thin wooden panels with his shoulder and his bare hands.

The damned woman was rude, churlish, and ungrateful. For such a small, delicate-looking kitten, she had quite a bite and a set of sharp claws. And when her temper was up, she was more beautiful and beguiling than she had any wretched right to be. He'd better walk away now and save that innocent school-house door from taking the brunt of his frustration.

Then he heard a stifled burst of laughter through the wood panels. He'd never been so confused by a woman in his life. Nor so aroused.

Chapter 11

ALL SOPHIE'S ATTEMPTS TO IGNORE THE STRANGER'S presence at the end of the lane soon proved impossible. Daily, the fellow's curious antics were brought to her attention, and rarely could a handful of hours pass without mention of the name Lazarus Kane.

He was witnessed playing cricket with Mrs. Finchly's sons, inspiring them, no doubt, to even greater depths of wickedness. He was apparently skilled with his hands, and he built a luxurious new birdcage for Mrs. Cawley's parrot and mended the cowshed roof for Dairyman Osborne. According to Henry, there could be only devious motives behind so much altruism. No good would come of it.

Villagers passing the repaired gate at Souls Dryft saw the place much improved, all by Kane's own hands and in such a short amount of time. The new resident must have wondered at the increasing number of ladies, young and old, who passed his gate each day while he worked in the yard without his shirt. At first, it was only one or two ladies scuttling by, averting their eyes, but very soon it grew to small flocks of four or five, who often passed more than twice in a single morning, and seldom a hurried step amongst them.

Henry secured promises from several folk not to attend the party at Souls Dryft. But as time passed, a strange thing happened. People began to form their own opinions without conferring first with Henry. One by one, they forgot their vows not to attend.

Even Lavinia weakened. Unfortunately for Henry, he made the mistake of purchasing his wife a new lace shawl that week. Now she complained of having no cause to wear that lace shawl, especially if he meant to stop her from attending the party and keep her trapped at home within the "moldy walls" of that fortress. She nagged at him for four-and-twenty hours, until he could take no more and told her she must do as she wished with her lace shawl—even strangle herself with it—but he would not accompany her to the party. In reply, she declared she would gladly go with Mr. and Mrs. Bentley.

"What can you mean?" he exclaimed. "My sister Maria will not go. I'm sure of it. She knows my opinion on the matter."

Lavinia replied smugly, "But as they are representatives of the church, she told me yesterday it's only proper they welcome the stranger to Sydney Dovedale."

Now Henry had no choice. "Unfortunately, thanks to my sister's betrayal, I must go and keep an eye on things," he stated. "If I stay away, the villain might think he gained a victory."

~⁂~

Once they were gone, Sophie settled in with a book. All was peaceful until Finn sat bolt upright in her chair, exclaiming, "I'm betaken with a desire to dance."

Sophie looked up warily over the top edge of her page.

"We should go to the party," her aunt added emphatically, already half out of her chair.

"I think we'd much better stay here."

"No, no, Sophie. We'll go to the party and dance." The lady began fussing over her dress, clearly afraid it was too plain and worn. "And I've nothing for my hair." She touched her lace cap with nervous fingers. "Lord! 'Tis so long since I attended a dance. Mayhap I've forgot the steps."

"Please sit down, Aunt. You upset yourself."

But Finn had her mind set. "Would you deny an old woman the pleasure of a good dance, when one has not been had in so long, Sophie? Surely you could not be so cruel! And you were always my favorite niece."

Sophie sighed heavily. She wondered if her brother could have got far along the lane yet. If he might be caught, Aunt Finn could go on with them, and she could return to the cookhouse alone. She finally fetched her aunt's woolen shawl, in case there might be a chill nip in the air.

"I don't know what's got into you this evening," she muttered. "If you should catch cold going out tonight…"

Aunt Finn skipped on ahead, already through the door while Sophie was still removing her apron and putting a guard over the fire. There was no time to find her best shoes or check her face in the mirror and, in any case, she thought, what did it matter? She knew her reflection well enough, and staring at it would change nothing. At the door, she pulled on her dusty boots but could find neither a bonnet nor her spencer. There was no time to look further. She'd just have to do as she was. As she ran across the courtyard in pursuit of her aunt, she looked for any sign of Henry, but he and his wife must have walked with unusual speed. Lavinia, of course, wouldn't want to risk the food all being gone before she got there.

"Hurry, Sophie!"

"I come, Aunt, I come!" she cried breathlessly. "I do wish you'd return to the cookhouse. We can dance there, and it'll be quite the same."

But the gleeful lady linked her arm under Sophie's, almost dragging her along the lane. "You, my dear, have spent too long dancing alone. You've read that book from cover to cover more times than I can count. 'Tis time to put all that knowledge to practice. There is no occasion to be fearful of the real article, is there?"

So her aunt had seen through her subterfuge all along.

"No need to blush, Sophie my dear," Finn exclaimed breezily. "'Tis healthy and natural to be curious. What *is* unnatural is to stifle it. I found that book among the possessions of my lovely captain many years ago and kept it as a souvenir of our affair."

The man she referred to as the captain was now the admiral—the same fellow who owned Souls Dryft. Almost thirty years ago, he and Finn enjoyed a scandalous love affair, much to her family's humiliation. She was not in the least remorseful and still mentioned her captain with great fondness, despite that he never wrote and apparently went on to enjoy other affairs, soon forgetting the young lady to whom he once swore undying love.

Henry referred to their aunt as "a fallen woman best left where she fell, because she'll only do it again, given half the chance." Sophie often imagined he thought the same of her.

And tonight, after so many years of relatively good behavior, Finn Valentine was apparently in the mood to cause trouble again.

They were at the gate in the next moment, and Sophie's wondering gaze swept up over the farmhouse with its repaired, repainted shutters. Underneath the new paint, it was still the place in which she'd spent a happy childhood. How long ago it now seemed since she and her siblings chased hens, piglets, and one another about that yard. She closed her eyes and deeply inhaled the sweet fragrance weeping from the orchard where blossoms still hung heavy, some trodden underfoot, merging with rich new grass and churned mud. When her father was still alive, the stables were full of farm horses, great solid beasts with docked tails, lively pricked ears, and fluttering nostrils. She still recalled the heavy, plodding thud of their massive hooves and the creak of their leather harness as they came home down the lane after working in the field all day. How gently they nibbled her fingers when she ran out to feed them treats and pet their broad pink muzzles.

Although Sophia had promised herself not to look for Lazarus, his face was the first she encountered looking back at her, his expression one of surprise followed by something else. Sophie sidled away into a shadowy corner, self-conscious in her old gown and muddy boots, but Aunt Finn, in her giddy mood, wouldn't be satisfied merely as a spectator. She soon wrestled free of her niece's clutches to wreak havoc at the cider barrel.

Henry shouldered his way through the throng, demanding to know what they were doing there. Sophie sorrowfully explained Aunt Finn's sudden desire to dance and added, if Henry promised to watch over the lady, she'd gladly leave.

"Nonsense!" he exclaimed. "You will take her home with you directly!"

As her brother moved away, she saw she was, once again, the target of Kane's dark, curious stare. Caught looking, he turned his head, but only partially this time, showing his profile as he talked to the rector.

He needed a shave and a hair trim, she mused idly. Someone ought to take better care of him. And then she chastised herself for those wistful fancies and reminded her inner hussy to behave. She'd already decided, hadn't she? The stranger was not for her, and she'd caused enough trouble for her family already.

But even the way Lazarus Kane moved made her quite unaccountably feisty. It was a long time since she'd danced with a young man, but she remembered what it was like. And if she let her imagination wander, she could feel herself dancing with him, his strong hand lightly holding hers, his attention riveted on her. She began to get rather overheated.

⁂

Henry bellowed for his wife, but Lavinia wanted to stay longer and wouldn't be removed unless he lifted her over his shoulder—an act at which stronger men than he would balk. Having found a small coven of like-minded complainers, she sat with them, holding court on the inadequacies of husbands, mixed in with some thoughts on fashion and the effectiveness of various lotions for wart removal. Sophie could hear her even from a good distance away and over the music.

Obviously frustrated, Henry now apprehended Aunt Finn and firmly seized her elbow. There was a brief scuffle, and Sophie watched her brother's face darkening, his gestures growing stiff as he lost patience.

"You perspire, Henry," Finn observed loudly. "You should worry less. Continue on this path, and you'll be dead before you're forty." She laughed and shook her finger in his red face.

Sophie hid a smile and turned her attention to the other guests.

She watched as Kane danced with the equine Miss Osborne and then the Misses Dawkins—one after the other. There seemed no limit to his charm or energy. Just as she was thinking how hot he must be under his ivory silk cravat, he loosened it. Then he removed his fine jacket to continue in shirt and waistcoat, but not once did he sit out a dance until the band took a short rest. At one point, as he passed near her, the torchlight flickered across his crow-black hair, and she saw it was damp with sweat and sticking to his brow. As he blinked slowly, a small bead of water dripped from his jet lashes. He looked up abruptly, and their eyes met.

A sudden scream, followed by a loud splash, shattered the opportunity for any conversation.

All attention was drawn to the water trough by

the cider barrel. There sprawled Henry, legs and arms dangling, his broad form half-submerged in the cold water. Aunt Finn stood calmly beside the trough, hands clasped behind her back, a large wet stain on the front of her gown. After a brief, stunned silence, the crowd broke into chuckles that soon swelled to a great drunken guffawing.

Sophie went to her brother's aid, as did Lazarus, but Henry wanted no help and insisted on climbing out under his own power as he furiously cursed his host. Aunt Finn would, ever after, claim it was an accident he ended up in the water trough, but not a soul believed it—least of all Henry. Crimson-faced, he hissed at Sophie, "You'll take her home at once."

But Finn protested she'd not yet had her dance.

"For pity's sake," Henry snapped, "no one is going to dance with you. Your dancing days are long over. You will return to the house at once. Indeed, we all shall."

He bellowed for Lavinia and turned on his heel, water squelching inside his shiny boots. The laughter now ended as most folk looked on in various shades of sympathy and disgust for Henry's unkindness to Aunt Finn. Sophie, heart fallen to her knees, prepared to apologize on her brother's behalf.

And then Lazarus said, "Miss Finn Valentine, would you do me the honor?"

He politely bowed his head and offered a hand to Aunt Finn. As if alerted by some subtle signal, the little band seated on a pile of hay bales nearby immediately struck up a tune. The crowd gathered around for another dance, forgetting the little scene around the water trough, and Finn, beaming anew, graciously accepted his hand.

Sophie could breathe again, but only somewhat unevenly.

With no further ado, Henry found Lavinia and steered her home, prodding at her with his cane whenever she snuffled in protest. He was so rattled he left Sophie behind. She took a few steps back into the shadows behind the cider barrel and waited for Aunt Finn to be done with her dance.

Chapter 12

NO ONE WATCHING LAZARUS WOULD GUESS THE STEPS he showed off tonight were, like his manners, all very newly learned. But it was worth the sore feet, he thought, to have Miss Sophia Valentine's sole attention.

The dance was coming to an end. He feared she would take her aunt and leave, so he desperately sought for some means to make them stay a while longer. He was saved the trouble when, suddenly, his partner claimed she had twisted her ankle. Helping her to a bench, he bade her sit and propped her injured foot up on a little milking stool.

She thanked him profusely. "You must tell my dear niece Sophie I cannot possibly be moved until my ankle stops throbbing. We must stay a while yet, I fear." Then she licked her lips and blinked her feathery lashes, tilting in a half swoon.

He studied the lady, his eyes narrowed, as she removed her lace cap to fan herself. "Please do stay and rest," he advised her. "I'll find your niece and inform her."

She reached for his sleeve, her fingers plucking it

like the strings of a harp. "You know, young man, this house once belonged to my brother. We all lived here then, when my nieces and nephew were children."

"Yes. Tuck told me."

"Sophie loved this house, never wanted to leave it. How she cried when we were obliged to move up the lane to that fortress. Jeremiah, my dear brother, was not a lucky man with money, you see, Mr. Kane." She sighed. "I fear his son is just the same. The ladies in this family have always suffered from their bad choices."

"I'm sorry to hear it."

"I must see my Sophie content, back at Souls Dryft where she belongs." She paused for a breath then added, "By the by, our hens are off laying, Mr. Kane. Perhaps you might spare some eggs, should you remember us tomorrow morning. Come early if you can."

He bowed quickly and walked away to deliver her message. As he neared the cider barrel, he caught part of a conversation between Sophie and her sister, Mrs. Bentley.

"Why could you not, for once, keep your tongue, Maria? Have I not suffered enough?"

"If you're so mortified by it, you shouldn't have written that advertisement."

"Believe me, I regret it now. It was wrong of me to post such an advertisement without thinking of the consequences. Now he came all this way and must be disappointed by what he found. I cannot possibly make amends for the wrong I've done to the poor man."

His heartbeat strengthened, and his feelings toward her warmed even further. She had no idea, of course, he'd been looking for her long before he learned of that advertisement.

The two women noticed him approaching through the flickering light of the rush torches, and Sophie immediately fell silent. He bowed and greeted the rector's wife, who commenced chattering to him as if they were already in the midst of a conversation. He waited for her to be done, but Mrs. Maria Bentley could talk for considerable length without pausing for breath. His nerves were in a frayed, delicate state. This stupid awkwardness he suffered in Sophie's presence might have been comical if he stopped to consider it—which he didn't. He was too anxious for her attention and yet too fraught with nerves to claim it. By her gentle admission, she had knocked his thoughts all asunder.

From the corner of his eye, he saw that long tail of honey-colored hair pulled over her shoulder while she fidgeted with the end of it, curling it around her finger. In the mellow, shimmering torchlight, that color was even more intriguing, a cornucopia of ever-changing tones and shades, too many to count.

Mrs. Bentley talked on with no end in sight, apparently forgetting the very presence of her sister. He scratched his neck and fitted a finger under his cravat, which, although loosened, still felt much too tight. The noise of the crowd was beginning to annoy him, and he was thirsty, his throat as dry as a bone.

Sophie was watching the dancers, her face turned away. A shorter frond of hair escaped her ribbon and fluttered against the side of her neck, just below that small ear. He wanted to brush that tendril aside with his uncouth fingers, as he'd done in the church when he ran into her. His fingers coiled into a fist, this time resisting the urge, but the idea of touching her again took rapid possession until every nerve within his body came alive, jolted out of a long, deep sleep.

When he let out a sudden, soft groan, Maria finally ceased her chatter. Her eyes widened in apparent alarm. "Mr. Kane?"

He was still staring at Sophie's neck and that thin sliver of golden hair. His hand flexed, prepared to do as it pleased without a care for propriety.

"Mr. Kane?" Maria persisted.

Sophie turned her face to look at him, and the stray lock of hair slid from his view. He coughed, one hand raised to his mouth. Her eyes were layered in the rich shades of an autumnal forest, pulling him in so far he heard wind-fallen leaves rustling under his feet—and her laughter, soft and breathless. He felt her hand, warm in his while he led her along to where the leaves were piled into a bed under the rich, golden canopy. There he laid her down, put his mouth to her ear, and whispered all his desires. The fantasy blossomed. He saw his hands removing her gown and her petticoats. Would she cry out when his lips took possession of her nipple for the first time? He stared and imagined he could see a sharp little peak there, pushing through the thin material of her old blue gown. He bit down on his lip. Lust, greedy and quick, soared through his body. When he entered her for the first time, would she arch her back as she did when leaning from the bridge to reach for a hawthorn flower? He could already hear her sighs and moans, could feel her breath softly brush his cheek as her body welcomed him in at last…and he drove himself deeper…and deeper.

Lost in his vision, Lazarus was quite unaware of his hand moving. Until she blinked, and the spell was broken.

"You must excuse me," he croaked, bowing very stiffly and almost double before hurrying away like a man with his boots on fire.

❧

"How very odd," Maria whined. "What can he mean by walking away like that?"

Sophie couldn't reply. She could hardly even breathe.

Because, in the darkness, his little finger had brushed against her hand.

Perhaps it was by accident alone. If his finger hadn't curled so slowly against her palm, she might have thought it was just that—a mistake. But she'd looked into his eyes and read thoughts that shocked her. Aroused her.

Now he walked out into the brighter light of the yard, where he stopped to talk with Jane Osborne. Sophie looked for her aunt and saw the lady sitting on a bench, clapping along to the music, one foot resting on a milking stool.

She moved quickly across the yard, but before she reached her destination, Farmer Osborne stepped in her path and playfully demanded a dance. She felt Lazarus watching her through the crowd, his regard still heated and lusty.

"Of course, Mr. Osborne." She accepted the elderly gentleman's hand and let him sweep her off for a jig.

Luckily, she hadn't forgotten the steps after so long with no opportunity to dance. When younger, she'd often enjoyed trips to the assembly rooms in Morecroft for the monthly balls. She and her sister would dress up in their best gowns and curl their hair. But that was a long time ago. These days Maria was busy with her own family, and Sophie stayed away from Morecroft as much as possible, rather than suffer being stared at. Tonight she felt a little stab of wistfulness for the old days. As she looked across the yard, she caught Maria's eye and smiled. Her sister was tapping her feet to the music, head bobbing, and suddenly it seemed like yesterday when they would giggle together in their bed and talk over the happenings at some ball or party, or gossip about other girls and handsome young men. Speculating on whom they would one day marry.

Certainly, she thought with a wry smile, Maria had never shown any fancy for clergymen, and she'd never imagined herself advertising for a husband in a farmer's gazette. Funny how life turned out.

Suddenly the dance was over. Breathless, still smiling, she stumbled directly into the arms of Lazarus Kane.

"There she is," exclaimed Aunt Finn, who had hold of his sleeve in her fingers as if she'd just dragged him across the yard like a naughty boy. "Mr. Kane wishes to dance with you, Sophie. He's been waiting all this time."

He looked slightly bemused, but then he smiled, and it lit up his entire face.

She couldn't very well refuse, could she? And since Henry wasn't there…

"I suppose I have time for one dance," she muttered. "And then we really must leave."

As Lazarus took her hand and led her into the line of couples, whispers fluttered in the air around them on all sides, curiosity swooping like a flock of seagulls over broken crab shells on the sands.

"Don't mind them," he muttered from the side of his lips.

"I don't."

He arched an eyebrow.

"I don't," she repeated firmly. It would be good for them all to see her dance with him, she decided. Then they would know there was no awkwardness between them and no reason for any further speculation.

The dance began. She tried to avoid his direct gaze but soon found it impossible. She could see her face reflected in his dark, satiny pupils as he looked down at her, rarely blinking.

"Ouch," she said when he stepped on her toe.

He mumbled an apology and promptly stepped on her foot again, his gaze still trained upon her face.

"You didn't seem to have this much trouble with your other partners," she observed curtly.

He gave a sheepish grin and turned her just a little too fast. "You have an extraordinary effect on me, Miss Valentine. As your aunt has already observed. A very clever lady."

"Will you please pay attention to the steps? And you're holding my hand too tightly." His palm was very hot and clammy.

"I don't want you to get away again."

She glowered at him.

He laughed softly. "You can stop pretending you didn't want to dance with me."

"I didn't," she objected. "I was forced into it by my aunt."

"Your aunt is a sweet lady."

"Sweet? Don't be fooled, Mr. Kane. None of the women in our family are sweet or delicate, despite appearances."

"Oh, I know you are not what you appear to be," he said with a wink. "Hold tight!" He spun her again, far faster than necessary. She tripped over her hem and fell against his torso, giving him the excuse to put his hands on her waist while she found her balance. "I bet you're a damn good card player," he added.

She was, as a matter of fact. It was a skill inherited from her aunt. "Mr. Kane, you are bold and presumptuous."

"How else can a man get what he wants out of life?"

She rolled her eyes to the starlit sky. "Thank goodness not all men think like you. Where would we be if everyone cast aside rules and propriety and forgot their manners?"

He leaned down to whisper against her brow. "I'd be with you, madam, and I know *exactly* what we'd be doing."

As much as she might like to misunderstand, his meaning was shockingly clear.

"Not dancing," he clarified with a grin.

She merely shook her head. She was unable to speak just then, still recovering from the stroke of his breath against her temple.

"You think me too forward," he added.

A slight understatement, she mused.

"But I like to get all my cards out on the table. I don't waste time."

She swallowed a groan of despair as he tossed her about again like a rag doll. All the other couples danced demurely and elegantly, while she felt as if she'd been dragged through a hedge by her feet.

"Your brother doesn't like me much, does he?"

Again she shook her head.

"Is that why you keep running away from me?"

"Certainly not. I do not run away from you, Mr. Kane."

"Yes, you do." He stuck out his jaw. "Five times now we've encountered each other in private. Twice you ran away. Once you simply backed away and hid behind your sister-in-law. The other times, you railed at me for helping you over a puddle and slammed a door in my face."

"I was...embarrassed. Mortified by your behavior."

"Nonsense. You're not embarrassed, Miss Valentine." He tightened his hold on her hand, almost squeezing the blood out of it. "You're afraid."

"Of what?" she scoffed, annoyed by his smug assumption.

"Of what you want from me."

Her lips parted, but she couldn't find the words to protest.

His eyes narrowed. "You're afraid of how badly you hunger for it and of what you might do to get it. I understand you've been known to take drastic measures in the past."

The music ended. She finally unwedged her hand

from his great paw. "Thank you, Mr. Kane. That was most amusing. Good evening."

"Thank *you*, Miss Valentine. Now this entire party was worthwhile."

"Worthwhile?" She scowled, hands raised to tidy her hair.

"I did it all for you," he added. "You were the only guest who mattered. I look forward to our next dance."

She replied hastily, "There won't be another."

"Oh, but there will. And the next dance will be much more intimate." He bowed from the waist and walked away, leaving her with two bruised feet and the horrifying realization she'd finally met someone as difficult and stubborn as she.

Chapter 13

LAZARUS STROLLED UP THE LANE THE FOLLOWING morning with a large basket of eggs, full of such neighborly good intentions he forgot how very early it was. The warm air was rich with fragrance. A pollen-heavy haze had already formed, so the sky was more gold than blue, and as he strode along, admiring it, he was too preoccupied to whistle his usual merry tune. Neither did he bother with the bell at the gate since, in his experience, no one ever answered it. Instead he went directly to the cookhouse. Finding the door ajar, he pushed it fully open with his basket, looked in, and saw the place empty.

Then he heard splashing and creaking. Curious, he walked around the side of the cookhouse and saw her by the water pump, bent over a half barrel, her hair falling loose over her face like a thick curtain. He stopped, frozen mid-step, and almost dropped his eggs. She pumped the lever again with one hand, and another abrupt gush of gleaming water splattered down over her bent head.

The fool woman was outside in only her shift.

What if some other man came there that morning and saw her? He suffered a sudden spur of hot anger, but his temper soon changed to something else when, having twisted and squeezed her long hair with both hands, she threw her head back. An arc of tiny prisms flew through the air to splatter the thin material of her shift, making a large patch down her back completely transparent.

He immediately looked away, but not many breaths had passed before he looked again. Now she stooped to wash her arms in the barrel, and the dampened shift clung to her hips, revealing a tempting hint of soft pink skin beneath.

His mouth was very dry, his heart thudding away as if it might, at any moment, burst out of his chest. He thought about backing away before she turned and found him watching, but his boots preferred the patch of stone upon which they stood.

You idiot! She'll turn and see you. Then she'll run and hide. And think you a rotten, lecherous cad. Which, indeed, you are.

He suddenly wished she *would* turn and see him there. He wanted to see her eyes. It was their attention for which he yearned, as much as a bird might for the first sight of snowdrops to mark the coming of spring.

Sophie washed her feet next, stepping into the half barrel and reaching down to splash water up her ankles and along her legs as far as the knee. Again, he was treated to forbidden glimpses: some merely taunting suggestions of what lay beneath that wet linen, and others so finely and clearly outlined by the clinging shift. He stopped breathing for a moment, forgetting his brain's need of oxygen, while other parts of his body were fully and delightfully nourished.

A swallow building its nest somewhere under the eaves of the cookhouse roof swooped low over his head, chirping irritably. He ducked but stayed, too mesmerized to leave yet.

She turned slightly and unknowingly treated him to further delights, for the front of her shift was also wet. The thin material clung to her breasts like a second layer of skin, following the full swell of their shape and revealing the darker circles at their peaks. As he stared, a drop of water fell like a tear to her left breast and dribbled slowly down over the lush curve. He felt that heavy heat in his groin, the excitement of the hunt, the anticipation of imminent capture. She was too assailable.

The swallow, a fierce sentinel, dived down again, narrowly missing his head, and Lazarus finally retreated. His pulse raced, pumping blood hard through his body.

❧

Some time later, Sophie entered the cookhouse. She wore a dry gown and carried her wet shift. Her aunt was fast asleep by the fire. No one else was up and about yet. Lavinia was still in her chamber, fussing over her appearance and her curls, as usual, while Henry, with no business to get him up and out of bed, she supposed was still snoring heavily into his pillow.

Sophie kissed her aunt's temple and then spread her shift before the fire to dry. As she turned her back to the hearth, she finally noticed the basket of eggs. Most of which were broken.

Wilson, the maid, came in carrying a milk pail. "The stranger brought eggs, Miss Sophie. He left them for you. Seemed in a hurry."

She flicked her damp hair back over her shoulders and stared at the basket of eggs, wondering how long he'd been there to make his delivery and why she didn't hear him come. She was very warm inside suddenly and feared she might have caught a fever.

❧

"Eggs, indeed! As if we need his charity," Henry muttered at breakfast later that morning. "Take them back to the blackguard, Wilson. Or better yet, send them with the steward. It wouldn't do to put you, a young maid, in his way. Mark my words, the fellow is trouble. Look how he cavorted about last night with one girl after another. No woman is safe in this village now."

"Except Sophia," Lavinia pointed out. "He doesn't want *her*."

Sophie bit into her toast with a loud crunch. She wanted to correct them all and shout he did, indeed, want her still. What good would it do? They would probably not believe her, and then she'd be forced to tell them how he'd kissed her...about the way he looked at her. She fidgeted in her chair, her skin warm, the heaviness of want starting in her belly again, as it did whenever she thought of his warning to her last night.

The next dance will be much more intimate.

"It seems he has designs on the Osborne girl," Henry muttered as he opened his copy of the *Racing Post*. "He means to get his hands on her father's pretty property, without a doubt, and she has no brothers or sisters to share the inheritance."

His wife wrinkled her small, round nose. "No one would want that plain creature for any other reason but the property. Lord, with those teeth, she ought to be pulling her father's milk cart up and down the High Street."

Henry rustled his newspaper, turning another page as if the contents of the last had mortally offended him. "The tailor in Morecroft informed me he fashioned an entire suit of clothes for the illustrious Mr. Kane," he grumbled. "Breeches, jacket, coat, shirt, and waistcoat. What's more, he was paid in full for his services, although the stranger arrived there in a very poor and shabby set of patched clothes that clearly belonged to someone else. The only item of clothing he did not purchase new in Morecroft were his boots, and these he was loath to remove, even while being fitted for his new clothes. The reason?" He paused for effect, glancing up over the top of his paper. "Because, according to the tailor, his boots were stuffed full of bank notes."

His announcement did not have the expected effect. Lavinia was busy complaining to Wilson about the crispness of her toast, and Sophie was deliberately not listening.

Aunt Finn offered jauntily, "He seems very fond of the widow Finchly and her boys. She would be a better choice for him than Jane Osborne, who is too young and desperately stupid." She turned to her niece. "Do you not agree, Sophie?"

Having just taken another large bite of toast, Sophie made much of chewing and swallowing.

"Of course, either one of the Misses Dawkins might stand a chance," Finn added cheerily. "They are lively creatures, although Amy Dawkins has the features of a squirrel with rather too many nuts in its cheeks, and the other one rarely has her finger out of her nose."

But the two Misses Dawkins and the grasping Jane Osborne were not the only hopeful, unwed young ladies in Sydney Dovedale, starved of new male company, who regarded the mysteriously wealthy stranger with eager speculation. They all knew he was in want of a wife, and now that Sophie was considered out of the running, the field was wide open. Already there were signs of a battle campaign being waged. The first to benefit were the milliner and the haberdasher in Morecroft, while new gowns and trimmings became matters of the utmost importance. Gowland's lotion and Steele's Lavender Water flew off the shelves quicker than it could be stocked, and a disturbing amount of powdered rouge was suspected of lending an unaccustomed blush to even the most immodest cheek.

"Amy Dawkins is the most likely to snare him," said Lavinia, finally forgetting her dispute over the toast. "She has her sharp claws out and won't let her lack of fortune or property stand in her way." She sighed heavily as she brushed crumbs from her bosom. "She's a dreadful, common little thing, with no fashion, but he seems to be making the most of all the female attention."

"I would rather not hear another word about his comings and goings," Henry exclaimed snappishly. "From now on, I will not hear that man's name mentioned in this house."

His wife stoutly reminded him he first began the subject. "You are altogether too red in the face, Henry. I hope you are not on the verge of apoplexy. I refuse to be a young widow, for black doesn't suit me at all."

He disappeared again behind the *Racing Post*.

Wilson brought over a letter, handing it to Lavinia, who snatched it away with her buttery fingers. She was growing more discontent by the moment and now claimed to be off her food that morning, although her empty, clean-scraped plate suggested otherwise. While supposedly engrossed in her letter, she threw out little criticisms about anyone and anything.

"This bacon is much too fatty. I believe that butcher deliberately gave us the worst he had yesterday. I know his wife is jealous of my new bonnet. It is very like her own except better and more expensive, which is quite plainly apparent when one looks closely." She reached over to spear another slice of inadequate bacon on her fork.

No one spoke.

"And now we expect my mama for dinner on market day," she announced, waving her letter.

Sophie groaned into her coffee, "Let joy be unconfined."

Lavinia's mother, Mrs. Dykes, was a frequent visitor to the fortress. She was smaller than her daughter and less stooped, but extremely stiff. Sophie suspected Mrs. Dykes had a cork leg, although it was never mentioned. She feared that one evening, if she had too much wine, she might feel inclined to shoot it with a dart to be sure.

Until Henry married, it was Sophie who managed the daily housekeeping affairs and thus was able, wherever possible, to curb some of his more extravagant spending. But now Lavinia insisted *she* take this role, she who had even less restraint than her husband and refused to discuss "vulgar economy." Whenever Sophie quietly tried to offer advice, Lavinia whined to Henry and to her mother that her place as mistress of the house was undermined. Mrs. Dykes, protective of her daughter's interests, had lately suggested, in countless unsubtle ways, Sophie ought to be sent away with a respectable family as a governess or nanny.

But Sophie had no desire to leave Sydney Dovedale or her little schoolhouse. When she ventured beyond that small world, folk had a tendency to stare and point at her scar.

"We must move everything back to the Keep today, for Mama would be appalled to see how we live, crunched up together like this," Lavinia exclaimed. "Surely the weather is fine enough now, Henry, and we might at least put a small fire in the great hall."

From behind his newspaper, Henry agreed their living quarters could be moved back to the main building, but even this was not enough for Lavinia. She insisted also on beeswax candles for the dinner table, not the cheaper tallow.

"The last time Mama dined with us, she commented on the use of tallow candles, and I was so ashamed. Is my mama not deemed worthy of the best candles, Henry? Each time I got them out, Sophia put them back again! But if it were any other guest, the beeswax would be got out without question."

He mumbled that she may choose whichever candles she preferred.

"I hear Mr. Kane is only five and twenty," Aunt Finn exclaimed abruptly, causing Henry to ruffle his paper angrily. "One wonders how he came by his fortune at such a young age. He must be either very clever or very wicked. Perhaps both." She chuckled. "Still, while some men are old before they mature"—she glanced at Henry's newspaper—"other men mature before they're old."

Sophie's mind drifted wantonly over the image of Mr. Kane as she saw him a few days ago, shearing sheep. He wore naught but those snug breeches as he bent over the protesting, squirming creatures, working with speed and efficiency. Each animal was shorn of its thick fleece before it knew what had occurred, and then it skipped off in delight, several pounds lighter.

She saw again the sweat glazing his thick shoulders under the afternoon sun, and the pronounced lines of muscle as he twisted over the sheep. She would like to run her hands over that torso, feel every mound and valley, know every inch of that terrain. He had dark hair on his chest, mostly across the upper planes then trailing away to a thin line that ran below the waist of his breeches. When he turned and stretched between shearing each sheep, she'd taken note of that vast breadth between his shoulders, and then the rapid narrowing, and lastly, the little dip in the small of his back just above his tight, round buttocks.

The next dance will be much more intimate.

Disgusted, she dropped another crust to her plate.

Only five and twenty! She'd guessed he was young,

but it was still a shock to hear his age confirmed aloud. A mere boy, for heaven's sake! No wonder he was so carefree when it came to the rules.

The devilish Mr. Kane was too young for her; yet he was also, oddly enough, many years too late.

Chapter 14

ON MARKET DAY, LAZARUS WAS OBLIGED TO ESCORT Miss Jane Osborne to the village square. How he came to invite the lady for a ride in his cart he couldn't remember, but it had something to do with a conversation they had at his party.

She was already waiting at the grass verge as his cart rattled down the lane at speed. The bonnet she wore was yellow straw with bulbous swirls of red-and-white striped ribbon. Although such things were still largely a mystery to Lazarus, he knew ladies took their bonnets and trimmings very seriously, so he was sure to compliment her on it as he drew his horses to a sharp halt. The lady looked up at him and beamed, stretching her lips over those enormous teeth. He was late, but now, since he'd complimented her hat, he was forgiven.

He knew enough about ladies to know…

Struck with an idea, Lazarus prodded Tuck with one elbow. "Get in the back and make room for Miss Osborne beside me."

"Why can't she ride in the back?" Tuck protested grumpily.

"Because she's a lady, ain't she?"

Tuck huffed and puffed and muttered under his breath, but he crawled into the back of the cart. Jane Osborne eagerly accepted the hand Lazarus held down to her.

"You're too kind, Mr. Kane," she giggled frothily.

And then they were off again, Tuck complaining loudly from the back of the cart. Lazarus slowed the horses to a prim trot and eyed the short, angular woman at his side. After a few minutes of struggle, he found something else to compliment. "Miss Osborne, that gown is a very becoming color on you."

"Why, thank you, Mr. Kane," she neighed excitedly, causing the horses' ears to twitch.

Behind them, Tuck grumbled and spat and glared at the woman who had taken his seat. She tittered, and her left hip shifted closer to Lazarus as they traveled over another bump.

"Best hang on to me, Miss Osborne," he told her. "I shouldn't like to lose you under the wheels."

Tuck muttered, "Cart would come out worse for it."

❧

There was so much noise in the market square he could barely hear himself talk, but Miss Osborne still laughed loudly at everything he said, even things that were neither funny nor meant to be. Her laughter held its own against the bleating of goats and sheep as they rounded the animal pens. With her hanging on his arm, his considerable strength began to wane before they completed a full promenade of the square. But he soldiered on, his eyes scanning the crowd for the sight of a certain small, prim face.

"Mr. Kane, I should like to have my fortune told."

He let Miss Osborne lead him off to the gypsy fortune-teller's striped tent.

"You'd best not come in with me, Mr. Kane," she giggled. "It would not do for you to know all my secrets, would it? Not just yet!"

When he smiled, it actually felt painful. She disappeared through the tent flap, and he looked around, searching.

Aha! There they were.

It was the same gown she wore to church, a light primrose color sprigged with a pattern of tiny flowers, over which she wore a pale blue spencer today, instead of her longer coat. Rather than wear her simple bonnet, she carried it by the ribbons, swinging it at her side as she strolled along behind her brother.

Just as his eyes found her, she was joined by her sister, the rector's wife. The two women walked side by side, and he saw Mrs. Bentley's mouth moving rapidly, as usual, while Sophie said nothing. She swung her bonnet idly as her warm hazel eyes searched the stalls for anything of interest. The two women stopped to peruse a selection of jams and pickles just a few feet from where he stood, but Henry, turning irritably to see where his sister had gone, caught sight of the enemy watching. He clasped his sister's arm, and the officious coxcomb pulled her away into the crowd.

Lazarus realized his jaw hurt, and he raised his hand to it, rubbing it slowly to ease the tension.

"Mr. Kane! We wanted to thank you for the splendid party." The Dawkins sisters sprang up out of the ground like weeds to stand before him and demand his attention. With one sister on either side, he was immediately penned in. "We so seldom enjoy an evening of dancing here in the village, Mr. Kane. Sydney Dovedale is rather a dull place, you know, for Mr. Valentine frowns on parties. He says they foster drunkenness and lewd behavior, so it is usually discouraged. Of course, there are dances at the Morecroft assembly rooms every month, but they're hardly worth going to, since one always sees the same people. Do you plan to attend the assembly rooms, Mr. Kane?"

Only half-listening, he replied, "I'm not much of a dancer."

"Oh, but you must come!" The most outgoing sister of the two moved closer. "We can tell you all about the people there, and we shall have laughs."

"And we saw you dance already, Mr. Kane," the other sister chided him shyly. "You danced all night long at your party."

He was straining to see where Sophie had gone, and then he caught sight of her again. She trailed behind her brother and sister, lingering to watch some piglets. She was smiling today, and on impulse, his hand went to his heart. He took a breath as his fingertips traced over the slight bump where that shard of metal rested under his skin—his Sword of Damocles.

The Dawkins girls had apparently followed his gaze with their own.

"I suppose it was a great shock to you, Mr. Kane," one of them exclaimed while tapping his arm with her netted purse, "when you came here expecting to marry Sophia Valentine and saw that dreadful scar."

"I've seen much worse."

"Worse? How could it be any worse?"

He knew they would never understand. Their world was a sunny, sheltered one. They couldn't know of life's horrors. They would never see some of the places he'd lived in. They probably didn't even know of the existence of rookeries—the slums of London where he was born. They didn't know what it was like to beg for food in the streets and alleyways. And they would never fight on a battlefield and see their friends blown to pieces before their eyes.

To these ladies, it seemed, that scar on Sophie Valentine's cheek was a hellish disfigurement, the worst thing they could imagine. But they'd never been to hell, had they?

"She was engaged once before, I understand," he muttered, low.

"Yes. Her beau gave her up, and serves her right too."

Her sister had the grace to blush at those harsh words. "Poor Sophia. Her heart was broken."

"But they say she jumped deliberately from that balcony. Mama says Sophia was always a wayward, disobedient creature. It serves her right Mr. Hartley broke the engagement."

Lazarus watched the distant, shapely figure hurrying along, the breeze pulling on her skirt. When she was hiding, he wanted to lure her out of her shell with kisses. When she was angry, he wanted to do more than that. Something about Miss Valentine brought out every ounce of his masculinity, even those parts a gentleman was supposed to bury with good manners. From first sight, his heart, and indeed his entire body, had nursed this curious idea that she belonged to him, needed him...whether she admitted it or not. Of course, his heart was a very unpredictable beast and, by most learned accounts, should have ceased to beat some years past, so he couldn't trust it to behave wisely.

"Do tell us, Mr. Kane, what qualities you look for in a young lady."

"Qualities?" he murmured, still distracted.

"What do you consider most attractive in a young lady?" the other Dawkins sister urged, her eyelashes quivering with mock timidity.

"A lady should have spirit and not be afraid to take chances," he replied, "or make decisions of her own. She should take control of her life and her own happiness."

Forgetting good manners, he abruptly left the two young ladies to follow Sophie through the crowd. So she had a broken heart, did she? This was why she kept her distance. She still pined for an old beau who had abandoned her.

He was distantly aware of the Misses Dawkins watching him go, and he heard one of them declare she didn't think him quite so handsome now as she did before. Her sister still allowed him to be an "interesting" fellow, if somewhat brusque and common.

Their chatter faded as he was submerged in the crowd, following Sophie. He slowed his pace. She seemed unaware of his presence behind her, but suddenly she lifted that ugly straw bonnet, placed it over her hair, and tied the ribbons under her chin, tucking that golden treasure away. Disappointment was as sharp as the broken knife blade lodged near his heart. She stopped suddenly, absorbed by a display of little clockwork ornaments, and he, rather than collide with her, stepped swiftly aside and walked on. As he passed, Lazarus raised his hand, prepared to tip his hat, but she stared down at the goods on display as if she didn't see him. So his hand dropped again, the gesture never fully developed. He lengthened his stride and hurried onward, furious with himself for being such a fool, but also with her for hiding away under her bonnet, denying him even the pleasure of admiring her hair.

Miss Osborne soon caught up with him, annoyed to find him gone when she emerged from the gypsy's tent. "What were you talking of with the Dawkins sisters?" she demanded.

He thought quickly. "The Morecroft assembly rooms."

"Lord! You don't want to go there, Mr. Kane," she exclaimed. "They're always full of the commonest riffraff. All manner of drunks and strumpets go there! It's the sort of place tawdry, desperate girls go to find husbands. I certainly would never be so frantic to find a husband as some of the women around here. The lengths they will go to…advertisements in the paper…" Miss Osborne's voice echoed around the marketplace, and he realized Sophie looked over at them. For just a moment, he was the target of her questioning perusal. Then her gaze lowered to her feet again, those disapproving lips pursed tightly. He wished he'd never given Jane Osborne his arm, but it was too late.

～

The rumors were confirmed, then. He was courting Jane Osborne. Folk said he'd dined with the Osbornes at least thrice and showed the young lady a great deal of attention. Jane Osborne was nearer his age, more suited to him in many ways.

With the noise of the marketplace churning in her ears, Sophie picked up a little clockwork bird in a cage and studied it as if it were the most fascinating thing in the world. It was very delicately painted, the eyes wide and staring, the tiny beak chirping at her.

"Good gracious!" Maria clutched her sleeve. "Is that James Hartley?"

She looked up as a jaunty, yellow-wheeled curricle rolled across the cobbles, traveling fast in their brother's direction. Absorbed in his own reflection in the butcher's bow-front window, Henry must not have heard his name shouted and was almost run over in the street. The great rumbling wheels came to a juddering halt, the horses close enough to bite holes in his hat.

"Valentine! I thought that was you. Almost mashed you to a pulp. Where have you been, old chap? Haven't seen you at the club lately!"

Sophie, realizing her mouth was open, quickly closed it and set the little caged bird down.

"It is!" Maria whispered in her ear. "It is he. And he doesn't look a day older." She grabbed her sister's arm tightly and drew her away from the market stall and across the square in unseemly haste. If this was any normal day, Sophie would have resisted, but with the memory of Jane Osborne's disdainful comment still ringing cheerlessly in her ears, she let her limp self be dragged across the cobbles, dignity be damned. Admittedly, she was almost as curious as Maria.

James Hartley leaped down from his curricle and exclaimed, "You're looking a little green about the gills, Valentine. Married life not suiting you? Although"—he paused, standing back to take in Henry's full figure—"somebody feeds you well."

"Bored with London again, Hartley? Aren't we too dull and provincial for you now?"

James laughed, the diamond pin in his cravat winking. "Must visit Grandmama in Morecroft once in a great while to replenish the pockets. And I just heard some most astonishing news while I was there, Henry."

"Indeed?"

"That your sister seeks a husband in the pages of the *Norwich and Morecroft Farmer's Gazette.*"

Fumbling in his waistcoat pocket for his watch, Henry avoided the subject of that advertisement. James looked around for something more interesting, and found Sophie and her sister standing nearby. His gaze hardened. It was only a subtle dimming of the merry, careless light in his eyes. Most folk would have missed it.

"It is all over town," she heard him say. "Such a strange thing. Especially since I thought she was resolved not to marry. At least, that's what she once told me."

Henry replied, "Yes, well...it *was* a long time ago."

"I suppose time passes, and we're all very much older now."

"And some of us are wiser. Well, I cannot stay and chat, Hartley. Good day. My regards to your grand-mama." Henry hurried away down the street, obviously keen to escape.

But Sophie came to a halt on the path. Guilt made it necessary to explain herself. When she'd posted that advertisement, she never thought it might come to James's notice. He was so seldom in Morecroft, the possibility never occurred to her. He surely never read a publication like the *Farmer's Gazette*. Someone must have pointed it out to him, probably one of his friends, to tease him.

"How pleasant to see you again, James."

"Yes," he answered sharply and squared his wide shoulders under that fine garnet coat.

"You look...very well."

"So do you, Sophia." His voice shook a little when he said her name, belying his stiff, unyielding demeanor.

Clouds passed over the sun, and grey shadows rolled at her feet. She was painfully aware of faces turned to watch the encounter, hands pressed to whispering lips and eager ears.

James held out his gloved hand. "Perhaps you will allow me to take you and your sister home. If you've concluded your business here."

It was a timely offer, since the first sprinkles of a summer shower had just made their presence known on her sleeves, and a fresh bite in the air warned more was to come.

Maria declined, since she had only a short distance to the rectory and preferred to walk. Thus, Sophie climbed up alone to ride with him in the curricle.

Chapter 15

THE HORSES CHARGED ALONG, JUST MISSING HENRY once again, who stumbled into the verge, holding his hat and cursing. Sophie squinted against the rain and looked back over her shoulder. The ribbons of her bonnet slapped her cheek. "I didn't expect you to see that advertisement, James," she murmured apprehensively as her hands clung to the seat for dear life.

"Really? I thought perhaps you wanted me to read it and come back again."

Her lips parted with a quick, startled exhale. A spark of panic sputtered to life in her chest. That damned advertisement!

"All the way here," he muttered, "I told myself it was merely a nice, quiet ride in the country, but my horse somehow made its way along the lane toward Souls Dryft, and as that old flint stone wall came into sight, the memories came back to me."

She relented with a small smile. It was good to see him again after all this time. When they were young, he used to come out to Souls Dryft and take her for rides like this. In fine weather, she would sit on the flint wall, waiting eagerly for him.

"Just like old times," he said, mirroring her thoughts aloud.

His genuine smile, which suddenly appeared, gleamed just as brightly as she remembered, and his eyes were that dazzling clear blue she imagined must surround tropical islands, those she only read about in books. The years between had been kind to James. They had mellowed his boyish, slender good looks into something more solid, something warmer. He always had charming manners, but now there was an ease about his gestures. He'd grown into his skin. Youth had its advantages, without a doubt, but there was also much to be said for maturity.

The wheels jolted hard over a deep rut, and her bonnet slipped back off her head. She grabbed the ribbons but didn't bother replacing it. Her pins had all come out, as usual, and cramming the straw bonnet back on her wet head would be pointless.

"I think your hair is darker now," James observed. "And—good Lord—it's positively wild!"

Flustered, threading her fingers through it, she replied, "Well, I have no ladies' maid, and I—"

He interrupted to exclaim, very gallantly, that she looked more beautiful now than she did at nineteen.

She looked away, her face so warm raindrops dried soon after they touched it.

"Henry is married now, I hear," he said jovially, as if he'd not noticed her embarrassment or the fingers suddenly raised to cover her scar.

"Yes, indeed. The house is rather crowded now and—"

"I must say, I never thought Henry would succumb. Where did he find her?"

"In Norwich," she replied curtly. "With her trotter stuck in a grate. I wish he'd—"

"Aha! Is she that bad? I did wonder why I never see her."

They rode on a while in silence, and then he stirred up the memories again, reminding her of the day *they* met, when he offered to climb a tree and pick a pear for her, but she calmly pushed him aside and climbed the tree herself. "That was the very first time I was rendered speechless by the sudden sight of your ankles. I decided immediately I was in love with you."

She rolled her eyes. "Yes, you did like to be in—"

"But you were surely a worthy target of my affections, a diamond of the first water."

He was full of sayings like these. Words were James Hartley's specialty, and he had some for every occasion. "Oh, really!" she chortled. "Even in my best year, I was never a great beauty, as you—"

"You stole my heart, Sophia. I could never tell what you were thinking."

Well, perhaps if he ever let her finish a sentence, he might know, she thought with a sudden spur of annoyance.

"You intrigued me from the start," he admitted. "Funny, scowling creature, often found behind a potted palm and flicking pieces of fruit from the punch bowl at people you disliked. Always plotting some mischief and taking that horrid little girl under your wing when she came here to stay with her aunt—what was her name?"

"Ellie Vyne," she replied curtly, knowing he remembered her young friend's name well enough, but since the Vynes and Hartleys had been feuding for years, he pretended ignorance.

James urged the horses even faster. She clung to his arm to save herself from being thrown out and crushed under the wheels.

"You decided you were *in love* with me, James Hartley, largely because your grandmama fiercely disapproved. As the niece of Finn Valentine, a notorious scarlet woman, I was the very last sort of girl Lady Hartley wanted for her grandson." She smiled slowly. "But you did like to tease and torment her, as far as— "

"I disobeyed the old dear to run after you to London. I suppose I was utterly spellbound by those mysteriously sad eyes of yours. Always hiding secrets. And when I asked you to marry me, you laughed, as if it were the funniest thing you'd ever heard, and said, 'Yes, let's! Let's do it soon, before I change my mind. We should elope to Gretna Green!'" He paused, the laughter gone. "I should never have let you slip away."

Sophie breathed deeply, sucking in the damp rustiness of the wet earth. "Young people grow up. You found other women to fall in love with." She hoped it was true. She wanted him to be happy.

Lips pursed, James nodded. "Just as my grandmama says, there are a great many women in the world. It would be foolish to pine over just one." He turned his face toward her again. "But quantity is not the same as quality, Sophia."

She thought of the young, raven-haired housemaid smiling wistfully up at him as he tweaked her dimpled chin. Had he been "in love" with that girl too? Perhaps she should mention what she'd seen that night at Lady Honoria Grimstock's ball, while she waited on the balcony and pondered her future. But what would be the point now, all these years later? Back then, everything seemed significant, every happiness so thrilling, every sadness completely dire, and every slight utterly unforgivable. How silly she was then.

She played with her wet bonnet ribbons, getting them in a tangle. "Souls Dryft is let again." They were just passing the tall iron gates of the farmhouse. The yard was empty today. Raindrops pricked the surface of the water trough and shined on the ivy that climbed the flint wall.

"Really? Let again? No one stays there long, it seems."

Her heart tripped. "No. Not for—"

"Damned place is haunted, if you ask me. Don't know why anyone would want to live in the drafty old place. Value's in the land, of course, not the old building."

She swallowed a small sigh.

"Do you suppose Henry will invite me to stay for dinner?" he chirped, grinning broadly, one subject exchanged for another without a second thought.

❧

From his own gate, Lazarus had a clear view of the crumbling old Norman fortress and the gatehouse that once kept out the marauding enemy, not to mention curious natives. Even in the rain, he watched for a good half an hour and waited for that fancy carriage to leave. But now the candles and torches were lit. It was plain the popinjay had stayed to dine.

"Ye comin' in or stayin' out all night?" Tuck hollered from the door of the house, stooping sideways under the low lintel. "Supper's gettin' cold."

The drizzle had now turned into a real "pelter," which got in his eyes and ran down the back of his shirt. "I'll be in."

He didn't like this. Not a bit. Jane Osborne had told him who the man was in the market square that day...Sophie's old flame. And when he saw them riding off together, the tightness in his chest became unbearable. He'd set out that day to make her jealous. The tables were turned.

⸻

Outside, the rain fell heavily now, and during silences in the conversation, it could be heard rattling against the shutters, burbling along the bumpy cobbles of the yard and splattering from the stone gargoyle spouts.

The precious beeswax candles, even in extravagant array down the length of the pitted old trestle table, were not enough to light the entire great hall, only the very center of it. The flames, under periodic bombardment from the many drafts, seemed almost ashamed of themselves and constantly bowed in apology for their woeful inadequacy. In the corners, dark shadows remained and closed in the dinner guests. A fire was lit in the massive hearth, but there was such a wind down the chimney, the flames ducked and danced, providing more smoke than heat. The faces of the dinner guests came and went in the unreliable light.

On this grim evening, Mrs. Dykes's dour, mournful appearance was oddly apt, as if she were another element of the storm. Henry's mother-in-law was a formidable creature in her severe black widow's weeds. She wore her graying hair pulled back in a tight knot that lifted the corners of her eyes and mouth into a rather terrifying grimace. While she dressed plainly, content to merge with the walls, her daughter preferred flamboyant colors and frills to accentuate her bosomy figure. This proclivity lent her the look of a dancing girl from the Drury Lane Theatre.

The two women stared at James Hartley in a fierce way, taking their attention from him only when Wilson brought around tureens and platters of food. Then they both looked away just long enough to choose greedy portions.

Mrs. Dykes had sold her house in Norwich to be closer to her daughter, and she now rented rooms in Morecroft. Like most things, they were deemed unworthy, falling far short of her expectations. She never failed to mention, during every visit to her son-in-law, the discomforts of her living quarters.

"It hain't in me to complain," she said, smiling distantly across the table at James Hartley, "although the rooms are *hawfully* damp in the winter and hot in the summer. They are, at least, in the better part of town, and one is close enough to visit one's daughter. When the roads are passable. It hain't so great a distance, even for an old woman with bad hips and weak blood. Traveling with the mail coach hain't no comfort, very often cramped with unsavory characters, but one withstands any trial to visit one's only daughter. I should love a private carriage, even just a small, jaunty little curricle, like what you own, Mr. Hartley. But one makes do."

Sophie looked at Henry, who merely slurped at his consommé and offered nothing to the conversation. Fortunately, the Bentleys had also been invited that evening, and Maria could always be counted on for some conversation.

"What news from Morecroft, Mrs. Dykes? Have you seen any new fashions there?" she politely enquired above the soup tureen.

The lady answered in a faint, disinterested voice. "One don't follow fashion these days, Mrs. Bentley, now one's a widow, of course." She sat very straight-laced and stiff in her black bombazine.

Maria's shoulders drooped in disappointment. Since she relied on news from larger towns when it came to keeping abreast of trends, Mrs. Dykes was really useful only as a conduit to such news. Loath to abandon the subject, she exclaimed, "I hear waistlines continue to fall. I'm sorry for it, as I do hate to wear tight stays!"

Aunt Finn declared herself heartily glad for the return of stays. "I never gave mine up, of course, but I saw many a young lady discarding stays who would be far better off"—and here she cast Lavinia a sly glance across the sputtering candles—"keeping herself restrained. Some bosoms are better off not being seen flopping about."

Sophie thought she would explode with laughter. The insult went over Lavinia's head, but not her mother's.

Mrs. Dykes glared at Aunt Finn with an intense, burning hatred. "Hain't the soup too spicy for you, Finnola dear? Lady Sadler recommends nothing but bland food for the helderly. It don't do no good to get them too lively with heavy seasoning, she always says."

Aunt Finn, who was surely no older than Mrs. Dykes, raised another spoonful to her mouth and, cooling it with her breath, blew several bubbles that spattered across the table.

"Such a pity you hain't got a French cook, 'Enry," Mrs. Dykes muttered as she dabbed at the spilled consommé with her napkin. "Lady Sadler swears to the proficiary of a French cook above any other."

Lady Sadler was a familiar name on her lips. Indeed, she used any excuse, stretched any topic, to include some anecdote about Lady Sadler, the wife of a retired judge and a former employer of Mrs. Dykes. The Sadlers, it seemed, were the authority on all things proper.

Sophie stole a glance at James and saw he was thoroughly entranced by Mrs. Dykes. Led by a wickedly dark sense of humor, he asked the lady many questions about the Sadlers, which she was only too glad to answer.

"Indeed, I've some right splendid news," she announced grandly. "The Sadlers have took a place along the seafront in Morecroft this summer for Lady Sadler's health. They bring all their daughters, Mr. Hartley, all unwed and at present unengaged," she simpered. "I defy you not to be in love with one of 'em while they're here. Wherever they go, they're much hadmired. Of course, they hain't got my daughter's complexion or her fine bones, but not everyone can be as fortunate as my Lavvy."

Sophie felt the tremors of James's stifled laughter. "I'm intrigued already, madam."

Now Mrs. Dykes turned her gimlet eyes to Henry.

"I took the libertary of mentioning to Sir Arthur Sadler our particular problem with Sophia. He'll soon sort her out."

Sophie exhaled. "Sort me out?"

"Sir Arthur will find Sophia a governess post." Mrs. Dykes smiled ghoulishly.

Sophie wondered why this dormant subject was suddenly raised again, but even as the question formed in her mind, she knew the answer. The scandal of her advertisement for a husband suddenly made it even more prudent she be sent away.

Mrs. Dykes continued, "It hain't like me to speak out of turn, but disciplinary is somewhat lax in this house, 'Enry. A really well-regulated family like the Sadlers hain't never suffered with scandal like what this one does."

James smiled dashingly at Mrs. Dykes and suggested that as soon as the Sadlers arrived in Morecroft, they must all come to his grandmother's house for an evening of music and cards.

"She does enjoy new company and would be excessively glad to meet you all."

Sophie winced. James always did love his pranks.

"You keep an 'ouse in London, sir?" Mrs. Dykes asked James.

He confirmed he did.

Gravy dripped down Lavinia's chin, but she was oblivious to it. "Henry won't take me to London. He says it's too much expense."

"Not even to visit the Grimstock relatives in Mayfair?" James asked politely.

"He's never taken me to visit them."

James leaned back in his chair to look at Henry. "Really, old chap? One should take one's lovely and charming wife to meet the noble Grimstocks."

Sophie tried to get his attention with her foot, to end his teasing for her brother's sake, but turning his handsome smile back to Lavinia, he exclaimed, "You would be the talk of the town, Mrs. Valentine. I daresay Henry fears you might be stolen away by an admirer if he took you out into Society."

Lavinia giggled and covered her plump lips with one hand.

"I don't have time to go to London," Henry snapped. "I have an estate to run."

Sophie drank her entire glass of wine in one swallow.

Mrs. Dykes shook her head sorrowfully and sucked on her teeth before giving this pronouncement: "Your sister's becoming a drinker, 'Enry. I knew it would come to this! Sir Arthur Sadler says an idle mind is too easily prone to over-hindulgence. A firm hand is what you lack here, 'Enry. With your parents gone, certain behavior has been tolerated, unchecked, for far too long, particular in light of…recent *hevents*."

Henry's face blossomed like a scarlet peony.

"The Sadlers have, in the past, helped several trouble-some young ladies like Sophia find good positions away from 'ome and in the bosom of good, proper Christian families. They'll surely find somewhere to put Sophia. Out of the way."

Sophie sighed so heavily she almost extinguished the nearest candle flame.

"What with that gypsy fellow down the lane, 'overing like a vulture…"

Sophie felt James watching her intently, his eyes cool and questioning.

The syllabub was served, but she couldn't enjoy a solitary spoonful, not while that nodding dragon sat across the table, trying to force her into another corner. Why did everyone assume they might organize her life? Soon they might drive her to a desperate act of mad violence with a meat cleaver. That cork leg would not stay attached long to Mrs. Dykes once Sophie began swinging something sharp in her direction.

As soon as she could politely leave the table, she walked outside for some fresh air. The wind and rain had stopped, coming and going with that peculiar eccentricity of an English summer, but it was still a chilly evening, and Sophie regretted leaving her shawl behind. It was too late to go back for it. They would all be discussing her now, as if she were a disobedient puppy leaving puddles on the rug. She hugged her arms and marched up and down the courtyard to stay warm, acrid smoke from the fireplace still clinging to her hair and gown.

"So this…gypsy…is the man who leased Souls Dryft?" James had followed her out into the yard and brought her shawl.

"Yes. He came here because of the advertisement. Just like you." Taking the shawl from his outstretched arm, she swung it around her shoulders.

"Not like me," he corrected her. "I have a prior claim. Besides, Henry says this gypsy changed his mind when he found you scarred."

That was a new one, she mused. Before, it was because her dowry was too small. Sophie turned away and walked toward the gatehouse.

James followed. "Where are you going?"

She stopped by the ancient stone and inhaled the calming scent of distant pine trees. The damp air was thick with it this evening.

Where *was* she going?

"What is all this about a governess post?"

"That's Mrs. Dykes…doing her best to be rid of me for her daughter's sake. I'm under Lavinia's feet here, and she resents my daily '*hinterference*.'"

James reached for her hand. "I can't decide who is worse, Lavinia or her mother. If I had any liking for Henry, I'd feel sorry for the man, but he makes his own problems." He looked down at her fingers. "And I can't forgive him for persuading you to break off our engagement, Sophia."

He never believed it was her idea to end their engagement. He preferred to blame Henry's influence. Ironically, most people in the village assumed James broke it off. No one could imagine Sophie Valentine, quite a commonplace woman even on a good day, would turn down the likes of a James Hartley.

"We should be married, Sophia. As it was meant to be."

He was so handsome and gallant in the moonlight. But it wasn't enough. People would think her daft, but she couldn't help it. She wanted more. The way he'd once touched that dark-haired maid in a crowded ballroom when he thought no one saw, had more tenderness, more heated desire in it, than the way he ever touched or looked at *her*. James seemed to think they belonged together, almost as if it were preordained, an item on a list to be crossed off. It wasn't because he had to have her, lusted after her, felt he would die without her.

Of course, if she thought practically, taking stock of her situation, marriage to James offered her much. At her age, it would be ungrateful, not to mention foolish, to turn him away without the slightest consideration.

"Kiss me, James," she whispered, wondering if it would feel different now they were older. She reached for his shoulders, but he gripped her arms and braced them so her hands rested on the lapels of his coat instead.

He was so painfully proper with her, when she knew he was not like that with other women. Oh yes, she knew about his reputation, but their one and only encounter on that billiard table ten years ago was initiated by her. He'd always treated her as if she might break, and the disappointment had led her to leap from a balcony.

"James. Just kiss me!"

With Lazarus Kane, she had not needed to ask. He hadn't given her the chance.

Finally James kissed her, almost missing her lips but for one southerly corner.

"Marry me, Sophia," he said again.

She sighed heavily, tears threatening at the brink. It would be a "good" match. No more money worries. Henry might even stop being angry with her, and she would no longer be the great disappointment, an embarrassment to be shoved off into the corner. She would escape this fortress and Lavinia. People would stop looking at her with pity in their eyes.

But she would have to leave behind this pretty village she loved. Then there was her schoolhouse—any good she'd tried to do there would be undone. And venturing back out into James's world...she didn't know if she wanted that again. Part of her would die forever. It must if she was to survive in that society. She remembered that evening by the balustrade, how she'd felt stifled and trapped. Of course, she was nineteen at the time, and many things seemed more dramatically wretched to her then. It might be different now.

"I need time to think, James."

"My darling Sophia. I shall be patient."

He was probably afraid she might do something drastic again if he forced a decision.

Chapter 16

THE GIFT CAME ON THE FOLLOWING MONDAY.

"Miss Sophie, Miss Sophie!" Wilson clutched a box in her hands and dashed through the waving flags of wet linen. "I just went down to the gatehouse to let Old Bob in with the fish cart, and this was sitting there for you."

She took the box cautiously in her hands. "Whatever...?"

"It has your name on it, miss, look."

Sure enough, her name was scrawled across the lid—badly misspelled. There was no note with it, no explanation. Sophie gingerly opened the lid. Inside, nestled in straw, there was a birdcage, complete with the model of a linnet seated on the perch. She recognized it at once from the market stall. There was a tiny key in the base of the cage, and when turned, the little bird let out a pert chirp, flapped its wings, opened its beak, and dipped forward, ready to take flight. But the door of the little cage didn't open, and the bird remained on its perch, ever ready to go nowhere.

She knew who sent it to her; there was no doubt. They'd not spoken since the dance, but somehow she knew he was responsible for this.

"Isn't it lovely, miss?"

"Yes," she whispered reluctantly.

"But what can it mean?"

Frowning, she handed the cage to the maid. "I suppose I'd better find out."

❧

The air that morning was fresh and warm as a loaf straight from the oven. The shrill larks, chattering blackbirds, and sultry wood pigeons, feeling the gentle, glowing sun on their feathers, greeted its rise with a full orchestral performance. The slightest of breezes carried a few stringy fleece clouds, just high enough to keep them from snagging on the treetops, and wildlife rustled, unseen and industrious among the hedgerows. Her feet, walking quickly through the long grass of the verge, disturbed a young rabbit and several butterflies, whose sudden nervous emergence caused her as much fright as she caused them.

She raised one hand to her forehead to shade her eyes and peered ahead to where a man was climbing a stile into the field beyond.

"Mr. Kane!" The name still sounded strange on her lips.

He stopped and looked back. She waved and quickened her pace, afraid he might disappear or she'd lose her courage, but he rested his arms on the stile and waited. Panting, she finally arrived beside him. "Mr. Kane, where do you go?"

His dark, thoughtful eyes studied her warm face. "I go to pick mushrooms."

"Oh."

"Will you pick them with me, Miss Valentine? If you have the time to spare, of course. I know you have far more important things to do than share a few minutes with a shallow young rake."

The invitation was spur of the moment, and she accepted just as speedily, not even waiting for his hand to help her over the stile. When he stood back, giving her room to pass through into the field, she saw him look away, pretending not to notice the little flash of ankle as she leapt from the stile. On his best behavior today, it seemed. He walked on into the field, leaving her to follow.

"You have no basket, Mr. Kane," she said as she quickened her pace to walk alongside. "You came out to gather mushrooms but have nothing in which to keep them."

"We can use your apron."

"Did you know you would meet me, then, and I'd wear my apron?"

He stared ahead. "So I didn't come out just to pick mushrooms. How astute you are." Then he smiled crookedly. "Too clever for me. But then I'm an ignorant fool who can't even read."

She ignored that comment. "You came out, Mr. Kane, to leave something at my gate."

"Did I?" He looked at her with eyes wide, feigning innocence. Very badly.

"Why did you buy me the caged linnet?"

He stopped, and so did she. "It reminded me of the little bird I saved from your schoolhouse. When you shouted at me for no reason and slammed a door in my face. Don't worry, I won't expect any thanks for this bird, any more than I got for my other favors."

She couldn't be angry with him, even if she wanted to. "You shouldn't give a gift to me, Mr. Kane. It's not proper. We are not engaged." She hesitated. "And Henry won't be pleased."

"Is Henry ever pleased?"

Sighing, she lifted a shoulder. "Not these days."

"Then I'm sorry for him. His life is passing by, and he can't enjoy a moment of it."

How strange it was that Lazarus Kane should express sympathy for Henry, a man he barely knew, yet James Hartley, who'd known Henry for years, couldn't spare him the smallest of pities.

"My brother thinks only of what he doesn't have. Of course"—she hesitated—"if I wished to be completely honest, I'm often guilty of that too."

He scratched the back of his neck and laughed low. "'Tis a human failing."

His black hair was almost in his eyes as he looked down at her. She felt the urge to reach up and stroke it back from his forehead. Needing something to keep her hands busy, she untied her apron and knotted the corners to make a sack for the mushrooms. Then they passed through a new gate into the covert. He held the latch for her, and she swept by, swinging her apron. Now he was behind her as they walked between the elm and chestnut trees, sunlight dappling the grass. She knew he was close. His breath came faster as their footsteps rustled along. Then she felt his touch. His fingertips moved her hair, where a loose curl rested on her shoulder.

She stopped abruptly and spun around. He showed her a caterpillar in his palm, laying the blame on that tiny creature, which must have fallen from the trees to her hair. But she saw the gleam in his eyes, and Sophie knew how it felt to be taken by surprise, kidnapped and held ransom by a sudden sensation, a desire that came unwanted, unbidden.

The only sound in that covert was of their feet through the grass, the warbling wood pigeons, and the occasional drowsy burr of a wasp.

He reached out his hand again and ran those wayward fingertips along another loose lock of hair that fell to her shoulder. There was no excuse to be had this time, no caterpillar or likewise impertinent insect.

Then he took his hand away quickly, as if abruptly remembering his manners and how she'd shouted at him before, and motioned her on ahead. She turned without a word and continued onward, glad of the shady trees to help cool her blood, although the peacefulness made her heart beat only that much louder in her ears. Why had she run after him? What did she expect to happen?

Something. Anything.

There was no avoiding it any longer. Her desire for him would not be quenched, and James's recent kiss only highlighted that great empty ache in her heart. Her skin prickled when Lazarus was near, the expectation of his touch almost too much for her sanity. It made her ashamed, this pointless hankering for someone so unsuitable. But she couldn't stop it. She'd given up trying. Surely, like a bad itch from an insect bite, it would work itself out of her soon, and she would recover from this foolish fancy.

At last they spied some mushrooms peeping out from the damp grass, and together they picked them, each newly discovered bundle bringing a small cry of delight from her lips as she swooped down to claim it before he did.

"When my strawberry beds bear fruit, Miss Valentine, you must come and pick them with me. Your aunt tells me it was once one of your favorite things to do."

She looked up in surprise and wondered when he'd spoken to her aunt.

"As long as you promise not to eat them all," he added.

She wiped an arm across her brow. "She told you of my lack of willpower?"

"Oh yes."

"Well, I was very young, and when I ate one, I just couldn't seem to stop." As a child, she'd eaten three times as many strawberries as she picked one day, and subsequently suffered a terrible stomachache. "I learned my lesson. Now I know when I've had enough."

He leaned against a tree and watched her, emerald shade and gilt spatters spinning across his face. "I hope so, because my berries will be the sweetest you've ever tasted, and you might be tempted beyond endurance."

"Pride is a sin, Mr. Kane."

He pushed away from the tree trunk, stepped over gnarled roots, and came toward her. "One of many." She could smell the warm earth on his roughened fingertips as they brushed, unbearably gently, across her lips. She was overwhelmed by it all—this onslaught against her senses.

Above them the leaves shivered. Branches creaked and danced, suddenly caught up in a jig.

"You shouldn't have bought me a gift," she muttered. "It's not..."

He leaned his head down to her, and his dark gaze caressed her lips, following the path of his fingers. And then, as if he saw it there all along, he satisfied the secret, clamoring need within her. Hands on her elbows, he drew her gently against his body.

She should protest. She had plenty of time.

But she said nothing. Sophie moved her lips toward him, just a little. Just enough.

He tasted her slowly, carefully. His hands cupped her face, holding her still, his fingertips in her hair. She knew she should object, but she was in a wayward mood today...here in the trees where no one could see.

Their mouths drifted apart, and her lashes flickered open.

She wondered if he did this often. It seemed likely he stole kisses from other women too.

Now his face was unreadable, and when she continued to study it, he suddenly stooped to pick another mushroom.

Think of something else, she chided herself. *Think practically*. He was ignoring it had happened. Perhaps she should do the same. Then she understood exactly what she was doing there, why she'd run after him that morning.

As he bent over and she searched her mind for sensible matters, she saw a stain on his shirt. He always wore the same clothes. Even to work on the farm, he wore the same breeches, and on any day of the week, he might be seen in that fancy, embroidered waistcoat. The shirt he wore today, with the sleeves rolled up, was made of rich silk. She remembered what her brother said about the tailor in Morecroft fashioning one suit of clothes for Lazarus, paid for by bank notes hidden in his boots.

"Mr. Kane, have you no other clothes but these?"

He glanced up over his shoulder.

She added, "I don't mean to offend."

Straightening up, he tossed a handful of mushrooms into her apron. "You don't offend. And yes, I have only one set of clothes. Why else do you think I take off my shirt to work in the farmyard?"

"Pure vanity, Mr. Kane?" When he laughed at that, she smiled. "Another of your sins."

His eyes were on her lips again, and blood hot with anticipation rushed through her. It was as if a dam had broken.

"Miss Valentine, I'm not a rich man," he confessed. "I know it might seem that way to you and to others, but my fortune is far from infinite. The money I have will soon be spent."

She was startled by the sudden change of subject. Lavinia, she mused to herself, would call it improper to talk about money with a man who was practically a stranger. What, she wondered wickedly, would Lavinia think of her question to Lazarus about his clothes? He hadn't seemed to care. Perhaps there was no "improper" in this man's mind.

"The admiral agreed I can live at Souls Dryft until the end of harvest," he added. "I'll pay my rent by managing the farm and maintaining the old house.

He'll take one-third of the harvest profit this year. The remaining two-thirds are mine."

His lease was only until the autumn. She felt her heart skipping too many beats. He wouldn't stay long, then.

It was strangely gratifying to be taken into his confidence.

"I saved a little of my army pay," he added ruefully, "but one shilling a day doesn't go far."

"You were a soldier?"

He nodded as they walked on. "An enlisted man."

She was silent, politely waiting for more.

"I was born fatherless and destitute, Miss Valentine, on the streets of London. I found work wherever it could be got, turning my hand to anything required"—his lip turned up in a wry smile—"not always on the right side of the law. When I joined the army, I hoped to turn my life around."

"You had no family?"

He blinked, and she saw a subtle hardening of his jaw, a tense movement. "A sister. A few years older than me. She died...in childbirth."

"I'm so sorry." She shook her head. "How awful."

"She was only seventeen. The sweetest girl..." He stopped, catching his breath. When he didn't continue, she asked his sister's name, and he told her, "Becky. She'd be twenty-seven now. Not a day goes by when I don't think of her."

"Yes, I'm sure," she muttered sadly, feeling for his loss and the loneliness he must have suffered. "What...what happened to her baby?"

He stopped and looked off into the distance. "I wanted to keep him with me, but I was only fourteen, just dismissed from my post a few months earlier, and I couldn't get work without a reference. That's when I joined the army. I left the boy with a woman I knew, but a few years later, I found out she was in the workhouse, and so was he. After I…got out of the army, I fetched him out of there and found him a place in a shop. They give him room and board for helping out, running deliveries—that sort of thing. He's doing well enough. Growing up. I send money when I can. Soon he'll start an apprenticeship." He looked down at his hands. "One day, perhaps, I'll tell him about his mother."

She knew she probably shouldn't ask, but she did. "And his father?"

His smile became further twisted; his shoulders flexed. "Perhaps I'll meet him one day, too. I've a few things to get off my chest."

"Yes." She didn't know what else to say about that.

"I thought, one day when I settled, I'd bring young Rafe to live with me." He looked up at the trees as another breeze shook the thick branches. "I'd like that." He paused, one hand to his chest. "Ah, but for now, he's better off where he is."

She wondered how it could be better for the boy to live with strangers. "You never knew your own father?"

"No. When I was young, I met an old man who helped me. I suppose he was the closest thing I had to a father—found me work sometimes, places to stay. When he died about five years ago, he left me his life savings. That was enough to set me up here after I got out…" He paused, his face dark, half-turned away from her. "After I left the army."

His story had tumbled out of him, as if he'd held it in too long, waiting for the opportunity.

"It doesn't matter to me, whatever you are," she said. "Rich or poor. We can be friends, I hope, no matter what our circumstances. For as long as you stay."

He looked at her oddly. "Friends?"

She stared down at the grass around her feet. "Are you still in need of a tutor?"

No reply.

"If so," she added, "I'd be glad to offer my services."

"How much will it cost me? You'll expect payment."

She clutched the apron of mushrooms between them. "No, no…good heavens! I would not accept anything at all." Her gaze drifted to his shirt. "You'll need some new clothes soon," she murmured. "Would you like me to wash it for you, Mr. Kane?" When he assured her he did his own laundry, she exclaimed, "I never met a man who did his own laundry. Can this be true?"

"Oh yes. As you once said to me, Miss Valentine"—he leaned toward her and teased gently—"I, too, have looked after myself all my life and managed to survive. Long before I thought to acquire a wife."

Now she looked down at her feet again.

"Forgive me," he mumbled. "Once a man's been rejected, he should know better than to make a fool of himself and mention it again."

She swung her apron bundle again and forced a cheery smile. "I wonder why you want a wife, since you do your own laundry."

"Well, there are some things I cannot do for myself." He coughed and looked away. "Not the way a wife can do them for me."

Her fingers picked at the knots holding the bundle

together. "There are many women in this village who would be glad to provide any service you need, Mr. Kane."

"Not quite all I need."

She bit her lip. They should not be talking of this. It was terribly improper. Henry would expire on the spot if he knew she was even alone with Lazarus Kane.

Chapter 17

SOPHIE VALENTINE WAS CLEARLY A WOMAN WITH secret passions and curiosities. Kane knew little about wooing, but there were other things he knew.

He shot another quick glance at her. She could have had a husband by now. She certainly didn't need to write an advertisement for one, but Sophie Valentine—the real one, the one she tried to hide—was looking for something more, something even she didn't understand.

They walked on together, slowly moving out into the sun again, and soon they were within sight of Souls Dryft, its crooked chimneys lifted to the sky like twisted, blackened tree trunks, and the waving, moss-covered roof defying Mr. Newton's laws of gravity.

"You've been very busy at the house," she said, her gaze following his. "It hasn't been so well maintained in years."

She was changing the subject.

He stopped walking once again. "Perhaps I can find some other way to pay you for those lessons you offered."

Sophie looked startled, a little paler than usual.

"Or are you interested only in the theory?" he added quietly.

She stared. "I don't understand."

Oh, yes she did. "One of your lessons for one of mine."

"Lessons?"

"Lessons in love, Miss Valentine. Repairs to a broken heart free of charge."

Her mouth flapped open, and she closed it again quickly

"I saw your book that day when it dropped from the chestnut tree. Remember?"

The prim schoolmistress shook her head, trying to deny what he'd seen, her eyes misting over, her face set in that stubborn, haughty way.

"When I heard about that advertisement, I thought you a woman of gumption," he added. "Now I see you're a timid female who daren't take on a man with a few rough edges and prefers instead to study the safe sketches in a book." He took the apron of mushrooms out of her hands and set it on the grass by his feet. "Well, madam?"

"I…I don't know what you're asking of me."

Moving swiftly, he captured her restless hands and drew her close again. "I promise to devote myself to your education, if you devote yourself to mine. I'll make it worth your while."

Much to his amusement, her eyes sparked with indignation, like little fireworks spinning and sputtering. "You're very sure of yourself, but of course you're a young man of twenty-five and can afford to be so." She sniffed. "The arrogance of youth!"

"Four."

"Four what?" she snapped irritably.

"Twenty-four."

She exhaled. "Oh, Lord!"

He laughed and tipped back on his heels. "I'll be twenty-five in September. Why? What's the matter?" When she shook her head, he laughed again and eased her closer until her breasts brushed the front of his shirt. He could feel her every breath, could smell the sun on her hair. His groin tightened instantly; his shaft thickened and grew. She did this to him without even trying. "How long do you need to make up your mind, Miss Valentine?" he whispered. "How long did you think before you put ink to paper and wrote that advertisement? How long did you think before you leapt from a balcony?"

She held her lips tight, playing the mute.

"Perhaps I'm asking you too many questions." Now he made his face solemn. Or tried. "Very well, then, I'll let you ask one of me."

A slight pause followed, while she apparently struggled for a question. Finally, she muttered awkwardly, "You took a great chance in coming here to marry a woman you'd never met. Why would you do that?"

"I take chances every day of my life, every morning when I wake and every night when I lie down to find sleep. I never know when it could be the last time I do so." He paused. "As it is for everyone, I suppose."

She nodded, but he sensed she'd barely heard. Her gaze passed over the branches above, searching for something.

"What is it to be, then, Miss Valentine? Do you

accept the offer of my private lessons in exchange for yours?"

She stepped back. "I don't…"

He waited, but she couldn't finish.

He picked up her apron, handed it back to her, and walked on across the field. After a moment, he heard her quick steps following him, her skirt brushing the long grass. He reached the stile and leaned there, waiting for her to catch up. "If you need time to consider, I'll give it to you," he said calmly.

❧

A swirl of lighter color broke through the darkness under his lashes and, as he leaned with one elbow resting on the wooden post, he was almost too casual.

"Thank you, Mr. Kane." She couldn't resist a little sarcasm. "I'm most grateful for the opportunity to learn the wondrous things you could teach me. I'm sure they're plentiful."

He grabbed her hand, brought it to his lips, and kissed it firmly. She tried to slip her hand from his, but he wouldn't relinquish it. "Time's up. What will it be?"

She inhaled sharply. "That was unfair."

"I said I'd give you time. Never said how much."

"You're a trickster, sir!" Again she tried to retrieve her hand, but the villain kept it and tugged gently on her fingers, drawing her back to him. She tripped the last small distance, until his lips were almost upon hers. "I know things are different where you come from," she gasped. "In Sydney Dovedale, gentlemen do not kiss ladies in public!"

His mouth hadn't yet touched hers, and now he pretended it was never his idea to kiss her again. "Is that your way of asking for a kiss, Miss Valentine?"

Her temper up, she jerked her hand away, but in that same moment, he caught her around the waist. He pulled her against him, holding her there tightly, her breasts crushed to his hard chest. Again he lowered his mouth to hers and pried her lips apart with his own. She felt his warm tongue pressing hers, seeking a response, demanding it.

The heat of his body melded with hers, and they became as one, locked together in an embrace surely too savage and improper. She dropped her apron of mushrooms as her hands moved up his thick arms to his shoulders and then to his neck, which was almost too broad for the span of her fingers. He slanted his mouth to hers, not giving her a moment to breathe. One of his large hands moved down over her hair and then lower, falling to her bottom. He shockingly caressed it in the same manner, urging her upward slightly to fit more securely against his hard groin. Her belly was very warm, and her bones softening, one by one. His hand squeezed her right buttock, fingers spread, gripping her with too much possession, too much strength. Although he'd been bold with her before, this was more than he'd ever dared. It seemed today he was determined to leave his mark on her.

As he expelled a harsh, shuddering groan, his lips finally released hers, and she slid back to earth, wilting down his body, her legs trembling against his iron-hard thighs. His eyes were closed, but hers were wide open, and her gaze drifted down to his breeches to where she'd felt that eager, jutting beast pressed against her thigh and her belly.

Shocked, she muttered his name in a curious, high-pitched, breathless voice.

He bent his head and pressed his lips to the rounded swell of her breast above her corset. She felt his tongue move wetly over the curve of flesh, and her nipple was instantly roused. It tightened under the layers of clothing, wanting his lips. She gasped and knitted her fingers through his sun-warmed hair. And then his mouth wandered a little lower, gently kissing the front of her gown, as if to pacify that frantic nipple in any way he could. Had there been no corset, no chemise, and no gown in his way...

Her legs weakened at the mere thought of skin-to-skin touching. With him.

"Forgive me," he said gruffly. "I'll never be so presumptuous again. At least, until we have an agreement about those lessons."

She said nothing. If he tried stealing another kiss—or something more than that from her—she just might give it. Her inner hussy was all hot and heavy. Any moment now, she could sink to her knees on the grass and be quite unable to find her feet again. Her back arched slightly with his big hand spread across her spine. She wanted to press her aching nipple toward his lips, but that would be wicked, asking for trouble.

He straightened, and his breath brushed her cheek. "The next time, it'll be your kiss, and there'll be no debate about who took and who gave."

She slid away, put up her chin to regain a little dignity, and straightened her frock. She stepped over the stile and tried to act as if this were a day like any other, as if she couldn't still feel the pressure of his fingertips on her flesh. He'd probably left her bruised.

"I see your ankles, Miss Valentine!" he reprimanded her, teasingly stern.

"Then don't look, Mr. Kane!" She felt extremely wanton now, after that kiss and his wicked caress. Most inappropriately giddy.

"You do have a very pretty pair of ankles," he remarked as he watched her skip down the other side. "I suppose you know that, since you flaunt them deliberately." His crooked smile somehow succeeded in being very warm and eager while still bearing a shadow of uncertainty—as if he were ready to duck away, fearing she might slap his face. What a strange mix of rough and gentle he was. He reminded her of a sweet-natured young dog emerging from puppyhood into a boisterous growing stage, and suddenly finding his paws and limbs much larger as he crashed about in excitement after a butterfly.

"Mr. Kane, you're too familiar."

"Miss Valentine, I haven't even begun."

She was tempted to laugh, but she managed a curt, "I shall expect you for a lesson tomorrow after the school day."

"And when shall I hear an answer from you? About these lessons I'm willing to give you in return?"

"When my brain has made an informed decision."

"Women have brains?"

She pursed her lips.

"Can it be true?" he asked again, blinking as rapidly as she had when he'd told her he did his own laundry.

"Oh yes, Mr. Kane. And, unlike young men, our brains are not led by any other part of the body." She curtseyed. "Good day, Mr. Kane."

Unfortunately, as her thoughts were in a pickle, she forgot her apron and remembered it too late to go back.

Her mind was spinning. What did she want now? A man she knew well, a man who curbed her naughty side and with whom a secure future was certain. Or a cocky young stranger who curled every hair on her head just by looking at her, and who kissed her without permission, in broad daylight on wash day, when her appearance must be a complete and utter mess. A man who tempted bad Sophie to come out and play. One was a gentleman who wanted a well-behaved wife. The other, apparently, was a lusty young bull who simply wanted her however he might get her and was shameless about both his methods and his motives.

How strange it was that suddenly she—a scarred spinster of almost thirty—had two men vying for her attentions. Perhaps, she mused, that advertisement was not so idiotic after all. She wondered idly if any other men would come in answer to it. Then she laughed at the idea, for truly she didn't think she could cope with yet another offer. It was all quite absurd.

Chapter 18

He came for his first lesson the following day and stood with unusual meekness in her doorway, head bowed, hands behind his back. It was half an hour since the last child had left, and she was sweeping up when his shadow fell across the wedge of afternoon sun at her feet.

"Am I too early?" he said.

No, you're ten years too late, my dark warrior. But she set down her broom and bade him come in, very politely, very businesslike. After that, he always said the same thing when he arrived, "Am I early?" Even when he was late and she knew he must have known it.

On his first afternoon's lesson, she sat him by the window, put a book into his hands, and told him to read aloud what he could for her, so she might gauge the level of his education.

"Street level," he replied with a charming smile. "That's where I was educated."

He was always very careful to arrive at the schoolhouse while no one else was walking by in the narrow, grassy horse path, and he left in the same cautious way.

Sophie thought it best his private tutoring continue in secret. She certainly didn't want Henry finding out and using it as another excuse to try closing her school.

The secrecy apparently suited Lazarus. He confessed he didn't like people knowing he'd had no formal education. For the first few lessons he applied himself diligently to the exercises she gave him. It did not take much, however, for his attention to wander. Even the sight of a centipede crawling on the window ledge would give him an excuse to set his slate aside and disrupt the lesson.

She tried to encourage an interest in books by reading aloud at the end of each lesson a chapter from *Tom Jones*, a novel she thought he would enjoy for its saucy humor. She sat beside him as she read, so he could follow the words on the page with his finger. Occasionally that finger would stray upward to stroke a curl away from her cheek or to straighten a crease on her sleeve. She did her best to ignore it.

"When do we get to the good part?" he said one day.

"Are you not enjoying the story, Mr. Kane?"

"Yes, but when does Tom get his Sophie?"

"Eventually. You'll see."

He sighed, taking the book from her and turning it over in his sun-browned hands. "But he must have all these trials and troubles first."

"Of course. Our struggles help build character."

He threw her a dark look. "I'm sure I could have done without my struggles."

There wasn't much she could say to that. From what he'd told her of his life, she knew it had not been an easy one. But she often sensed there was more he had yet to confess. She didn't want to pry for fear of chasing him away just when they were becoming friends.

"I think I deserve *my* Sophie now." His lips, formerly solemn, parted in a wily grin.

She rolled her eyes.

"After all I've been through," he continued, "it's time I had my reward. 'Tis only fair I have a little happiness in my poor, sorry life. And you need some in yours. I knew that the first time I laid eyes on you."

Her heartbeat slowed, thickened. Somewhere outside, a dove cooed lazily. The sun drifted down below the treetops and broke into millions of dusty specks that danced through the window.

He lifted her fingers to his lips and kissed the tip of each one, so gently she thought her heart would stop completely.

"I knew you were mine even then. But it took me a long time to find you again."

"You had only to walk up the lane," she replied crisply, and thought of that sunny morning in May when he caught her reading her scandalous book in the chestnut tree.

He laughed and looked down at her hand. "Oh, I had farther to come than that. My adventures would fill a book twice as long as poor *Tom Jones*."

She pulled her hand away, pretending she needed it to tidy her hair. Letting him hold her hand for too long made her wicked urges excessively feisty. She was supposed to be reformed these days and a good deal wiser. She was respectable now, prudent and demure at all times. At least she could put on a good façade as long as she kept Lazarus and her growing feelings for him hidden away, like the way she kept that naughty reading material tucked out of sight within the pages of more suitable books.

His empty hand dropped to her knee and rested there. It was heavy and warm. She should have told him to move it. Instead, she said, "We haven't finished the chapter." *He can never concentrate on one thing for long,* she mused.

His fingers spread, moving upward, rubbing her thigh gently through her gown and petticoat. "Are you wearing your French lace drawers again today, Miss Valentine?" he whispered.

"No."

His lips turned down slightly at the corners. "Pity. I'd like to see them again. Study them more closely."

"I'll be sure to let you know next time I wear them." She meant to be sarcastic, but his mouth quickly turned up again into a grin, and she knew he'd taken it seriously.

"I think that's the end of today's lesson." She stood and cleared her throat. "Good evening, Mr. Kane."

He watched her a moment through narrowed eyes, and then he, too, stood. "Until tomorrow, Miss Valentine."

She bit her lip and nodded. Until tomorrow. So many hours away.

He was very close, the hot male scent of him surely rubbing off on her gown. His hand stroked up her left arm almost casually and briefly rested on her shoulder before sliding down her spine. He kissed her cheek softly and then turned away.

She suddenly wanted to call him back and put her

arms around him. But he was walking toward the door, his broad shoulders framed by the dying sun. She blinked, and then he was gone. She felt oddly adrift now he was not there at her side. There was a hollow ache in her belly, and she could not catch her breath.

His lessons, she realized then, had become the brightest part of her day. His company amused her, entertained her, even when he was badly behaved. Especially then. She could never let him know that, or it would go directly to his big head. It would encourage him when she should be doing the opposite. She didn't want any further scandal, did she? He was a young, charming stranger, never still, never idle, but also probably never long fixed on one idea or one fancy.

As she'd said to him, she'd met his type many times before in her youth. He was too busy enjoying life, too young to settle. Even if he thought today—this hour—he wanted her, tomorrow he could change his mind, and then where would she be?

Only minutes after Lazarus had left, she heard the familiar sound of her brother's cane swishing at the long grass, his boots squeaking, his heavy breaths puffing along. By some miracle, he'd just missed Lazarus.

"Henry! What—?"

"I decided to come and see for myself what you do here so late."

She glanced up at the sky as she came out through the low door, closing it behind her. "I didn't realize how late it was." This was true. Each day, her secret pupil kept her a little later, which wouldn't do at all. It was unusual, however, for Henry to put himself out by walking to find her. He must want her for some very important reason.

And almost at once, she learned what it was. "James Hartley tells me he means to pay court to you again."

She let the iron latch fall with a clatter. "Yes."

"And you've agreed to consider a marriage proposal."

Turning, she walked back along the horse path, and Henry followed. Usually her brother had a brisk stride, but today he was easily out of wind, and she had to slow her pace for him. "Hmm."

"Good."

Surprised, she looked at him. "You hate James Hartley."

"*Hate* is a very strong word, Sophia. James and I had our differences, 'tis true. But may I remind you, Sister, you're soon to be thirty, and no other man is coming to Sydney Dovedale to marry you."

"No, you need not remind me, but you just did. Thank you."

"What I'm trying to say, Sophia"—he stopped her, one heavy hand on her arm—"is you must consider this proposal very seriously. It could be your last chance. Marry Hartley and become a respectable wife at last."

Sophie was relieved. Clearly he came to find her there so they might talk out of Lavinia's nosy earshot—not because he suspected her of anything untoward.

They walked on. "Did James ask you to talk to me?" she said softly.

Henry denied it, but she would not be at all surprised. She couldn't be trusted to make her own wise choice, could she? Needed a man to set her straight.

With a gusty sigh, she looked up as the slow-burning sun exhaled the last of the daylight and began to sink, like a fire ship on the horizon. "I suppose my only other choice is to go away as a governess for the Sadlers." She was joking, of course.

Henry rumbled along behind her, beating at the grass with his cane. "You are exceedingly fortunate, Sophia, that so many folk are willing to help you out of your situation."

Her "situation" being that of an unmarried woman, almost thirty, scarred, truculent, and burdened by past scandal.

"I sincerely hope you're not nursing any ideas about Lazarus Kane," he added suddenly.

She laughed, high and silly. "Why ever would I?"

"He has not spoken to you?"

"About what? You told me he doesn't want to marry me." She shot him a sideways glance. "Why would he try to engage me in conversation?"

"Just make sure he doesn't," Henry snapped. His face reddened, and he mopped his sweaty brow on a linen handkerchief. "As you say, that villain has no reason to approach you or converse with you on any matter. I hope, should he try, you will immediately inform me. If you're on the verge of an engagement to Hartley, we can't have another scandal to upset his grandmother."

Sophie watched his waistcoat buttons straining, his swollen fingers dabbing frantically at that broad, glistening brow. She was tempted to laugh, but she felt sorry for her beleaguered brother, so she linked her arm in his and helped him along the lane.

Chapter 19

LAZARUS MOVED SLOWLY THROUGH THE CROWD, enjoying the bustle and smell. When he thought of all those rich pockets crammed together, unsuspecting and untended, he was reminded of his misspent youth. But he was a new man now, there to find livestock, not to use his light-fingered skills. Tuck had already picked out a fine-looking ram to add new blood to the flock and was now perusing a complacent line of cows. The old man had lost some of his inherent doom and gloom today, because he was in his element here at the sale, moving among his "kind," with nary a dainty female in sight. His eyes gleamed like the sun through a damp, early morning fog, and he temporarily forgot his limping shuffle. Instead, he swayed along with relative ease on his bowed legs, hands in his pockets, the ever-present, dusty cap pushed back from his forehead.

He passed a long row of farm horses and came to a dappled grey standing apart and alone in the corner, gently cropping away at the grass. He stopped, and the animal raised its graceful neck to drop a curious muzzle over the top slat of the fence. Its solemn brown eyes blinked soulfully.

"That's a riding mount," Tuck muttered depreciatingly, coming up behind him, "for a lady. Won't do ye no good."

Lazarus petted its long muzzle and watched its ears prick up. "She might like a horse to ride. You told me she was a good horsewoman."

The old man shook his head and propped his cap even farther back with one broad thumb. "That were a long time ago. Ain't seen her on a horse in years." They both knew of whom they spoke, just as they both knew any caution of Tuck's would be treated with polite impatience then disregarded in as warm a manner as any well-meant advice was ever ignored.

Lazarus leapt over the fence and examined the horse, lifting its feet, running his hands down the tendons. The horse was a sturdy animal, but it had a beautifully arched neck and a certain refinement in the way it held itself. He knew good blood when he saw it.

"I thought we came 'ere for the farm beasts," Tuck mumbled to no one in particular, arms resting on the fence. "That one won't earn its keep, will it?"

Lazarus straightened up, one hand resting on the grey's firm rump, the other stroking its neck. He could already picture Sophie on its back, riding around his paddock as he watched and admired.

A loud cry suddenly echoed around the field, causing everyone to turn and cease their conversations. A very large fellow elbowed his way through the crowd. His big, bald head shined in the sun's rays like a lighthouse beacon.

"Russ! Is it you? After all this time!" He had a round, ruddy face with a bulbous nose. His head and neck were as one, a thick column shooting up out of his dirty collar like a large thumb from the hole in a glove. The two hands he raised over the fence toward Lazarus were almost the same size as the head they moved to embrace, and they clutched the younger man's ears with clumsy fondness. "Don't tell me you've forgot your old friend?"

"Chivers! What are you doing here?"

"I should say the same to you, eh? This is a long way from where I last saw you."

"'Tis good to see you, old friend. Come back with me."

The giant declared he didn't want to get in the way and was only passing through, but Lazarus insisted. "It'll be a pleasant change to have one of my own about the place."

Chivers looked over at the dappled grey and wanted to know whom it was for.

"My wife, Chivers. My *trouble and strife* as we'd say back home in the rookeries." He grinned. "Not that she's agreed to it yet."

❧

Chivers filled the farmhouse kitchen with his great bulk. His presence overflowed the crooked walls, and his roaring laughter was surely heard for half a mile down the lane that evening. Tuck had gone up to bed, and the two old friends shared a bottle of brandy that rested now three-quarters empty on the table between them. It was six years since they'd last met. They'd fought together in the army and become close as brothers. Now, as Lazarus considered that broad, scant-toothed smile, he realized how much he'd missed the friendship. There was no need to pretend for Chivers. He would see through the sham, in any case. He was a solid, trustworthy, unchanging fellow, and he either liked you or he didn't. If the latter, you were very unlucky; if the former, you had a faithful friend for life.

"After all this time, to find you here in such a quiet little place," Chivers exclaimed again, looking around by swiveling the top part of that head-and-neck apparatus. "You've a right cozy home here, Russ."

Lazarus was aware of his good fortune, and even felt a little guilty about it. He sat up and reached for the brandy bottle. "'Tis harder than I thought, this being a gentleman."

Chivers drank and let out a burp that threatened to shake the stone walls of the cottage. "You mean to settle down at last?"

"That all depends on Miss Valentine."

"She's the one, then? The angel you saw on that balcony once? The one you always talked of finding?"

He nodded.

"Tell me about her."

He struggled to describe her, but it was a long time since he'd drunk like this and, with the brandy taking effect, he soon ran out of adjectives. "She's a fine filly," he mumbled. "Thinks herself too grand for the likes o' me to ride, but I'll show her." And he swallowed the brandy in one gulp, bolstering his own swagger.

The big fellow's face crumpled with teasing laughter.

"Set your mind on it, eh? You always set yourself a high target."

"You'll see why, Chivers…when you meet her."

Chivers shook his massive head slowly. "I'll be gone tonight on my way. You won't want the likes o' me around."

Lazarus protested with brandy-induced passion. "You can stay here as long as you like, Chivers. I've plenty of room. You can even have a bed of your own." He stared at his boots and burped. "Besides…you're like family to me."

They were silent, then, until Chivers said, "I'm glad you got out o' that prison hulk, Russ. Thought you'd be carried out in a box or dumped at sea."

"I was."

Chivers looked at the bottom of his empty cup and then lowered it as his friend's declaration slowly registered. He swayed in his chair, leaning over to place his heavy hand on the other man's shoulder. "Dead?"

"You see before you a ghost, Chivers. Ol' *Lazarus* raised from the dead at last."

The big man's eyes were like saucers. The great expanse of his brow rippled in bewilderment.

"I lay with all the other corpses one morning when they lifted the hatches. There were always plenty of dead men. They tossed me overboard with the others. That's how I got out of that stinking place, head first and stone…cold"—he hiccupped—"dead."

Chivers's face showed a slow glimmer of understanding. He pointed to his friend's chest. "The old wound? They thought it done you in, like they always said it would?" Then he laughed again, celebrating the victory as if it were his own. "Fooled the buggers, eh, Russ? Thought you were dead, did they?"

Lazarus sobered up briefly and put a finger to his lips. "So don't tell you saw me, or they'll"—he hiccupped again—"think you mad and send you to Bedlam."

Chivers's laughter bounced around the walls. "Lazarus back from the dead. Well, you should never have been locked up in that place anyway."

He looked down at his hands clenched around his knees. "A man died because of me, Chivers. Every debt has to be repaid."

"But that drunken ass attacked you first—with a knife—and you had no weapon but your own hands. He would 'ave killed you right enough."

He closed his bleary eyes, thinking back to the foggy night in a tavern when one of his fellow soldiers, upset over a game of cards, came at him with a knife. War with Napoleon was finally at an end then, and they were all celebrating but still on edge. The savagery of war was burned deep into their darkened souls, and the tavern that night had been a powder keg, too much wine the fuse that lit it.

He was arrested and tried for the death of the man who attacked him. He would have been hanged, but his sentence was changed to transportation. Then he was sent to one of the disease-ridden hulks anchored off the coast, where he waited for a seaworthy ship to carry him off to Botany Bay. A ship that never came. When he was mistakenly tossed overboard with the dead bodies, it was mostly sheer strength of stubborn will that carried him back to land in the grey light of a new day. Thus he was reborn.

For now, at least. Until the Devil came for his due.

"Others weren't so lucky," he muttered as he stared down at the toes of his boots and thought of old man Kane, the fellow who'd looked out for him when he was a boy on the rough streets. Kane had died on the hulks, but before he was sentenced, the old man told his young friend where his "nest egg" of stolen loot was buried. He'd wanted him to have the use of it to start a new life. After his own escape, Lazarus retrieved the money and stuffed it into his boots. Not a day passed that he didn't think of his benefactor and hope he approved of the choices he'd made. In a way, he'd spent that money for both of them, given them both a new life.

"This is a long way from the rookeries and the battlefield," Chivers observed sleepily. "A nice fire and a bed o' your own. We never imagined such things, did we?"

"No."

"'Tis quiet here. Peaceful. You look a proper gent now."

You look a proper gent now. Those words echoed around his foggy head. Apparently he didn't look a proper gent in Sophie Valentine's eyes. She'd kept her word about the reading and writing lessons, but she'd also kept a discreet distance. Most of the time. Once in a while she put her hand over his fingers to guide his chalk or his quill, and Lazarus lived for those moments, as if they were all he had to keep his heart pumping. It was a sorry state of affairs to be so in need of her slightest touch.

The determination to win her over burned inside, a rush torch never extinguished, but still he couldn't read her thoughts, and that bothered him like a splinter in his thumb. He caught an occasional glimpse of the true Sophie under that prim act, but she had developed the skill of closing herself off. She enjoyed her secrets. Damnable, vexing wench.

"Stay with me, Chivers. Help me on the farm. There's plenty to do with the harvest, and I could make good use of a fellow with your strength. I'll pay you from my share of the harvest yield."

The fellow considered, frowning. "I should move on. Not good at staying in one place."

"Neither was I. But I grew accustomed to it."

So Chivers stayed. He wouldn't commit to a lengthy sojourn, but for now, he'd help his old friend in the fields.

Lazarus was grateful for the extra pair of hands, and he enjoyed the chance to chatter with a friend after so many months of living among strangers. There was no fear with Chivers, no doubt, no suspicion, and no struggle. They knew each other well, all the good points and all the faults—and they didn't judge each other. It was a blessed sort of freedom to have the big man's easy company. Lazarus retreated slightly into old ways and manners, setting aside the awkward trials of being a "gent."

The villagers didn't know what to make of this development. One stranger was bad enough, but two—one of them being such a monstrous sight—was too much to be absorbed. Over the next few days, Sophie heard all the gossip and saw how Henry fed upon his neighbors' doubts, dourly warning them the village would soon be overrun with similar types.

"Where one crook comes, others soon follow," he solemnly predicted. "This village has seen the last of peace and tranquility. Now we're a destination for villains of every shape and size. He will gather his compatriots around him and spread his wickedness like a blight across our pleasant countryside. You see...it has already begun."

There were rumors of drunken revelry at Souls Dryft, and Mrs. Flick claimed to have seen Chivers bathing in the stream by the mill. While it might be shocking enough to know the fellow bathed at all, this was not what caused her to run screaming back to the village. Rather it was the surprise of stumbling upon his supine, hairy form, sunning itself among the bull rushes without a stitch of clothing. She never quite recovered from it and, ever after, avoided long grass, exclaiming it gave her the vapors. Even her husband—God rest his soul—had had the decency never to reveal his nakedness within her sight, she exclaimed.

Chapter 20

IT WAS JAMES'S IDEA TO ATTEND THE MORECROFT assembly rooms. Sophie did not want to go, but when Aunt Finn gladly offered to come along as chaperone, Sophie couldn't disappoint the lady.

"I do so love to watch the young people enjoying themselves," Finn cried. "I promise I shall be very good and not flirt with any young man, no matter how handsome or how much he reminds me of my dear captain."

"Very well, Aunt. But no gin. Leave the flask at home."

Finn blinked her pale golden lashes. "Goodness, Sophie, do you think I can go nowhere without it?"

James dutifully arrived at the appointed hour, having borrowed his grandmama's barouche to drive them there in grand style. After helping each lady up into the carriage, he took a swift, critical appraisal of their attire. Sophie saw it but excused him. She knew he couldn't help himself. He would, no doubt, be disappointed, but although her muslin frock with the primrose sprigs had seen better days, it was her best.

She'd dressed her hair in a simple knot and wore a pair of small amber earrings. She had no other embellishments, and when his narrowed blue eyes focused momentarily on those tiny amber chips, her heart wilted under his disapproval.

"These were a gift from my father, James."

"Oh." He smiled quickly. "How…quaint."

As for Aunt Finn's appearance, it was not the sort of thing one could take in all at once. Her gown was black gauze over bronze silk, very low cut to show an astonishingly pert bosom of which a woman half her age would be proud. Around her throat she wore a black velvet choker decorated with amber stones. But one's eyes went almost immediately from her bosom to her head, atop which she carried a silk, turban-like affair that tilted precariously for a foot and a half above her pale curls. At some point, it might have been fashionable, Sophie thought, making excuses for her beloved aunt—or perhaps she was merely ahead of the trend. Finn was not the sort to care either way. She wore what she liked, whatever caught her eye and her fancy. Poor James eyed that turban with suspicion but dared not speak a word against it.

The monthly assemblies were held above the Red Lion in the High Street, in a long, echoing room with a dais at one end for the musicians and frail gilt chairs set about the edges for those who didn't dance. One large chandelier shook and swayed from the ceiling when the dancing became particularly rowdy, and there were more candles in iron sconces, casting a soft light on warm, merry faces. It was all much as Sophie remembered it from her youth, and when the music vibrated through the boards under her slippers, she felt that old spark of excitement.

It was crowded on that summer evening. Their arrival might have gone unnoticed if not for Aunt Finn's extraordinary hat. James tried to act as if she were not with them, and Sophie wanted to laugh, glad her scar, for once, was not the first thing people pointed at.

But her amusement was quelled almost immediately when she saw Lazarus Kane at the far end of the narrow room, dancing with Sarah Dawkins. He'd not mentioned any plans to attend the assembly rooms. She quickly chided herself for expecting him to tell her all his comings and goings. She was only his tutor. It was none of her business where he went or with whom he danced. The flighty, distractible young man was free to do as he wished.

She tightened her hold on James's sleeve as they moved through the crowd, and he looked down at her, smiling, his hand on her fingers. But a lump came up in her throat, and when he asked her to dance, she could only nod. He steered her into the line of dancers, and she kept her gaze on the floor, counting steps in her mind and moving through the motions. James was an accomplished dancer. He deftly masked any mistakes she made without ever losing his smile. She was intensely thankful for his skill and hoped no one noticed how he got her through the two dances. Once the set was over, she returned quickly to Aunt Finn, who handed her a glass of wine.

"My dear, did you see Mr. Kane is here, dancing with Sarah Dawkins?"

"No." Such a wicked liar she was.

"Over there…Oh, now he's dancing with that dreadful creature Amy Dawkins. What sin can he have committed to be so punished by both sisters?"

"Plenty, I'm sure," she muttered, determined not to look in their direction.

James squared his shoulders. "They must let anyone in these days."

He'd seen Lazarus only once, from a distance, but the man was not the sort one might mistake for anyone else. He simply exuded energy and an easy, carefree charm. Every woman in the room was trying to catch his eye. Sophie felt their seething, squirming desire, hidden even behind wildly fluttering fans.

"Standards truly have gone downhill," James mumbled sourly. At first she thought he was still complaining about Kane, but when she looked up, he was staring across the room at a young woman in an apricot gown. A riot of dark, mahogany curls bounced around her pretty face as she danced exuberantly with her partner.

Sophie cried out in surprise, "Ellie!" She had not known her friend would be there tonight. "I thought she was still in London."

"Apparently not." James sniffed. "I daresay they threw her out. Probably offended royalty again."

"She did not write to tell me she was coming into the country."

"It would not occur to her to warn anyone. She is a thoughtless, careless, unguarded girl. Why you ever formed a friendship with her I'll never know. She can be only a bad influence."

Sophie chuckled. "Yes, James. Isn't she wonderful?"

He glared down at her.

"I wish I could be as brave," Sophie explained. "I must confess I've lived vicariously through her exploits over the last ten years, since I've had none of my own. Her letters are tremendously entertaining. If one can overlook the atrocious spelling."

A smartly dressed gentleman with graying temples and a rather distinguished mien now approached their little group and addressed Aunt Finn with a low bow.

"Finnola Valentine. However many years has it been?" His lips were quite thin and firm when he first arrived before them, but now, as he rose from his bow, they seemed unable to maintain that solemnity, and parted in a tentative smile.

"*Fitzherbert Derwinter,*" she exclaimed, one hand going to her velvet choker. "Can it be? I hardly recognized you."

"You're just the way I remember." His eyes crinkled up at the corners. "Perfection cannot be improved upon, of course."

Finn laughed at that, her monstrous hat tilting further askew. "And what brings you back to Morecroft after all these years? We were never quite grand enough for you, surely?"

"My wife is visiting family nearby, and I'm here tonight escorting my daughters. There"—he pointed with bob of his head—"you see them, I fear, making exhibits of themselves. They share their mother's love for dancing. Once they heard about this place, they could not be dissuaded against coming, despite my best efforts."

Sophie turned to watch the two young, golden-haired Misses Derwinter enjoying themselves with gusto.

"And how have you been, Finnola?" he asked. "No husband here tonight?"

"Good Lord, no!" Her shoulders heaved dramatically. "I have managed to survive this long without that particular menace."

"Well," he said with a sigh, shaking his head. "I tried, but you wouldn't have *me*."

"Not strictly true, Derwinter." She chuckled. "It wasn't you—it was the institution of marriage I had no fancy for."

"Pity. I would gladly have made an honest woman of you."

"Alas, I was destined for infamy." Then she added thoughtfully, "What fun we might have had if you weren't such a pious stuffed goose."

The man laughed softly and shook his head again.

Finn seemed suddenly aware of her niece watching this exchange with great curiosity, so she drew her forward for an introduction. "This is my Sophie."

He bowed again.

"My brother Jeremiah's daughter," Finn clarified. "And, Sophie, this is Fitzherbert Derwinter of Derbyshire." She tossed a coy grin at the tall fellow. "He won't dance, so don't waste your time waiting for him to ask. I learned that lesson."

The introduction then moved on to James, but Sophie, glancing across the room, was watching Kane surrounded by adoring females of all shapes and sizes, and she began to wish she had the courage to walk up to him tonight. Would he notice her presence among all the other, prettier faces? Another cup of wine or two, and she just might forget propriety. She might become as bold and carefree as her aunt or Ellie, and tell him exactly what she needed, what she wanted.

The current dance ended, and a few seconds later, Ellie Vyne ran across the room to embrace her warmly. "My dear Sophie, how well you look!"

James took a step back, as if he thought the young Miss Vyne might somehow get stains on his clothes.

"Why did you not write to tell me you were coming?" Sophie exclaimed.

Ellie shrugged, her eyes shining with merriment. "I only just decided, on the spur of the moment. My little sisters are being too bratty for words, and Papa is trying to marry me off again. London is dull, dull, dull, full of fussy, old pudding-faces who look down their fat noses at me." She demonstrated, holding a pretend lorgnette up to one bright eye. "And I realized how much I missed my aunt and all my friends here."

Sophie knew Ellie had recently called off her seventh engagement. That was most likely the reason for her sudden flight to the country. Ellie had no fancy to be married or to ever do what was expected of a young lady. It was a great frustration to her stepfather, Admiral Vyne, and whenever she was in his bad books, she sought refuge with her aunt Cawley.

"I can stay only a few weeks. The Duke of Ardleigh has invited me to go to Brighton with a small party next month, and I think I might. He is an amusing old fellow and very naughty. Papa will disapprove of my having no chaperone, but I very much doubt he'll pry himself away from his brandy to come after me."

"But, Ellie—"

"I know it's not entirely proper, but then what is? After a certain point, a woman can't get into much worse trouble." She laughed gaily at her own misfortunes. "We may as well be dead now, if we can't have any fun. I'll just go and expire quietly in a corner, so as not to cause anyone to fret about me, shall I?"

Behind her, Sophie heard James make a small, tight sigh of disgust.

"Hartley," Ellie exclaimed, suddenly noticing him there. "You're still hanging about the place then."

Sophie cringed.

"Disappointed, Vyne? Sorry your spells and curses failed to put me in my grave?"

Ellie looked him up and down. "You're taller than I remember. And didn't you used to be fat and spotty?"

"Certainly not."

She cocked her head and batted her long dark lashes. "I must be thinking of someone else."

"I'm sure," he muttered and glowered down at her. "Your acquaintances were always vast and indiscriminate."

"I suppose it was some other arrogant, imperious bugger, then. Amazing how many there are about."

James mumbled something under his breath and stalked off. Ellie quickly linked her arm under Sophie's, demanding to know all her news.

For once, Sophie had a great deal to tell.

Chapter 21

LAZARUS HAD GONE TO THE ASSEMBLY ROOMS ONLY because he overheard Mrs. Bentley at the cobbler's that week, babbling on about Sophie's attending with Mr. James Hartley.

He knew the moment she entered the place, but he kept his gaze from admiring her. Finally, during a pause in the dancing, he allowed himself a glance in her direction. At that moment, she stood with her back to him, Hartley's hand cupped under her gloved elbow, claiming possession. It seemed to confirm the rumors of an imminent engagement. But she'd said nothing to him about it.

Why should she? He was nothing to her but a lowly young man who came to her for lessons. A young man who'd probably been too forward. But he didn't know how else to be. Subtlety was not his way, and time was not on his side.

Now, when he looked for her again, she was chatting away with another woman, their heads bent together in a conspiratorial fashion. Suddenly the dark-haired one looked up, caught his eye, and grinned. He knew then they were talking of him.

"Honestly, you'd think she wouldn't dare show her face after the scandal of that advertisement," Amy Dawkins exclaimed, her voice rising shrilly from somewhere in the region of his right shoulder. "Some women have no shame. Just like her aunt, of course. And poor Mr. Hartley has even agreed to pay off her brother's debts. I daresay they would have bled you dry of every penny, Mr. Kane, had she got her hooks into you, too."

So the popinjay was paying off Henry Valentine's debts. Interesting news, indeed. While Henry was too proud to accept coin from *him*, he took it readily enough from a Hartley. No doubt, between gentlemen, they had a different name for it, but where he came from, selling a woman for money was one thing only.

His temper flared quickly, induced by the spiteful whispers of Amy Dawkins and encouraged by his own white-hot jealousy.

He abruptly strode up to the curly-headed young lady who'd grinned at him, and interrupted her conversation with Sophie by asking her to dance. The lady accepted his hand with only a slight hesitancy. As he whirled her away, his shoulder knocked against James Hartley who, having watched his rival approach the two women, speedily returned to stand over them. Lazarus did not stop to apologize.

∼

Sophie swallowed a breath of Ellie's perfume as they swept by. Of course he'd spotted Ellie Vyne in her flattering apricot silk. Half the men in the room were probably in love with the delightfully sociable young woman.

"Did you see that?" James hissed, his expression one of superior, pinched disdain. "He deliberately knocked into me, the blackguard."

"I'm sure it was an accident," she replied.

"Accident, indeed!" His eyes followed the dancers down the room. "I might have known Vyne would be attracted to him," he muttered. "Birds of a feather. Not a jot of propriety. Perfect for her."

Sophie struggled not to be envious of her friend, but it was hard indeed. "They are of the same age," she said softly. "Both lively and open-hearted young people."

"I don't suppose it has occurred to you, that for a young woman of reduced circumstances, she gets about the country with remarkable ease. You know Admiral Vyne is in debt and has almost been forced to sell Lark Hollow."

"She never mentioned it to me, but then money has never mattered to Ellie, and I don't believe it matters that much to you either. You're just looking for things to criticize about my friend, as always. She's always gotten under your skin."

The dancing couple looked over at them, and Ellie laughed, throwing her head back as if her partner had just told the most amusing jest.

James sneered and quickly turned his back to the dancers, pointedly giving them no more of his attention. It was then he spied a group of acquaintances nearby, and Sophie gladly gave him leave to join them. "Don't worry, James, I have Aunt Finn to keep me on the straight and narrow."

He looked dubiously at her aunt, who was still talking with the very sensible-looking Mr. Derwinter.

"Very well. I'll be back momentarily." She watched him hurry away through the swarm of overheated bodies, and for a while, she tried to pay attention to Mr. Derwinter's conversation with her aunt. But she sensed she was intruding. She slipped back slightly and soon found herself surrounded by prettier gowns, younger women with ringlets, and painted faces. The gentlemen looked down at her and immediately, upon seeing her scar, looked away again. Someone stepped on her foot, and another spilt wine on her frock. Behind her, whispers slithered through the crowd.

"Is *that* her? Surely not. That plain little woman?"

"Don't be deceived by her mousy looks. She's a dreadful trollop, and no man is safe…"

"What can a man like James Hartley see in her?"

"On a billiard table, so they say…"

"Look at that dowdy gown! Well, you know they're practically penniless now, for all their Valentine pretensions."

"Throwing herself at Hartley for his fortune…"

"You heard, of course, about the Billiard Table Incident…"

"One would never think it to look at her…"

"An unrepentant hussy…"

Her face throbbed in the heat, and she couldn't find anything to do with her hands. In the way, once again, she began to feel nauseated, penned in, suffocated by thick layers of perfume.

And suddenly a hand gripped hers.

He tugged, and she followed, slightly dazed. In her panic, she hadn't even realized the music had changed.

"Dance with me," Lazarus said. His arm around her waist, he spun her in a rapid circle, and cooling, soothing air rushed by. "Put your other hand on my shoulder."

He held her close, his fingers spread against her back, his other hand firmly clasping hers. Usually, a gentleman asked politely before he held a lady's hand and danced with her, but Lazarus Kane did it his own way.

"This is a waltz," he informed her proudly.

It was a scandalous dance she'd only heard about. Very soon they were the destination of every startled, questioning eye—the subject of every whisper. She could not see where Ellie had gone. As he swung her around, clumsily knocking into other dancers, she laughed. It burst out of her in a rush of giddy relief after feeling trapped by the crowd moments earlier. "Are you sure these are the right steps?"

"Uh hmmm."

She laid her cheek to his strong, firm shoulder. She had no choice, she assured herself, for he whirled her around so fast she could barely keep her toes on the ground, and without his strength to hold her upright, she feared she might fall to the floor in an ungainly mess. "Where did you learn?"

"Dance lessons."

"From whom?"

"The landlady here at the Red Lion Inn. She was most obliging."

I'll bet she was, thought Sophie dourly. It seemed there was no shortage of women willing to tutor him. "Is she young and pretty…the landlady? I suppose it was an excuse to hold her close."

He spun her faster, until they bordered the dance

floor. And then they were in the corner, where, as they turned again, he blew over his shoulder, extinguishing three small candles in their sconces. Now he drew her to a halt in that shadowy corner. Her gown swung against his legs, and he held her tightly, in a manner that would never be seen in the finer ballrooms of Society. "I learned it in case I needed an excuse to hold *you* very close, Miss Valentine. I came to marry you, remember? Before you so rudely rejected me."

"What *are* you doing?" she exclaimed. "Everyone is looking!"

"Let them look."

"Mr. Kane!"

"My God, you smell wonderful." He leaned into her, sniffed her hair and then her cheek. She prayed no one would see them in that darkened corner. "You stir my appetite, Miss Valentine. Give me something, anything to stave off this hunger." She felt the size of that hunger as his groin pressed against her thigh. "If you had any idea what you do to me, you would take pity."

"I can't…" What did he expect of her, in public, in a room full of people? "What is it you want?"

"I want to know when we'll begin *your* lessons, Miss Valentine. I believe I've been patient enough. Give me some assurance, a promise to start soon."

"Please take me back into the dance."

"When you answer my question."

He held her hostage in that corner. She daren't look over his wide shoulder to see if anyone was watching. "Very well. Soon."

"Soon? How soon?"

"Within the next week. Now dance on...*please*."

"Name the day." His voice deepened, and she felt his large shaft again, just as insistent as its master. "Or I will."

"Wednesday," she gasped, plucking it out of the air and knowing she was sealing her fate at his hands.

He leaned down to whisper in her ear, "I'm sorry, Miss Valentine, to take these extreme measures for your attention, but I can't help myself."

"A consequence of extreme youth," she replied dryly.

"And of your stubborn refusal to admit you find me desirable, which, coupled with your sheer, unbearable, sweet-scented loveliness, makes me wild. But you know all that, of course, being so much older and wiser."

In the next moment, they were out again on the floor, moving with a few couples who dared participate in the new dance.

He was the sort of man who got away with anything, she mused. He didn't seem to understand that ladies were never meant to talk about their desires or acknowledge their needs and wants in that regard.

"What did Ellie tell you about me?"

"A great many things."

"Don't believe half of them. She's a mischievous soul."

"Like you, then, my lovely and wanton Miss Valentine."

He should have had two dances with Ellie, she realized. A proper set was two dances. Yet he'd come for her instead, breaking the rules. Very few men would give up a second dance with her friend.

Sophie pressed her cheek very briefly to his shoulder

and tried to hide her blushes. "We must never dance together again. People will notice."

"What will they notice?"

"Don't be a fool. You know what I mean. You *know*." And then, giving up, she tipped her head back to look up at him. "You just said it very succinctly—and arrogantly."

He smiled, and warmth flooded his face. Those clever, all-too observant eyes were a deep, rich brown tonight.

"It cannot possibly do anyone any good," she added. "It's only lust. And very unwise for either of us to pursue. I'm not the right woman for you, and you are definitely not the right sort of man for me."

"My body, Miss Valentine, takes issue with that statement. See?"

He moved against her, shameless.

"I'm trying to make you see good sense," she hissed. "Wretched man!"

"Good sense has nothing to do with it. This is pure desire. It's all animal."

Sadly, he was right. Passion sparked between them with the slightest touch. Yet they were so wrong for each other, completely unsuited. Where James corrected her wild streak, Lazarus encouraged her rebellious tendencies, and that could be very dangerous, indeed.

"Don't worry," he murmured, "I won't ask you again to marry me. I have my pride to consider."

Her heartbeat faltered. "Thank goodness," she managed tersely.

"But a lover has more fun than a husband, in any case. All the pleasure and none of the responsibility."

The man was utterly infuriating, incorrigible. She could have protested, but she knew it would be a waste of breath.

"You may as well give in to me," he whispered, confirming her worst fears. "It's only a matter of time." Oh, dear Lord, he had just let the tip of his tongue trail across her brow. Had anyone seen?

"You taste as good as you smell," he murmured, his voice hoarse. "I'm going to feast on you, Miss Valentine. Soon."

He spun her even faster. They danced up one side of the hall and down again, because Lazarus forgot how to negotiate a corner turn. But Sophie didn't mind at all. It couldn't last forever, could it? She may as well make the most of this stolen pleasure for one dance.

He brought her back to her aunt and kissed her hand with rather more exaggeration than necessary. James strode over with a thunderous frown on his handsome face, but before she could introduce the two men, Amy Dawkins came running to claim Lazarus for the last dance of the evening.

"Why did you dance with him?" James demanded crossly. "And *that* dance of all things?"

"Don't fuss, James." She was still more than a little breathless. "You're beginning to sound like Henry." With one trembling hand, she struggled to tidy her disordered hair. No one had seen what he'd done. No one had seen him taste her damp skin.

"Your brother cares for your well-being, Sophia, as do I. What that gypsy cares about is plain to see, and it is not your well-being."

She was amused. Henry and James had never got

along, even at university when they first met. Yet now, they'd put aside past differences to join forces against the outsider.

"You've heard, of course, what people are saying about his past, Sophia. He has no family, no background, no breeding. He evidently came by his coin through no legitimate means. He is rootless, a wanderer, a drifter."

"I hear a great deal of unfounded speculation from people who should worry about their own lives and spend less time—"

"Now he has a houseguest who, so they say, walks about with no clothes."

She was giddy from the dance, blood rushing through her veins, and she snorted with laughter.

"I thought Henry said the gypsy changed his mind about marrying you when he arrived in Sydney Dovedale and found you scarred. Why would you dance with him now?"

"Actually, it was I who turned him down. Mr. Kane *did* want to marry me." She supposed it must be the effects of the waltz still spinning through her, but she no longer cared what anybody knew about anything.

"I don't understand."

"It doesn't matter now, does it? I turned him down, and no man would ask the same woman a second time."

He glared at her. "*I* did."

"Yes, but…that's…" The giddiness was fading. "You're different."

There was a long pause while James digested this information. Finally, he snapped, "I insist, Sophia, you never speak to the man again."

He was agitated—more so than she'd ever seen him. Neither Henry nor James liked any threat to their carefully ordered world, and Kane was a young upstart who, in their eyes, got above himself. They did not believe—as she did—he had as much right to be there as anyone.

But dormant rebellion once again stirred inside the unlikely form of Sophie Valentine.

"James, you should really stop being so stiff and pompous."

He scowled at her with his lips parted, his face reddened. "I suppose this attitude tonight can all be blamed on the defiant, obstreperous manner of your friend Vyne." His blue gaze darted back and forth until he saw the very object of his scorn approaching them again. "Here she comes now, damn her."

"Don't worry, James." Sophie laughed, patting his sleeve. "I'll protect you."

Ellie Vyne returned to her side. "Mr. Kane is remarkably charming, is he not?"

"Most people think so."

The young woman suddenly exhaled a small groan and ducked behind James, whose tall form made a useful screen, despite his reluctance to be used in such a manner. "For the love of all that's holy, stand still, Hartley. Don't let that wretch with the yellow hair see me. I promised him a dance two years ago, and he's never forgotten, but he has the most dreadfully bad breath."

Sophie laughed. "I think it's too late to hide."

Her friend cursed broadly, and James exclaimed, "Perhaps you would not garner so many unwanted followers, if you acted with decorum and stopped running about all over the place. A young lady should learn to sift the wheat from the chaff and not dance willy-nilly with every man who asks."

"Sakes, you are a pompous tick, Hartley," Ellie grumbled.

"Thank you."

"It wasn't a compliment."

"Any criticism from your lips I take as an accolade. If I ever met with your approval, I'd know instantly I was doing something wrong."

She laughed. "Rest assured, Hartley, you're just as tedious as you ever were. You're in no danger of my admiration."

Sophie interrupted jauntily. "Would anyone like some more punch?"

She was ignored. "If you are always so right, Vyne, and I am so wrong, how is it you are the one cowering out of sight to avoid a gentleman you have no doubt strung along for your own amusement in the past and now drop like a hot coal the moment he is no longer a novelty? Do you see me hiding? Do I ever find myself in scrapes from which I cannot extract myself with dignity?"

Ellie sighed as she grabbed his sleeve and peered around it. "Of course not," she exclaimed, her tone matter-of-fact, "but we can't all be like you, or no one would ever have any fun, and we'd all die of boredom."

He shook his head, his mouth pinched.

Sophie knew he was being a hypocrite. James had his fun, but they weren't supposed to know about it. People like Ellie Vyne and Lazarus Kane annoyed him because they were open about their failings and indiscretions. They didn't care what people thought of them. To James, appearances were very important, no matter what went on behind closed doors. In many respects, despite his wealth and advantages, he was a prisoner of his world. And he wanted Sophie to be one too.

❧

On the way home that evening, Aunt Finn removed her turban and revealed a silver flask concealed under it. "I need a sip after the shock of seeing Fitzherbert Derwinter again."

James stared grimly out at the road as it tumbled by.

"Was he really one of your beaus, Aunt Finn?" Sophie asked.

"Oh yes, but he didn't have gumption. I wanted a man who danced and didn't care what he looked like doing it. Shame really. I might have been rich, then, my dear, had I married him." She touched her niece's knee with one delicate gloved hand. "But money is far from the everything men—and some women—think it is. Ah"—she sighed pensively—"if only they knew…"

Sophie silently echoed the sentiment, following her aunt's gaze across the barouche to James, and thought what a waste it was—all that beauty wrapped up so tightly and so elegantly, desperately afraid of losing a little control and giving in to passion.

"Your little friend Mariella Vyne has grown into quite a stunning creature," Aunt Finn exclaimed.

"Yes." Sophie smiled. "I fear for the hearts of gentlemen everywhere."

Across the carriage, James sniffed. "I fear for their sanity."

There was a short pause, and then Finn leaned close to whisper, "Now what is this I hear about a great big fellow running around stark naked at Souls Dryft?"

"It is nothing for you to worry about."

"Oh," came the forlorn reply, "what a pity!"

Chapter 22

THE FOLLOWING MORNING, SOPHIE PAID A VISIT TO Mrs. Cawley's cottage to see her friend and catch up on more news. By then, Ellie had heard all about the advertisement for a husband, and even with a headache from too much punch the night before, she teased Sophie without mercy.

"Now your extremely charming Mr. Kane came all this way in answer to it, why do you keep him waiting?"

"The extremely charming Mr. Kane is precisely that! He flirts with every woman in the village"—she lowered her voice to whisper as her friend poured the tea—"even your aunt."

They both looked over to where the elderly lady was napping by the fire, her feet up on a little tapestry stool. And they chuckled together.

"How can anyone take him seriously?" Sophie added.

Ellie threw an extra lump of sugar into her teacup and stirred carefully so as not to wake her slumbering aunt or irritate her own sore head. "Who said anything about taking him seriously?" She leaned across the tablecloth, gripping her friend's hand and squeezing it lightly. "Stand up for what you want. Seize every opportunity, for we will never be younger, Sophie, than we are today."

Sophie sipped her tea and felt excitement stir within her breast, the wicked gladness that comes from hearing convenient advice. Advice that told her to do precisely what she wanted. Ellie Vyne was always very useful for dispensing this particularly pleasing sort of wisdom. Probably why James Hartley was so determined to dislike her.

❧

"You caused quite a stir at the assembly rooms with your flirtatious behavior," she said to Lazarus on Wednesday afternoon when he came for his lesson.

"Everything about me causes a stir," he replied cockily.

"You have a high opinion of yourself. I've warned you before about pride and vanity."

"Can't help it if I'm the most interesting fellow in this village. *Some* folk"—he gave her an arch look—"have nothing else to do but gossip about me."

"Is that so?"

"And they have nothing else to stave off the boredom, because they daren't let themselves trust a man who can give them exactly what they want. More, in fact, than they ever dreamed."

She sighed. "It must be quite a burden for you, Mr. Kane."

"Hmm?"

"That massive male..." She temporarily lost her train of thought.

"Massive male...?"

"...vanity of yours!"

He laughed good-naturedly then made a pretense of studying his slate, holding the chalk awkwardly in his thick fingers. "Are you engaged to that idiot?" he asked suddenly. "Your friend Miss Vyne said you were not, but Miss Amy Dawkins thought you were."

How easy it was for him to ask her questions, she thought. He just blurted them out, probably as soon as they popped into his head. All sorts of improper questions he had no right to ask and she shouldn't answer.

But she did. "I am not engaged. Not yet."

"Ah." He was still looking down at his slate.

"As for Amy Dawkins and her gossip...folk here like to talk. If there's nothing to talk about, they make it up."

He shook his head. "How do you live in such a place where everyone pries into your business and speculates freely on what they don't know?"

"I suppose one gets accustomed to it," she replied. "I like to think, Mr. Kane, there is some good in every soul. No one is completely faultless, so I forgive them their sins."

"Very nobly said," he muttered skeptically. "Very pious."

"Now will you proceed with the lesson, Mr. Kane?"

"Would you forgive my sins too?"

She hesitated, looking down at his bent head. "I suppose it would be hypocritical of me not to forgive you."

"But you don't know what they are. They'd shock you right out of your frilly lace drawers."

With that comment, he reminded her, yet again,

of what he'd seen on the first of May when he caught her climbing out of the chestnut tree. With nervous fingers, she checked the prim knot of hair at the nape of her neck. "Do pay attention to the letters, Mr. Kane. Once again, your 'b' has become a 'd.' And I have no idea what that mark is supposed to be at the end. The tail of the 'y' goes downward and to the left, not to the right." Sometimes she thought he did it deliberately. Even Matthias Finchly applied himself more diligently to his letters.

"If you sit on my lap, I daresay I'd learn quicker." He shifted back slightly, offering her his knee.

On this evening, there was something in the air. The sky was very pink, casting a warm, rich light through the schoolhouse window, painting everything so it looked brand-new. For several weeks now, he'd attended his lessons, but each day he came later—just like the night itself—making her wait for him just a little longer every time. It was only a few minutes, but she was aware of it and wondered if he did it deliberately to see if she'd wait.

Because she did. Much to her chagrin.

"If you stopped your mind from wandering, you'd learn quicker, Mr. Kane."

When he looked up at her, she felt his dark eyes measuring the distance to her lips. "You don't believe in reward as a motive?"

This grown man was her most ill-behaved pupil to date. "You might at least make an attempt to be slightly less transparent in *your* motives."

"'Tis only a knee. Come. Sit, woman."

"Thank you. I prefer to stand."

He grinned. "So you can run away if you need to?"

She tipped her chin. "Why would I need to?"

"It's Wednesday, Miss Valentine. You promised we'd begin today."

Finally, with a sharp gasp of frustration, she lowered herself to his knee. She glanced anxiously at the window, fearing someone might pass by. She didn't let her mind dwell too long on what she was doing. Surely it was all quite harmless. As he said, it was only a knee.

He put his left arm around her waist, and she felt his leg tremble slightly.

"Am I too heavy?"

He shook his head and laughed low. His strong, thick thigh flexed under her bottom, and she bit her lip as a surge of excitement traveled quickly into her womanly core. With his right hand on her knee, he slowly began to caress, wrinkling her muslin gown. "What would you like first, Miss Valentine? Where shall I begin your tutoring?"

But she didn't know what she had to choose from, so how could she say where to start?

"I know you've had some experience," he added softly. "You're not a maid."

Of course, he would have heard by now she was a fallen woman. No doubt Amy Dawkins couldn't wait to tell him the story.

"It was only once and very brief," she replied, her voice tense. "I'm sure your experience is much greater."

Suddenly, he placed his right hand on her breast, cupping it gently through her gown. Spreading his fingers, he caressed the full mound above the edge of her corset. "Pity we haven't enough time to take this off, Miss Valentine. But perhaps there is another way under your armor."

He slowly gathered the folds of her skirt and petticoat, lifting it inch by inch until it was over her knee, her stockings exposed. Then the frilly lace trim of her drawers.

"Miss Valentine," he exclaimed, beaming. "You wore them for me. My favorites."

She sighed and nodded.

His fingertip explored the tiny pink-ribbon roses that decorated the lace edging, and his thigh muscle tensed again beneath her. She heard his breath catch. If she closed her eyes, she could imagine she felt his pulse throbbing just as hard as her own.

Slowly, his fingers traveled farther, along her drawers, under her gathered skirt and petticoat. "Stop me if I go too far, Miss Valentine. This is our first lesson, after all, but that French lace is in danger of making me forget caution."

Again she nodded and squirmed a little with the first tremors of impatience.

"You will tell me if I'm too audacious?" he asked.

She licked her lips but remained silent.

"If you would like me to continue, you must kiss me."

Leaning closer, she waited, but he made her reach for his lips. So she moved the last little distance to give him her kiss and thus permission to continue.

His hand slipped higher between her legs until it came to the little slit in her drawers. She held her breath, watching the sunlight drip over the window ledge. His fingertips poised there at the apex of her thighs. If she moved just slightly, his fingers would brush against the material and slip through the gap to touch her flesh.

"May I?" he asked, waiting for another kiss.

She turned her head and pressed her lips to his again, longer this time, more insistent, silently pleading.

His fingers parted the little slit to find her sex eagerly waiting.

More gently than she expected, his fingers stroked her, while his other hand held her waist. She heard his breath quicken. She swallowed hard and tried to be still in his lap, but the sensations he roused with the touch of his fingertips were far more intense than anything she'd experienced during her own explorations.

"You're already wet, Miss Valentine." She detected a slight tremor in his voice, but she still daren't look at him.

"Yes." He'd made her that way the moment she sat on his knee, the contact of his body with hers something that never failed to cause her these problems. Often it was only the idea of touching him that made her melt like this.

Her pulse was beating so hard in her ears she could barely hear herself. Thick strands of hair already fell to her shoulders again, wayward as their mistress.

He took his fingers away, and they rested on her knee, sticky and warm against her stocking. She parted her legs, silently urging him to continue.

"Tell me what you want, Miss Valentine. Tell me what you need."

But how could she say it? "More of that."

"More of what?"

"What you just did," she muttered tightly.

"My hand here again, Miss Valentine?" Once more he touched her through the slit in her drawers, but lightly, teasing—a tantalizing whisper of his roughened fingertips. His gaze ripped into hers, and she couldn't look away. "On your—?"

She interrupted, kissing him again, fiercely this time, to stop him saying the word aloud. He was so coarse, she thought, shivering. She shouldn't encourage this. It was wicked. James would never say such a thing to her.

His fingers withdrew again and tickled her inner thigh, drawing circles slowly, idly. "Tell me about James Hartley."

"What about him?"

"It was he, wasn't it? The man who had you?"

She sighed. "Yes."

There was a pause, and then, "Was he good?"

"Good?" Frustrated that he was delaying their lesson to talk about James, she exclaimed tartly, "You mean, did he attend church regularly?"

His eyes narrowed, and his jaw tightened. "If you want me to continue, Miss Valentine, you'll answer me. Did he please you?"

She sat very still, her legs parted, liquid longing seeping out of her. "No, if you must know. It was over in moments, before I even knew it."

He suddenly swept her falling hair aside with his left hand, leaving her neck exposed. She closed her eyes and felt his lips there, his teeth gently nibbling. She knew he'd feel her pulse, fluttering recklessly—a caged creature looking for a way out, so desperate it would harm itself.

"Breathe, Miss Valentine, or you'll faint."

She exhaled, feeling foolish.

"That's better. Can't have you fainting on me, can I?"

She shook her head.

"Look at me," he whispered. Confused, she looked at his face, and he gestured downward to the straining bulge in his tight breeches. "One day, if you progress well in your lessons, you can have that," he whispered, his breath blowing on her overheated skin as he leaned close.

"What makes you think I want it?" she demanded archly, amazed yet again by his sheer impertinence, the brazen expectation that no woman could resist him.

"This does," he replied, slightly hoarse as he touched her again through her drawers, sliding a finger over her pulsing wetness.

"Oh."

"But you can't have all of me yet," he added gruffly. "And I can't have all of you."

So he meant to tease her this way. Very interesting. Much better than illustrations in a book.

Thinking of which…

"Would you like me to kiss you there?" she asked.

Now it was his turn to be shocked. "*What?*"

"I saw it in the book."

❧

It took Lazarus a moment to remember. Ah yes, the book he caught her reading once. He gazed at her full, soft mouth with its slightly pouty upper lip and felt his manhood jerk like a stallion wanting out of its stall to chase a mare in season. The schoolmistress was trying to take control of these lessons, and if he wasn't very careful, she just might tempt him into letting her. But he must set the pace. This was his seduction of her and not the other way about.

"Perhaps next time," he managed finally. "Today is your turn."

"Oh." She looked pleased.

And she very soon would be.

"Shall I continue, Miss Valentine?" he asked politely.

She nodded, sitting very primly in his lap, evidently enjoying the game. From the waist up, she might have been seated at a piano, about to give a recital.

He turned his cheek, waiting. Finally remembering the procedure, she kissed it, giving the sign to continue. Then he moved his hand back between her thighs, almost immediately entering her with one finger. She was soft as satin, very hot and overladen with stifled desire. He felt it pounding through her, fluttering against his finger, and he didn't know if he could restrain himself from taking more.

When she closed her eyes, he told her to open them again, because he wanted to see their color. And then he slid a second finger inside her, caressing in and out, driving her to each new wave of rapture but never letting any wash to shore. She moved her hips, and her back arched. He wanted to pull her astride his lap, take her now, fully, the way it should be done, and clearly the way it never had been. But he had to wait. He had to be patient.

"Kane!" It was a demand, spat out with the urgency

of a woman unraveling faster than she knew how to handle it.

With the pad of his forefinger, he pressed upward to the crest of her womanhood. He watched her bite down hard on her tongue, and then he slid his fingers partially out again, leaving her balanced precariously at the rocky peak. His hand cupped her sex, holding her, savoring the moment of possession.

She cried out, gasping, gripping his shoulders, digging her nails in. Slowly he slid his fingers into her again, working her intently, the broad pad of his thumb gently rubbing her heated crest, taking her over that edge until she collapsed against his chest, her knot of hair—like the rest of her—completely fallen.

Thus ended Miss Valentine's first lesson at his capable, ungentlemanly hands.

Chapter 23

SHE HAD ENOUGH LINEN IN ONE CHEMISE TO CUT OUT the pattern for a man's shirt, as long as she was careful and didn't waste any. Sophie was not much of a seamstress, her stitches big and clumsy, usually requiring they be picked out and resewn by her aunt, but she was determined to do this herself and not seek any assistance.

"He can't go about in that silk shirt every day," she exclaimed. "This will be much cooler for the summer heat."

Aunt Finn smiled at the soft mutterings from the other side of the great hearth. "You're making a shirt for Mr. Kane?"

"Yes. He needs one."

There was a short silence, and then her aunt said, "There is an extra curl in your pretty hair these days, Sophie. And I like to see it loose more often. It makes you look much less careworn."

Sophie felt a broad smile pulling at her face, but she daren't let it out to play. She knew what caused that curl.

Her aunt sighed heavily. "I hear James Hartley has proposed marriage again."

Well, that wiped away the temptation to smile.

Her family had mixed views about James. Maria—ever the romantic—had high hopes for her sister to be in love, and Henry, transparently eyeing the financial advantage of such a match, reminded her she should think of the family. It was, as he told her, the least she could do after all the trouble she had caused. Henry didn't like James, but he could ignore many things if coin was at hand, as indeed they had daily proof in the shape of Lavinia, and his circumstances were more dire and desperate now than they were when she was nineteen. If the "problem of Sophie," as his mother-in-law called it, could finally be solved without forcing her into a governess post, he would be glad of it. He certainly wouldn't discourage Sophie's wealthy suitor from coming to the fortress almost every day and escorting her about in his curricle.

But when together, she and James talked mostly of their memories, for the past was all they had—the present being such a changeable, odd thing, and the future too far away. Sophie didn't remember everything quite the way James did. His memories were well embellished with gilt paint, but little truths occasionally shone through, peeking out between the extravagant, curling fronds of his enlarged stories.

She was still studying her stitches and sighed pensively. "James lives in the past. Our golden youth."

"But your woman's heart is elsewhere now."

Sophie folded the half-finished shirt and stuffed it away in her sewing box. "Wherever my heart is, it hardly matters. A woman of almost thirty must be practical."

With a half hour still to wait before James arrived, she looked for her book. *Fordyce's Sermons for Young Ladies* was on the mantel where she previously left it, knowing it was never in any danger of being picked up, much less opened, by Lavinia. But the little book she kept hidden within it was gone.

"Aunt Finn, have you seen my book?" She searched the shelves nearby, but the slim volume was nowhere to be found.

"I saw it earlier," the old lady offered genially.

"Where?"

Finn beamed. "In the fire."

"In the fire?"

"It fell in."

"*Fell in?*"

"From my hand."

Sophie ran for the poker and prodded among the ashes in the great hearth, but she was too late. All she could retrieve was a tattered corner of the leather-bound cover. "What on earth possessed you?" she cried.

"It was chilly in here, and we were running out of coal." The elderly lady lifted her shoulders in a pert shrug, not unlike those Sophie was prone to giving when caught in some misdemeanor. "You spent far too much time with your nose in that book. It was not healthy."

Still gripping the poker in one hand, Sophie stared down at the smoldering ruins. Well, that was that, then. No more theory.

"I wish you two young people would get a little

wind in your sails," Aunt Finn exclaimed suddenly, and Sophie knew the lady wasn't talking about her and James. "I want my old chamber back at Souls Dryft—overlooking the orchard in the back of the house, facing south. I spent many a delightful afternoon in that orchard when I was young and terribly in love with the admiral. He used to come through the hole in the orchard wall, the one your father never got around to mending, and I'd wait under the plum trees. Of course, he wasn't an admiral then, just a merry, blonde-haired captain. The most stunning specimen of manhood." She fell back in her rocking chair with another sigh, a sweet, soft breath of yearning for a long-passed summer. Finn was a small, delicate creature with wide grey eyes and white hair that was once pure gold. There was a look of angelic innocence about her, which made those tales of erotic adventure even more shocking. "This family, naturally, was appalled"—her lips turned up in a mischievous smile—"because he was a man with a rakish reputation."

"Then he left you and broke your heart." Just as Lazarus would leave, she thought, so it would be just as well never to fall in love with him. It was only lust, of course, what they had.

"But my heart still beats," Finn replied, "so he can't have done it much harm after all. Now I take comfort in some very blissful memories of our stolen hours together, and I regret nothing, nor do I begrudge him a single kiss." Her steady gaze rested on her niece's face. "If not for him, I might have grown old with nothing to remember. I might have been married to someone like Fitzherbert Derwinter, a good enough fellow but rather dull. Like your Mr. Hartley. Oh yes, I had my share of offers." She chuckled, her pale ringlets shaking jauntily under her lace cap. "But I never met a man to compare to my captain. Had I never known that pleasure, I might have been willing to settle. I might have been trapped in an unhappy marriage like many we see around us. So, no, I have no regret, and I'm more grateful to my captain than he knows." She leaned forward again and placed a small hand on Sophie's knee. "He left me with a very precious gift, and I would not, for all the world, have forgone that delight."

Sophie smiled. "Then I'm glad you had such a love, Aunt Finn, and he left you with wonderful memories." But the captain also left her aunt alone, a ruined woman, she thought acidly. He took his pleasure and left. It was frustrating that her aunt forgave him so easily. Finnola Valentine generally saw through men as if they were glass. For some reason, however, the lady held no bitterness in her heart for the captain, as if, whatever he gave her, far outweighed any suffering she knew as a consequence of his brief love.

"I hope, my dear Sophie, you won't let your own chance for happiness slip away. Our Mr. Kane tells me he might not remain long in Sydney Dovedale. If he found a wife, he might stay, of course."

Curiously enough, her teeth ached at the thought of Lazarus ever leaving the village, but he'd told her his current agreement with the admiral was only until the end of harvest. Perhaps he grew bored already in Sydney Dovedale and would soon take flight again.

Their conversation ended shortly after, when James Hartley arrived, as promised, to take Sophie out in his curricle again.

❦

Kane had seen those yellow wheels go racing by his gate again, churning up mud and scattering wildlife. He waited until the curricle disappeared under the gate-house at the top of the hill; then he grabbed his shovel and ran out, while Chivers kept vigil from the wall.

❦

It was a cool, overcast day following a night of rain. The trees shimmered, their branches bent under the weight of raindrops hanging from the leaves like crystals from chandeliers. The long grass at the verge was sodden, the lane soft, churned over by hooves. James drove at his usual speed, and Sophie wondered vaguely if he gave any thought to her comfort on that small, slippery seat at his side. She felt her life hung in the balance in that wretched curricle as they careened along the wet lane. At nineteen, she would have shrieked for joy and urged him ever faster; at twenty-nine, she had the foolish desire to get where they were going in one piece. Apparently, she mused, Ellie Vyne was quite right when she suggested men did not mature at the same pace as women.

As they whipped along, traversing wet, unsteady ground, the curricle squeaking and shuddering, the horses clopping along at full speed, Sophie tried dissuading him from planning an evening's enter-tainment at his grandmother's house. The more she thought of it, the more certain she was of imminent disaster. Lavinia and her mother would be in their element in the presence of such wealth and "superiority," and their delusions of grandeur would, doubtless, be ten times more painful to endure. Then there were the benevolent Sadlers, so worshipped by Mrs. Dykes, with their team of marriageable daughters and their devout eagerness to save the world from stray fallen wenches. James had insisted on inviting them along, just to amuse himself and his grandmother. And to tease Sophie about that governess post—out of the way—Mrs. Dykes was so keen to arrange for her. He seemed to think her only option, if she wanted to escape Mrs. Dykes's plan, was to marry him. Naturally, he liked to see himself as a knight in shining armor, and she wouldn't want to spoil his illusions.

Just as they approached the gates of Souls Dryft, there was a bump, a lurch, and then an abrupt, rocking halt. The horses whinnied and shook their heads against the bit, as if to say they were done with this idiocy, and James eventually admitted they were stuck. The left wheel was sunk in a deep rut. For a moment they were suspended, the small equipage tilting at a treacherous angle, and then there was an ominous crack. James fell sideways, slithering along the leather seat. He clung on for several seconds, until, with another deafening crack, the wheel finally broke under the strain, and he found himself sitting in the muddy lane.

While he cursed and threw his whip, Sophie tried desperately not to laugh. But to see the ever-elegant, always-spotless gentleman in such a state was almost too much for good manners and new maturity to bear. To make his humiliation much worse, the gates opened and Lazarus came out, along with his large friend, their faces just a little too concerned and amazed.

Chivers tried to help James out of the mud, while Lazarus came to her side of the cart, arms raised. She was quite a bit higher than she should be, due to the angle of the stricken vessel, and leaping down herself would probably twist an ankle. It would most definitely leave her with muddy shoes and hem. Although she chided herself for thinking of a little twisted ankle and a spattering of mud when poor James was in a far worse state, she thought it would be petty to refuse the arms she was offered.

The young rogue's hands were tight around her waist, fingers spread, and when he lifted her down, he took his time about it, letting her body slide slowly down his, inch by lingering inch.

"Your friend should drive his horses with greater caution," he muttered.

He held her a few inches from the earth, making some excuse about not wanting her to walk in the mud, and kept her against his body so she felt every breath he took, every movement of his muscle. She marveled once again at his strength, for he didn't even break a sweat as he carried her toward the grass verge by the gate. Slowly.

Her private tutor, she thought with a little shiver of wicked delight. Her secret.

On the other side of the broken curricle, James was still scrambling to his feet, slipping about in the mud, loudly cursing and refusing the help Chivers offered.

Chivers gave up on the surly gentleman and turned his attention to the horses, petting them with a kindly, soothing hand. Kane finally lowered Sophie the last few inches and suggested his friend could mend the wheel if they waited a while.

"It looks like more rain," he added, gazing up into the grey, mottled sky. "We'll stable the horses here to keep them dry, and you can take shelter inside."

James sulked, sticking out his lower lip and pulling on his silk cravat with muddied gloved fingers. "We should go back up the hill," he muttered as the rain fell like arrows around them.

Sophie looked askance. Her feet wouldn't be warm and dry again for hours, and her hair would frizz. Not that she was vain about her hair, but, good Lord, a woman had to have something in her favor, something that didn't make her cringe when she looked in the mirror.

"I could ride Speedwell, and you could take Foxglove, if the people here could lend us saddles," James snapped.

Lazarus replied swiftly, "My horses work on the farm and are not for pleasure jaunts. I don't keep spare saddles."

"Oh, for pity's sake, let's go in!" Sophie turned and marched through the gate before James could stop her. In fact, she was curious to see the lady's horse which, according to rumor, Lazarus Kane had recently purchased despite his claim of owning only farm horses. She strode across the wet yard and glanced casually toward the loose boxes, but no horse looked out. The familiar warm smell of horse and hay, however, filled her up with pleasant memories of youth, and she was tempted to run in and see for herself. Alas, she presently had two other fractious beasts to worry about.

They eyed each other at the gate, predatory and square shouldered.

Lazarus waved his hand toward the house. "After you. *Sir.*"

Chapter 24

RAIN CLOUDS FOLDED AROUND THE CHIMNEYS AND buffeted the crooked roof, casting their shadow over the yard and through the windows. Only the fire in the main hearth gave out any light, and this is where Tuck stood, heating a kettle of water.

"Miss Sophie!" the old man exclaimed.

The house was just as she remembered it; almost nothing had changed. Even Tuck seemed to have the same patch on his breeches. Walking to the fire to dry her skirt, she heard the door open again.

"Tuck! You're still here?"

"Mr. Hartley," Tuck mumbled with a distinct lack of enthusiasm. "Where else would I be?"

"And now you have another new master. I wonder how long this one will stay."

She glanced over at Lazarus and saw him stiffen, hands behind his back, feet apart—a man on guard. "Long enough," he spat.

James smiled coldly and pulled off his gloves. "Just until the harvest is in, so I hear. There can't be any reason for you to stay after the work is done."

"Don't trust all you hear."

Now they looked at her, both accusatory. She ignored the tension and that they knew, all too well, who everyone was, and said cheerily, "You've not been properly introduced. James, this is Mr. Lazarus Kane." She nudged his elbow, prompting. "Mr. Kane, this is my old friend, Mr. James Hartley."

They did not shake hands. The eyes of Lazarus Kane grew darker, which Sophie hadn't thought possible until then.

"Are you making tea, Tuck?" she asked. Ah, yes, tea! Always the perfect solution. The old man muttered he supposed he could make tea. If she wanted it. He'd actually been heating the water for his aching feet.

"That would be lovely." She tugged James out of his coat and spread it by the fire. "Once the mud has dried, I can brush it off. It won't be so bad."

While she fussed over him, James reverted to a sulking boy, and Lazarus strode to the hearth, where he rested one arm along the mantel while watching in dour silence. No one sat, although she urged James to rest his leg, for he was limping very badly now.

Taking a deep breath, she sailed forward into the still, angry silence. "Well, isn't this weather bleak? One would hardly know it for summer."

Only Tuck managed a belated, "Aye."

The air was taut as a drum. The conversation, as she forced it out, falling in clipped, slight sentences, splintered on impact like icicles on stone. Sophie, deciding they were all being quite ridiculous, soon stopped trying to find topics of mutual interest to discuss. If Lazarus chose to hover here like a sharp-eyed, black-haired bird of prey, then so be it. She was tired of trying to prevent people making fools of themselves; she had her own madness to tend.

When the tea was ready, she offered to pour it, and Lazarus shrugged, as if he didn't care what she did. She handed him a cup, which he wouldn't take and, in coldly refusing it, wouldn't even look at her but kept his gaze fixed upon the fire, his hands clasped behind his back.

James thanked her profusely for his cup, even though he disliked tea and seldom drank it.

"Mr. Kane, you're not from around these parts?" he asked suddenly, breaking into another long silence.

"No," came the terse reply.

"From another county? Do I detect a note of the Cornish tongue? Or is it Welsh?"

Sophie turned to look at Lazarus, also curious. He merely shook his head.

"Somewhere far from here?" James persisted.

"I've lived in many places. Never called any home for long."

"Ah. A man much traveled, then. Quiet, nondescript Sydney Dovedale seems an odd destination for a young man well traveled."

Sophie took offense at the adjective "nondescript" applied to the village she loved, but James didn't see her scowl, as he was too busy preparing his next offensive.

After a pause, during which rain rattled at the windows and both men smoldered with sullen unease, James continued. "I hear you have quite an interesting past, Mr. Kane."

Sophie almost dropped her cup. She felt the air

move as the man standing by the fire tipped from one foot to the other, restless and agitated.

"Interesting past?" Lazarus spat the words from the corner of his mouth.

"Perhaps you've been in trouble with the law? That would account for your having traveled about so much." Then he smiled, as if he were teasing.

"I don't know which rat hole you frequent to get your information, but you'd best not go nose first down it again, or next time you might find it bitten off."

"I beg your pardon. Do you threaten me?"

"I warn you, *sir.*"

James wisely backed down. "As you advise, I won't pay heed to all I hear."

Sophie once again offered their host a cup, which he refused just as sharply as he answered James's questions, and then she was truly annoyed. He had no right to treat her so. She slammed the teapot down on the tray and felt his eyes on her, hot and angry...and something else, almost as if her display of temper gave him satisfaction. She turned to James and said merrily, "Do you stay long in Morecroft this summer?"

"Yes," he replied, "I think I might remain a while yet. I've been too long in Town, and the air here is so much fresher, more convivial to good health. And Grandmama has begged me to visit her more often. She does so enjoy my company."

Lazarus muttered something very low, which she ignored.

"I've not seen Lady Hartley in many years."

James made a sorrowful face. "Too many years."

"I'm not certain your grandmama would consider it too many," she remarked dryly.

Lazarus wondered aloud what took Chivers so long to mend a wheel and marched outside to see for himself.

James now apparently felt safe enough to sit, taking a chair beside hers. "The man is barely civilized," he muttered in her ear as he propped his injured leg on a bench. "Are you sure he's not American?" he huffed. "I wouldn't be at all surprised."

Tuck began banging pots and pans about.

"He puts on no airs and graces, but he's usually very polite," she replied firmly. "And he's done many favors around the village."

James sneered, "Well he certainly got above himself coming here to answer that advertisement. How old is he, in any case?"

"I have no desire to talk of it, James." She sipped her tea, acting as if this were a perfectly normal situation, another afternoon visit between friends, where polite gossip could be exchanged and harmless laughter shared. "I would like to forget that advertisement was ever written."

He laid a hand on her knee, and she looked down at his well-tended fingernails. He touched her as if she were a young child under his guardianship—a touch meant as much to calm as to reprimand. "But it brought me back to you, so there was some good in it, my darling Sophia."

The door opened, and Lazarus returned. His stern gaze instantly went to that hand on her knee. She stood, as if she'd been about to do so anyway, and set her cup down. "Mr. Kane, I believe I left my apron with you," she exclaimed, having sought urgently for some reason to stand up, and then clutched desperately at the one cause she could find. "When I lent it to you for the mushrooms."

He stood just inside the doorway, arms swinging slightly at his sides. He was wet now from the rain, the shoulders of his shirt sticking and transparent. "In the pantry," he muttered.

"Oh." She was already walking toward it, when he set off in the same direction, moving rapidly. "I'll get it," Sophie exclaimed irritably. "I can get it for myself."

"But I know where it is. You'll never reach it."

He was too close behind her. She couldn't turn and go back to the safety of her chair, and his forward momentum was unyielding, the breadth of his shoulders once again startling when close. Her courage in both hands, she tripped down into the pantry, and he followed.

❧

He watched her as she stood with her back to him and he let her speak first.

"I see you fixed the gap in the orchard wall."

The pantry had one small window with old, diamond-shaped panes, through which the dull, weary day spilled in a quilt pattern. Rain spattered lazily against the crooked glass, and silver splinters of reflected light shimmered through her hair.

He stared at the nape of her slender neck. "Tuck told me the local children steal fruit," he managed to say. He wondered if she stole it too, and let the door shut behind him.

"The orchard produces a great deal of fruit," she murmured. "You should make jam so it's not wasted. Do you...do you know how to make jam?"

"No." He stood so close now his thighs brushed her skirt.

"You could ask one of the village women to help you."

He placed his hands on her waist. "Like Miss Osborne?"

"No. She makes the worst jam. Everyone knows it. Her jam leaves a sour taste on the tongue."

"But you," he whispered as he lowered his lips to her neck, "you leave a sweet taste in my mouth."

She spun around, her back to the shelf, and he moved closer until there was no space between her body and his. He needed the feel of her, the taste of her, the scent of her. Every day when he woke, she was the first thing on his mind. Sometimes he could barely get through the day until their lessons in the evening.

"Why are you still riding about with that popinjay in the silk cravat?"

"He's an old friend."

"What am I, then?" It choked out of him, because he hadn't realized, until that moment, how angry he was with her for still seeing James Hartley.

"You're a new friend. Or I thought you were. I'm beginning to doubt it when you continually seek to cause me problems with your outrageously forward behavior."

"Why? Because unlike the rest of you I don't hide my feelings?"

"I wish you would," she exclaimed under her breath. "You're doing no one any favors by being so transparent. Not me, and especially not yourself. James Hartley is not a good enemy to make."

"As if I care what he thinks."

"Well, you should, for heaven's sake!"

"As your friend Miss Vyne would say, what's he going to do to me? Blind me with the gleam of his boots?"

She groaned, eyes shining with frustration, her cheeks pink. "Do you take nothing seriously, foolish man?"

"I take you seriously."

"Indeed, you do not, or you wouldn't act this way in front of others." She put her hands to her face. "Good God, I wish I'd never started this with you. It can only end badly. I don't know what I was thinking to encourage you!"

He dragged her hands from her face and held her wrists tightly so she could not pull them away. "I like you in a temper," he breathed.

"You also like challenging the rules and causing trouble."

"No more than you."

"Nonsense," she protested.

"Why did you bring him into my house, then? You must be bored again, like you were when you wrote that advertisement."

"*You* caused his wheel to break," she whispered frantically. "I don't know how, but you did it."

"He drives like an imbecile. Perhaps in future he'll learn caution, before someone gets hurt."

"*I* could have been hurt!"

"No. I knew what I was doing. I always do, don't I? Haven't you learned to trust me yet?" His lips brushed hers very gently and felt her shiver, the pulse in her wrists throbbing too fast. "What is it you wanted in here again, Miss Valentine? Best remind me, because I'm already distracted by other thoughts."

Sophie's eyelashes fluttered against her cheeks. "My apron."

"You suddenly had need of it?" He looked down at her pouting lips.

"I just remembered," she replied tautly.

With his left hand, he reached up behind her, onto the shelf, where he'd left it folded neatly. The motion brushed the muscle of his chest up against her right breast and forced her farther back, trapped between the shelf and his body. His other hand went to her waist, fingers splayed, and greedily followed the deep curve under that thin bit of linen and petticoat. He wondered if she wore her lacy drawers today. He hoped not, since she hadn't expected to meet him.

Through the closed pantry door, he could hear James Hartley complaining, while Tuck gruffly told him to sit still and rest his ankle before it swelled up any further.

For a moment they were still, listening. He was so hot for her he might have taken her there and then, right where she stood, leaning against his pantry shelves and cursing him under her breath again. But Lazarus had promised himself he'd make Sophie marry him before he gave her everything she wanted.

Suddenly, she rose up on tiptoe, her lips seeking his even as the last curse died away on her tongue. The conflicted woman touched his face, drew him down to her, and those soft lips timidly explored his. Then he felt the damp tip of her tongue drawn along his lower lip, seeking a way in, unsure of itself. His mouth opened on hers, and his hand swept upward from her waist, following her ribs until it rested just below the weight of her bosom. He paused, but she kissed him now with unladylike fervor. So he cupped his hand around her breast, and immediately the grinding need multiplied. She wore no corset today, and he felt her pert nipple against his palm. He squeezed her breast and groaned deeply into her mouth.

She pulled back, looking down at his hand where he was fondling her. "I can't," she muttered, breathing hard so her breast thrust itself into his hand, telling him what she wanted even as her words tried to deny it. "Not now…like this…with James…"

"Still can't decide between us?" He ducked his head. His lips closed around the small peak through her gown, and she gasped. Her hands gripped the edge of the shelf against which he held her. It was almost too much for him—not being able to taste her fully through the material. He could enjoy only the teasing feel of that hardened nipple swelling and ripening under his hungry suckling. He could feel the passion galloping wildly through her, and his own desire was raw, explosive. He stopped, grabbed her right hand, and led it to his groin, where she could touch his arousal, feel it growing hard and hot against the front of his breeches.

"I'm in need of you," he growled, standing as still as he could, letting her explore the shape of his cock. Even without his lips around it, her nipple hardened, protruding through the dampened patch on her gown. He longed to let his tongue sweep over it again.

Instead, he rubbed it gently between his fingertips, trying to control his own savage need. She closed her eyes, her breath shuddered, and her hand pulled him closer. His sac ached, and blood rushed to his shaft. It certainly approved of her touch, he mused. Her hands were small, but thorough and curious. His fingers tight around her nipple, he bit down hard on his tongue, keeping another groan from spilling out.

Now he heard James stumbling across the flagged floor, demanding to know how long it took to find an apron. The door handle—an iron loop—shook and twisted, but the door wouldn't open.

"On damp, rainy days, the door sticks," he murmured.

"I know."

Of course she would know, he realized. But she hadn't stopped him when he shut the door.

His rival thumped hard on the old, scarred wood panels, cursing.

Lazarus swiftly made a decision, knowing he couldn't let her go without giving her something more than her apron. He lifted her onto the lowest shelf, which protruded a good few inches farther than the others, and then he crouched, sliding her skirt up to her hips. If she was going riding with James today, he'd make certain she thought of him the entire time. She was holding her breath again, as she often did in moments of excitement, but he knew he would soon make her expel a cry of pleasure.

And scant moments later he did. His mouth only had to touch her between her thighs, and she was gasping softly, her hand knocking a small jar of mustard from the shelf. He wished he had more time with her today, but this quick servicing would have to do. His hands held her thighs apart, and his tongue lapped at her almost roughly through the slit in her linen drawers. He brought her to a series of hard, trembling orgasms, pleasuring her diligently, while her gentlemanly suitor banged on that door. Her fingers gripped his hair and pulled hard. He laughed softly and drank from her as she trembled into his mouth and her thighs tensed under his hands. And when he felt the last of her stifled sighs, he finally looked up.

"Can he do that for you?" he demanded, his hands still on her thighs, his shoulders still holding her knees apart. "Has he?"

Flushed, Sophie pushed him back and slid down from the shelf. She adjusted her skirts and tried to get her breath back. "If I have splinters on my derriere now, it's your fault!"

The pantry door handle rattled frantically.

He grabbed her by the arms. "Does he?" He knew the answer but needed to hear it from her. If she confessed aloud that he, Lazarus, gave her something no one else did, perhaps then she'd be forced to realize it herself.

At least he knew she didn't wear her fancy lace for James Hartley.

She wiped a loose hair from her cheek and tucked it behind her ear. "He reads poetry and brings me flowers. Do you?"

Poetry and flowers? Is that what she wanted? No. She thought she *ought* to want them. It was all "oughts" and "shoulds" with these people, he mused.

He wouldn't let her pass, but kissed her again. His lips caressed her mouth, taking greedily, giving generously, knowing she would taste herself on his tongue. Only when she began to struggle and fuss did he let her go, by which time James was cursing at Tuck, demanding he find some way to get the door open.

"You're a very brazen young man," she reprimanded Lazarus in a low, breathy whisper as she glanced down at the creature straining in his breeches.

"Humble fellows like me have to be that way," he whispered. "Otherwise, we'd never get what we want. Ma'am." He tugged a pretend forelock.

She grabbed her apron, but he stood in her way again, his feet spread. "I look forward to our next lesson. You're coming on very well, Miss Valentine."

Her prim little nose stuck in the air. "I'd like to go now."

Still looking at her, he reached back and opened the door. Like everything else—including her—there was a trick to it.

She clutched the folded apron to her bosom and hurried out.

❧

"What were you doing in there?" James demanded as he hobbled after her.

In reply, she held up her apron, still not quite composed enough to answer.

He fell back into the chair and eyed her folded apron as if he could read her guilt upon it.

Lazarus emerged from the pantry and went to fetch Doctor Swift from the village, who returned with him to examine the wounded man and diagnose a slight sprain. As Sophie suspected, his pride was hurt more than anything, but James was furious—almost as if he would rather have a broken leg.

Sophie was feeling guilty and finally agreed to attend the planned soiree at Lady Hartley's to placate him, even if it meant watching her family be publicly disparaged for his entertainment. She deserved it, she decided, for being wicked and allowing Lazarus to do those things to her—and relishing it thoroughly—while poor James stood only inches away. The chance, the recklessness of it made the encounter only that much more enjoyable. She couldn't imagine what came over her.

"I don't like that wretched, insolent-eyed gypsy," James exclaimed bitterly as they rode back up the lane in Doctor Swift's carriage. "I'll find out why he came here. I'll get to the bottom of it and expose the truth."

"The truth? He was a soldier who fought for this country. What do you expect—?"

"I don't like the way he looks at you. He was an enlisted man. All manner of rogues enlist to escape debt or criminal punishment, or to abandon family obligations. He could have a wife and children somewhere. Or a dozen little bastards he refuses to acknowledge."

Uneasy, she laughed and assured him he was worrying too much. Mr. Kane's presence at Souls Dryft mattered not one whit, she lied yet again.

"Why?" he demanded coldly. "Can you tell me he hasn't continued pressing his suit? I suppose it was coincidence that pantry door should stick with you both on the other side of it."

She pressed her thighs together. "What does that matter?" she replied sharply. "I told you I turned him down when he came here. There can be no occasion for prying into his past."

But James was moody, not easily put off the idea. "This former employer of Mrs. Dykes's—a judge's wife, is she not?"

"Sir Arthur Sadler is retired, I believe. Why?" Anxiety flipped and tumbled through her belly.

"I daresay he could help uncover that blackguard's true past."

Things had got out of hand that day. For so long they'd managed to keep their relationship a secret, but if they continued along such a wayward, impetuous path, unable to keep their hands off each other, they could soon be exposed. From now on she must maintain a safer distance from Lazarus. For his sake.

But, as she suspected, this proved to be easier said than done.

Chapter 25

Sun beamed brightly through the schoolhouse window, and the children were too restless for books and slates. She'd brought in her little caged linnet to teach them about clockwork mechanisms, but this, too, was beyond their attention span today, especially with the school term soon to end.

"It's a fine day for flying a kite," Matthias Finchly announced suddenly, and his brothers joined in rowdy agreement. Lazarus recently helped them all make kites, and it was now the most popular thing to have. Long, heated discussions were held about the merits of one another's kites and whose might fly the highest.

She was just about to suggest a nature walk out to the oak at the crossroads, when the distant rumble of a cart drew the Finchly brothers to the window.

"'Tis ol' Tuck," they shrieked in unison, having craned their necks around to see what lay at the head of the horse path, and the other children scrambled to see out, screaming delightedly. Someone knocked at the door, and Sophie quickly ordered the children back to their benches while she went to open it.

Lazarus Kane was on the doorstep, shirtsleeves rolled up, one brawny arm holding something behind his back.

"Mr. Kane!" Unfortunately, despite her plan to avoid him as much as possible in that small village, Sophie woke up each morning thinking of Lazarus and went to sleep every night with the same ideas running through her restless mind. As for her dreams, thinking of them now as he appeared at her door caused Sophie a great deal of discomposure. Like any habit, he was very difficult to give up.

He revealed what he'd kept behind his back, offering it with a flourish: a small posy of larkspur, pink germander, and white bellflowers. "I picked them along the lane," he told her with an amusing amount of pride. "Many happy returns of the day, Miss Valentine."

Somehow he'd learned it was her birthday. Did he also know it was her thirtieth, which officially made her an old lady?

"Thank you, Mr. Kane." She accepted his flowers very formally, conscious of the children watching.

As he smiled at her, his arms braced in the frame of the door, one foot on the step, he appeared to be waiting for something. A kiss? Surely even he knew better than to expect one at that moment, surrounded by children.

Oh, but she wanted to kiss him.

Her heartbeat raced around a corner, out of her clutches. The moment she saw this tempting man under her chestnut tree two months ago, she swore she wouldn't throw herself onto the mercies of the unknown again. Yet she was falling. Now, in that moment, she knew it; she was falling over the edge again. He was no longer just a moving, breathing study of the illustrations in that naughty book. He was real. He was a real man. And when she couldn't see him, when something happened to prevent their lessons, she missed him terribly. If she never saw him again, she didn't know what she'd do.

It was the worst possible moment to lose her head like this, when she ought to keep her distance for his own good.

"Is there something else you wanted, Mr. Kane?" she uttered stiffly with a frown.

A slow grin worked across his lips. "Why, yes, Miss Valentine." He paused. "I thought the children might enjoy a picnic today."

No sooner did the children hear the word "picnic" than they were up again, pushing past her, tumbling out into the sun with kites carried overhead and ribbons streaming.

Momentarily thrust aside by the rush, Lazarus waited until they were all out in the lane, then he lunged forward, one boot crossing the threshold, and whispered, "You've been avoiding me."

"I told you I've been busy these last few evenings and had no time for your tutoring."

"Busy with Hartley?"

She wouldn't answer. In fact, she'd spent most of her time with Ellie Vyne, enjoying her friend's company while she had it.

"I don't know any poetry, but I did bring flowers," he reminded her with a wink. "Come out and play with me, Miss Valentine."

Again, she didn't know how to cope with the intensity

of her feelings, so she was angry and snappish. "Did the children know about this picnic already, by chance?"

His grin widened. "I might have mentioned something…"

"How dare you interfere with my school day!"

"Tuck made sausage pies. Your favorite."

"Oh."

"They're still warm," he added. "But if you don't want any…"

She muttered hastily, "I suppose we might enjoy an afternoon out. This once."

"Yes. We don't have forever."

It struck her as an odd thing for him to say, and it cast a shadow over his smile just before he turned away and walked off down the path toward the cart. But the sky was cloudless, a blushing expanse of pale blue. It was not the sort of day in which anyone could be morose for long. Besides…sausage pies…

As she grabbed her bonnet from the hook by the door and followed him down the lane, she wondered idly how he discovered her love for sausage pies. Tuck was already helping the children and their kites into the cart, and the ruckus was supervised by Ellie Vyne.

Of course, who else would tell Lazarus Kane all her deepest secrets?

Ellie saw her and waved jauntily, knowing full well she was a meddling menace. Sophie sighed and shook her head.

Soon the cart was full, the children piled in, Ellie attempting to keep some order over the proceedings and having little success. Molly Robbins ignored old Tuck's protests and frowns and climbed up to sit beside him at the front of the cart, where she made herself comfortable and chattered away happily about the joys she anticipated in the day ahead. Tuck, generally of the opinion that children should be seen and not heard, was about to toss her into the back of the cart with the other children, when she beamed up at him, showing off the large gap between her front teeth. He then showed her his own gap, and thus a bond was formed and the little girl permitted to stay at his side.

Sophie tied her bonnet ribbons under her chin and, still holding her posy, stepped up to the cart. Lazarus waited for her, his foot on the wheel. As she glanced left, she noticed a small grey mare tied behind the cart. Its silver mane gleamed, and its ears were pricked. It was the riding horse she'd heard about. Was this another of his schemes to tempt her into bad behavior?

"I can make my own way," she said and lifted her skirt over one arm to climb up into the cart.

Without a word, he walked up to her, put his hands around her waist, and lifted her easily up over the side.

"Well, really!' she exclaimed, merely because she ought to complain, not because she was at all put out. He swung himself up beside little Molly, and the cart lurched forward into a bumpy, rattling journey up the lane. The grey mare trotted merrily behind.

"You put him up to this," she accused her friend.

Ellie blinked innocently. "I cannot think what you mean. It was all his idea. Besides, no one should be shut inside on such a lovely day, even an old curmud-geon like you." She wagged her finger. "Remember, we shall never be younger than we are today!"

Only a short while later, they rumbled to a slower

pace and joined a second, smaller cart, this one holding two passengers and a large basket of provisions.

"Aunt Finn?" Sophie exclaimed in amazement. Her aunt seldom ventured so far from the fortress on hot days, but there she was, the lace lappets of her bonnet blowing in the playful breeze as she sat beside the giant Chivers and chattered excitedly.

The carts turned off the road and took a slender, bumpy, winding lane for about a mile before Lazarus climbed out to open the gate into his meadow. Once they arrived at a pleasant spot, strewn with daisies and buttercups, which overlooked the valley and the village below, the cart came to a halt and was unloaded. While Sophie and her friend spread out the blanket, Lazarus took the horses into the shady covert where a pleasant little brook rambled lazily by. She observed his quiet, gentle way with the horses and felt a sweet yearning deep inside. Perhaps his gentleness meant so much more because he was not soft by nature, and when he laid a kind, compassionate hand to anything, it was done with a true desire to show tenderness, not because it came easily to him. His rough, callused hands could be remarkably soothing, as she knew.

Once he was done with the horses, he gave the children their kite-flying instruction, but as the sun reached its peak, the breeze died away, and several kites came to a sad end, nose down in the tufted grass. Undaunted, Lazarus and his friend soon had other games underway to make up for the disappointment, and there was much shrieking, screaming, and tearing about. But even Tuck didn't seem to care about the noise. He sat under a tree and showed Molly Robbins how to make a good whistle through that gap in her teeth.

Sophie was the quietest of the group on that glorious, sunny afternoon. As she felt a great, heavy weight pressing on her chest, she stifled tears that hovered constantly on the brink and sat silently on the blanket, her face half-shaded by the brim of her straw bonnet, with no sign of the bubbling commotion within.

We don't have forever, he'd said to her. Did that mean he planned to leave after the harvest? He'd told James, in her hearing, he considered no place home for long.

Or it could mean he planned to marry that twittering ninny Jane Osborne. Any wife, it seemed, would do. After all, this was a man who came in answer to an advertisement, knowing almost nothing about the woman who wrote it. He was a well-traveled man with a mysterious past, a jack-of-all-trades, a trickster who knew how to play her like an instrument.

But he'd warned her that day when they picked mushrooms he wouldn't ask *her* to marry him again. *Once a man's been rejected, he should know better than to make a fool of himself and mention it again.*

He was a man who never stayed anywhere for long, never set down roots, probably never formed deep attachments with women. He would leave her, just as the captain left Aunt Finn alone with her gin and her memories.

So many doubts and fears swirled about her mind, and she couldn't concentrate for long upon any; therefore, none were satisfactorily resolved. Some of the things James had said about enlisted men stuck in her thoughts like a spur of goosegrass. Lazarus could come and go with ease, leaving people behind as he went. Look how easily and quickly he settled in the village and won over its residents. Only a man accustomed to meeting new people in new places could adapt so smoothly.

Sophie had no appetite for the picnic. Her head ached, and she considered moving to sit under a tree, but when Lazarus trotted over and dropped to the blanket beside her, she no longer wanted the shade. He stretched out his legs, crossing them at the ankle, and leaned back on his elbows.

"On a day like this," he said, "a man can almost forget his worries."

"Do you have many of those, Mr. Kane?" He never seemed to let anything bother him unduly, or for long.

He must have caught the sharpness in her tone, for he squinted at her, nostrils flared slightly. "Just a small one that vexes me."

"Only one? You're fortunate."

"It's been avoiding me of late, a stubborn, secretive creature, but I'll get the better of it."

She scowled and looked away. Chivers, Ellie, and Aunt Finn joined them on the blanket, chatting and laughing together.

"You ought to sit in the shade," Lazarus said to her. "You look hot."

"I'll do as I please!" she snapped. "I managed very well without your advice for thirty years, and I daresay I can manage again. When you're gone."

"Why? Where am I going?"

"How should I know? You have the freedom to come and go as you please, unlike some of us."

"Nothing stops you from taking flight, Miss Valentine, but your own cowardice."

"How dare you!"

"Pity I didn't know you before you jumped off that balcony. Then, I daresay, things were different." He leaned over to tickle her cheek with a long grass. "You lost your gumption."

She batted the grass away and glared at him from the shadow of her bonnet brim. "At least I'm not an arrogant, thick-headed man who gets distracted by a passing butterfly and cannot sit still for five minutes together, or devote himself long to one idea."

"*What the Devil…?*"

"I've heard you boast you're a jack-of-all-trades, always traveling and learning something new." Her temper mounted under the midday heat. "I suppose you've never stayed long enough in one place to finish what you came there to do. I daresay, wherever you start a new life, you soon grow bored and abandon it."

He studied her for a moment as he chewed on that long blade of grass. "What brought this on? Oh, I see—I'm not going anywhere. You can let your brother know that, and your fine and fancy dandy too. Whatever they try to dig up about me."

"Do as you please. I'm sure I don't care and never did! Dreadful, impertinent man."

Aunt Finn's eyebrows flew skyward, Ellie began to hum rather tunelessly as she poured out the cider, and Chivers fidgeted with his piecrust. Lazarus reached for a plum and bit into it with rather more savagery than necessary. Ha! She'd finally made him angry.

"Your brother not likely to join us today, ma'am?" Chivers asked.

"Henry Valentine would never approve of a picnic. He would think it uncivilized," Lazarus muttered. "Henry Valentine prefers games with high stakes to kites and cricket."

Chivers looked interested. "A sharp or a flatt?"

"A flatt. Definitely."

"What do you mean?" Sophie demanded.

Chivers explained, "There's two kinds of gamblers, ma'am. A sharp what wins, and a flatt what always loses to a sharp."

She glared at Lazarus. "How do you know my brother loses?"

"Because I once overheard a conversation about his debts your brother wishes I hadn't." He tore off another lump of fruit and chewed it angrily. "I wish I never heard it either, since it set him against me from the start."

Sophie understood then why Henry had taken such a fierce dislike to Lazarus. That dreadful pride would always be Henry's downfall. Her temper quelled for now, she searched the grass by her hand for a four-leaf clover. Despite the tone of their conversation, her body still leaned toward Lazarus. Like a flower toward the sun.

She decided she'd sat there long enough, suffering the closeness of his body and all the temptations that entailed, and leapt up and ran across the grass to organize the children in a dance.

❧

Lazarus closed his eyes tight against the sun and leaned back on his elbows. Evidently, Henry or that arrogant peacock, James Hartley, had been whispering doubts in her ear. Well, they wouldn't chase him out, no matter what they threatened. Let them uncover every crime in his past. He'd face it. This was the end of the road for him; he was done with traveling, done with running. Now he'd do whatever it took to hold on to what he had, what he wanted more than anything in this world.

Sophie.

Chapter 26

WHEN IT WAS TIME TO RETURN TO THE VILLAGE, AUNT Finn had wandered off into the grove of trees and couldn't immediately be found. It was decided Tuck and Ellie should supervise the children in the cart while the others split up to look for her.

"I should have hidden your gin today," Sophie muttered as she swung her bonnet by its long ribbons and stomped through the bracken. She was well aware of her aunt's love of games, particularly hide-and-seek.

She heard a twig snap behind her and stopped to look over her shoulder. There was Lazarus, just a few steps away, leading one of the cart horses and the little grey. "We were supposed to split up and search," she exclaimed.

"I didn't want to lose you, too."

She thought he looked remarkably handsome under the dappled shade of the trees, almost too much to take in. Their brief quarrel had changed something between them. She sensed it, read it in his face. Whether it was good or bad, she had yet to decide.

"Tuck has taken the children back to the village in

the big cart. Chivers will find your aunt," he said calmly as he came closer through the bracken. "He can track anything. Nose like a bloodhound."

"Your friend is a gentle fellow."

"Looks can be deceiving. Like yours."

That made her smile…just a little.

"You ride sidesaddle, Sophie?"

Now she realized he'd saddled the little grey for her. So he did keep saddles! She felt nervous suddenly. "I…I haven't ridden in years."

Without another word, he helped her up onto the horse, her right leg over the pommel, left foot in the stirrup.

"I've missed having a horse to ride," she said. "We can't afford to keep animals unless they work on the land."

"That's why she'll stay at Souls Dryft." He smiled and flicked hair out of his eyes as he handed her the reins. "Come and ride her whenever you fancy."

He *was* staying, then. Had he found a wife?

She dampened her lips and cleared her throat. "Miss Osborne will not be pleased you keep a horse for me to ride."

"Is that all you ever worry about? Who will and will not be pleased?"

"I believe someone should be concerned about Miss Osborne."

"But why should it be you?"

He was pushing her, she realized, trying to expose her jealousy. Apparently he thought he could flirt with every unmarried woman in the village and owe no one any explanation. Not even the woman he tutored privately in matters of the flesh. "Do you not dine often at the Osbornes?"

"To meet with Mr. Osborne," he replied easily. "I like the old fellow."

"Oh."

"As for Miss Osborne, since Chivers arrived, she's kept her distance."

She petted the horse's neck, drawing her fingers through the silver mane. "I'm sorry people can't accept your friend without judging on appearance."

He swung himself up onto the other horse and sat well, at ease on the big mount even without a saddle. "Shows me the true colors of some folk. That's all."

With a nudge of his heels, he steered his horse forward, ducking under the lower branches, and Sophie followed through the dappled sunlight. She couldn't remember the last time she'd ridden a horse. It must have been before she and Maria were sent away to that wretched ladies' academy. Back then, there was no greater pleasure than to ride out alone through the shady covert. In the spring, the ground was sprinkled with bluebells, as if little bits of sky had fallen to earth, and in the autumn, under the gilt-draped chestnuts, she and Henry once enjoyed mock sword-fights with sticks they found.

Sophie rode along at her own pace, and enjoyed a wondrous sense of freedom and independence—a very rare and precious gift, indeed. For a while, there was no conversation, just the shiver of a slight breeze through the leafy canopy, the sleepy coo of wood pigeons, and the steady thud of hooves. The sunlight was heavy today, thick and damp with nature's perfume, and the atmosphere heavily laden with pine from the tall evergreen columns that bordered her brother's property in the distance. But the air pooled here under the chestnut trees and lost its stinging heat.

She urged the mare forward in a quick trot, and as they came out into a wider lane, she drew alongside Lazarus. As she'd noted before, he was not a man who required noise and chatter to pass the time, but was perfectly content to ride along, admiring this beautiful day and sharing her company. They were riding back toward the lane and the cart, she realized, but they were traveling the long way round, and he was in no hurry. Neither was she.

She pulled ahead of his horse and turned left, leading the way off the path and back under the trees. He followed. Her breath quickened until there was almost no difference between the in and the out. Farther into the trees she took him, remembering the way she used to ride alone when she came here to get away from chores or hide from punishment. Once she'd called it her "emerald cave," for it was jewel green from floor to sky, a mass of leaves and moss and soft grass that seemed to curl around her like an eggshell. Whatever possessed her to take him there, she didn't question it for long. The need to show him was too great, the desire to share that secret with him almost overwhelming.

They dismounted and walked down into the tranquil hollow where moss-garbed roots rose up out of the ground and reached around them with curiosity. The sky was barely visible now through the thick leaves and close branches, but where some sun trickled through, it painted slender columns of silver dust that hovered in the still air and dotted the ground with ghosts of fallen stars.

Sophie gathered her courage and turned to find him close behind her. She didn't have to say anything. Those strong arms were already around her, his mouth lowering to hers.

"Tell me what you want," he whispered as he always did at the start of their "lessons." He held her tightly, and his lips pressed to her hair, waiting.

She never knew what to ask for, because her entire body pleaded like a selfish child, wanting everything all at once.

"Sophie." He spoke her name as if it were a plea for mercy. "We don't have forever."

There it was again. What did it mean?

Her hands went to his arms tentatively; her fingers stroked the pleats of his rolled shirtsleeves, then higher to his broad shoulders. They sank slowly down into the moss, and she closed her eyes when she felt his stroking hand on her hip and the side of her thigh. Here at last was a man not afraid to touch her as a woman should be touched, not as if she were a child to be restrained or a girl to be mollified out of a temper tantrum. She lay back in the moss. His lips were on the swell of her bosom and moving lower, kissing her through her gown. He slowly lifted her skirt and chemise higher, until she felt the air on her stockings.

"Lazarus." She whispered his name, her hand resting on his hair. She wanted to say she loved him, but she held it back, too afraid of leaving herself vulnerable, leaving her private thoughts as unguarded before him as her body.

Warm lips caressed her thigh, and then a damp, gentle tongue drifted across her skin.

Today there was no hurry. He took his time to tease and cajole. She held her breath, and her fingers tightened in his black hair where his exertions in the sun had left it hot and damp. He shifted his weight and slid farther down. Then his hands gently but firmly pressed her thighs apart.

Chapter four: Arousal of the Female. He was expert at it. Oh, Lord, was he expert at it!

Of course, not being a reader, he would have learned from practice, but she pushed that thought aside hastily, not wanting to think of him pleasuring other women.

For too long it seemed to her he merely gazed upon her sex, as if in worship, making her wait until she burned inside. Then his mouth finally touched her where she yearned for it. At last she released a breath, a quivering, excitable sigh. His tongue moved over her, stroking gently. Then it was inside her, taking her intimately, and his trembling hands pressed on her thighs as she felt his excitement keeping pace with her own. She succumbed in the next gasp and arched against the sun-spattered ground, lifted herself to his mouth like an overeager strumpet, and then sprawled with that glorious, exultant weariness.

What was the word for it? Ah, yes. In her aunt's informative little book it was called a climax. He made it happen twice more for her after that, until she was a quivering, breathless puddle, and then he lay over her, his upper body supported on his forearms, and leaned down for a kiss. His tongue met hers and stroked it. She tasted herself on his mouth, a muskiness that mingled with the sweet plum he'd eaten earlier.

Feeling rejuvenated, she pushed him over and sat up. Her hair fell loose down her back. "My turn. It is my birthday, after all!" She gave him no time to argue but rolled him onto his back and stripped his shirt over his head.

"Careful. Don't tear it," he warned. "It's the only one I've—"

She kissed his nipple, and he lay still, like a pagan sacrifice. Her tongue darted out and swept over the tiny point nestled among the soft fur of his chest. She closed her lips on it and suckled gently. His soft groan of approval encouraged her further. She climbed to sit astride his hips, and licked and nibbled at his bare chest, her hair falling over them both.

And when her fingers found that small bump over his heart, she finally found the courage to ask, "What is this?"

He held her finger. "A bit of broken knife lodges here. The surgeons can't remove it without killing me. So there it stays."

"A broken knife?"

He looked away for a moment and then back at her, his eyes darkly penetrating. "It was a fight…six years ago. The other man died…a fellow soldier."

Sophie reclaimed her finger. "He died?"

"He attacked me with that knife, but I had no weapon, only my hands." He held the objects up for her perusal. "When I hit him, he fell back onto a stone hearth. He died later."

After all these weeks of wondering, the truth came out so suddenly.

"They sent me to a prison hulk off the coast."

As her aunt always said, some secrets were better off kept secret. She tore her gaze from his wound to his face and tried to keep her own countenance composed. "But you're here."

"They thought I was dead one morning—sometimes it looks and feels as if my heart has stopped—so they threw me overboard with all the other corpses. Disease is rife in those damp, fetid prisons. Men die every day." He reached for her hand again. "I swam to shore and promised myself if I lived long enough after that, I'd pay recompense for everything I ever did wrong, every mistake I made in my life."

Lazarus resurrected. Of course.

"They tell me I should have died long since." He laughed gently. "Yet here I am. The physicians say that bit of blade will move one day, and then I'll be dead"—he clicked his fingers—"just like that. Snuffed out like a candle."

He spoke so casually, it shocked her. But now she knew why he was always so busy, moving on to another thing before he'd finished the one before. He didn't want to miss a moment of the life he had left. She understood that—oh, yes, she understood. *We do not have forever.*

He folded his arms around her and held her against his wounded chest, her cheek on his shoulder. "Now I told you this, I don't want you to watch me with those big, panic-stricken eyes, expecting any moment might be my last. I believe in living for the moment, taking every chance that comes…without fear." He slid his hand to the nape of her neck and then higher, under her hair, so he could pull her up and press his lips to hers.

She kissed him back, wanting to erase the sadness that ripped into her heart suddenly. But he didn't dwell on the darkness, and already he had turned to happier thoughts.

"When you tempt me like this, you bring out the worst in me," he said, his voice hoarse, his hands running down her spine to her bottom. "You bring out the devil in me."

She was thrilled to hear him confess the power she had. When she licked his chin, the stubble tickled the tip of her tongue.

"Whatever will you do to me next?" he whispered wearily, as if it were all so inconvenient.

"Whatever *you* would like," she replied, smiling as she sat astride his body, her fingers trailing over his chest. She couldn't think about what he'd just told her. It was too much, too painful, and she wanted it gone, erased by those decadent sensations she'd discovered at his hands. As a child, whenever she was crying, her mother gave her toffee to chew. She soon found one could not cry and chew toffee at the same time. The pleasure replaced the hurt.

His hands tightened around her waist, and he lifted her down onto the grass beside him. Now propped up on one elbow again, he took her hand and led it slowly to that hard, ravenous creature now freed of his breeches. "Here is one new thing I can show you." He'd never trusted her with this before.

She nibbled his lower lip with tender excitement. "Show me what to do," she whispered.

He guided her hand to his manhood, showing her how to hold and caress it with a steady motion. Once she was confident enough to take over, he returned the favor. He slid his hand and fingers under her petticoat. When she gasped out his name, he covered her mouth with his and drank from her greedily. His hips bucked frantically, and he pushed his manhood into her hand until she thought she could feel it inside her, the friction of those warm, throbbing ridges against her inner walls, thrusting and withdrawing, taking her like a battering ram. His hand quickened between her thighs, and she heard the breath as it gushed out of him, escaping over his lower lip, as her body once again reached that joyous peak.

But he was still hot, rigid iron in her hand. Even as her tremors faded, he was pulling away, his fingers around her wrist to stop the motion, a fiercely intent expression on his face.

This time, however, she wanted to see him lose control. He'd watched her surrender helplessly, and now she would do the same. When she resisted his hand, tightened her hold, and continued the motion, he grunted, part laughing and part angry. But she was a determined, stubborn woman, and today she was on a mission. He gave up. Under her firm strokes, he swelled, expanded. Then his head fell back. He arched, grabbed her shoulders to steady himself, and at last he jerked, spilling in a rapid rush, her hand still clasped around his shaft.

Minutes later, he looked down at her, distraught. "I've ruined your frock." He groaned and fell back to the moss, one arm across his forehead. "I shouldn't have done that. I promised myself I wouldn't spend until…" The words fell away in a sigh.

She watched his lashes pulsing against his cheeks and thought him the most beautiful man she'd ever seen. How many women had he known, she wondered, savagely jealous. "When was the last time you had a woman?" she blurted as she sat up.

His answer was coy. "A while ago."

She pouted. He laughed and raised one hand to stroke her warm cheek. "Not since I saw your lacy drawers climbing out of that tree. I've been a good boy since then, ma'am."

"That's a matter of opinion." They both chuckled, and she slowly spread one hand over the hard planes of his chest. She reached inside herself for the courage and finally said it, releasing the words into the air, just as he once freed the bird trapped in her schoolhouse. "Make love to me. I want all of you."

His breath stilled. "No. Not yet."

What was he waiting for? Did he want her to beg?

"It has to be just right," he added softly, thoughtfully.

"When will that be?"

"Soon." He grinned. "I hope. That depends on you."

She didn't understand. He lay before her, stretched out with his arms behind his head, his manhood finally at ease but no less inspiring.

Sometimes when she stopped to consider the intimate things they'd done together, her face was so hot she felt certain other folk would look at it and read all her guilt. But despite these "lessons," what did she know about Lazarus Kane?

He could drop dead at any moment. He'd killed a man with his bare hands.

He'd killed a man with his bare hands.

She'd marveled often at the strength in his hands. From the very beginning, she'd sensed their restlessness, the dangerous capability that thrummed through those thick, powerful fingers.

This dark, dangerous warrior had come for her at last. As a foolish, harebrained girl, she'd never realized exactly what that meant. But a dangerous man—a true warrior—did not suddenly become tame and harmless overnight. A man-eating tiger could never become a kitten.

The air seemed too thick and still suddenly, over-brimming with things that ought to be said, questions that should be asked and answered. But the pleasures of that afternoon still lingered in her warm bones, and she didn't want to spoil them.

Back to practical matters. "I'll wash my skirt in the stream," she said.

When they finally emerged from the emerald hollow, riding again side by side, the sky was aglow with melting sunset that slowly covered the last, lingering, forget-me-not innocence of a cloudless afternoon. They didn't speak. What was there to say?

All the way home, they left the conversation to Chivers, Ellie, and Aunt Finn. But little glances passed between them as the small cart rumbled gently along and the little grey clopped neatly behind. They shared his secret now. Soon they would have a past to talk about; for now they had only a few shared moments to recall, but it was building, and they learned new things about each other every day.

So what else did she know about Lazarus Kane?

Despite his unconventional, bold, "improper" ways, he was, underneath it all, a man of generosity, tenderness—when he chose to use it—and boundless courage.

And fatal secrets.

Chapter 27

JAMES WAS WAITING BY THE GATE WITH TWO HORSES harnessed to a brand-new phaeton. In all the excitement, she'd completely forgotten tonight was the evening at Lady Hartley's. Aunt Finn certainly hadn't bothered to remind her.

"Oh, Lord!" the lady now exclaimed, all innocence. "Mr. Hartley appears a trifle sour, Sophie."

He must have ridden up to the fortress to fetch her, and then, finding her gone, his suspicious nature took him directly to Souls Dryft. Lines of anger were etched deeply across his usually smooth brow.

"Yon milksop's here again," Chivers confirmed sourly under his breath.

Ellie snorted with laughter until Sophie threw her a look. The last thing she needed was James being even more furious than he clearly was already.

"I shan't go," Finn resolutely declared. "I have better things to do with my evening. Chivers promised me a game of cards here."

"Aunt Finn, you must come. Henry will expect—"

"Henry can expect until the cows come home and go out again."

If James wasn't standing there, waiting, Sophie, too, would gladly have missed the evening—made some excuse.

She held her bonnet in her lap, and the frayed ribbons twisted around her fingers. She didn't think she could stand up, let alone climb down from the cart. In her current state, everything was thrown askew, inside and out, and she wanted to curl up and hide. It was unfair of these wretched men, she thought, to pull her about like this. Or was she the one pulling them about? It was, after all, her advertisement that started this.

A few feet away, James glowered at her and made twitchy gestures. He took a step closer, but Lazarus was there first, his arms reaching up to her. Her hair, now without ribbon or bonnet, cascaded over her shoulders and across his face while he let her slide down his body until her toes met the ground.

"Thank you," she breathed, her hands lightly pressed to his shoulders. When he didn't immediately release her, she heard James complaining about the time. Still, those hands remained around her waist, reluctant to give her up. Her pulse skipped like a spring lamb, and when she raised her eyes slowly to his, what she saw there made her want to run away. His desire was savage, even brutal. But what else should she expect from her flesh-and-blood warrior? He was no fantasy she could control with her imagination. He'd come to find her—to carry her off over his shoulder. What had she expected to happen next, after he rode off with her into the horizon? For him to sit her down and make daisy chains, or let her sketch his silhouette? No. There was only one thing he had in mind when he came to steal her away. It was what conquering knights did.

"Don't…" she gasped in a frantic whisper, "don't kiss me." She had a real fear he would do it just to incite James. The touch of his strong, unpredictable hands made her tremble. His breath warmed her temple, and when she blinked slowly, her lashes brushed his jaw. Much too close. What did her warrior care? He'd killed a man with those same hands. He could do it again.

In the corner of her eye, she saw James waiting, growing steadily more irate. She felt the tension in the air, the unspoken aggression, and turned quickly to slip out of those dangerous hands and step gingerly across the rutted lane to James and his carriage.

❦

Lazarus escorted Miss Vyne back to her aunt's cottage in the village, and she obligingly filled him in on Sophie's history with Hartley.

"He's been in love with her for fifteen years," she'd said with a pert sigh, "or at least he thinks he has. James Hartley is accustomed to getting what he wants, because he's filthy rich, as well as handsome as the very Devil." Then, after a short pause, she threw him a shred of comfort. "But he's also the stupidest man alive if he thinks he can get Sophie by forcing her into a corner. That's the very worst thing he can try. A wild animal, when cornered, will strike. I hope he's prepared. Of course, I could have told him he's wasting his time on Sophie, but he'd never heed my advice. Pity, really. I have much advice to give, and people so seldom follow it."

He looked at her warily. "How did you become so clever and fearless at your age?"

"Out of necessity," she chirped. "Same as you did, I suspect."

He said good evening, saw her into the cottage, and then rode home.

When he entered the farmhouse, Chivers and Finn Valentine were in the midst of a game of cards.

"Why did you let her go with Hartley?" Finn wanted to know at once.

"I'll let her make her choice. I won't force her decision." He tried to make light of it, remembering what her friend had just told him. He shrugged in a lazy, careless fashion, which was far from what he felt. "She'll do what's best for her."

The lady sighed dramatically and got out her gin flask. "Now you'll just have to wait and see if she comes back, you young fool."

Lazarus slumped in his chair, one hand to his chest.

Chivers watched his friend thoughtfully. "You all right? You look done in."

He shook his head and winced.

Chivers pushed, "Did you tell her?"

"Some. Not all. But soon I will."

"You must be head over heels in love with that woman, you bloody fool." Even as Chivers cursed his friend, it was with a soft, chiding care, like that of an impatient older brother.

But Lazarus gave a sheepish grin. "I want her to know the truth. All of it. Whatever happens."

"Then I was right, and you are in love," Chivers grumbled. "Or mad as a March hare."

"Perhaps both."

"But, Mr. Kane," Finn cried, "my Sophie has been waiting for you all her life. And now you've let her go off with James Hartley."

"I think your niece has had enough people telling her what to do. It's time she made her own leap of faith."

Finn exclaimed, "She did that once before, and look what happened."

"Yes. It brought me to her when I would otherwise never have known her."

"I don't mean her advertisement. I mean the balcony, Mr. Kane, when she jumped from it."

"So do I." He stood abruptly, walked to the window, and looked out on the ink-splotched evening sky. He wished her back again in his embrace, but he knew he had to let her go. She had to be there by her own choice, or he'd never have the courage to tell her the whole truth about his past. Today he'd told her a great deal, but he had yet to tell her the most important detail of his life—the first moment he saw her.

It happened on one moonlit night almost eleven years ago, when he was an under-gardener who stayed out late, trimming ivy. He'd seen her on that balcony and stared up at her, bewitched. If he hadn't been so distracted that night, watching the beautiful girl on the balcony above, he would never have left his ladder out.

But he did. When she jumped, she hit her face upon a rusty nail that protruded from that ladder. He was promptly dismissed from his post, and if it hadn't been for his sister, he would never even have known her name.

It was all his fault she was scarred.

He felt certain she could never forgive him for that

mistake, but he'd come there to make amends in any way he could. If only she'd let him.

Aunt Finn knew none of the turmoil in his heart, declared him a fool of the highest order, and refused to speak to him for the rest of the evening. Eventually, before it was full dark, Chivers took her back up the lane to Henry's fortress, and Lazarus sat alone with his head in his hands, past mistakes preying heavily on his mind.

❦

James said little as they rode into the dusk. He was plainly angry, and she wished he'd let it out rather than keep it locked away.

"We had a picnic," she said, "for the schoolchildren."

She caught the quick, sharp flick of his furious gaze as it lashed sideways like a whip.

"I forgot the time," she added. "I should have gone home to tidy my hair, at least."

"At least," he snapped.

She sighed and brushed at the damp grass stains on her skirt. "I suppose even my best frock wouldn't compete with the famously elegant Misses Sadler's, whom we shall meet this evening. Certainly won't meet your grandmama's standards."

He rested his forearms on his knees, the reins slack between his fingers. "Sometimes, Sophia, I think you deliberately like to upset my grandmama."

"It's easier than meeting with her approval."

His lips pursed and then snapped open to mutter a curt, "I don't like your running about the country-side like a stray cat. Like that Vyne girl." He sat up straighter. "And I agree with Henry. That school is a waste of your time."

"You've discussed me with Henry?"

"Of course."

She turned her face away and remarked softly, "I think I liked it better when you hated each other."

And I think I'm in love with Lazarus Kane. She couldn't quite reconcile herself to the idea. After all, he was a mere boy, impetuous and probably attracted to things that weren't good for him. *Was it love or lust? Or both?*

"If I see you with Kane again, Sophia…"

"There is no harm in it. The children like—"

"…I *will* put a stop to it. I suggest you act with decorum in future and don't encourage that man. He ought to know his place."

She sighed and looked at her hands in her lap. She didn't want to bring Lazarus trouble. He must be made to understand the peril he courted by pushing James's temper and overstepping his "place."

Chapter 28

THE SADLERS—THEIR EIGHT DAUGHTERS, TWO MAIDS, a valet, a butler, two footmen, and a coachman—had arrived that week in Morecroft. Mrs. Dykes had taken it upon herself to show them the sights and entertainments, such as they were, and soon found herself fully utilized in this and many other, less-gracious capacities: shepherding the listless daughters about and standing ever ready to demean herself as necessary in the task of carrying boxes, finding lost bonnets and gloves, walking lapdogs, and disposing of the little gifts those lapdogs left behind on the pavement.

Tonight, she took the greatest of simpering pleasure in providing, through her own "connections," this social coup of an evening's company with Lady Ursula Hartley—the most consequential person in Morecroft.

Sophie expected nothing more from the evening than a few grim laughs and possibly a generous measure of humiliation, but she was curious to meet the Sadlers, especially those eight daughters who were supposedly so fine and well behaved.

In the drawing room, as soon as they entered, James

was whisked away to be introduced to the Misses Sadler—the five that were present this evening—and Sophie was escorted to the couch. She was obliged to sit between Sir Arthur Sadler, who had a habit of reaching for his knee and finding hers instead, and her sister-in-law, who worried constantly about her new gown being crushed by the proximity.

Their late arrival caused quite a stir. Her sister was already certain they'd had a fatal accident in James's new phaeton, and Sophie's bedraggled, windblown appearance did nothing to dispel that fear immediately. Lady Hartley's piercing grey eyes quickly assessed the dirt on her shoes, the grass stains on her skirt, and her unbound hair, but no one mentioned it. Sophie took her seat on the couch with as much grace as she could muster and silently lamented her bare arms as she took note of all the long white gloves. Even if her gown and shoes had been clean and her hair pinned up, she was hardly dressed for an evening party. But she had to make the best of it.

For the first half hour, Lavinia and her mother were too awestruck for much conversation. To dine in the company of Lady Hartley was the sort of achievement for which they lived and breathed. Sophie knew anecdotes of this evening would pepper their speeches for the next ten years, and they would find any cause to throw in a tidbit about the pattern on Lady Hartley's china, the luster of her pearl earrings, even the "charming" tricks of her yappy, ill-tempered pug.

The Sadlers evidently considered themselves on a near equal footing with Lady Hartley and far above Valentines. Lady Sadler was a slight, shrunken creature with a head that never seemed quite upright, and skin so pale it was almost transparent, like thin paper. The lady bore a shocking resemblance to a corpse, Sophie mused. As for her daughters, Sophie had seldom seen such a dull group. All were tall and reed-thin with sallow features and despondent shoulders. The Misses Sadler looked as glad to be there as Sophie felt inside. The eldest daughter was very elegantly attired and very straight, as if set in strengthening plaster to correct a twisted spine, but she had an empty prettiness—the same that must once have graced her frail mother's face. The three youngest daughters had not come out that evening but remained home with the servants.

Maria made some attempt to engage the young ladies in conversation, prying for details about fashionable trends in Norwich, but it was usually Lady Hartley who shouted across the room to answer her questions. Since Maria was always rather scared of that lady, she soon gave up. After that, the conversation was left almost entirely to Lady Hartley and Sir Arthur, both of whom had a fondness for their own voices.

Sir Arthur was a stout fellow with a large, fleshy nose, bristling eyebrows, and yellowed teeth. His booming voice, abrupt as a foghorn, curled Lady Hartley's hand-painted wallpaper, and his breath singed the falling curls on Sophie's head when he suddenly boomed in her ear, "So you're the little lady causing all the trouble, eh?"

Her stomach clenched like a fist. Every eye, including those of the mostly disinterested Misses Sadler, swung in their direction. She opened her mouth, but only a very tight sigh escaped.

Mrs. Dykes spoke up in her softly menacing voice, "We're most grateful to you, Sir Arthur, for your hassistance in this matter. We're quite done in with worry about poor, dear Sophia. Hain't we, 'Enry?"

Lady Sadler looked up, her pale eyes red rimmed and always, it seemed, on the verge of tears. "Something dreadful about an advertisement…for a *husband*?"

Mrs. Dykes apologized to Lady Sadler for the sad state of her son-in-law's family. She explained the regrettable Sophia's unfortunate habit of causing mischief, and her complete carelessness regarding the consequences. "The sooner she's safely far away and put to good use in some capacitry or other, the better off we'll all be. Especially dear Sophia."

Sophie toyed with the idea of thrusting a cushion into Mrs. Dykes's mouth and wrestling her to the ground.

"I hear you're the wayward gel who caused Lord Grimstock a hernia." Sir Arthur's voice rattled the candelabra.

It was the first time she'd been accused of that, but she supposed she might as well be blamed for this too. Why not?

"And you're the gel that got caught in a compromising position with that young fellow. On a billiard table, no less. I'd have tanned the young blighter's arse if I found it sticking up in the air, make no mistake." He roared in Sophie's ear, "And yours too, missy."

Across the room, his daughters flinched delicately. In the process of averting eyes from their father, they succeeded only in meeting one another's shocked, startled glances, so there was very nearly a nervous giggle or two among them. Lady Sadler moaned softly and tipped forward, as if she might be sick upon the carpet, while Mrs. Dykes rapidly fanned her face for her, and James's grandmother suddenly became enthralled by the diamonds on her pug's collar.

Lavinia, being familiar with that story but not with the name of the young gentleman involved—certainly unaware of his presence in that very drawing room—smugly assured Sir Arthur, over Sophie's head, this was indeed the same hoyden who continued to bring shame on the family and cared not one jot about it.

Now the young Misses Sadler stared at Sophie with the sort of morbid fascination reserved for an exhibit of Egyptian mummies, but she was glad to provide them with some entertainment, since they could get none elsewhere that evening. If she was in their shoes, she would be equally enthralled by the scarlet hussy in their midst.

The very improper subject of Sophia's behavior was soon raised again...most particularly, the solution for it. Now it was revealed that, since the Sadlers recently lost their old governess, Mrs. Dykes had persuaded Sir Arthur to let Sophia fill the vacancy immediately. It seemed the Sadlers planned a move to Bath, where Lady Sadler's poor health might benefit from the cures. And they meant to take Sophia with them.

Much to her bemusement, every minutia of the trip was already sorted. For the journey itself—Sir Arthur informed her in an ever-increasing octave—Sophia would sit behind the carriage with the luggage, and there was more than enough space for her living quarters in a very small box room in the attic of the house they'd purchased. Sir Arthur went on to add that the window of her room couldn't be opened, but if she required additional airing, she might leave her door open, and it wouldn't cause much bother. She would not require coal in that room, for it was so high up in the house it would surely capture all the rising heat. They were concerned about the expense of an extra mouth to feed, but he thought that, with some creative measuring, an adequate portion from each meal might be eked out for a governess, especially one who—according to Mrs. Dykes—ate like a bird and was very small.

For five pounds a year, plus room and board and two half days off a week, Sir Arthur thought Sophia should be excessively thankful.

Mrs. Dykes closed her fan with a snap. "I do 'ope I hain't exhumed my place in making these arrangements on your behalf, 'Enry, but something hought to be done. For Sophia's sake." Her mean little eyes were downcast in an attempt to seem demure, but her lips were thin and very tight, her claw-like hands curling, ready to snag the fur of her prey and drag it off to feed her young.

Lavinia chirped, "She should be grateful, mama, but she won't be. She never is. She's surly, rude, and extremely quarrelsome." She bounced about in her seat, untethered bosom almost hitting her on the chin. "Since the stranger came to Sydney Dovedale, she's been worse than ever."

"Eh?" Sir Arthur turned his quizzing glass to that plump and restless bosom. With his free hand, he reached for a pear on the console table behind them. "Stranger? What stranger?"

"A gypsy with no manners or breeding, Sir Arthur. And since he came to the village, it has upset everything and injured my husband Henry's health quite dreadfully."

Henry and his now-dolorous expression were swiftly examined through Sir Arthur's quizzing glass, which was, with little delay, returned to Lavinia's generous bosom.

"The stranger," she squawked, delighting in the attention, "came in answer to Sophia's advertisement for a husband, and now we cannot be rid of him."

James joined in, sitting forward on his chair. "Indeed, Sir Arthur, we wondered if you might be able to help uncover the fellow's background for us. I suspect there is some criminal history, for he is most reluctant to talk about himself."

Sophie felt her teeth turn to sawdust in her mouth. She looked at James, but he avoided her gaze and continued. "We don't like to have any man among us who is dangerous and likely to cause trouble. Clearly this man, Kane, does not belong in Sydney Dovedale."

"A criminal, eh?" Sir Arthur's voice boomed out, shaking the wood paneling around the walls. Even soot, dislodged by the sound, spattered down the chimney in loosened chunks and darkened Lady Hartley's ostentatious statuary mantel. One eye gleamed at Sophia through the quizzing glass he held in place with a lopsided squint.

"He's dark as a devil, Sir Arthur," Lavinia exclaimed. "One only has to look at him to know exactly what he is."

They all agreed fervently for several minutes.

When the murmuring finally died down, Sophie offered a quiet suggestion to the room in general. "Shouldn't every man be given the benefit of the doubt?"

Sir Arthur reared back. "I see you're a mouthy wench, madam." He took a loud bite of his pear and instantly cried out in agony. "Damned tooth!"

His wife looked vaguely interested but offered no solace for his pain. That was left to Mrs. Dykes, who passed him her handkerchief, which had a little clove oil on the corner. "One's a martyr to the tooth-hache oneself, Sir Arthur," she explained.

Muttering low curses, he pressed the handkerchief to his sore tooth, and no more was said about criminals and wenches with too many opinions. For the time being.

⁕

Later, when they were all standing about on Lady Hartley's tiled foyer, waiting for carriages and fussing over coats and mantles, Sophie realized she'd left behind her shawl. Rather than bother one of the staff, she slipped back to the drawing room to find it. The door was ajar, and James was already discussing their guests with his grandmother.

"Good Lord, what wretched women—the Dykes woman and her daughter! Thank heavens I'm hard of hearing."

"But you were entertained, Grandmama, were you not? I knew you would be."

"And that's why you invited the organ grinder and her monkey?"

"Couldn't resist."

"It seems Valentine no longer blames you for what happened to his sister."

"We have an agreement to put all that aside for Sophia's sake."

"Surely you're not still pining for that indecisive creature?" she snapped. "As I told you before, you were far better off when she broke the engagement. And all this latest business about an advertisement for a husband!"

"Yes. Indeed."

"I hear Henry's so deep in debt they threw him out of his club. I caution you, boy, never lend him any money."

James made no reply, but Sophie heard the gentle chink of the brandy decanter.

"Henry Valentine is a shifty blighter," the old lady continued, "and I suspect it wouldn't be the first time a woman in that family was sold for coin. Look at the demirep aunt, a notorious concubine and not in the least repentant. As for Sophia, I've seen chimney sweeps in smarter attire. And a brush seems curiously absent from her possessions."

"Well, all that will change, Grandmama…soon."

"Surely you don't plan to renew your attentions to that hussy! After what she did before."

"I won't lose her again, especially not to a man like that! With Sir Arthur Sadler's help, I'll soon be rid of that young devil at Souls Dryft. That'll teach him not to get above his place."

"Henry Valentine is after your money!"

James answered with a slurred confidence, "I prefer, Grandmama, to think of it as an investment. For my future happiness. And for Sophia's."

"Do be wary, James. That girl has very sinister eyes. Cunning. Reminds me of a tinderbox waiting for a strike."

"Don't worry, Grandmama. Sophia will realize I am the right choice for her. She must."

Deciding to forfeit her shawl—hot enough without it now, in any case—Sophie returned to the foyer.

Lady Hartley lent the services of a coachman and her barouche box for the journey home. Sophie was crammed in between Lavinia and Henry, with Maria and Mr. Bentley seated across the carriage, but she suffered the discomfort rather than risk injury or worse along a dark, bumpy road in a phaeton driven by James in his cups. For the first two-thirds of the long journey home to Sydney Dovedale, Maria chattered eagerly about the events of the evening, the gowns of the Misses Sadler, the decoration of Lady Hartley's drawing room, and the elegance of her menu, as if none of the others were there to see it for themselves.

"How funny, Sophia," she said finally, "Mrs. Dykes should take it into her head to make arrangements for you to go to Bath."

"'Ilarious, h'aint it?" she agreed somberly.

"I fail to see the amusement," Lavinia protested.

"But don't you know?" Maria exclaimed. "Sophia is going to marry Mr. Hartley."

"Am I?"

Henry grumbled, "Isn't it time you thought of the good of this family? Hartley is the best chance *you* will ever have."

Lavinia began to perk up. "When Sophia marries

Mr. Hartley, then we shall have cause to go to London, Henry. We'll need a house in town, then, shall we not?"

Henry changed the subject. "You might at least have made an effort with your dress this evening, Sophia. Or is that disarray another of your protests against society's many ills?"

She looked down at her grass-stained skirt and was abruptly reminded of her glorious afternoon with Lazarus. A great, surging warmth flooded her veins. Like good wine, it made her dizzy, even made her feel invincible. It was surely dangerous to feel that way. He did that to her all the time.

He had done so much for her already. What could she do for him?

Chapter 29

THE CART WHEELS ROLLED RAPIDLY DOWN THE ROAD as the horses moved at a steady clip. Chivers had urged Sophie to sit in the back, but she insisted on riding beside him on the front seat, one hand hanging onto her bonnet, the other around his arm.

"I don't know what Russ will have to say about this," the big fellow grumbled. "I shouldn't have let you talk me into it."

"You're a good man, Mr. Chivers. I'll pay you well for bringing me."

But he didn't want payment. He was willing to take her, he said, only because he'd heard how stubborn she was, and he knew she'd find some other way to go if he refused to help. "I didn't want you getting into trouble, did I?"

"Of course not." She smiled up at him and then looked away down the road as it stretched between flat fields and clusters of greenery. "Is it much farther?" She hoped not, for her backside was already sore from the journey, and as much as she hoped it would soon be numb, it had not, so far, obliged her.

"There." He pointed with the whip. "Just over the next dip to the right."

She saw a tall church spire surrounded by rooftops of slate and straw. It was a larger place than Sydney Dovedale, the roads much more frequently traveled and, therefore, well kept. As they neared the main street, there was a general sense of bustle: creaking carts and rattling carriages passing them at greater speed, people shouting greetings to one another, dogs barking, and tradesmen singing out their wares.

Chivers slowed the horses to a trot. "Now we can't stay long, missy. Remember, I must get this cart and the beasts back before Russ knows they're gone."

"Don't you worry, Mr. Chivers. You won't have to perjure yourself for me."

The cart drew up before a busy coaching inn across from the church. Sophie gave Chivers a handful of coins for some beer while he waited, and then, tidying herself with nervous hands, she clambered down, straightened her skirts, and hurried over the cobbles. Her eyes scanned the shop fronts and signs. It felt odd to be out alone in a strange town without Henry or her sister, or James dragging her along on his arm, but today she was a woman on a mission, and so she quelled that moment of uncertainty and put up her chin. Let people look at her scar all they wanted, if they had naught better to look at. She was a thirty-year-old woman marked by adventure, and that was all there was to it.

After a few inquiries, she found the haberdasher's shop down a narrow alley and stepped inside to the accompaniment of a little bell attached to the door. The shop was larger than it looked from the outside, with rows of cupboards and shelves to explore and a long table for measuring cloth. She waited while two other women were served, and then asked the proprietor if she might have a word with his delivery boy.

"What's he done now?" he exclaimed as he rolled his eyes to the heavens.

She hastily assured him the boy had done nothing wrong, and she explained her mission.

He turned and bellowed into the back of the shop, "Young Master Rafe, come out here."

A small boy emerged, carrying a broom three times longer than himself. Like his uncle, he had thick, black hair, but Sophie was surprised when that curious, slightly cross face looked up, and she found a pair of light blue eyes staring at her instead of the knowing dark gaze she expected. She felt nervous suddenly. Lazarus had told her very little about his sister or her child, and she knew he might not appreciate her going there to see the boy. Men could be difficult when it came to family pride, as she knew too well.

"This lady has come to see you," the shopkeeper explained. "She's brought a message from your uncle."

He gazed up at her scar. "Are you a pirate?"

"Yes," she replied solemnly.

"Can I sail on your ship?"

"Perhaps one day. But first, would you like some lemonade?"

∽

They sat in the small tearoom by the church, she with a china teacup, Rafe with a glass of lemonade and a large, sticky bun.

"My uncle's a soldier," he said, feet swinging.

"Yes, he was. Now he's a farmer."

"Why?" He screwed up his small face. "Don't he want to kill people anymore?"

"I think not. I think he had enough of being a soldier."

"How d'you know, missus?"

"I'm a friend of your uncle's." She felt inside her purse. "I've brought you something."

"What's it?"

She smiled at his impatience and passed him an envelope. "There's money in there for you. But try to save it."

"Why?"

"Because you'll need it later, so don't spend it all on silly things."

"Why?"

Oh, Lord! She never had much luck teaching this principal to her own brother, so why she thought she could teach this boy of ten was anyone's guess. "I suppose, since it's yours now, you may do as you wish with it," she said with a sigh. It was money she'd been saving for a new gown and a few underthings from Norwich, but this boy needed it more than she did, and she knew Lazarus would never take money from her. This was the only way she could help them at the present time, with James and Henry breathing down her neck, watching her every move around him.

"I'll put it in me boots, like me uncle done."

She sipped her tea. "Good. As you think best."

"No one ever says that to me, missus."

"Nor to me," she replied wryly.

Rafe guzzled his lemonade and smacked his lips.

"Do you like living here? Are the people kind to you?"

"'S all right," he sputtered and wiped his mouth on his sleeve. "Better than the work 'ouse."

She nodded as she watched his small, expressive face.

"One day I'll live with me uncle. He said so."

Sophie thought of Lazarus struggling to make a new life for himself in Sydney Dovedale, trying to set down roots and put his past behind him. But even if he wasn't recaptured and sent back to that prison hulk—or worse—that piece of blade lodged by his heart could finish him off at any minute. And here was this boy, waiting for a home and a real, loving family. She could see Lazarus in the boy's face and imagined him as he must have been years ago. He'd done the best he could for his sister's child. It must have worried him unbearably…what might happen to Rafe.

"If your uncle said it was so, then I'm sure it will be," she said, but her heart ached. Perhaps she shouldn't raise the child's hopes. "When was the last time you saw your uncle?"

"Last winter," the boy chirped. "He brung me a mince pie."

"He brought you a mince pie."

"That's what I said he done."

"*Did.*"

He scowled and fidgeted in his chair. "That's what I said he done did."

"Don't spill your lemonade."

"You're a bossy one, ain't you?"

"Women are supposed to boss men and little boys about."

"Bet you don't boss my uncle about. He wouldn't never put up with it. He don't like ladies."

"Doesn't he?"

He swept out his arm in a dramatic gesture. "Steer clear of 'em, he said to me. Steer clear of the lot of 'em."

She laughed. She couldn't help it. "Yes. He was right to warn you."

"He's going to marry an angel."

There was something else in his face, something she recognized but couldn't quite put her finger on. She set down her teacup and said carefully, "An angel?"

"He saw her once, when he was a boy. The angel was high up on a balcony, the most beautiful thing he ever seen. And he knew he'd marry her one day, just as soon as he founded her again."

"Why? Where did she go?"

"She fell, didn't she? She fell from the balcony and broke her wing."

Sophie looked over his head, through the tea-shop window.

Jump, jump, jump, and I'll catch you.

"Oy, missus. You've gone all white as a daisy. Can I 'ave another bun?"

She swallowed, looked at him again, and nodded.

It couldn't. How could it be?

Suddenly she remembered what he'd said to her in the church once. *Take a leap, Miss Valentine, and I'll be there to catch you.*

Where had he come from, and how had he known? He'd claimed to be searching for her, but she'd dismissed that as another charming lie. Even when he stole that very first kiss under the chestnut tree, he'd seemed familiar to her somehow—a part of her once lost, now found again.

❦

A soft wind blew across the field, only occasionally giving respite to the thick, hot air and ruffling the long grasses with an idle caress. But Lazarus worked on without pause, perspiring under the merciless sun, a man intent on punishing himself. With another swing of the scythe, he cut another bundle of hay and then another. He never looked back to see how far he'd come, or looked forward to see how far he had yet to go. That was always a mistake, so he'd learned.

Chivers sat a while by the hedge with a jug of cider, but Lazarus swung on, moving steadily through the field, the motion unbroken. He kept one eye on the lane, watching for a certain woman to pass by the hedge, carrying her basket or spinning her bonnet as she often did. It was two days since he'd had sight of her, several more since they last spoke or he had the pleasure of touching her.

Sometimes he wondered if he'd made a mistake on the day of the picnic, when he rode with her into that emerald glade. Perhaps he'd frightened her off when he told her how he got his wound. But she was stronger than she looked. She was steel inside, and there was no yielding until she was ready to make her choice.

He wouldn't want her any other way.

❦

She turned about anxiously and studied her reflection in the looking glass with a stern critic's eye. "It's kind of you to offer, Maria, but it is a little too young for me."

"Nonsense!" her sister replied. "Once I've brought it in for you and added a trim, it will look brand-new."

It was a pretty gown, in white muslin with little sleeves edged in pearl, and a rather daring neckline—unless one had the foresight to tuck a little lace. Unfortunately, it was similar to the gown she wore the night she leapt from a balcony, and it brought back the memory of how excited she'd been to dress that evening as she anticipated the many delights of a ball. She never wore her lovely gown again after that. It was spattered with crimson drops, and someone must have burned it. That gown belonged to the lost youth of her life, and she was now filled up with sadness for it—for that lovely gown that must have had grand hopes and dreams, the expectation of many fun excursions with charming partners. Worn only that once, now it was ashes.

Maria dropped to her knees on the carpet, the pincushion clutched in her hand. "Oh dear! It is the fashion now for more embellishment at the hem, and this is a little plain."

Sophie looked out through the casement window, to the view of her sister's garden and the lane beyond. The little scene was picturesque, the window flanked by a yew hedge, and Maria's genteel flower beds were now blooming with color. The rectory was a pleasant, cozy home. The parlor was tidy, cool, and peaceful, with a delicate, unobtrusive pattern on the wallpaper, silhouettes above the mantel, and comfortable chairs arranged for intimate conversation. Mr. Bentley's books waited nearby on a small Pembroke table, and the cushion, where he sat when he joined his wife, was shyly dimpled. How nice it must be, Sophie mused, to share an evening in company with someone who was there by choice—someone who enjoyed spending his time with her, even if it was just to sit quietly and read a book or admire the garden together.

Love. Such a small word with such a devastating effect on the person who suffered it. Love had turned Maria from a vain creature whose head was filled with dancing and the latest fashion, into a busy wife and doting mother. Into a woman who gave away her once-precious gown to a sister for whom she wanted only the best.

Lady Hartley, probably under duress from James, had invited Sophie to her summer ball. She knew she ought to go. Invitations for the event were much sought after, and one's appearance there was usually the sign one had "arrived" in the grander society of the county. James was very anxious for her to make a better impression on his grandmother this time. She wished Ellie was still there to give her that little extra burst of confidence, but she had already gone away to Brighton. Her feet never settled long in one place. One day soon that girl would wear herself out, thought Sophie with a sad smile.

She looked at her reflection again and turned her face so the scar wasn't visible. Once upon a time, she loved parties and lived for balls, the nervous excitement that preceded them, the satisfaction of being admired in a new frock, trying a new style of hair. Just like James and his memories, her sister's altered gown took her back there, to that joyous, untroubled season. But there was one thing different. Sophie had changed. Never in her youth would she have passed up the opportunity of dancing at a ball, yet she knew now what a disappointment it could be. That tomorrow, when the candles were snuffed and all the fallen flowers swept up, everything would be just the same as it was before.

When James first came back for her, she thought these feelings meant she'd missed him, but now she knew it wasn't that. It was a sweet, sad yearning for times gone by, a part of her life she could never know again, like coming to the end of a good book. But there was new life ahead of her and a new beginning. A new story to discover.

Since her visit to little Rafe, she kept thinking about his story of the angel on the balcony, and she wondered why Lazarus hadn't told her. He'd told her everything else, so why not that?

She stared out through the parlor window again and watched the breeze flirt with the leaves of the chestnut trees that bordered the common.

Perhaps she'd let her imagination run away with her. Perhaps it was merely coincidence he told his nephew that story.

"Love becomes you, Sister," Maria said suddenly. She had removed the pins from her mouth and was looking up at her from the carpet. "I've never seen you look so well as you do of late. Even Mrs. Cawley commented on it yesterday…that your complexion glows and your hair shines. And I see"—she sat back on her heels, smiling broadly—"you've taken to using curling papers in your hair again."

"I do not use curling papers!"

Maria was smug and wouldn't hear any denial, but it was true. Sophie didn't need curling papers when her hair took on a life of its own lately, twisting about of its own accord.

"Well, it's no surprise to me, Sister, you won back Mr. Hartley's admiration, and when you're his wife, I do hope you won't look down on us here in Sydney Dovedale."

She took a breath. "But I haven't yet agreed to marry James Hartley."

Maria's lips formed a small, round "O."

"In fact"—she took another breath—"I'm not in love with James. He's not the one who curls my hair."

"But…"

"You know who does." She felt certain those little bolts of lightning were bright enough even for her sister to notice.

After a short silence, Maria exclaimed, "But…he's expected to marry Jane Osborne. She'll be quite comfortably well off when her father dies, and she has no brothers to take the farm in hand. She'll need a capable husband, unless she means to sell."

Sophie's gaze drifted back to the window through which she could see sheep grazing on the common and a gaggle of ill-tempered geese chasing Mrs. Flick along the bridge.

"He's not going to marry Jane Osborne. He told me so." And she believed it. He didn't tell lies. There were just some things he kept to himself, but he didn't tell fibs.

Maria resumed her pinning. "But how could you marry a stranger? To be sure, he's proven himself quite amiable. He's made a very good impression on my dear Mr. Bentley and apparently he believes himself in love with you…Oh, do keep still, Sophia. Quite distraught with love, according to my Mr. Bentley. He thinks you an angel come to save him. But really, as I said to my Mr. Bentley, James Hartley has everything you could possibly want and is a far better prospect."

Her heart skipped, faltered. *Quite distraught with love.* Lazarus had never spoken to her of love. Yet he'd told the rector.

Then we don't exist to people like them? People like her—up there?

Jump, Jump, Jump, and I'll catch you.

Foolish man. Why could he not have said it to her?

Because she hadn't been able to say it to him, perhaps.

Or something else held him back. Thanks to his little nephew, now she understood what it was. He'd been told, long ago, he didn't exist to people like her. Despite his outward bluster, he was still a boy inside, and he had to know for sure how she felt before he could be brave enough to tell her he loved her.

Chapter 30

TUCK ENJOYED HIS CUSTOMARY NOON NAP IN THE trapped sunlight of the window seat, chin on his chest and gentle snores emitted every other breath. Lazarus had just come in to find some luncheon. Weary after a long morning that started hours before most folk were up, he was pouring two mugs of ale from the jug in the cool pantry, when he looked up and saw Sophie through the window. For a moment, he merely stared. Then he realized it was no daydream or the effects of too much sun. She was in his yard, peering in at his pantry window and bouncing up and down.

He thought something terrible must have happened, and so he hurried to the door and let her in.

She leapt down the crooked step and flew by him like a ghost in a thin white gown that was distinctly out of place in that farmhouse. "You should wear a coat," he exclaimed, too surprised for any other greeting.

"It's August."

"But it's too…" He wavered, his own sudden prudishness a mystery to himself. "Like a nightgown."

She walked in a nervous circle and hugged her arms. "Miss Valentine, is there…?"

"It was you under the balcony, wasn't it? On that night when I jumped. You were there, a boy trimming ivy. Is that the house where they dismissed you without a reference?" It all came out in a tumble of sounds, frantic and uncontrolled.

The moment had come, then. He'd never quite been able to tell her.

"It was you," she persisted.

"Yes. It was my fault." He cleared his throat. "I left the ladder out, because I was so distracted." Just like that, there it was.

The clock beat gently on the mantel, and the hens outside in the yard cackled like old gossips gathered on market day.

She was staring, lips parted, cheeks flushed. He couldn't bear it. She must hate him now. He waited for the blows to come, for the tempest of her anger to rain down on his head worse than ever before. Nothing came.

"After it happened, Becky told me your name. I always swore I'd find you one day and make amends. That's why I came here to find you."

She frowned. "Your sister knew my name?"

"Of course. She worked at the same house."

Again she walked in a circle—first left, then right. "But it wasn't your fault," she said finally. "I heard that other man tell you to leave it. He was angry with you for taking so long over the ivy. He made you leave the ladder behind."

He couldn't think. All the other events of that

evening and the following days had obscured much of the before memory, the details.

Suddenly she took hold of his arm, a clump of his shirt captured in her fingers, and she pulled it so hard the stitches snapped at the shoulder. "I'm so sorry. I should like to marry you, Mr. Kane. At your earliest convenience." It came out in a breathless rush, and she kept her eyes on his torn sleeve as she said it, afraid apparently to look any higher. The "sorry," he realized, must be for the sleeve, not for wanting to marry him. He hoped.

He felt the flagstones moving under his boots. "I am forgiven, then?"

"Of course, you're forgiven."

Somewhere nearby, he heard Chivers whistling.

Her lashes raised another infinitesimal distance. "I know you won't ask me a second time, so I'm asking you. Marry me. Please."

Reeling, Lazarus choked out a startled, "Yes?"

"Yes?" Again her lashes fluttered, struggled upward, her eyes now reaching as far as his lips. He saw the little nervous swallow that worked up and down her slender throat.

"Yes," he managed. The nagging ache in his belly finally began to subside. "But...are you sure?"

In answer, she pressed a kiss to his mouth, and as she fell slightly against his length, his fingertips gingerly grazed her hips. Scalding desire roared through every sinew and muscle. He was tempted to lift her in his arms and carry her to bed, there and then.

"How soon can we be married?" he croaked out.

"The banns must be read in church three weeks."

"Then three weeks it is." He supposed he could wait that long. He'd waited more than ten years since the first moment he saw her. He clasped her tightly in his arms and kissed her again, hoping to stem the trembling—hers and his.

"I think your friend is thirsty," she whispered shyly, reminding him of Chivers, who stood just inside the door, one hand on the iron handle.

"So am I." He scooped her up, arms wreathed tightly around her, and buried his face in her hair, drinking in the soft lavender scent.

"Mr. Kane…" It was half laugh, half gasp. "May I stay here? Now? I want to live with you."

Startled, he drew back and gazed down at her.

"I don't care about the three weeks," she added. "I'll keep house for you until then."

He wasn't sure he understood. "Are you rushing into this because you fear changing your mind again?"

She shook her head, and her amber hair gleamed in the sunlight through his windows. "There is Aunt Finn, of course. She must come too. Is that all right?"

All right? Of course it was all right. He would have agreed to anything just then.

"Shall I go out and come in again, Russ?" Chivers inquired gruffly from the doorway.

They both laughed, and Lazarus urged his friend to come all the way in and celebrate with them. A moment later, they woke Tuck from his nap, and cups of ale were drunk all round, the old retainer muttering his usual groatsworth about wives and the woe they caused. Today, however, he said it with a smile, and confessed he was glad to have some of the old family back at Souls Dryft, especially if it meant the "young master" would finally get out of his blue-devil mood and stop to smell the flowers once in a while.

Lazarus gazed down at the beautiful woman in his arms, the woman who'd agreed to be his wife. His wife. The thought skipped through his head and then down to his heart, stamping about on weak legs like a newborn calf. He'd expected her to run from him when she found out the truth about her accident. To his shock, it seemed to have the opposite effect. If only he'd known that sooner, he could have saved them both a great deal of time and anguish.

❧

"Impossible! Quite Impossible!" Henry paced before the cold, dark hearth. "How could you do this, Sophia? To sneak about…"

"It was not done deliberately to hurt you, but it is done, and there's no going back." The sense of having finally taken control of her own life was almost overwhelmingly satisfying, and she couldn't help sounding a little smug. "Lazarus is meeting with Mr. Bentley now to ask for the church in three weeks…"

"Three weeks?" He looked her up and down. "Why so much haste? And what the Devil are you wearing?"

"Because I cannot wait any longer, and neither can I ask him to wait, since I already dillydallied over my answer, which was rather unfair of me, considering it was my advertisement that brought him here." She paused. "And no, Henry, there is no child—yet."

He flushed scarlet.

"And this is a ball gown of Maria's. She was altering

it for me, but I don't suppose I'll need it now." She felt a little sad about that, but it passed with surprising swiftness. "And I'm moving back to Souls Dryft today," she added. "I see no reason to wait, since we're now formally engaged and…"

"Have you taken leave of your senses? You cannot move into that house before you're married."

"I'll be his housekeeper," she said firmly.

Henry paced quickly back and forth, and his boots squeaked in protest. "I suppose he wants a dowry, but I won't give that crook a penny. You do this entirely against my wishes and without my blessing. After all these years, when I sheltered you from the world, this is how you repay me? By taking up with that villain, a charlatan who came here with naught but a boot full of bank notes, acquired through no honest means? This *Lazarus* is not what he pretends to be, as I always suspected."

"Are any of us, Henry?" she exclaimed. "Are any of us what we pretend to be?"

He didn't know what to say to that.

"You told me he didn't want to marry me, and it was a lie. I knew that when you told me, but I didn't want to upset you. Why did you try to keep us apart, Henry?"

"I did it for your own good. I'm your elder brother, and I'm supposed to protect you. Well, I wasn't there that night when you jumped from a balcony, but I could certainly keep you from making this mistake."

Sophie walked around the long trestle table to gather her temper and her thoughts. Outside, the day was bright and warm, but inside this ancient fortress it was damp, and the chill seeped into her bones.

"He came here to make a new life," she said, her voice unsteady, hands clasped before her. "And I…I'm in love with him." She wanted to laugh hysterically. "I mean to protect him in any way I can, and you know how stubborn I am." She knew Henry wouldn't hurt Lazarus, if by so doing he would also injure her. Despite their differences and their bickering, they did love each other, however hard it was, sometimes, to bear. "I need a home of my own, Henry. I cannot stay here and get under Lavinia's feet any longer. Surely you understand."

As he stood with his back to the empty fireplace, he exclaimed, "It will not last. You know nothing about each other."

"I know more about him than you knew about Lavinia."

He passed over that quickly. "He is uneducated and common, makes no distinction of rank, understands nothing of good manners and propriety. Just like our mother, you're ruled by your heart."

"I'd rather be ruled by my heart than my purse." She sighed and put out her arms to him, stepping closer.

Henry brushed her hands away. "If it's true you've developed some fondness for the villain, you'd best advise him to leave this place at once, for even if I abide by your wishes and leave the blackguard alone, James Hartley is another matter. He won't rest until the truth is exposed. "

She took a breath and pressed her palms together. "James must have been at a loose end and suffering ennui to come back here looking for me, but he'll soon find another woman to distract him again."

"I warn you again, Sophia. I shan't take you back

when you change your mind or Kane changes his. Nor shall I encourage this mistake by funding it. As you brew, so shall you drink."

It was no more and no less than she expected, but perhaps she'd held on to a small glimmer of hope. Alas, her brother's anger was largely fueled by disappointment. He'd wanted her to marry rich James Hartley for purely mercenary reasons. Henry didn't understand love matches—never had and never would. He couldn't even forgive their own mother for turning her back on Grimstock wealth when she eloped with their father.

"You need a new waistcoat, Henry," she said, shaking her head. "You'll take someone's eye out when one of those buttons pops free." With that parting, sisterly comment, she left his fortress.

❧

Lazarus was in the field again, haymaking under the balmy, late-afternoon sun. He didn't hear or see her until she was almost upon him. The crisp rustle of the hay and the rhythmic whisper of the blade accompanied her progress as she approached. Her beauty, as it always did, caused him to catch his breath, and his hand went to the scar on his chest as it pinched. In the past, she always stood by the hedge and watched, but today she climbed over into the field and walked toward him.

"Since you're still working out here like a stubborn bull, I decided to bring supper to you," she exclaimed. Now he saw the basket she carried. Her hair was tied back in a long braid, and she'd changed into her old blue gown with an apron over it. "Will you stop a while and eat? You work too long and too hard. Tuck tells me you've been out here all day."

Mother Nature, he wanted to lecture her, didn't wait for a man to rise late and go to bed early. There was always work to be done. But when she smiled at him, too lovely to resist, he set down his scythe. "I suppose I can stop a while."

"The hay will still be there in half an hour," she said, taking his hand.

They strode across the field to a haystack. Her hand was warm, soft, and dry in his. Sometimes he worried he held it too hard and might crush her small fingers. "What did Henry say?"

She removed her apron and handed it to him. "Dry your face."

Slowly he rubbed it over his head and shoulders, and then they sat together in the shade of the haystack while she unloaded her basket and passed him a pork pie and the small cider jug. He watched her face, her hands, and the little stray curl of hair against the side of her neck.

He reached for her hand suddenly and brought it to his lips. "You've not kissed me in several hours." He squinted up at the position of the wilting sun. "Must be five or six hours I've been without."

"Is that a rule, then? That a wife must kiss her husband every so often?"

He nodded and wondered if she'd dare—out here in view of the lane. She didn't leave him wondering for long and planted a harmless kiss against his warm temple.

"Not good enough," he whispered. So she bent

another few inches and put her lips to his. They were unbearably soft. His supper cast aside, he eased her down against the hay. His hands cradled her head, and his mouth covered hers, taking it fiercely. It came over him swiftly, this need to feel her kiss again, to remind himself she was real and not a dream.

"Tell me what Henry said."

She sighed, and her breath cooled his sun-warmed cheek. "Exactly what we knew he would say. I'm on the path to hell and damnation."

He felt her hands on him suddenly. Of course, he knew she was a lusty wench, but...here? Where anyone might stroll by the hedge and see? He laughed huskily. "The sun's gone to your head." But he made no move to prevent her as she unhooked his clothing and slid her hands inside.

"I disagree cordially." She wriggled under him, "'Tis not the sun, Russ, 'tis you. Against all my efforts, I've fallen in love with you."

Her words squeezed around his heart and stopped it for a breath. Then it pounded back to life. She was so beautiful, lying there beside him with hay caught in her hair, her eyes heated with longing, her lips parted and dewy pink. He couldn't speak. A sob of unmanly happiness was stuck in his throat.

He checked quickly over his shoulder and saw the lane was empty. The sun drifted down through the treetops, the sky was calm, and the air was thick and still. Resting on his elbow, he looked down at Sophie and longed to understand her, all her thoughts and fears. He grew thick, heavy, and hard at once under her steady strokes.

Her warm gaze wandered over his mouth as it hovered above her. "I'm hungry," she whispered. "I want to taste you."

"I'm not your husband yet," he reminded her.

Her hand cupped his sac. "That didn't stop you tasting *me*, several times."

"That was different. I was trying to sway your decision." He grinned briefly. "I had a proud, stubborn wench to win over."

"So now you won me, you no longer have to try?"

Again he lost his voice as her fingers caressed his hot, swollen crest.

"Shall I stop?" she asked softly.

He moved his hips closer, and her hand closed around his sac again, gently squeezing. Eyes closed, he swallowed another deep groan. "Sophie!"

Now her hand swept up his length again, her fingers wrapped tightly around him, and he exhaled a shuddering breath. She repeated the motion, and he forgot entirely where he was. The dying sun was no match for the feverish heat she conjured with her hands. He throbbed, aching with the need to release and yet not wanting to end it. Every drop of his blood seemed to rush to that one body part. She leaned down, and he felt her exploring tongue, then her soft lips on his crest. He gasped and shuddered. At some point he'd wrapped her braid around his fist, and he clung to it, the muscles in his weight-bearing arm tense with strain. He let her sample him as long as he could, and then he pulled her up. He was too close to spilling. Her eyes were wide open, watching him with interest.

"Aunt Finn is spending tonight with Maria at the

rectory," she whispered. "Chivers and Tuck have gone to celebrate at Merryweather's Tavern by the common, and we have the house to ourselves for several hours at least."

"What is it you suggest, Miss Valentine?"

"What do you think I suggest, Mr. Kane?"

"I'm almost afraid to say it. Is this how house-keepers generally behave?"

She laughed softly, the sound rippling through her body and into his. "It's how this one behaves. I'm very thorough, Mr. Kane."

He observed her solemnly, and one hand stroked her hair. "Lucky for me," he said.

Chapter 31

THE HOUSE WAS EMPTY AND THE AIR FILLED WITH scent, for at her request, Tuck had filled every container capable of holding water with those dark, purplish-red wild roses that grew up the garden wall. The blooms were abundant this year and almost covered the grey flint stone.

Before she could protest, Lazarus swept her up and carried her over the threshold, not even losing a single breath.

"It's not our wedding night yet," she pointed out as he set her down again.

He hesitated then laughed. "It feels as if it is."

"Yes." She began removing his shirt, but his rough, square hands came down over hers.

"We shouldn't…"

"But I can't wait. I want you now!"

"Well, you're a bossy little madam, aren't you?" His hands tightened over hers.

"You taught me to express my needs and to stop hiding them," she reminded him.

His eyes narrowed, but she still felt that smoky heat

of the warrior's raw desire on her face. It was almost comical when he tried to be a gentleman, suddenly concerned with propriety.

"Will you remove your own clothes?" she asked sweetly, "or shall I do it for you?"

At last, he relinquished the task to her eager fingers with only one further caution. "We should not. We should wait another three weeks, until the ceremony."

"Do stop chattering, Kane. It's most distracting."

He kissed her before the last word was fully out, but this interruption she didn't mind. She felt the drowsy effects of the sun's heat that day and all that heady rose fragrance, and she let him take over, allowed his lips to take possession of hers.

Her fiancé's hands sought the hooks to her gown, earnest in their task but fumbling.

"Let me," she whispered, and he did. She turned her back to him as she undressed. The only sounds were those of his agitated breath and the low, crackling fire. Her gown crumpled to the floor, and she stepped out of it. She heard the soft, pleading moan of her name on his lips. She felt his hand brush her hair aside and then his eager breath, warm on the nape of her neck as he struggled with her corset laces. Her chemise slowly slid down over her hips, silently joining her discarded gown. She closed her eyes as his arms immediately came around her, those rough-skinned hands that so fascinated her, reaching for her bared breasts. His lips were on her neck, his groin pressed hard against her behind. Not knowing what to do, she laid her head back against his shoulder while his hands moved over her body, exploring and fondling without asking permission. He took freely, knowing what he wanted.

Maria and Lavinia were right; he certainly didn't have the hands of a gentleman. But her feet were on the ground, and there was no inclination to run away or escape. Except into his arms. And his ungentlemanly hands.

"I love you," he whispered and reached into her heart and soul with his gentle admission.

And she knew how glad she was he'd come to find her, how relieved she was she'd waited.

His tongue licked the scattered pulse at her neck. His hand cupped her breasts, and his teeth nipped her earlobe. She sank against his chest and reached around to feel him, to free him from his breeches. "Let's go upstairs," she gasped.

He shook his head. "Here will do." As he sank back into a chair before the low, flickering glow of the fire, he eased her down astride his lap, and then his hands caressed her arms, her back, her hips, and her thighs, continuing the determined exploration. When his fingers moved between her legs, she groaned with joy.

∽◦∾

Sheer, white-hot pleasure roared through his veins and spun around inside his head. The low purr forming in her throat suggested he pleased her. He could hear and feel the rapid throb of her heart as he nuzzled her firm breasts. He tickled her hardened nipples with his eyelashes and gently rubbed them with his palms. When she tossed her head back, arching her body and offering her breasts to his mouth again, he knew she was about to reach her peak already. Her skin gleamed in the firelight, a gratifying shade of pink. Her nipple was taut and erect, and she wanted his lips on it now, apparently, unless his ears deceived him and she was not, in fact, begging him with breathless desperation to take it. He held back to prolong the pleasure.

"Russ!" she cried out. "Please! I want you."

He laughed low, cradled her to his lap, and fell forward, slipping from the chair to his knees on the crumpled pile of their clothes. Her skin was pure luxury—satin and silk, so soft it melted in the heat of his body.

"Are you ready, then, Miss Valentine?" Because he was. In one fluid motion, he thrust and fell forward from his knees, covering her mouth with his to halt that shocked gasp. For a moment, they lay still while her heart beat hard and fast against his chest. He was not even completely sheathed yet. Her eyes fluttered open, met his heated gaze, and held it. He began to move, pressing farther with more care, resisting the powerful urge to thrust again, not wanting to hurt her. She was small and very tight but warmly welcoming. Inch by inch, he filled her at last.

❦

Sophie thought there must be something wrong. Surely he was too large for her, but he was patient, careful. When her hands rested timidly on his buttocks, she felt them tense with the strain of holding back, so she caressed them and stroked his back, anxious to help. And then when he did thrust, she gasped again in shock, and her body quivered under his.

He withdrew slightly and then immediately reentered, watching her eyes all the time. As he repeated the motion, she learned the rhythm, and her body gave as well as received. It became a slick, pumping motion, the friction causing sparks they both felt, a sensation they couldn't get enough of.

She curled her legs around his hips, and a symphony of startled gasps and moans accompanied his every thrust and withdrawal. The pleasure swam through her blood like a school of tiny fish, darting this way and that, shooting upward toward the sunlight. She was shameless, utterly lost.

❧

Lazarus slid his hands under her bottom as wild heat raged through his veins and his limbs, inspiring him with the need for complete and utter possession.

As he felt her trembling at his mercy, the half moons of her fingernails digging into his back, he took her nipple in his mouth and thrust again and again. A few harsh breaths later, he thought his skull must have separated from his brain as a sensation stronger than any he'd ever felt ripped through his tight, rigid body and flooded out of him.

At last, the angel was his, and he was ready to let her take him up, if this is how it must be. But a few minutes later, he was still alive. He opened his eyes and looked down at her flushed cheeks and wet, smiling lips. Her back was still arched, and her full breasts quivered as the last waves of her own pleasure lapped through her. Slowly she raised her lashes and met his gaze.

"That was lovely, Kane. Again, please."

Even with her legs wrapped around him, and despite the complete abandonment she exhibited only seconds before, she was now a prim, bossy Valentine again.

Still breathing hard, Lazarus gazed down at her and thanked his exceptional good fortune for this very wanton, wayward fallen angel.

✎

She woke slowly, keeping her eyes closed and reality at bay until the last possible moment. Aware of a new scent invading her pillow, she tried to think what it might be, and then she remembered. That scent was of another body beside her own, the scent of a man.

Eyelids still not yet raised, she made a careful assessment of her inner workings and her body parts. She finally concluded she was sore and aching, but she would live, surprisingly.

Finally she opened her eyes and discovered his face, two-thirds pressed into the pillow, mouth partially open. His hair was a rumpled mess, some of it sticking directly up in the air. Jet-black eyelashes twitched and fluttered against his cheeks. Even in sleep, he was restless. Of what did he dream this morning? Of her? From the coarse words he mumbled into that pillow, she sincerely hoped not.

But how young he looked while he slept.

He lay above the sheet, sprawled out naked on his front. There was not a scrap of fat on his body. Every part was well used, from the astonishing width of his shoulders, to the narrow waist and slim hips, to the taut buttocks, hard, lean thighs, and full calves. And, of course, there were those parts not visible while he lay on his front—in particular, that part of him put to very good use last night.

So this was what it was all about. This is what it should be like. It was more than she'd ever dreamed, this blissful completion, this loving. She'd never trusted like this, never let herself go as she did now.

She wanted to throw open those shutters and cry her happiness to the wind.

She wanted to touch him again, but it would be unfair, surely, while he slept. All she could do was stretch out beside him and wait.

Or not.

She inched her face along the pillow and blew gently on his eyelids. At least this way, if he woke, she could claim it was an accident.

He stopped cursing in his sleep. His hand, tucked under the pillow, withdrew slightly and then was still.

She dampened her fingertip and carefully drew it across each of his eyebrows, following the relaxed curve. He groaned and mumbled in his sleep again, something about "giving that bleedin' gent a right smackin'," and she hastily took her hand back. She glanced down the length of his prone form to his hip. Perhaps she could just slide her hand under that curve and...

In the next second, she was flat on her back and he was over her, laughing.

"You were fast asleep," she protested. Her heart pounded madly.

"Never," he told her. "I'm always alert, even when"—he leaned down to kiss the tip of her nose—"I may not appear to be."

"I'll bear that in mind." She gasped as she still hadn't caught her breath. "'Tis a very sneaky trick."

He grabbed her wrists and held them up over her head. "As long as you behave yourself and I don't catch you up to no good, you've no cause to fear." A slow grin broke across his lips.

"I am not very good at behaving myself."

"I noticed."

He lay with his legs between hers, holding them apart, and she felt the bold, broad head of his erection already poised to enter her again. It pressed at the threshold, throbbed there, taunting her. Apparently that part of him never slept deeply either.

He held his upper body a few inches above hers and asked casually, "Is there something you wanted from me, then, ma'am? I can't help noticing you were eager for my attention this morning."

She writhed and rubbed her soft, eager womanhood against that hard, male brawn.

"Is that what you want?"

She groaned. Her hands struggled to get free of his grip. She wanted to grasp his buttocks and urge him in, but he held himself taut above her, his muscles tense. And then he kissed her eyelids slowly, one at a time as he laughed throatily. He moved his elbows to resettle his weight. The sheet whispered as his thighs slid farther apart, holding hers open. "I think my fine lady is insatiable." He shook his head. "What shall I do with her?"

She still couldn't say the word, although she wanted to. Fortunately, he took pity on her. His question was rhetorical when he asked it, and a few seconds later, it was also entirely moot.

Chapter 32

SOPHIE SAT HIM IN A CHAIR BY THE WINDOW, WHERE sunlight streamed in.

"Now be still," she cautioned.

"It might hurt." He folded his arms. "You might slip and draw blood!"

"Oh, hush!" She pulled his head back and began ruthlessly trimming his hair, while he muttered low complaints and one foot tapped nervously. "Have you never been to a barber?"

"Never. Why would I want another man fussing over me, probably stealing my money while he has me at the point of a knife?"

She laughed. "Such distrust! Where have you lived your life before now, that you think that way?"

"I told you. I was raised in the rookeries of London. Or rather, I raised myself. Mostly."

"But for your sister."

He said nothing.

"And that old man who was like a father to you." She ran her fingers through his hair, fascinated by the juxtaposition of pale and dark. "The one who left you his money when he died."

"Hmm. Are you done?"

"Not yet. Where did he die? On the hulks?"

His eyes were half-closed, but she knew he was watching her from under those jet-black lashes. "Yes, he died on the hulks," he snapped. "Before he was sentenced, he told me where he'd buried his money—his nest egg, as he called it. Wanted me to start a new life with it. Now, are you done yet, woman?"

"Have patience. I know there's no trust where you come from, but is there no patience, either?"

"Very little. Even for beautiful women."

"Flattery will get you nowhere with me, Kane. Now be still!" Curling locks of black hair drifted to the flagstones at her feet and then blew about in the breeze through the open window. While still, the strong lines of his face reminded her of the carved profile belonging to one of those ancient crusading knights sleeping in the church crypt. In her opinion, he had a very fine nose, even if Mrs. Flick did think it lacked nobility. What did that old bat know?

"Tell me more about your sister," she said quietly.

"Nosy, aren't you?"

"I'm also the one holding the scissors."

He groaned and closed his eyes all the way now. "She was seduced by some fancy gent who abandoned her when she was pregnant. I never knew his name. She wouldn't tell me."

"And she was only seventeen."

"Yes. Three years older than me."

"Did she look like you?"

"S'pose so. She was dark like me."

She stopped trimming. "She worked at Lady Grimstock's." She felt cold suddenly, despite the sun.

"I told you that already. They tossed her out when she told them she was pregnant."

Just then, Aunt Finn peered in through the window. "Sakes! What are you doing to that poor man, Sophie? You mean to leave him bald?"

Alarmed, Lazarus tried to leave his chair, so she held him down by the shoulders. "She teases you, fool." Her heart was racing, her mind still trying to put everything he'd told her in order. She closed her eyes and saw James Hartley stopping to whisper in the ear of a young, dark-haired maid. No, it couldn't be. Her imagination had always been too lively.

Suddenly, she leaned down and kissed his brow. He reached one hand up to the back of her head and drew her forward until her upside-down lips met his. At once she felt the heaviness of desire again. Yes, better. *Don't think bad thoughts. Enjoy what you have, Sophie! Chew your toffee. Besides, what good would it do now to speak of what she'd seen and tried so many years to forget?*

Don't dwell on the past. It was all gone now, and they must look ahead to the future.

She'd written to James that morning. It had not been easy to explain in words that would not make him angry, but she didn't want him hurt. She'd known him a great many years. Even during his long absence since her accident, she'd thought about him often. She would always care about James and want him to be happy, but she knew she wasn't the woman for him.

She tried fitting all that into her letter. Her dearest hope was he would move on with his life.

She straightened up and pushed her thoughts of James aside. "Now for the razor, I think."

"I'll shave myself," Lazarus protested, but she wouldn't allow it. She prodded him up out of the chair and instructed him to remove his clothes.

❦

His fingers curled around the edge of the old copper bathtub, feeling the dimples and dents. How many previous bathers, he wondered idly, had put themselves at the mercy of a woman with something sharp in her hand? Then he felt the warm soap she rubbed on his face, and shortly after, the first sweep of the razor. She was quite accomplished. Nothing to worry about, then.

Or was there? Where did she acquire this skill? By practicing on her past lover?

Damn you, James Hartley.

With the tip of her finger under his chin, she lifted his face for another sweep of the razor. He swallowed carefully. It was very hard—this trusting. It was also very hard not to be jealous. However, Lazarus was determined, a fighter, and he would beat it back. He wouldn't let it get in the way of this happiness. What did the past matter? They would have a fresh start with each other.

In the yard, Tuck and Chivers were preparing the cart for a journey to Sydney Marshes, where they planned to visit a farm sale. Aunt Finn was excited to go with them today, enjoying her new lease on life. Lazarus heard the familiar rusty groan of the gate, wheels rumbling over cobbles, rioting hens clucking irritably, and then they were gone. Doves chortled in the dovecot, the hens quieted to a low cackle, and the piglets in their mother's sty grunted, merry and content.

The last pass of the razor left his face smooth. Sophie wiped it carefully with a towel and then laid a cloth over his face and ordered him to keep his eyes shut.

"What have you done to me?" he mumbled from beneath the warm, damp cloth.

"Made you *almost* look respectable."

He gripped the edge of the tub and listened to her steps move back and forth. Having sat still for half an hour under her command, he was now restless, his blood surging, his mind eagerly sending the message to his body they were alone again.

She beat him to it, however, for when he was finally allowed to look again, she'd already removed her gown, and now let her long hair down from its tidy knot. The beauty and abundance of that hair still shocked Lazarus whenever it was unbound. It fascinated him that so much wildness could be restrained inside that demure knot.

"Is there room for me?" she asked as she stood naked before him, her skin gleaming.

If there wasn't room, he thought, he'd cut off a damned leg to make it.

She stepped in and lowered herself into the water between his knees. "'Tis my turn," she said. "I need my hair washed."

He eagerly grabbed the lump of soap and lathered up. "Now you're at *my* mercy," he exclaimed.

"Don't get soap in my eyes, Kane."

He paused and looked at her sitting in the bath, her knees drawn up to her chin and her small, heart-shaped face surrounded by all that stunning hair, the ends of which just dipped in the water. She tried, did Miss Sophie Valentine, but it wouldn't work with him. Not since he'd seen her go from proud, haughty schoolmistress to reckless, wildly abandoned strumpet.

"I'm minded to start nowhere near your eyes," he remarked coolly.

"I asked you to wash my hair."

"I think, madam, you need a good cleansing all over." Her imperious little chin lifted another inch.

He sat up, causing a swell of water that slapped against the side of the bath and over the rim. "You've been a very naughty young lady. Do you want people to look at you and know what you've been up to with your humble, lowly lover?"

She pursed her lips, and her eyes sparked with a sultry amusement.

"They'll smell my scent on you," he added. He brought the soap slowly up the side of her leg to her knee, and his heated gaze held hers. "'Tis time for your ablutions, my lady, to wash off all the evidence of your wicked, saucy exploits."

"You'll spill all the water out at this rate!" she warned.

He knelt and sat back on his heels. The water just covered his hips. "This won't work," he muttered, eyeing her clenched knees. "You'll have to spread them out."

She observed him warily through wavering lashes.

"There's not enough room," he added. "Do you want the job done properly, madam?"

"Very well, Kane! Get on with it, then. The water will soon be cold."

"Thank you, my lady!" He tugged an imaginary forelock. "I'll do my best." He slowly pressed the soap between her knees and then down along her inner thigh into the water.

Her lips parted; her eyelids fluttered. A very slight sound sputtered out of her mouth, but it was more laugh than protest, no matter how she tried to maintain her serious expression. Her cheeks colored charmingly, and he, besotted, almost let the soap slip from his hand. He looked down at his arm in the water, to where the dark curls on his forearm spread and drifted, pulled about by the slight current he was causing with his motion. "Best start here," he muttered, clutching her knee with his free hand so she wouldn't close him out.

Not that she even tried. His "housekeeper" placed her arms along the edges of the copper bath, and her fingers grasped at the rim just a little too tightly. As her shoulders sank lower against the side, her eyelids finally closed all the way.

"Oops, I lost the soap," he muttered.

"Fancy that!"

"I'd best see if I can find it." He moved his hand now without the soap.

Her eyes flashed open and treated him to a warm caress of hazel. "You won't find it *there*," she purred.

He grinned slowly and slipped his fingers inside her.

She bit her lip, her back arching slightly, her hands tightening around the edge of the bath. More water lapped up and spilled over onto the flagged floor. His fingertip found her sensitive core and gently teased it, while he looked down at her and felt his own desires quickly mounting. She would exhaust him if they kept up this pace, but he wasn't tired yet—far from it.

⤦

She leaned back and gave herself up to his caress, her knees falling against the sides of the tub. She glanced down at the water between her legs, where it lapped in small waves around his gently moving arm. When her eyes rose to his again, she found him watching her with that keen, voracious intent. He leaned down to kiss her moistened lips and then served each nipple in the same way, leaving them pert and gleaming against her pale skin, like delicate pink shells left behind on the wet sand by a retreating tide. As each little ripple slipped over those treasures, stroking them in the same way he stroked her sex, they grew harder, riper. Her breasts bobbed just above the surface, and she felt his eyes upon them, ready to devour her.

She sat up, unable to wait longer, and his hands slid under her arms. He lifted her astride his hips and lowered her so swiftly onto his erection, she cried out at the suddenness of this penetration. Today he gave her no time to adjust but held her tight, his mouth wide over her breast, sucking her nipple with the greed of a starving man. As he grasped her bottom, he thrust upward violently, madly. She was his captive, his plaything.

Water lapped over the edge of the bath as she rode her dark, conquering warrior, held her breasts to his mouth, and laughed. Each time with him it was entirely new, a different level of sensation that lifted her on a cloud. Never had she known this or even suspected such a deep, exhausting pleasure existed.

❧

She could look at her reflection now without flinching. If not for that scar, she might have married James and then been desperately unhappy. If not for that scar, she would never have stayed here and written an advertisement on impulse. Russ might never have come here and kissed her as no one else ever had before. How odd he should have played such a significant role in her life, long before they ever met. It was almost as if, that night alone on the balcony, she'd known he was there—her warrior—watching and waiting. And the only way to cross the divide between them was to take that jump.

One morning while he still slept, she saw the crooked letters marked inside his boots where they lay discarded on the floor by the bed. *R. Adamson.* When she first heard Chivers call him "Russ," she thought it was a derivative of Lazarus, but now she realized it must be his real name—Russ for Russell, perhaps. For some reason, she dared not ask. How ridiculous she should be afraid to ask, she mused grimly. That was the result of sharing a bed with a man who was almost a stranger. It was a little late and uncomfortable now, after the intimacy they'd shared, to suddenly ask his name.

Then she found the letter, and looking forward to the future was no longer possible without addressing the past.

While cleaning the upper floor of the house, she'd

come upon his unlocked trunk and, being of a curious nature, couldn't resist looking inside to search for more clues about his past.

When her fingers discovered the folded paper, hidden down the side of the trunk, she drew it out to examine it.

Aha! A love letter from a past amour, perhaps! A *billet-doux* he kept tenderly. Would there be a lock of her hair inside? Was this the woman upon whom he practiced and honed his skills? She thought of the brassy-haired landlady at the Red Lion in Morecroft—another of his conquests, no doubt.

She opened the paper and found faded words sprawled in a hasty, familiar slant.

There was no signature on the paper, and she had time to read only a few lines, but she knew that writing—knew it well. Before she could even adjust her thoughts, Russ was below, calling her name. She put the letter back and closed the trunk lid.

The words she'd read circled her mind, expanding as if they shouted at her. There was no ignoring it now, no further shoving the idea away to a dark corner of her mind.

His sister's name was Rebecca, and she'd worked at Lady Grimstock's house. She was very dark, like Russ.

And the writing on the letter belonged to James Hartley.

Somehow she regained her feet and made her way down the crooked stairs without stumbling, no sign of any guilty prying on her face. She hoped.

Later that evening, she raised the subject of one day bringing little Rafe to live with them.

He looked at her, sudden surprise streaking across his face, but then his eyes dimmed. "You wouldn't mind?"

"Of course not. One day he'll have cousins. It would be nice if they all lived here together."

"Perhaps." His free hand went to his heart, the fingers spread over that little bump.

It tore brutally into her happiness, that he didn't expect to live long enough to see his children grow up. He worried about leaving her with those responsibilities.

Life was not fair, she thought angrily. Here was a young man who should have years ahead of him; yet, one night, he could lie down to sleep, and if that little bit of broken blade should move while he slept, he would never open his eyes again. Well, he had her now at his side, and every day would count.

She thought again of that letter hidden away in his trunk. Should she mention it to him? No. She'd deal with this on her own. She had a letter to write to Lady Honoria Grimstock.

Chapter 33

MARKET DAY WAS THE FIRST TIME SHE SHOWED HER face since she moved to Souls Dryft as "housekeeper." Aunt Finn advised her to hold her head high and thumb her nose at those spiteful few who were bound to gossip unpleasantly, but as accustomed as she was to rumors about herself, she didn't like hearing folk talk badly about Russ.

Even as they set up their stall at the market, Amy Dawkins swept by in the company of Mrs. Flick and whispered just loud enough to be heard, "They say he paid Henry Valentine five hundred pounds for his sister. He bought her like a woman"—she lowered her voice to a hiss—"of the streets."

"Nonsense! Henry paid the stranger five guineas," Mrs. Flick replied, "to take Sophia off his hands and end the scandal. Henry had no choice once he found out what they were up to together. I knew about it, of course, the moment I heard how they waltzed together at the Morecroft assembly rooms."

"Mama says Sophia's loose morals and opinionated misbehavior are a demonstration of the chaos that results from an education granted where it was not required."

Due to their notoriety, they soon had many customers, who came primarily to assess the situation and were thus trapped into making a purchase by Russ and his excellently persuasive chatter. Amused and proud, Sophie watched him make the most of their curiosity to lure them in and sell his fruit. He had an odd sort of charm he didn't even seem fully aware of. Probably a good thing too, she thought, or else no woman would be safe. She felt a quiet sort of contentment watching him work, knowing he was all hers. He threw himself into the task of shopkeeper just as he did anything, whole-heartedly.

While he was thus preoccupied, Sophie spied James Hartley in the crowd, approaching slowly until he stood a short distance from their stall. His handsome face was marred with a scowl, and his angry gaze stabbed at her like prongs of a toasting fork. She wished he'd been the one to break off their engagement ten years ago; then she wouldn't feel this guilt now.

She slipped away from Russ and walked around the baskets of fruit to meet James. Better get it over with, she thought.

He began at once with a heated accusation. "Do you know what a fool you've made me look? Yet again?"

"I'm sorry, James, but I—"

"I could give you everything."

Except what she needed most of all.

He took her elbow in his gloved hand. "I'll forgive

you for this error in judgment. I suppose he tricked you somehow."

She tried to move her arm away, but his grip tightened.

"Come with me now, Sophia, before he drags you down with him. I can forgive you for this transgression, but I can't continue excusing it to my grandmama forever."

"Surely my actions have no importance to Lady—"

"They will, when we marry."

"Marry?" she burst out in surprise. "But I've already accepted Lazarus."

"I'm willing to overlook your mistake."

"Mistake?"

"Sophia, I've loved you for fifteen years at least."

"Yet you spent the last ten of those away from me." She meant to say he didn't know her anymore, not the way he thought he did. Too much time had elapsed.

But he took her statement as an accusation. "It broke my heart when our engagement was ended. For a long time I was angry with you for listening to your brother and throwing me over. We can put that all behind us now. Let me make those years up to you, Sophia. Don't stay with him. Come back to me. I can give you so much more."

She was astonished he could be so willing to forgive her and take her back. But on reflection, she realized there always had been a tender, vulnerable side to James. He usually kept it well hidden from the world, but she'd witnessed it on more than a few occasions, when he thought no one was looking. He wanted her back because he truly thought she needed him, that he could take care of her. But the love he felt for her was not the passionate, all-consuming fire she shared with Lazarus.

Poor James, she thought, sadness beating slow wings in her heart. He was a rich man who could buy anything he wanted in life. Anything except love.

His lips trembled, but he managed to calm his tone. "You'll never go through with it. It's just like you, Sophia, to make such a sudden, irrational decision, which soon you'll regret."

"I'm not leaving him, James. I'm sorry."

"For the love of God, Sophia, I put aside everything to come back for you when Henry asked me to. I came back to save you."

She pulled her arm away. "Henry asked you to come here?" So that was it. She'd thought it strange he should come to find her again after ten years.

"He wrote to me about your unhappiness and the advertisement. He told me he regretted breaking off our engagement."

"Oh, James, *I* broke it off. It wasn't Henry. It was my choice. *Mine!*"

He stared at her, uncomprehending.

"And he encouraged you to return, James, because you'll soon turn thirty-five, with access to your full inheritance. I'm afraid your grandmama was right about that. I love my brother, but I have no illusions about his failings when it comes to money."

She turned and hurried away between the stalls, but there was no escape. Wherever she turned, she heard the whispers.

"It is well known around Morecroft, Mrs. Cawley. I heard the stranger demanded five hundred pounds from Henry *not* to marry Sophia. Once the ransom is paid, he agrees to leave the village, so the incident can be hushed up."

"'Tis too late to be hushed up, surely."

"Sophia will be sent away to Bath as a governess, and Henry hopes the entire affair may be forgotten."

"She's such a quiet girl…"

"But she takes after Finn. Blood will always out. And you know what…"

Jane Osborne screamed when a well-aimed plum knocked her new bonnet sideways. Almost simultaneously, several other ladies were likewise assaulted by flying fruit, and they all ducked for cover, wailing in distress. Within moments, the market was in an uproar. Someone opened the latch on a sheep pen, and then a number of crates were broken open, releasing a cackle of excited hens into the fray. A dozen guinea fowl made their rattling, chortling cacophony as they mysteriously rampaged free from their cage, and Amy Dawkins, in haste to escape an ill-tempered billy goat, tripped backward into the village pond.

No one, of course, had any proof as to the identity of the culprit, although they all had their suspicions. Sophie would later claim to be nowhere near at the time, for she walked home early from the market that day, not waiting for Russ and her aunt on the empty cart, as she needed the time alone with her thoughts.

⤷⤶

It was a quiet, subdued meal at Souls Dryft that evening, none of the usual merriment in evidence. Chivers apparently thought he might be to blame for the change in mood and mentioned he must soon be on his way. He thanked Russ and Sophie for their hospitality, but it was time for him to move on—he didn't want to outstay his welcome.

Sophie quietly urged him to stay, at least for the harvest. "We're grateful to you for all your hard work…" She trailed off, and her gaze moved to Russ, but he let her speak. He never interrupted her as certain other folk did. In fact, he often pressed her for an opinion, waiting to let her talk. She swallowed hard and added, "Of course, the decision is yours…whether to stay…or go."

The fire crackled softly in the hearth. Finally Chivers cleared his throat. "I can stay another few weeks, then. To help get the harvest in, Russ."

"Don't stay just for that," he said. "If you need to leave, we'll manage here."

"If your lady has no objection," said Chivers calmly, "I'll gladly stay on a while."

Sophie smiled and nodded. "You'll always be welcome here. Whenever you need a place to stay."

Russ looked down at his fingernails.

Good. She wanted him to know she wasn't afraid of what he was or where he came from or the company he kept.

"Thank you, ma'am," said Chivers. "That's very generous of you."

"You're a dear old friend. Of course you're always welcome."

Aunt Finn pulled her chair up to the table, brought out a pack of cards, and began to shuffle them with a dexterity that continually surprised both men but not

Sophie. "If you mean to stay, then, Mr. Chivers, you'll want another chance to win back the pennies you lost to me, I suppose."

He laughed. His broad face crumpled as he looked at the little lady with the sharp eyes and the quick fingers. Sophie began clearing the plates and cautioned him to watch his pockets, although it was too late for that. In the past two nights, Aunt Finn had practically emptied them for him.

Russ picked up a knife and toyed with it. After a while, he got up and went out to chop some wood to expend some of that pent-up energy.

⁓

Later, when he came to bed, having no further cause to delay, he paused outside the bedchamber to listen. He couldn't hear her moving around, so perhaps she was asleep. He carefully lifted the latch and went in. He wasn't sure how to handle what had happened in the market that day, but he knew he ought to say something about her temper. Soon he would be her husband. She would be his responsibility.

She was seated on a long bench by the window, finishing little details on a sketch by the light of that great, round moon. He thought of the dandy, Hartley, as he stood in the market square earlier and watched Sophie, like a dog pining for a lamb chop. He ought to give that pretty fellow a good beating. One of these days, if he was pushed far enough, he just might.

"What did Hartley say to you today?"

He heard her small gasp of frustration. "Naught."

Hands on his hips, he turned away and padded

across the creaking floor to the small hearth where she kept the little caged linnet. It took pride of place there, beside a vase of open-faced roses, their stamens dripping gold dust to the mantel.

He swung around again to face her. "You caused that ruckus today in the market square, wench."

"*Wench?*" Her eyes narrowed. "You wouldn't deliberately try to cause a quarrel with me, would you, Kane?"

He said nothing. What could he say when she sat there so prim and proud with that long, honey-colored hair spilling across her shoulders, her linen chemise almost transparent in the moonlight? How could he still be angry? After all, Sophie was now his, whomever she belonged to before.

Yet there was a veil between them. Still she hid secrets behind those watchful, hazel eyes. He knew she'd been prying through his trunk, and she'd written a letter to London. When he asked her about it, a guilty pink had instantly covered her face, and even when she said she'd written to a relative, he didn't know whether to believe her. She was holding something back.

"Why did you leave the market today without me?" he demanded.

"I had a headache and couldn't stand the noise."

He ground his jaw. "Or couldn't stand to hear what's being said about me?"

"What *is* being said?" Now she pretended to be unaware of it.

"That your friend Hartley has uncovered my past and means to chase me from the village."

There was a still, breathless pause. She stopped sketching. "Will you have to leave now?" she asked quietly. "If James…I don't want you to leave, but if you're in danger…"

"I'm not leaving. I've run too long and too far already." He leaned one arm on the mantel, and his finger rubbed the bars of the little birdcage. "He won't chase me off. I told you that."

"Then we'll fight him together."

He turned his head to look at her again, amazed once more at his good luck in finding her—afraid he didn't truly deserve all this. Perhaps it was selfish of him to keep her, to cause her all this trouble. "James Hartley is filthy rich, is he not?" he demanded gruffly.

She sighed, agreeing he was.

"Handsome too."

"Beauty is bought by judgment of the eye."

He walked across the chamber, put his hand under her chin, and lifted her face so her eyes couldn't hide. "You think him handsome?"

"I think you're far handsomer."

"He's much better dressed."

"You're much better *undressed*."

❧

Much to Sophie's relief, he took the hint and finally stripped off his breeches and shirt. She returned to her sketch, and eventually he came up behind her again to look over her shoulder. "Is that me?" he asked, sounding bemused.

"No," she replied dryly. "It's some other man who works on the yard with his shirt off."

Suddenly he touched her hair, and she realized he had her brush in his hands. "May I?" he asked very quietly.

She said nothing but bent over her sketch, and after a slight pause, he drew the brush down gently through her hair. She closed her eyes. The brush strokes were firm and steady, that soft sound the only noise in the room apart from her own heartbeat fluttering in her ears. With one hand he briefly caressed the back of her neck before lifting her hair again for another pass of the brush. She could smell the warm night air and fresh-cut wood as if it permeated his skin and seeped out with his sweat.

Now he put down the brush and used his fingers. He ran them slowly back from crown to nape, gathered her long hair into a tail, held it and then let it fall, like a child mesmerized by a new toy. She exhaled at last and turned to look at him.

Before she could speak, he pressed a finger to her lips, and she tasted his salt. "May I?" he said again.

She waited. He sat astride the bench, his front to her back. Her silence, apparently, was acquiescence, and the sketch drifted out of her hands to the floor. He tugged gently on the sleeves of her chemise until they slid down over her arms, and then she felt the air on her breasts, her nipples already taut with the anticipation of his touch. His tongue traced a pattern on her neck, tasting her in a slow, meticulous fashion before moving slowly along her shoulder.

It was almost like a man enjoying his last meal, she realized.

The chemise crumpled to her hips, and slowly he freed each of her wrists from the fallen sleeves. His body shifted closer, pressing against her so she felt every part of him, the heat and strength, the hard maleness. When she shivered, he didn't ask if she was cold; he simply put his arms around her, wrapping her tightly, his lips in her hair and his inner thighs enclosing her hips. And between them—his bold erection. She felt it through her thin chemise like a ridge of hot steel pressed to her lower back. She writhed a little as his fingertips gently circled her nipples and his lips continued along her shoulder. Each kiss lingered longer and a little wetter. Then one hand moved down to her belly, pausing there a few tantalizing breaths, fingers spread, before it slid lower, under her chemise. Pleasure flooded her veins and her limbs. He curled his torso to her back, and a soft growl shuddered out of him and against her hair.

"Bear my child."

In response to those three words, her body throbbed with need. She sensed this night it would serve that special service, an anointed vessel for his seed and his life. Biting her lip, she rubbed her bottom against him, wanting him desperately. She felt the dampness on her chemise from his arousal and her own. He suddenly scooped her up, one arm around her waist, and bent her forward while he positioned the pulsing head of his erection against her slippery sex and pulled her chemise aside impatiently. His breath seared her skin in quick waves as he urged her to kneel before him on the bench, and in the next moment, she was filled.

He rocked forward, his feet on the floor. She flexed under his arched body and gasped as his thighs bent, shifting muscles pushing against her legs. One arm held her firmly around the waist as he thudded into her. It was a primitive coupling, a need they both had that night, simply two creatures with the same basic desire under the silent, silver moon. She opened to him, welcomed him with tearful gladness, and he spent lushly, hotly as he ground onto her, the possession complete.

She might not know how long they had physically together, but that night they made their own forever.

He lay down with her in the bed, his arms tight around her body, her head cradled in the powerful embrace of his warm chest. She listened anxiously for his heartbeat, and whenever she thought she heard it falter, her eyes opened wide, staring into the moonlight until that steady rhythm returned again and finally rocked her back to sleep.

Chapter 34

A FEW DAYS LATER, SOPHIE HEARD THE BELL AT THE front gate and went out to find her brother standing there.

She wiped her hands on her apron and crossed the yard with a wary step. "Why have you come, Henry? To give me another lecture and remind me I'm a fallen woman who cannot be saved? Or just to get out of the house and away from Lavinia? You must have a bee in your unmentionables again to bother coming here."

"You may find all this highly amusing, but your behavior, Sophia, has caused great outrage and upset." He sounded breathless, and he clutched at the bars of the gate, wincing. "Might I come in and sit?"

She wanted to refuse, but the look on her brother's face was such, she thought he might collapse there and then, so she opened the gate. Worried, she led him inside out of the sun's heat, where the stone walls and floor of the house kept the inside temperature cool even at the peak of summer. She fetched him a mug of ale from the pantry, for which he muttered his thanks and drank thirstily. Once recovered enough to speak again, he surprised her with the following: "We're invited to dine with Lady Hartley on Saturday."

"I don't care to go."

Henry clasped the ivory knob of his cane in both hands and leaned heavily on it. "Nevertheless, it will do you good to be among elegant company for a change. Perhaps you forget how to behave now you live among crooks and degenerates. Your wild behavior at the market, I hear, was something to behold."

"I take it Lazarus is not invited to—"

"Certainly not. He's not fit company for Lady Hartley. He will never belong in our world. You may as well face that fact."

She picked up a corner of her apron and nervously began cleaning the windows. "I know you told James about the advertisement. You brought him back here."

"I did what I thought was best."

She sighed. "But, Henry, I won't change my mind. Not this time."

He was reflected in the small, crooked panes, and she watched him irritably fiddle with his hat. "Obdurate, belligerent woman," he mumbled. "I hope you realize James Hartley is quite determined to save you from this mistake. He has uncovered some interesting facts about your Mr. Kane."

Sophie faced him bravely. "I don't care a tinker's damn what he and Sir Arthur find with all their prying. They might look to their own lives before they seek to destroy his. And the same goes for you, Henry."

Red-faced, he stumbled to the open door. "How do you think it affects me to walk down the street with everyone knowing my sister lives here in sin with a man? Housekeeper, indeed! Ah, but perhaps you do not care how it affects me. You never did care about anyone but yourself."

"Henry, that is unjust."

"Is it, Sophia? Whom were you thinking about when you made *this* decision? Certainly not me. Not even Lazarus Kane, for whom you will bring only more trouble." He carefully negotiated the step up into the yard, ducked his head below the crooked lintel, and then he was gone, cursing at the hens to get out of his way.

❧

The barley was waist high, a silver mass of heaving, rippling waves that gleamed under the sun. Lazarus liked to sit on the wavy roof of his house and gaze out over the fields to see the results of all that hard work finally coming to fruition. Beyond the acres of barley, wheat, and cut hay, there was pasture where the sheep, which once struck him as so mournful and defeated, now roamed about with as much cheer as sheep ever roamed. The cows had coats like velvet and placidly cropped away at rich grass, swinging their tails at the impertinent flies. In the paddock, the new farm horses enjoyed a rest before it was time to be put to harness again. And in the orchard, on the southerly side of the house, fruit trees bloomed in such great abundance he wondered why he ever fixed that hole in the wall. There was more than enough fruit to go around.

Aunt Finn, strolling among the fruit trees, gathered

wind-fallen bounty and sang ribald songs, daydreaming of a long-ago love affair. Throaty doves echoed her tune as they flew between the dovecot and the chimneys of the house, and Tuck, shoveling dirt out of the loose-boxes in the yard, whistled along through the gaps in his teeth.

The chestnut trees in the distance, where Sophie once dropped a book on his head, were at the peak of their green glory, and spiked fruits ripened in clusters between the leaves.

And there she was, sitting on the flint wall below his high perch, reading a letter that came for her that day all the way from London. He'd wanted to ask her about it, but she took it off immediately to be alone while she read it, and he let her have that privacy. He couldn't think whom she might correspond with in London, but it made him anxious.

Now she'd finished reading her letter, slid it away in her apron pocket, and began to watch the little grey mare who, despite her diminutive size, skipped about among the great farm horses without the slightest fear, teasing them with flicks of her proud tail.

The wedding was now a few days away, and neither of them spoke of it anymore. It hovered there, waiting, slumbering like a moth in one corner of the window, undisturbed until someone swiped at it viciously with a broom.

It was almost as if they were waiting for something to come along and spoil it.

He knew, then, as he watched her sitting on the flint wall, he loved her more than his own life. The thought of losing her worried him more than one day being recaptured.

❧

"I'm dining in Morecroft tonight with Henry," she said as she watched him harness the cart horses.

He said nothing, busy pulling the horse's tail through the crupper and then hunkering down to fasten the girths.

"I'll be back by morning, but I expect it will be very late, so you'd best not wait up."

For a few moments his mind was empty, as if she had pulled a cork and all his thoughts splattered out onto the cobbled yard. "Don't go."

"What?"

He swallowed. If she went through that gate with her brother, he'd never see her again. They'd keep her away from him. But he didn't repeat his request. He reminded himself, again, it must be her choice if she stayed.

"I have to go," she said softly. "It's important, Russ."

"Is it something to do with that letter from London?" He was angry she still kept secrets—even after he told her all his.

"Yes," she admitted finally. "But I can't tell you more than that, so please don't ask me."

He straightened up slowly and patted the horse's hindquarters, looking at her.

"I will be back by morning," she repeated.

He turned away and muttered, "You'd best not stay out in the field too long today, then, or you'll be tired." He couldn't keep her prisoner, could he? They must learn to trust each other.

But don't go. Stay. Please.

He'd never been afraid of anything in his life, but he was afraid now; he feared losing her.

Sophie stepped back and ran a hand over her long braid. "Going to be a hot day."

He nodded, unable to speak without betraying his shamefully weak emotions, and got on with his work.

❧

She decided to wear the gown Maria had altered for her. It would be a shame to waste it, and she must look her best tonight. Had she any armor, she would have worn it, but muslin and lace would have to suffice. Around her neck she wore a string of coral beads that once belonged to her mother, and with Finn's help, she managed to get her hair tamed into the reasonable facsimile of a ladylike coif, complete with a few ringlets over the ears and the last-minute addition of forget-me-nots picked from the verge by the gate.

When Lady Hartley's open barouche arrived in the lane that evening, Henry looked out and exclaimed, in some begrudging surprise, that she was "almost beautiful."

She smiled wryly and told her brother to stop flattering her or she might think him ill, or possessed.

Maria, seeing her gown finally put to good use, remarked in excitement at how well she looked, and even Lavinia was moved enough to say that, if she were not so dreadfully tanned by the sun, she might actually be presentable. If she wore a little powder. And darkened her brows.

Mr. Bentley asked quietly after her aunt's health.

Sophie assured him Aunt Finn flourished like the crops in the field.

"And Mr. Kane?" he asked. "He is well, I hope?"

"Yes." Her voice quaked, but no one seemed to notice. She knew what they were all thinking: she'd dressed up tonight for James Hartley; she'd "come to her senses" at last.

Well, they were right about the latter, wrong about the former. Now she had all the pieces put together in her mind, there was no more doubt and no more fear. But it was all up to her.

She kept her small beaded purse in both hands, because it contained the most important accessory of all. Tonight was the decisive battle in this war, and she would fight to the bloody end for the man she loved.

When they arrived at Lady Hartley's, Sophia was unpleasantly surprised to see so many other guests, where she'd expected only her family. Mrs. Dykes was there in her gloomy black widow's weeds, with Sir Arthur Sadler beside her. His wife and the battalion of daughters were also dragged out again—a row of sallow, unhappy faces. There was still not one expression of animation among them. Wooden puppets might have shown more life.

Sir Arthur already held court in his booming voice, and the moment she appeared in the drawing room, he glared at her through his quizzing glass, as if she were an insect retrieved from his port.

James was drinking heavily. He greeted her with a bow that leaned slightly to the left, and his lips almost missed her gloved fingers completely. "Sir

Arthur has much to tell us that I think you will find interesting, Sophia."

"Oh?" Her hands tightened around the little beaded purse she carried.

Of course she knew what this was about. The very moment she saw them all gathered there, she recognized this dinner party as an ambush.

Dinner was served almost immediately, and James took her arm, steering her wildly so they almost bumped into the elegantly carved acanthus scrolls of the door frame. "Sir Arthur has made enquiries regarding that man Kane. He has quite a tale to tell."

"Really? With eight daughters and a sickly wife, he has nothing else——?"

"You will listen to what he has to say, Sophia."

She looked at his fingers biting into her upper arm. "I'm disappointed in you, James. I thought you above scrabbling in the dirt."

He released her arm and held out her chair, eyes downcast, lips dry.

Lady Sadler had very specific requirements for food and seldom ate anything too brightly colored or highly seasoned. Her meat had to be cut up in very small bites, and nothing of a rounded shape or unpeeled could be set upon her plate without causing her undue alarm and severe palpitations. Sir Arthur, on the other hand, ate everything in sight, peeled or unpeeled, skinned or unskinned, and left his wife's ministrations to whomever else was at hand. In this case, it was Mrs. Dykes who assumed the responsibility of Lady Sadler's digestion. She sat beside her at dinner and pressed the lady to take only the softest and palest of foods, and even occasionally lifted the fork to the lady's lips or offered her a sip of water.

Once the first course was served, Mrs. Dykes prompted Sir Arthur. "Do continue your story about that man named Kane." She glanced quickly at Sophia. "It was most fascinating."

Sir Arthur eagerly obliged. "A wretched creature of innumerable depredations…"

Sophie toyed with the purse in her lap, one finger running over the beads.

"…born into poverty and he embarked on an early life of crime…"

She stared at the little hairs protruding from his nostrils, and his yellowed, leering teeth.

"…a thief, a brawler, a confidence trickster, a cheat, and a blackguard of the lowest order. In and out of prison all his life…"

His monocle gleamed brightly, reflecting the light of Lady Hartley's candles, so each time he moved his head, a flare of white flame replaced the eye behind the glass.

"I understand he became an inmate of Newgate Prison…"

Across the table, Miss Sadler was picking at her food, elbows tight to her thin sides. James, his eyes bloodshot, gestured for the servant to bring more wine. Lady Hartley's hands—two bejeweled, scrawny creatures—stroked the furry head of her lapdog, over and over again, and Mrs. Dykes ran a slow, lizard-like tongue across her lower lip.

"…but his last sentence was commuted to transportation. He was sent to a prison hulk near Deptford."

As soon as Sir Arthur paused for one sip of wine, Sophie wrapped both hands tightly around her purse, took a deep breath, and said suddenly, "I daresay a man born into that life has very few opportunities to rise out of it."

Silence descended on the dining room. Even the plaster cupids flying about Lady Hartley's high ceiling paused their frolicking to look down and listen.

She didn't think she'd ever heard her voice sound quite so loud. Everyone was staring at her, shocked by her bold words.

"Should we not look for ways to help rather than condemn a man simply because he was born in poverty?" she added.

"I'm afraid, Miss Valentine, you take a liberal view, along the lines of the reformer Grey Bennet and that Fry woman." The way Sir Arthur spoke their names made his feelings clear in regard to them and their reforms. The red veins on his cheeks looked ready to explode. "I did not know you were a woman of mouthy opinions."

"I only wish I could do more than have an opinion. I wish I might help those poor souls."

"Poor souls? Had you sat before these degenerates so many years, as did I, you would take a different view."

She couldn't stop herself, and more words spilled out over her tongue. "Surely every child born should have a fair chance at life. We cannot all be wealthy, but we can all be informed."

He sneered. "I begin to think you had better not come to Bath after all, young woman." He turned to a gray-faced Mrs. Dykes and complained that she'd described Sophia as a quiet, mousy girl. "We don't need these radical ideas influencing our daughters," he added sternly.

"Yes, Sir Arthur," Sophie explained with a great deal more merriment than she felt, "although I'm a woman and not entitled to them, I have my own beliefs and ideas."

"Forged by the heart, no doubt," Henry muttered into his wine, "instead of the head."

She continued, "So it would not do to bring me to Bath after all."

Mrs. Dykes grew irritable and flushed. "Do allow Sir Arthur to finish his tale about this wretched criminal. One hain't 'alf intrigued to hear how it will end." Her teeth formed an ugly grimace.

Sophie stood and thrust her chair back. "Would you hunt him down for your own amusement? What if he's begun a new life to make amends for the old one? Is he always to be condemned for where he was born?"

"Sir Arthur says this fellow has never lived an honest day. He has deceived and harmed many," James shouted, almost knocking his wine over. "For that he must pay. This is not merely about where he was born, Sophia!"

"But you don't know all the circumstances. His crime may be a...a moment he has regretted ever since, when he made a mistake. A rash, reckless mistake." She closed her eyes, seeing his fist strike a man's face...seeing the man fall back and hit his head on a stone hearth...and all the blood from his own wounded chest, where that knife remained stuck, darkening his uniform. Horror made her throat tight.

And then she saw that ladder again, rushing out of the dark toward her. "For that one mischance…something he never intended…what price could he ever pay to recompense? Nothing could undo it. He surely knows that." She exhaled finally and opened her eyes.

Mrs. Dykes gasped scornfully. "Like what I told you, 'Enry, your sister's a drinker."

"Not yet, madam, but I've made my own share of mistakes and misjudgments. And lived to regret them bitterly." She held her head high so they would all look at her scar and remember. Today she was a pirate—as a certain young boy called her—and pirates did not hide their scars; they flaunted them with pride. "We all have our sins to repent and mistakes in our past." Her words fell like a shower of hot sparks into the stone-cold silence. The Misses Sadler finally appeared alive. Their eyes danced with glee, and their noses twitched. She remained standing, astonishing even herself with the strength of her feelings in that moment. "We all have secrets, do we not? Lapses in judgment?"

When Henry looked up to find her watching him, he fumbled with his wine glass and spilled a few blood-like drops across Lady Hartley's pristine tablecloth.

"We all strive to better our circumstances," she went on and turned her eyes now to Lavinia and then Mrs. Dykes, who glared back at her in fury. "Why should some be forbidden that chance?" Finally she turned to James. "That diamond pin in your cravat could provide an education for at least one poor child—like that man you're all so keen to condemn—and set him on a path to greater things. Would it not benefit all of us to help those born into circumstances worse than our own?"

Again there was silence. Then Lavinia said, "I do wish she'd sit down. She's putting me off my dinner, and I'm sure I don't feel guilty for what I have. I deserve it and more too, which I would have if certain people were not so tight with the purse strings!"

Sophia cursed at her with words some folk around that table had never before heard. The Misses Sadler inhaled as one creature.

"Is that Latin or Greek?" Lady Hartley asked, slightly frustrated by the inadequacies of her ear trumpet.

Lavinia bristled, and her tight curls trembled with indignation. "Well! To be so spoken to! Me! A well-brought-up young woman from a good family!"

Suddenly her husband snapped at her to be quiet, and they all looked at Henry in surprise. "I believe my sister's point," he said slowly, "is no person *deserves* it more than any other."

And Mr. Bentley—gentle, peaceable Mr. Bentley—quietly and somberly stated, "Miss Sophia raises many good points. It would behoove us all to consider our advantages and help others less fortunate. She is perhaps a little impassioned in her speech, but the message is one with which I concur most heartily."

Her mouth open, Maria swiveled in her chair, gazing upon her husband in wonderment and growing quite giddily pink.

Lady Hartley appealed now to Sir Arthur. "What is that dratted girl saying? Why is she standing in the midst of dinner?" She raised her voice for the table in general. "Is she foxed?"

Sir Arthur cleared his throat loudly, and his voice boomed out, filling the impressive space of her elegant dining room. "All this chatter is gibberish, young woman. But it matters not one whit, in any case. This Kane fellow has been dead five years, at least. Died on that hulk, apparently." He snuffled with scornful laughter. "The Devil caught up with him in the end, as he always does. The Devil always gets his due."

Sophie felt her knees buckle. She pressed her hands to the tablecloth. Dimly she heard Mrs. Dykes protesting he may not be dead, but Sir Arthur was adamant, and of course, he was never wrong. The man was dead. He decreed it to be so.

"Furthermore, it cannot be the same young buck living nearby," he added, "for Kane was an old fellow—in his eighties."

Relief touched her like gentle, warm, summer rain. She belatedly remembered her manners, stammered an apology into Lady Hartley's ear trumpet, and left the room.

Kane—of course, that must have been the old man who helped him, the man who was almost a father to him. So Russ took that name when he escaped to make a new life. It was a tribute of sorts, and no one but she knew his real name…the name written in his dusty, old, scuffed boots.

Chapter 35

SOPHIA CROSSED THE FOYER AND KEPT WALKING, through the front door of the house, down the steps, and into the street. It was the grandest street in Morecroft, and she'd walked it many times but never alone. A few people turned their heads as she passed, but she looked at no one. Tonight she was escaping again, but this time she knew where she was going. The beaded purse tucked under one arm, she quickly stripped off her long gloves and let them fall. From now on she would touch life directly.

James followed. She heard his unsteady footsteps slapping and tripping along the pavement, his angry shout for her to wait.

Finally she stopped by a lantern, because she had a stone in her slipper. As he approached, he stooped to retrieve her discarded gloves from the pavement. The amber lantern light cast warm waves of gold in his hair. She breathed hard, and her bare fingers tightened around her small purse.

He was, fortunately, moving beyond his angry, drunken stage into a morose sulkiness. "I suppose this means you still don't know what's good for you." He must have seen the tears in her eyes. She felt them—great, hot droplets hovering in her lashes.

But she wasn't sad. She was too many other things now. A passion stirred inside her, more deeply felt than anything she'd known before Russ Adamson's first kiss—before the first caress of his fingertips. She blinked and shook a few of those teardrops loose, and as they rolled slowly down the curve of her cheek, she said, "Jump, and I'll catch you."

"What?"

"Nothing. Just…thinking."

He grumbled, "You always did too much of that."

She wiped her tears on the back of her hand. "Whom did you take to your grandmama's summer ball instead of me?"

"Miss Sadler. Hannah. Not a bad girl," he mumbled. "Knows a good thing when she sees it." He smirked and tucked her gloves away inside his evening coat. "Nothing like you."

"I'm sure. To be honest, I wonder what you ever saw in me."

He shook his head. "Sometimes I wonder the same. It was one of those evenings, I daresay, when the candles are bright, the air is warm…"

"Yes." She knew exactly what he meant. "Strong punch, dancing, and candlelight are a deadly combination with a great many unhappy marriages to answer for."

Unsmiling, he said, "If he ever hurts you, that blackguard will rue the day he met me."

"He will never hurt me, James."

"How can you be sure?"

"Because I know him. And I...I love him. Don't cause any more trouble for us. Let him be. Everyone deserves a second chance."

But he turned his head, his lips pale, nostrils flared.

She stepped off the pavement and walked across the road to the small park with its border of black iron railings. Again he followed her, stumbling over the cobbles and stubbing his toe on the curb.

She sat on a painted bench, closed her eyes a moment, and tempered the fleeting instinct to run away. The gate squealed, and then he was there at her side, dropping to the bench with a groan. "What has got into you tonight?" he mumbled.

This time he couldn't blame her behavior on the iniquitous Ellie Vyne's presence, she thought.

Her fingers blindly played with the beads on her purse. "Do you remember, James, the little dark-haired housemaid who worked for Lady Grimstock in Mayfair? Do you remember her?"

"Maid?" he grumbled sourly. "What maid? She had many."

"I wasn't certain of her name, so I wrote to Lady Grimstock to be sure." She paused for breath. "Her name was Rebecca Adamson." Now she opened her eyes and looked at him. "Do you remember her now, James?"

He stood abruptly and moved away to lean against the railings. "How am I supposed to remember one maid from another?"

"Don't you, James? Truly? You should—"

"Why the Devil should I remember a housemaid?"

Slowly, carefully, every word sharp as a pin, she told him, "I saw you that evening, when I stood on the balcony waiting for you to bring my shawl. I saw you stop and talk to her. And she looked up at you with two big, dark brown eyes shining with adoration. Her name…was Rebecca."

"Well, then," he blustered as his hands clasped the railings, "if you say that was her name, I suppose it must have been."

"She had a baby, James."

There was a long, heavy silence.

"It was your baby."

"Don't be ridiculous!"

The branches above his head trembled in a sudden breeze, and he raised his shoulders as if he felt a chill. She walked up to him slowly. "You knew. You could have helped her, but you turned your back."

"Oh, for pity's sake, what makes you think it was my child?" he roared.

She looked up at his moonlit face. "She died, James. Did you even know? Didn't you care what happened to her after your actions got her dismissed?"

He blanched, every ounce of heightened color fading instantly.

"She died giving birth to your child."

He backed away and blustered, "I suppose this is one more of your great causes, is it? Unwed girls getting themselves into trouble."

"That sort of trouble takes two people, James." She suddenly opened her purse and passed him the note she'd recently found in her lover's trunk. At first he wouldn't take it, so she pressed it into his clenched hand. "There is no signature, but I recognized your handwriting at once. For proof, I wrote to Lady Grimstock and asked if she remembered the name of that dark-haired maid who was dismissed because of a pregnancy. She did remember, of course." She sighed. "She has a memory like an elephant, especially when it comes to other people's transgressions."

He stared down at the crumpled letter. She didn't know whether he was reading or simply staring emptily. "Where did you get this?"

"From Rebecca's brother."

"Rebecca's...?"

"He doesn't know who you are. I won't tell him. I just wanted you to be aware of what you'd done—to face up to it after all these years." He kept his eyes on the letter. His shoulders sagged. "You could have helped her, James. She reached out for your help, but you pushed her aside with that cold, miserable little letter, telling her you could do nothing for her except send her money."

For a moment he was silent and still, staring beyond the letter. "I was too far from London when I heard," he murmured finally. "She had someone write to me. I never knew she was with child until then."

"She died, James, with only her brother at her side, and he was a boy of fourteen, just dismissed from his post without references."

"I...I didn't know she died." He thrust the letter back into her hands. "When I returned to London, I went to the last place she'd lived, and the people there knew nothing." Briefly he covered his eyes with one trembling hand, and then he shook his head. "Who is he...her brother?"

She licked her lips. "I think you guessed that somewhere in these last few minutes, because you must know why I showed you that letter and what I'm going to ask of you."

He said nothing, just stared.

"Leave him be, James. Stop this persecution. You owe him that much after the great wrong you did to Rebecca. I'll never tell him who ruined his sister, but in return you'll let him go on with his life and be loved."

He stumbled away from her, returned to the bench, and sprawled clumsily on it, head tipped back. Moonlight danced over his brow and limned his proud nose and sharp chin. She'd seen that haughty profile in Rafe's small face when he looked up at her and called her a bossy woman, but she hadn't recognized it then. And the little boy's blue eyes—those were James Hartley's eyes.

He hadn't asked anything about his son, she realized. Should she tell him? It would upset Russ. James had no space in his busy life for a bastard son, one he could barely admit was his own flesh and blood, and Russ loved the boy dearly. She wouldn't want to risk James getting any ideas about taking the boy away.

But was it right to keep his son away from him? Surely, as the father, he should know the boy lived.

And then what would Russ do if he discovered the identity of the "fancy gent" who ruined his sister? She must break the news to him very carefully, choose her moment wisely.

So for tonight, at least, they were all better off as they were. One day soon, when things were calm and settled and tempers had died down, she could let her husband tell James himself. That might be best. Her loyalties now must lie with the man she was about to marry. Let Russ, who had struggled all these years to keep the child safe, decide when the time was right for little Rafe.

"That's what you came here tonight to ask me?" James said suddenly. "That's the only reason you came, isn't it, Sophia? For him."

"Yes."

"You dressed up like that because you knew I'd have to do anything you asked when you looked so beautiful."

"Well, I tried my best."

"I almost don't see your scar tonight," he muttered.

No, but he *did* see it, and he always would, because he looked only with his eyes and didn't see beyond. Yet. One day he would learn what was important. She had faith in it. Now that she had found love, she wanted everyone to know the same happiness.

"I haven't lost you"—he soothed his own pride—"because you were never really mine."

"No," she admitted frankly.

"I was in love with you, though. Wasn't I?"

She shook her head. "You will know when you fall in love. *Properly* in love. You'll understand then."

He glared at her, still sulking and confused.

"He lost his sister, James. You owe him."

Finally he groaned, one hand to his forehead. "Very well, then, Sophia, you may have your gypsy. I won't interfere."

She wanted to cry with joy and relief, but she couldn't let him see how scared she'd been. "Thank you. I wish you good luck, James. May you find happiness of your own."

And she walked out of the park.

&

Lady Hartley once again loaned her barouche for the return journey to Sydney Dovedale. The travelers were subdued. Lavinia sulked up a storm, and her mother was so angered by her thwarted plans, she could barely breathe. She'd hoped for a union between Valentine and Hartley, one that would shoot her daughter into the upper rungs of society at last, but that opportunity had now slipped out of her grasp. And it was all Sophia's fault—and Henry's for not silencing her shockingly opinionated tongue.

Across the barouche, Mr. Bentley and his wife sat quite snugly, Maria occasionally pointing up at a bright star overhead while clinging to her husband's arm, her face laid against his sleeve. On her other side sat Sophia, who also looked up at the stars, searching. Finally her gaze swung down and reached across the crowded carriage for her brother.

Tonight was supposed to be his chance to be rid of the stranger. Yet he didn't seem very upset it failed. He'd even taken her side for once.

I believe my sister's point is no person deserves it, more than any other.

He met her gaze suddenly and raised his brows, questioning.

"Thank you, Henry," she said, her voice little more than a whisper blown across the carriage.

His head bowed slightly forward, and she thought

he almost smiled. "As you said, we all have our mistakes...regrets."

Lavinia immediately forgot her sulking. "Don't speak to her, Henry. If she married a Hartley, we would have a carriage of our own and not have to borrow. We would have a house in town. It's all her fault!"

"No, my dear," he replied firmly. "It's mine."

"Why would you say such a thing?"

Henry removed his hat and set it on his knee. "Because we're in debt, my dear. From now on, we must learn to live a little better within our means." The words finally out, he winced, fumbled for a stubborn white curl that kept falling to his brow, and then replaced his hat, signaling the discussion was over.

It was a day, apparently, for many truths to come out.

Chapter 36

ALTHOUGH SOPHIA HAD TOLD HIM NOT TO WAIT UP, and even though, in that terrible empty place in his heart, Lazarus feared she was gone for good, he did wait up. What was the alternative? Go to bed without her?

The hours passed. Owl hoot turned to lark song, and the light came up, but she didn't return. He must have closed his eyes to rest them and eventually fell asleep in his chair before the fire, for Tuck woke him with a poke to the shoulder in time for breakfast.

An hour later, hard at work in the rick yard as he layered wheat traves into a stack with a violently wielded pitchfork, something made him look up. Odd. He thought he felt rain, but the sky was pure blue, innocent as a forget-me-not. Then, as he turned to swing his pitchfork yet again, he saw her, walking along the lane with her hands behind her back. She wore that flimsy white party frock, he noted sourly, showing off her curves. Her long arms were brown now after working beside him in the sun. He thought she looked guilty, but then she often did, he realized, resting his pitchfork. She often looked as if she'd just done something she shouldn't. Or was about to. It was one of the first things that drew him to her, when he tried to see what she hid behind those lashes—what she'd been up to.

Feet apart, pitchfork held across his thighs, he watched her approach, taking in every detail and committing her to memory before she slipped away for good.

As she finally came closer, the words burst out of him. "You've come to tell me you're leaving to marry Hartley. You needn't have bothered."

"No. I suppose I needn't have bothered, you surly ingrate," she replied tightly, "but since I'm here, you may as well have this." She held out a white, folded object, which she'd kept behind her back.

He scowled at it, dubious. "What is it?"

"A shirt. I made it."

"Why would you do that?"

"I begin to wonder myself. So much blood and sweat has never been lost over one foolish shirt." Then her brave voice faltered when she added, "But no one else should have the wearing of it."

Sweat dripped from his eyebrows while he fought for something to say.

"And I'm going to marry *you*, Kane, whether you like it or not."

His heart began to beat again. The creases slowly melted away from his brow, and then he threw his pitchfork down, exhaling heavily. He actually felt as if he might cry, so he wiped his face quickly with one hand, as if he were perspiring. "That dandy could give you more than I ever could. Much more."

"But not what I need."

Tongue tucked well into his cheek, he cautiously took the offering from her hands and examined the clumsy stitches and rough edges. "Will it fit?" He glanced at her, saw her lashes flicker and the little swallow in her throat.

"Of course." But from the look on her face, it hadn't occurred to her until now.

He read her thoughts clearly.

At last they were no longer hidden from him. The veil was gone.

His heart actually hurt, pierced by the surprise joy of this gift, over which she must have struggled and suffered many pricks with her needle. Thrusting it back into her hands, he briskly removed his old silk shirt, and when he caught her glance at his chest, he teased, "You didn't go to all this trouble just to see me without my shirt, Miss Valentine?"

"There you go again, Kane, with your pride and vanity."

"And *your* lust."

"We'll come to that in a moment."

He pulled the new shirt over his head while she watched. Almost immediately, the sound of ripping stitches brought the action to a halt. She circled him impatiently and pulled on the material to force it over his shoulders, determined it would fit. The poor shirt barely contained his shoulders, stretched tight across his chest, and yet was curiously more than sufficient in length, hanging almost to his knees. He looked down and tried not to laugh. She was silent, vexed, chewing her nails. He spread out his arms, ignored the ripping, and exclaimed, "Perfect!"

Their eyes met, and they both laughed.

"Now," he said as he closed the distance between them, "I suppose this is when I tell you I love you."

She nodded, her hands and forearms pressed lightly to his chest.

"I love you, Sophie," he breathed, looking down at her. "I don't want to be without you, not even for a minute of the time I have left."

Again she nodded, lips pressed tight, eyes shining.

"Now it's your turn to tell me," he added sternly, all business, "what *you* need."

She slid her soft arms over his shoulders and then around his neck, urging that he bend down to her. "I need you," she whispered. "I want you. I love you."

He grinned and moved her even closer, until there was nothing left in their way.

༄

After the wedding feast, when the guests had all gone home, the newlyweds strolled in the garden at Souls Dryft, and Russ plucked one of those late, deep-red roses from the flint wall, tucking it behind her ear. Then he leaned back to admire it. His eyes traveled slowly and appreciatively over her face. "Did you make the right choice?" he asked softly. "You won't change your mind tomorrow?"

She pouted. "You think me so flighty and changeable?"

"You do have a reputation for changing your mind."

"But I waited all these years for you."

He chuckled, and she felt it rumbling through his chest where she leaned against it.

"Do you know how hard it is to keep falling all

that time, Russ, waiting to be caught? But I knew you had to come soon. I couldn't have lived another day without you." She lifted on tiptoe to kiss him.

His fine, knightly nose rubbed hers.

"Aunt Finn will be safely wrapped up in bed within ten minutes, fast asleep in another ten." She smiled saucily. "Chivers spends the night at Merryweather's Tavern, and Tuck has gone to visit his cousin in Yarmouth, so he won't return tonight."

"Is that so?" He set her back at arm's length. "Why do you tell me this?"

She laughed, and red petals fell from her rose to the sleeve of her gown. "You may do whatever you wish with the information. I merely apprise you of the fact that, in half an hour, we shall have the place to ourselves."

"Twenty minutes," he whispered. "I can't read, but I can add."

"How clever you are! My best pupil."

A breeze kicked over the wall and teased the climbing roses. For the first time in her life, Sophie had her shawl around her shoulders when and where she needed it. As she gathered it around her now to ward against that little nip of chill air, her smile widened until it became a chuckle.

I've grown up, she thought. *Finally*.

At the risk of sounding smug, she even quite liked herself.

⁓

The villagers of Sydney Dovedale never could reach an agreement on how it happened that Sophie and the stranger fell in love. As the years passed and memories faded away completely or became untrustworthy, the story of how he first came there changed, depending on whoever did the telling. Some said he purchased her from an advertisement in the *Norwich and Morecroft Farmer's Gazette*. Others said she shot him with an arrow, piercing his heart like Cupid. That, they would say, is why he has that little bump there, on his chest.

The poor man never seemed to have a shirt that fit, and neither did any of his sons, which was very strange, as they did well enough for themselves and lived more than comfortably. They would never be rich, like his wife's noble Grimstock relatives, but they didn't appear to mind.

She teetered on the balustrade, considering the distance to fall, but the future stretched before her, and she must take a chance. So she leapt into the night, her white ball gown fluttering around her with the tragic grace of a bird's broken wings.

Below, just emerging from the shadow of a boxwood hedge, a young man prepared to collect his ladder when he looked up at the sound of a slight cry. On instinct, he put out his arms and caught the falling woman.

Never had he laid eyes on such a creature of beauty. "Are you an angel?" he asked, breathless. "Are you here to save me?"

She laughed. "But, sir, 'tis you who saved me!"

And so, having rescued the maiden, he kept her and walked away with her into the night.

At least, that is how Sophie always told the story whenever their children asked why some people called her "a fallen woman."

The Wicked Wedding of Miss Ellie Vyne

by Jayne Fresina

**When a notorious bachelor seduces
a scandalous lady, it can only
end in a wicked wedding**

By night Ellie Vyne fleeces unsuspecting aristocrats as the dashing Count de Bonneville. By day she avoids her sisters' matchmaking attempts and dreams up inventive insults to hurl at her childhood nemesis, the arrogant, far-too-handsome-for-his-own-good James Hartley.

James finally has a lead on the villainous, thieving count, tracking him to a shady inn. He bursts in on none other than "that Vyne woman"...in a shocking state of dishabille. Convinced she is the count's mistress, James decides it's best to keep his enemies close. Very close. Seducing Ellie will be the perfect bait...

Praise for *The Most Improper Miss Sophie Valentine*:

"Ms. Fresina delivers a scintillating debut! Her sharply drawn characters and witty prose are as addictive as chocolate!"—Mia Marlowe, author of *Touch of a Rogue*

For more Jayne Fresina, visit:

www.sourcebooks.com

Lady Amelia's Mess and a Half

by Samantha Grace

⬱

Jake broke her heart by leaving for the country after sharing a passionate kiss.

Lady Amelia broke his by marrying his best friend.

When she returns to town a widow—pursued by an infamous rake, Jake's debauched brother, and just maybe by Jake himself—Lady Amelia will have a mess and a half on her hands.

A sparkling romp through the ton, Lady Amelia's Mess and a Half *delivers a witty Regency romance in which misunderstandings abound, reputations are put on the line, and the only thing more exciting than a scandal is true love.*

⬱

"Clever, spicy, and fresh from beginning to end."—Amelia Grey, award-winning author of *A Gentleman Never Tells*

"A delightfully witty romp seasoned with an irresistible dash of intrigue and passion. Samantha Grace is an author to watch!"—Shana Galen, award-winning author of *Lord and Lady Spy*

For more Samantha Grace, visit:

www.sourcebooks.com

A Gentleman Says "I Do"

by Amelia Grey

Her writing talent is causing all kinds of trouble...

The daughter of a famous writer, Catalina Crisp has helped her father publish a parody that makes Iverson Brentwood's whole family the talk of the town, and not in a good way.

Because he's the reality behind the story...

Furious and threatening, Iverson storms into Catalina's home, demanding satisfaction, but the infamous rake has finally met his match. With her cool demeanor and intense intelligence, Catalina heats his blood like no other woman in his notorious history...

Lady Maggie's Secret Scandal

by Grace Burrowes

❧

Lady Maggie Windham has secrets

And she's been perfectly capable of keeping them... until now. When she's threatened with exposure, she turns to investigator Benjamin Hazlit to keep catastrophe at bay. But the heat that explodes between them makes him a target too. In a dance between desire and disaster, it's not always clear who is leading whom...

❧

Praise for *The Soldier*:

For more Grace Burrowes, visit:

www.sourcebooks.com

About the Author

Jayne Fresina sprouted up in England, the youngest in a family of four girls. Entertained by her father's colorful tales of growing up in the countryside, and surrounded by opinionated sisters—all with far more exciting lives than hers—she's always had inspiration for her beleaguered heroes and unstoppable heroines. For more information, visit www.jaynefresina.com.